The Flesh of Kings

The Flesh of Kings

The final battle begins *after* Armageddon

A Novel

M. B. Lemanski

iUniverse, Inc.
New York Lincoln Shanghai

The Flesh of Kings
The final battle begins *after* Armageddon

Copyright © 2007 by Michael Lemanski

All rights reserved. No part of this book may be used or reproduced by any means, graphic, electronic, or mechanical, including photocopying, recording, taping or by any information storage retrieval system without the written permission of the publisher except in the case of brief quotations embodied in critical articles and reviews.

iUniverse books may be ordered through booksellers or by contacting:

iUniverse
2021 Pine Lake Road, Suite 100
Lincoln, NE 68512
www.iuniverse.com
1-800-Authors (1-800-288-4677)

Because of the dynamic nature of the Internet, any Web addresses or links contained in this book may have changed since publication and may no longer be valid.

This is a work of fiction. All of the characters, names, incidents, organizations, and dialogue in this novel are either the products of the author's imagination or are used fictitiously.

ISBN: 978-0-595-43275-2 (pbk)
ISBN: 978-0-595-68213-3 (cloth)
ISBN: 978-0-595-87615-0 (ebk)

Printed in the United States of America

And I saw an angel standing in the sun; and he cried with a loud voice, saying to all the fowls that fly in the midst of heaven, Come and gather yourselves together unto the supper of the great God;

That ye may eat the flesh of kings ...

—Revelation 19:17–18

Prologue

The first of many aftershocks struck Jerusalem right at suppertime. It was a Wednesday, nothing special. Full drinking glasses spilled, and water sloshed in the pools of fountains. Several ancient clocks stopped, marking the time. 6:44. Midwinter, it was well past dark; the temperature, a brisk forty-seven degrees Fahrenheit; skies steel gray, an unbroken overcast. Ergo, cloudy, not bright, no stars out tonight. For nearly half a minute the earth moved underfoot, side to side, during which the shake, rattle, and roll didn't grow, didn't ebb. Indoors, loose books were dislodged, some china broke. A train ride was more jittery. And then it stopped.

Given the antiquity of the place, casualties were ridiculously few, mostly stampede victims trampled by their fellows fleeing to God knows where. Trying to outrun an earthquake made about as much sense as chasing a parked car. Overall, damage to the Old City was similarly minor. There were scattered power outages, none lasting more than a few hours. Atop Mt. Moriah it was another story altogether.

Directly facing the Golden Gate, a jagged, foot-wide fissure snaking down its golden crown now marred the glimmering Dome of the Rock. And there was more, discernable only from a distance. A tilt. Not much, no more than a degree, and from a distance all cosmetic. Within the rotunda, however, the ancient mosque's troubles multiplied.

The impeccably carpeted flooring of the inner and outer ambulatories had sunk in stretches to an irregular depth of a meter or more. Girders had collapsed in on the Well of Souls, rendering the sacred stairway impassable. Holding valiantly, the magnificent arches supporting the cupola and the gilded pillars supporting the arches in a geometrically perfect circle intermittently creaked and groaned with structural fatigue. Deeper, the shrine's anchor struts and pilings had been critically weakened. Secular engineers at the scene had no choice but to shut it down, pending repairs. Even so, their most optimistic prognosis was bleak: the Dome of the Rock was mortally wounded. On the bright side, the rock itself, on which so much depended, over which countless lives had been lost, hadn't suffered a scratch.

Curiously, no other buildings comprising the Haram esh-Sharif, including Al-Aqsa Mosque, had sustained more than chipped paint and falling plaster dust. For the holy men of the Waqf, it was small consolation. The Dome was everything. The Dome *was* Jerusalem. Understandably, the Waqf trustees ordered absolute secrecy on the matter. It leaked out, anyway.

Rumors of the Dome's potentially deteriorating condition spread through politically charged theological circles like wildfire, reaching Rome shortly after midnight. The Holy Father was awakened and briefed. He pronounced the news *ne tumultus quidem*—roughly, "Not my problem"—and went back to sleep. Others were more enthusiastic. Virtually overnight, the Internet was transformed from an information superhighway into a global forest of burning bushes.

Jihadist radicals cried sabotage, alleging a Zionist plot, pointing to the absence of comparable damage to Jewish shrines in and around the sacred city. The Temple Mount Faithful celebrated the Dome's distress as an unimpeachable sign from God, urging that the site be leveled for safety's sake, eagerly renewing their drive to erect a third Jewish temple in its stead. Bellicose Christian sympathizers likewise delighted in the Dome's sudden turn of fortune, proclaiming it the fulfillment of prophecy, one way or the other. All three so-called fringe groups mobilized to welcome the End of Days. Secular authorities were less inclined to do so, endorsing the status quo, even as otherwise insignificant aftershocks occurring almost daily further crippled the sagging Qubbat. Cost estimates to restore it soared.

In the interests of peace under the auspices of UNESCO, a billionaire French philanthropist of Jewish extraction organized a Dome restoration fund based in Paris, securing generous pledges from the oil-rich emirates of the Persian Gulf. As the fund grew, so did street demonstrations by Temple activists, both Jews and Christians, augmented by professional agitators. Their attempts to block the delivery of hydraulic jacks and structural reinforcement equipment at the Dung

Gate led to clashes with police, turning bloody. Four days of rioting ensued before the Israeli Defense Forces restored order.

The worst instances of arson, vandalism, and looting were recorded outside the walls of the Old City in East Jerusalem's poorest districts, fueling Arab fears of Israeli government complicity, which had been whipped to a frenzy by Islamist propaganda. Off-the-shelf graphic accounts of Jewish and "crusader" atrocities against Muslim women and children swept the West Bank and Gaza Strip. To forestall retaliation, the borders were sealed, further delaying critical repairs to the Dome's ailing infrastructure by barring most of its Arab labor force. Arguably, two subsequent developments, one fathering the second, sealed the Dome's fate.

First, a prominent, pro-Temple televangelist in the United States publicly identified the French philanthropist as the Antichrist, citing the billionaire's wealth, strong ties to the United Nations, and his obvious "Jewishness." Keying on this insight, the minister scripturally affirmed that the Apocalypse was underway as of 6:44 PM on the date of the initial Makhtesh Ramon quake less than a month earlier. However arrived at, this assessment gained widespread acceptance among politically active Anglo American millennialists, who pressed Washington and London to call for an immediate investigation of the UNESCO-administered Dome of the Rock Restoration Fund.

Unfortunately, back in 1984 the United States and the United Kingdom had withdrawn from UNESCO—the United Nations Education, Scientific, and Cultural Organization—to protest the agency's over-politicized policies. As a result, U.S. and UK legal efforts to financially unmask the Antichrist were stymied, lending additional fodder to evangelical suspicions, culminating in a renewed media blitz against chronic UN corruption. Already racked by scandal, reluctantly invoking the articles of due diligence, the embattled secretary general himself commissioned an independent audit of the nascent but richly endowed fund, formally suspending disbursements until the examination was completed, urging all possible speed. Official Israel deferred to the wisdom of international due process.

Thus, the second nail in the Dome's coffin was but an extension of the first, for the audit rapidly exposed massive fraud and bid-rigging. At the same time, none of it was unprecedented or even particularly remarkable with respect to large historical reclamation and renewal projects. Nevertheless, outrageous sums had been bled from the endowment solely to reimburse its director's elaborate fundraising junkets, not all of them project related. He'd clearly been using the Dome as entrée to a variety of other profitable ventures throughout the Muslim world. Whether his actions were shrewd or execrable, one doesn't amass personal billions by strict adherence to the rules. Apocalyptic Christian and Jewish Temple activists were vindicated when indictments were handed up to the International Criminal Court at the Hague. The pillaged fund's bank accounts, quite healthy and robust otherwise, were ordered frozen. The Dome languished. She had vocal supporters worldwide, but their lungs were pretty much the extent of their support. Religiously ambivalent historians, anthropologists, and architects cried with one voice for sectarian differences to abate long enough to shore up her difficulties, a temporary reprieve pending juridical release of funds for more concrete relief. Opponents blocked these initiatives, insisting on peaceably awaiting the judgment of the Hague—nothing personal.

On Good Friday of the following year, during commemoration of the Passion on the Via Dolorosa, the overtaxed hydraulic jacks holding the crumbling Dome erect finally failed. Under a towering cloud of dust billowing up from the Temple Mount, witnessed up close by tens of thousands in Jerusalem, hundreds of thousands from the surrounding hills, untold millions more via television, Qubbat al-Sakhra fell. Final terror followed, leaving no part of the globe untouched.

Chapter I

Bling. The masked intruder ransacked every nook and cranny, every conceivable hiding place. *No bling.* A sinking feeling set in as he emptied the bookshelves. Guilt stabbed at him, but desperation drove him on. One row of spines didn't budge; it was locked tight. Tugging off his right glove with his teeth, he felt around the shelf's underside with his fingers until he found the button. *Bingo.* The false panel unlatched and opened to reveal a safe. "Combination," he demanded.

Receiving no answer, he angrily turned to a middle-aged couple. They were hog-tied on the carpet, both gagged. Dancing candlelight played on their faces, and their emaciated and blue-veined skin was like crinkled paper. The intruder's guilt stabbed deeper. He stepped over to strip the tape from the man's mouth, eliciting a moan. When there was no other response, the intruder raised a hand to threaten another beating—not the man, his wife. One of her eyes was already swollen shut and darkly purple, though the intruder had barely tapped her. He backhanded his own kids harder. *Had.* Racked by a coughing spasm, the former Hollywood producer with a Midas touch for satire hacked out the safe's combo. As he did, the bloody-black spittle drizzling over his chin made the intruder draw back sharply. *Plague.*

Unwilling to replace the gag, the intruder returned to the safe. After he spun in the numbers provided, it opened without further ado. Inside were bricks of mint-fresh cash. These he tossed away without giving them a second thought. Next, loose stock certificates, bonds, and real estate deeds rained out by the handful. The intruder gritted his teeth. "Where's the bling, man? Rich white folks always got bling."

The homeowner's eyes were scorching. "No bling, blood, not in a coon's age."

As he emptied the safe of more worthless paper, the thief's hand paused inside before bringing out an elegantly slim .32 caliber handgun, very shiny. At first, he didn't seem to know what to make of it. Then he fumbled to eject the clip. Five bullets. He scratched his neck under the ski mask with the gun barrel. He was sweating buckets. "These real?" he asked. The question was not as obtuse as it might have seemed.

"Only one way to find out," his captive replied. It was a dangerous taunt. Slamming the clip back in place and cocking the slide, the thief whirled around to drill the muzzle into the man's cheek.

"Oh, God, yes, do it!" the plague-ravaged man unexpectedly urged. "Cartridges are pre-war. I've had them for years. No, wait. My wife first. She means everything to me."

"*What?*"

"We've not been able to drum up the courage. Go on, get on with it! Squeeze the trigger."

The thief was incredulous. His ears plugged up, all strength draining from his legs and shoulders. The gun suddenly weighed a hundred pounds. Staggering back, he fell on his butt. Unable to breathe, he couldn't peel the mask off fast enough. "It's not like that," he gasped. "I'm not like ..." He came perilously close to tears. "I just need a can of milk."

The couple regarded him compassionately, the husband only briefly. "All you can think about is yourself ... *nigger?*" It struck the thief as terribly funny.

Flicking on the safety, he lobbed the piece onto the rug midway between them. "Believe it or not, I used to live in a house bigger than this," he said, "more fly." Reclining his head back, Julian Quinn chuckled. "My *other* car was a Bentley. My housekeeper drove a Hummer. I gave it to her for a birthday present ... *my* birthday."

"I know who you are, knew it from the way you move," the old man said, further surprising Julian by pulling his arms from behind his back. He'd somehow worked them free. In a flash he had the gun cocked point-blank, right between Julian's eyes. "The league's single-game rushing record, wasn't it? And on a broken ankle. The Mighty Quinn. You were something to watch." He let out a coughing sigh. "God damn you for the coward you became."

Abruptly diverting the gun, he shot his wife in the head before turning the gun on himself.

Julian fled the walled Tudor estate in Bel-Air the same way he'd entered: over the front gate. There was a sign out front warning that the place was protected by a sophisticated security system. All the mansions in the neighborhood had them, equally or more sophisticated, the kind of sophistication that went out the window when the energy grid failed, not that it would have made any difference. What good were alarms when there was no one listening? The gunshots, absent a hellacious scream, were another matter. They announced that someone had real ammo, and bullets of that sort were worth beaucoup bling. Next to spent cartridges, gunpowder—the good kind—was the most sought after commodity in the Zone. The other kind had a habit of blowing your hand off. A while ago, someone had knocked over a government warehouse full of experimental black powder. Or, more likely, it had been planted there. The street price for home-loads fell precipitously, even as the term *one-armed bandit* took on an entirely new meaning.

Dropping down on the other side of the gate, Julian was glad for the fog. It limited visibility to under thirty feet, increasing his odds of steering clear of the roving press squads, assuming they didn't see him first. They had NVG. The squads *owned* the night. Being out this late after dark, Julian was pushing his luck. His saving grace, if he still had it, was breakaway speed, world class. He'd not put it to the test in a long time, not since the arthroscopic surgery on his left knee before the war.

The war was now in its seventh or eighth year, depending on how one chose to calculate it. The front was half a world away and hadn't moved in the last three years, not significantly—a few kilometers every few months, this way and that, back and forth, no end in sight. The mantra certainly hadn't changed: "We fight them over there so we don't have to fight them over here." *Yep*, Julian thought despondently, *here we fight each other.*

For the moment, as he stole into the deserted mist along Sunset Boulevard, he had slightly more pressing concerns. He had to get to the Jaycees before they closed up shop.

There were essentially two powers in the Zone: the press squads and the gangstas. One was as anathema to staying alive as the other. The Zone was what was left of LA County, from the Valley in the north to the Orange County line in the south, the edge of the baking desert east of the Barrio to the coast. North and east, the high mountains formed a natural barrier, impossible to cross on foot with small children or old people, and hoofing it was the only way. There were still cars and trucks, of course. They were everywhere. The 405 was a parking lot from Skirball to Rosecrans. All the freeways and most of the surface streets were glutted. No one was going anywhere without juice, and a single gallon of gasoline, if you could find it, cost more bling than one man could carry.

In the south, white vigilantes calling themselves Minutemen patrolled to keep out the riffraff. The Minutemen didn't ask questions. If you were a reasonably healthy male between the ages of fifteen and fifty and they caught you, it was the same as being pressed—a long, cramped, seasick voyage to the God-forsaken battlefields of the Middle East. Everyone else of color, dead or alive, was dumped back inside the Zone like so much garbage.

Within the Zone, the press squads were the last remnant of organized government, and their sole purpose was harvesting warm, plague-free bodies for the war effort. Getting pressed offered the benefit of a full belly to those with a short-term outlook.

As for the second power in the Zone, the gangstas, they preferred to think of themselves as businessmen and were, in fact, the last refuge of capitalism in the Zone—food and meds for bling. Bling was any precious metal or stone. The exchange rate was determined at the time of the transaction, buyer beware. The gangs operated their territories as unofficial concessions granted by the military. Approach them without bling or enough of it, and you found out why they kept their concessions, but not until you were shanghaied and delivered to the nearest military recruiting station.

The Tongs held Downtown, and the Crips had South-Central. The 18th Street Gang ruled East LA. La Raza controlled the Valley, and the Packers ran West Hollywood into the canyons. Smaller outfits with questionable street cred operated the smaller neighborhoods in between as closely held subsidiaries of the greater powers, of which the Jaycees were by far the biggest and the baddest. Their fief was West LA, Brentwood, all of Santa Monica, and Venice. LAX was a boneyard of grounded commercial aircraft roamed by packs of wild dogs interbred with coyotes. The beach communities, from the marina down to Palos Verdes, were up for grabs, nothing worth holding—bad water, incubating disease. The mosquitoes were murder. Deadly parasites never before seen could strip a body to the bone within a few days, no maggots required. The parasites fed on the worms, too. When the pumping stations failed, billions of metric tons of raw sewage had backed up, all flowing into the sea, washed there by the rains. A day at the beach without a hazmat suit and a respirator was unsurvivable.

More safely inland, you could join a gangsta gang, for protection and camaraderie if nothing else, but the price of admission was steep—your soul. And if you had a wife or a girlfriend, that too. They became community property. Children, especially boys? You betcha, the younger the better. They were the future of the gang.

Turf wars were a regular occurrence in the Zone, but they were typically mild: skirmishes, really, to keep tuned up. The real prize was the Red Cross relief convoys, sporadic these days and always under heavy guard, that crossed over the Vincent Thomas Bridge from the Port of LA. Terminal Island was still under military control. It was also where the press ships put in to take on fresh conscripts, which made venturing anywhere close to San Pedro a dicey proposition, even for a banger. Caught off-turf, a gangsta was as good-to-go as any other civilian without perfect papers, and the only civilians with papers already worked for the military.

A permanent Red Cross relief camp was set up at San Pedro's Ports O' Call Village, once a harborside enclave of tony shops and restaurants. The parking lot was now a massively overcrowded tent city with a hospital powered by portable generators to treat the sick: plague victims, mainly—poor wretches who hadn't been, or couldn't afford to be, inoculated before the blowback. Resorted to in a desperate attempt to break the stalemate on battlefields far, far away, the residue of germ weapons had been carried on the jet stream—indiscriminate microbes that wreaked havoc all across the fruited plain, but primarily in densely populated urban areas where poverty was high and clean water scarce. Plague quarantine was the officially stated reason for the Zone's existence, conveniently sealing off "the hood" for easier pickings by the press squads.

Danger-fraught miles away from the overworked aid station, too many to contemplate, Julian continued through the fog along the UCLA campus—what had been a campus—passing a tattered recruitment poster stuck to the chain-link fence. It was a picture of Uncle Sam pointing a finger. The caption read, "JOIN UP NOW // HELP SAVE OUR WAY OF LIFE." *How funny.*

Julian was sorely tempted to cut across the overgrown track-and-field practice grounds before remembering that they were haunted. Superstition aside, this was the site of the whole country's last anti-war rally before martial law was imposed. Counter-protesters had overwhelmed the pitifully small rally and bricked its leaders to seize the microphone. "Traitors!" one of the brickers had screamed over the loudspeakers. "Get it through your thick heads! We're fighting for our freedom!"

Campus police and National Guardsmen in riot gear then dispersed the demonstrators on both sides with tear gas and beanbags. When the smoke cleared, nine people lay dead. Bricking was the same thing as stoning, except with bricks, and the brick typically stayed in your hand until you were done. No arrests were made, no investigation undertaken. The nationwide gas riots that erupted soon after foreclosed that possibility. Ten dollars a gallon, up from four dollars over the span of a few weeks, made everyone lose it everywhere, but especially in the gas-guzzling Southland. Not to put too fine a point on it, but the brickers at UCLA were not entirely without *casus belli*.

At the start of the semester, a proudly westernized coed from ostensibly friendly Dubai had strapped on twenty pounds of home-cooked explosives mixed with an equal weight of ball bearings and quarter-inch wood screws marinated in some kind of fast-acting poison, then waltzed into the registrar's pavilion on the last day to switch classes. There, leaving a triple-digit body count behind, she entered Paradise, crying in her native Arabic, "Remember the Dome!" The chemistry program was immediately cancelled, but the football team met for its regular practice. Under incredibly tight security at the coliseum that Saturday, during expansive, tear-filled applause for the National Anthem, the lower ten tiers of stands between the 40s, directly above the visitors' sideline, were incinerated by a splash bomb of home-brewed napalm disguised as a Gatorade barrel.

The visiting team was from the University of Michigan. Their quietly efficient trainer for the past twenty years, Adnon "Adam" Kazzari, a third-generation U.S. citizen known for his love of bacon and pepperoni pizza and otherwise as American as apple pie, had secretly reinvented himself as a born-again disciple of Mohammed after the collapse of the Dome of the Rock in Jerusalem mere months earlier. Caught fleeing the stadium, he happily joined Allah while taking out a half-dozen officers of LAPD's vaunted SWAT. The bomb was concealed in the team-autographed pigskin he clutched.

A litany of similar stories, many worse, swarmed the country. Within any single news cycle one report interrupted the next—*bada-bing, bada-boom, boom, boom*, and *boom!* Live television and radio fed the madness until it became a simple numbers game: so many here, so many there. People stopped going to work, stopped sending their children to school, stopped leaving their homes altogether. Being close to a group out in the open or gathered in any well-known enclosure was like wearing a bull's-eye. Wall Street crashed, sending the economy into an irreversible meltdown. Innocent nobodies with swarthy, Mediterranean features or olive skin tone were gunned down on sight until they had the unmitigated audacity to shoot back. Anarchy. An unsettled Congress threatened impeachment proceedings against the president and his entire cabinet for their abysmal failure to serve and protect.

And then all broadcasts stopped, and the Internet fizzled out—no power, not even emergency signal power. Precisely what or who was responsible lost relevance. The minions of the Antichrist were everywhere, behind every dark corner, even lurking in broad daylight. No one was safe. Then came the freak mega-storm, packing winds of more than two hundred miles per hour that wiped out the strategic petroleum reserve in Louisiana, along with the rest of the entire Gulf coast's pumping and refining capacity.

Hundreds of thousands of dead bodies from Houston to Jacksonville and all the way down to Miami and the Keys were left to bloat and rot, never recovered, never buried, creating a contagion of deadly bacteria that seeped into the water table, killing millions more. By then already tightly rationed, all remaining energy production was nationalized to feed the Pentagon. Uncensored print was outlawed, not that there was any ink left one way or the other. If Jesus didn't return soon, there'd be nothing to come back to. Who could blame him if he didn't? No one could fix this, not now.

Julian caught himself and prayed hard for forgiveness. He had no right to despair. What the Lord gave he could take away. All of creation was here solely at his pleasure, *for* his pleasure. Julian shuddered, as he always did when undisciplined, unholy thoughts crept into his mind, and yet the question would not go away. Was it possible that God took pleasure from this? *Teach us, Lord, yes, but for how long must we suffer the answer?* Julian's only comfort lay in his father's wise words: "The Almighty is from everlasting to everlasting, Julian. Our short struggle here doesn't register on any meter that could possibly interest him. And that, Julian, is the miracle, because despite his greatness, he deigns to pay us notice, as small and insignificant as we are. How do we know? How else? The Bible tells us so."

As he deeply inhaled the putrid fog, Julian's faith was refreshed and renewed. *Thank God for the Bible.* Without it, nothing made any sense whatsoever. This was all part of a grand plan, however incomprehensible to mortals. He recalled more of his father's loving advice. *Suffering makes us strong, then stronger, then strongest!* Horrible, glorious battles must await in heaven, Julian decided, requiring great strength, and Earth was the proving ground, like the two-a-day gridiron drills Julian knew so well, hated, and missed so much. *Come quickly, Jesus. I'm getting out of shape.*

Girding himself against what awaited more presently, he increased his pace, disappearing behind the thickening curtain of brackish, swirling mist rolling in from the coast.

Chapter II

"How I'm supposed to know this is real?"

The banger continued examining the shell in the firelight with a lit menthol cigarette in his lips, not looking particularly impressed. He was tired and cranky. Julian was the last one up. He'd barely made it before closing time. A half-court hoop game was going on at the other end of the blacktop. Concertina wire topped the twelve-foot-high chain-link fence, leaving no easy way out. A line of flaming torches was mounted along the building, and idle gangstas huddled around warming fires in fifty-five-gallon drums scattered around the schoolyard. Some gangsters were dancing. A boom box blared a hip-hop classic about a time few here were old enough to remember. D-cell batteries were about the only thing in the Zone not in short supply; there were warehouses still full of them in Carson. The fires made the fog beyond the fence glow red.

Barrington School, off Wilshire, was the Jaycees' depot in this sector of their turf. They maintained better stocks at their main drag on Santa Monica's Promenade, formerly an al fresco mall of trendy stores and cafés close to the beach. But things there got too wild at night, which was always the case in a place with too much liquor and meth and too few girls. There were no women here at Barrington, thank God, which helped keep the peace. Any women still here were too smart for that. There was no chivalry in the Zone.

"What are you, deaf? I'm talkin' to you!" the banger chastised Julian.

Julian cursed his mind for drifting. Lout or not, the lead banger was no one to dis. He wore a Muslim prayer cap in surreal contrast to a sparkling silver crucifix dangling from his ear. Julian didn't know him and didn't want to. The earring, though, was familiar. It had once belonged to Julian. "Where's Priest?" he asked.

The banger tilted his metal chair away from the table. "There's been what you call a change of management. Corporate didn't like the way this franchise was being run."

There'd evidently been a rift in the Jaycee hierarchy, and Priest had come up short. Literally, Julian realized, spying a severed head on a spike at the edge of the firelight. As always, from the heights of the Ivory Tower, it wasn't the fall that killed you. Lifting his torn and soiled shirt, Julian pulled out the pristine .32 tucked in his belt. The basketball game immediately stopped until he detached the clip, laying it on the table. Priest's successor unhappily picked it up and sniffed the barrel.

"Smells like maybe an hour."

Julian nodded. "Thereabouts."

The banger loaded the single cartridge Julian had proffered in the clip. "Got more?"

"Got milk?"

The banger looked up. "Family man?"

Julian swallowed.

The banger smirked. "It don't mean shit to me, B," he said, reinserting the clip. As soon as the retracted slide sprang forward the banger pointed the gun at Julian's heart, then raised it and fired, bursting the distant basketball in mid-flight off a fade-away jumper. The players were pissed but got over it, not that the shooter gave a shit about their gripes, either. "Real enough," he remarked smugly, "only now you got nothin' I need."

Julian worked his jaw to ease the ringing in his ear. "You got the gun."

"I can take this for free, and ain't a god damn thing you can do about it."

Julian sighed with disgust. "At least Priest was fair."

"The priest went soft. Didn't make his numbers. Maybe you're holdin' out on me." Unexpectedly flinching back in his chair, the banger had a sudden epiphany. "Whoa, hold up! I know you."

Julian's stomach knotted. "I don't think so."

"Oh, yes," the banger declared. "Yo, dogs, we got us a celebrity." Glancing over, none of the others betrayed any recognition. "LA Saints number 26. MQ, dogs, the Mighty Quinn. Y'all blind?" He waved off their ignorance. "Too young."

"What about you? Did you play?" Julian asked sarcastically.

"The game I play," warned the gangsta, "you go down, you don't get up." But then he softened a bit. "Varsity corner at Sepulveda High the year you made Super Bowl MVP, the last year before the shitstorm. Five TDs—two on the ground, three in the air. Man, you were greased lightning, you know that? Best spin move in the game, maybe of all time. Still got it?"

Julian himself didn't know the answer to that one.

"Nah, too old, I guess," the banger suggested with more fervor than Julian appreciated. "Dang, homes, where'd it all go? You're like skin and bones now."

Hearing so made Julian slouch even more.

"How old you are now, Mighty? Must be like, what, thirty-two, thirty-three? Closer to thirty-five?"

"Twenty-nine," Julian answered absently, scratching his thick beard, which now had sprouts of white. "Month before last."

"Still got the ring?" the banger asked lustily.

Julian scoffed. "What do you think?"

The banger let it go, continuing to stare, to measure him. "Give him anything he wants," he directed one of his underlings, "as much as he can carry."

Julian's eyes widened. On his best day, Priest was never *this* generous. "Why?" he asked more guardedly.

"You caught me in a good mood. That could change."

The underling beckoned Julian to follow him, which was even curiouser. Before, they'd always brought the purchase out from somewhere inside the school, authorized personnel only, and all that. "You gonna look a gift horse in the mouth, B?" the underling quizzed him impatiently. Julian hesitated only long enough to drop the remaining two .32-caliber cartridges on the table.

The gang leader regarded them with amusement. "So ... you *were* holding out on me."

"I ain't lookin' for charity, chief," Julian replied. "God bless you all the same."

He was stopped one final time on the way inside the school. "Yo, MQ," the head banger called. "How'd you get caught in the Zone, man? You had it all."

Julian's glum answer came as he went on, not turning. "I wasn't paying attention." Then, moving on for the door with more spring in his step, he asked his escort earnestly, "You got canned milk? Whatchu-call-it, baby formula would be better, if it's still like, you know, sealed." His escort opened a door and pushed him through.

"We got everything you're ever gonna need." And the door closed.

Back on the blacktop, the head banger opened a footlocker brimming with bling and tossed in the nickel-plated .32 and cartridges with complete disinterest as a black helicopter suddenly thundered overhead just above the rooftops. There were a bunch of them with searchlights, sweeping over all parts of the Zone. A moment later a Humvee and three empty troop trucks pulled up to the school along Barrington Avenue, lights out, creating zero alarm among the gang members. A boyish lieutenant, blond and freckled and in desert camos, entered through the gate and was smartly saluted. "What's our count, First Sergeant?" he asked the head banger, who had stripped off his gang colors to don a DCU, his own desert camouflage uniform.

"Sixty-two, all on ice under heavy guard."

"Not bad, Sarge—two over quota," the lieutenant said with delight as the "gangstas" on the blacktop efficiently armed themselves with assault rifles and sidearms previously hidden. "Well done, guys. Right on schedule."

"This is a helluva lot easier than the other way, LT," one said. "Too bad word'll get out."

"Things'll get back to normal in a few months. Memories are short. Anyone with half a brain got out of the Zone when the getting was good." A switch was thrown, and racks of portable arc lights lit up the schoolyard brighter than day. The lieutenant saw the severed head on the spike without reaction. "Casualties?"

"Just him," said the sergeant, taking out his earring and shedding the prayer cap. "They called him the priest. God knows why. Once he went down, the others became sheep."

"Anyone special?" the lieutenant inquired. The sergeant thought about it, then shook his head. Heavy boots shuffled up the street from Wilshire, and more soldiers took up positions outside the fence. A subordinate handed the lieutenant a bullhorn. "All right, let's have a look at 'em."

The five-dozen-plus-two prisoners were herded out of the building, wrists flexi-cuffed behind their backs, all terribly frightened. The light was blinding. Many had been beaten, their lips split, noses broken, faces contused. Julian Quinn, the last in, was among the first out. Favoring his side and limping, he now knew why he'd not run into any press squads on the way over. Like a blithering idiot, he'd waltzed right into their trap, fooled completely. A no-talking order was repeated as the captives were formed into two motley rows for inspection. As he paced in front of them, the boyish lieutenant raised his bullhorn.

"You men are now the property of the United States government," his voice echoed chillingly across the schoolyard. "Until further notice, the rules are simple. Resist or in any way disobey, and you and the man next to you will be shot. Do not speak unless spoken to, and then answer plainly and truthfully. Otherwise, keep your mouth shut at all times. Now, is anyone hungry?" he asked with a disarming smile. "Let me see a show of hands."

This was, of course, impossible. The little dude on one side of Julian, balding and stubble-faced with a beak for a nose and a bleeding gash across his eyebrow, made a pathetic noise way down in his throat. Julian stepped on his foot for naught. "I've not eaten a crumb these four days, Captain," the sot blurted. His accent was Eastern European.

"Step forward," the lieutenant invited. After hesitating briefly, the man did. The lieutenant summarily shot him in the head. "Now, you." Julian's heart leapt into his throat. The sergeant quickly whispered something to the lieutenant. Obeying the young officer's head flick, the man on the other side of the gap was tugged forward. He fell to his knees, his whimpers silenced by a single report. "*Am I getting through?*" the lieutenant bellowed over the bullhorn. Complete silence. "Excellent." He lowered the horn, then raised it again. "Oh, and welcome to the army. I know you'll do us proud."

The crackdown and roundup was Zonewide, massive, and tightly coordinated. Spies on the ground had furnished pinpoint intelligence. Months and months of uncontested gang hegemony over the Zone had lulled everyone into complacency, although at heart no one was surprised. How could they be? Deception was an organic property of the ruling military theocracy; deprivation under the guise of local independence was an age-old ploy since Roman times, making it that much easier to conflate conquest with liberation.

Executed flawlessly by the command authority, the surprise show of force netted in excess of forty thousand newbies in a single night after filtering out the physically unfit and terminally untrainable. Being rejected was no favor since, for the rejects, it meant transfer to the forced labor camps outside Victorville that made uniforms, boots, and non-lethal combat accessories. Those otherwise judged unfit lay where they fell, much like the two sacrificed on the Barrington School blacktop to encourage good order and discipline. Air power neutralized any remaining pockets of resistance, the fiercest in Hollywood. Huge fires now raging throughout the Zone would be left to burn themselves out.

Assessing the scene from the air by helicopter, Colonel Ken Rittenour, the operational commander, called off the fleet of Navy "smokers" plying the coastal shallows from Zuma to Redondo. They'd laid down enough "fog." The mild onshore breeze had cooperated better than forecast. Mop-up procedures could now safely go ahead.

Rittenour, at age forty, was a grizzled warhorse with sun-baked leather for skin, nicely accented by a gray buzz cut, high and tight and always regulation. Puffy bags under his eyes suggested he slept rarely and never soundly. He'd only been in LA for a week and would depart on the next day's high tide, taking with him the reluctant replacement troops now on their way to processing from all across the Zone. Obedient herds of them in leg irons—pathetic rivers of men joined by smaller tributaries—passed beneath the chopper's skids as bulldozers farther ahead plowed a path through the legions of abandoned vehicles on the main thoroughfares and freeways.

Following a fifty-seven-day zigzag voyage over the unpredictable seas of the Pacific and Indian Oceans to put some meat on their bones and make them righteous, the newbies would be put through basic in-country, then given empty rifles to form a Potemkin line—scarecrows of the Apocalypse—solely to influence enemy recon. They could expect to live for as long as their audience bought the ruse. No actor ever had better incentive to deliver a strong performance.

The enemy, howsoever Washington chose to define it, employed similar tactics, which only served to prolong the stalemate. The trick was figuring out which troops were real and which were props, making the war itself an illusion. In truth, there hadn't been any real fighting in a couple of years, mainly because it took almost as many legit troops to prop up the props and keep them in line as it would to attack the other side—toy soldiers in a holy game of Risk in which losses counted for less than little. Both sides continued to hold the nuclear option in abeyance. It could be exercised only once—after that, all bets were off. Both sides laid claim to a divine mandate, both awaiting spiritual intercession, neither willing to put its claim to the ultimate test, each accusing the other side of serving the Antichrist, each with persuasive arguments, pro and con.

For his part, Colonel Rittenour sorely missed the clarity of proper soldiering, when duty and honor in search of glory were his bulwark against doubt, his armor against regret. Alas, the days of the noble warrior fighting for a cause greater than himself were over, if ever there had been such a cause. Today it was all empty slogans sprayed by self-sanctified charlatans from protected strongholds far removed from battle and the dreary attrition of the thousand-mile-long front. Perhaps it had always been thus, all of which was too far above the colonel's pay grade to waste time contemplating. He'd already left instructions for what he wanted chiseled on his grave marker should he merit one: "HE DID HIS JOB." Even in a perfect world, which this was not, it was the best an old infantryman, twice widowed and childless, could hope for.

Checking off the final item on his list, the colonel tapped his pilot with a gesture to wrap it up and return to base at the Seal Beach Naval Weapons Station.

As Rittenour's chopper swooped in over the twinkling lights of the sprawling nationalized petroleum refineries surrounding Signal Hill in Long Beach, Corpsman Felix "Nacho" Angel was reporting for his nightly shift at the Seal Beach processing center. A former bantamweight club fighter with a passion for body art, Nacho was the complete antithesis of his surname. He had been written up countless times for his sadistic treatment of newbies, an offense which, in and of itself, was striking, since the rules were vague, to say the least, and corpsmen weren't held to the Hippocratic oath. Even his fellow medics gave him a wide berth. For whatever reason—and no one doubted he'd had a hard life—this Angel was bad to the bone, a condition no kind words or friendliness could moderate.

The break area for the medical corps also served as their locker room. A group of four was hovering over two others at a table, playing a heated game of Ship-Captain-Crew with dice cups. Apparently, banging down the cup with gusto positively influenced the roll. At his locker, Nacho changed into an unlaundered white smock flecked with dried blood. Wordlessly, he muscled his way to the table and stole a cup. Shaking it vigorously, he asked, "How many this batch?"

One of the medics checked a clipboard on a peg. "Our lot? Just over four hundred."

Nacho slammed down the cup, then tilted it up so that only he could see what lay beneath. Two fives and a three. Only one sequence worked. This he memorized, singling out whoever got the number for special attention. Then he scooped the dice into the cup, set it upright, and left.

"He always does that—one roll before shift," one of the others said. "How come?"

"Do you really wanna know?" another asked. All silently agreed it was a mystery that best remained unsolved. Angel was nutty. Besides, it was no skin off their nose.

In better times not so far distant, the conscript-processing stockades at Seal Beach could have passed for the line at a busy post office or the DMV, perhaps a ride at Disneyland, except that in this case, the customers were all naked. Under the soaring, elliptical roof of a vast hanger two football fields long, divided into eight sections of cold concrete floor, the newly pressed had hungrily devoured candy bars laced with a behavior-management drug to keep them pliable. This was just a teaser. The heavenly aroma of cooked food was piped in from an unseen mess—savory meats with thick gravy, high-carb sides, buttery corn, and seasoned greens rich in vitamins—as a further enticement for compliance. Some wept, ankle chains clanging as they slogged forward in line. Snipers on the catwalks ensured they didn't riot to get to the food before they were invited. Huge, elevated plasma screens ran inspirational video chock full of patriotic themes heavy on religious subtext, replete with hymns sung in tight close-up by sensuous, blemishless women with glossy lips and only the most tasteful hint of cleavage. Prisoner erections were involuntary, largely drug-induced; ejaculations were frequent and messy.

A military physician worked the front of each line, making a swift examination—eyes, ears, nose, throat, rectum—not bothering to replace gloves in between. Here, also, each conscript had a sequential number painted on his chest that was not easily washed off in the showers. Attempts to do so were severely punished.

Barely aware of his surroundings, tortured by hazy self-contempt, Julian Quinn was second in line from the doctor when the man in front of him inexplicably puked up his guts and collapsed in a grand mal seizure. As he writhed and shook, eventually expiring, the doctor took his time completing the paperwork. An argument sprouted up over the numbering scheme. Had the man died pre-examination or post? The doctor strongly asserted pre, but "355" had already been painted on the deceased's chest. The doctor was livid. One of the armed guards had the perfect solution, tossing the medic a handy roll of duct tape. Yanked up with a layer of skin and gobs of chest hair, the tape rendered the number indiscernible. The doctor was cajoled. "Close enough for government work." And the corpse was dragged away.

Julian was next up, examined, and numbered 355. Waiting for him at his next stop was Nacho Angel.

Chapter III

Within sight of the hanger, Colonel Rittenour was dropped off by a Humvee at a Quonset hut among a colony of others. It was his temporary command post. Amid the rattle of line printers and teletypes inside, the boiler room of metal desks with wireless field computers was dominated by a Plexiglas status map of the Zone and staffed by busy clerks and radio operators. As he swaggered to the back, Rittenour was given a stack of dispatches, mostly encouraging. The whole idea of impressments bothered him, though given the war's plunging popularity it remained a necessary evil. The colonel's bailiwick lay in the netherworld of unconventional operations, typically behind enemy lines, initiatives the brass weren't eager to acknowledge. Rittenour had remarkably few medals as a result, and medals were all the rage. The task of cleaning out the Zone had fallen to him mainly because the Pentagon didn't know what else to do with him. In a war without fighting, not on any scale, Rittenour was a fish out of water. Tonight's exercise had been given to him as a pacifier. Now that it was a wrap, he was once again bored out of his gourd, the menacing downside of command efficiency.

Absently perusing the reports along the way, Rittenour noted that the blinds of his office windows were closed, a light on inside—not the way he'd left things. He angrily jerked open the door to find a civilian behind the desk, his back to the door, pouring from a pocket flask.

"For Pete's sake, close the effing door!"

Coming from an uninvited guest, the command was irritating. Rittenour kicked it loudly shut, then mellowed. The amber liquid was contraband, best kept from the prying eyes of his staff. Possession was a hanging offense ever since passage of the temperance laws and their zero-tolerance enforcement. It was a very moral country.

Turning with the two glasses, Morton Parmister extended one. Rittenour accepted.

"*Salud*," Parmister toasted him.

"Bite me."

Rittenour belted his down. Parmister was less hasty.

A senior White House advisor without portfolio, a troubleshooter, Morty Parmister was somewhere in his mid forties and patently unremarkable, save for a put-on, buttery Southern accent he turned off as it suited him—these days purely fashionable, genteel. Regardless, Parmister didn't move and shake through the circles of power; he slithered; always there where he needed to be, then not, the go-to guy in a crisis—a fixer. All that aside, or because of it, he was Ken Rittenour's best friend, his only friend. "Solid work tonight, as usual," Morty complimented. He always started that way. "How do you feel about it?" He always asked that, too.

Rittenour gruffly plopped down on a chair, gesturing for Parmister not to be stingy with the flask. "I don't have feelings. I have orders." He was anxious to pound down a second tot but stopped. "I'm guessing you didn't fly all the way out here to buy me a drink."

Parmister took the desk chair. "Good guess. I need you back doing what you do best."

Rittenour grunted. "About time. Spill it."

Parmister pulled a well-worn valise onto his lap and unzipped it. "A new face has popped up," he said, "stirring up trouble, talking peace."

Rittenour snorted. "The gall of some people."

Parmister dropped a top-secret dossier on the desk. Pushing his glass aside, Rittenour opened it, thumbing through the contents. Other than an assortment of surveillance photos, it was short on specifics. The target was no one Rittenour recognized. "Looks young. Arab or Jew?"

Parmister shrugged. "We put him in his early thirties, charismatic, politically astute. Calls himself Janus Philio. Says he's a rabbi one minute, then claims to be a Christian, Muslim, Buddhist, Hindu, Sikh—can't decide."

Rittenour frowned. "Calls? Says? Claims?"

"We can't get a fix on his background," Parmister said. "Just sort of showed up in Galilee about a month ago from out of nowhere."

Rittenour eyed his guest cynically. "That ought to get a few rumors going."

Parmister was less amused. "He's milking it for all it's worth, too, drawing big crowds."

Rittenour lost interest, pushing the file away. "He'll fizzle. They all do."

"Opinions vary," Parmister said ominously.

Pondering this, Rittenour pounded back his second round. "That serious, huh?"

Parmister shrugged. "Why gamble?"

Rittenour dipped into a pocket for his cigarettes. Lighting up, he languidly exhaled at the ceiling, fully knowing Morty disapproved. "When do you want it done? I can fly out tonight."

Fanning away the smoke, Parmister shook his head. "This one's tricky. We don't need a martyr on our hands, and he's got a lot of light on him. Get creative. There's time. This cannon fodder you rounded up tonight is top priority. You'll get the particulars over there. Don't worry—you're the man." He returned the dossier to his valise. "It'll keep." Pocketing his flask, Parmister moved for the door. "You look beat, Ken. Get some rest."

Rittenour stayed in his chair, faced away, gloomy. "How did it get to this, Morty?"

The question stopped Parmister cold at the door. "What?"

"What we're doing to our own people."

Parmister pursed his lips and changed the subject. "When you get to Haifa, call me. I'll fly over. We'll do lunch."

"There is no Haifa."

"Oh, right. My bad. Aqaba, then. Call me."

The conscript infirmary, adjacent to the processing hangar, was a series of big tents with grass floors. Here, semi-lucid and almost universally banged up, the newly pressed were patched up—open wounds stitched or stapled and minor fractures set—before their bare buttocks received a cocktail of shots from injection guns. There was no anesthesia, and any with more serious injuries had long since been sorted out to be sent God knows where.

The lines outside the tents were long but orderly, kept that way by surly MPs with cattle prods and nightsticks. The temperature had dropped precipitously over the last few hours. Cold leg irons with an eighteen-inch chain between turned dreams of escape into a duck-waddling exercise in naked futility. One unwisely vocal captive prattled on about a return to antebellum slavery. He was silenced by a cattle prod jammed up a highly sensitive orifice, forced to crawl on all fours.

Within one tent, Corpsman Angel was just finishing up with a "patient" when he spotted the current lot's #355 pass through the entry flap. He was being directed to the next available medic when Nacho called out, "Over here. I'll take him."

The supervising physician glanced up from an old travel magazine, pulling his music headphones from one ear. "There's plenty," he said.

"He's mine," Nacho insisted.

The doc caved, reaffixed his headphones, and returned to his magazine. "Suit yourself."

An MP nudged Julian Quinn in Nacho's direction with a nightstick. A sextet of MPs were posted inside to discourage unruliness. Often, they were obliged to help hold a subject down for treatment. Wails and screams were the ambient noise from this and surrounding tents, a big reason the doctor here liked to wear headphones. Julian robotically shuffled toward Nacho's table in a funk, his chains softly rattling. His pupils were dilated, his eyes half closed. The candy bar had stolen his strength, along with his will. He strained to bring the corpsman's name tag into focus. "*Angel*," he managed breathlessly. Somewhere in his clouded brain a synapse fired, autonomically stretching his lips into a goofy grin. All around him, the MPs exchanged knowing smirks.

Out beyond the lights of the infirmary compound, Colonel Rittenour's Humvee rumbled in for a surprise inspection. The colonel had driven himself, arriving without fanfare. Killing his headlights, he lit a cigarette and took a moment to take in the scene from a distance. What caught his attention and would have escaped it, had he not stopped precisely here, was a naked man on all fours, chained at the ankles. Brutally kicked and electrocuted for fun offline by a pair of guards on either side, he was in a world of hurt. Hell itself would have been a welcome reprieve. Had his tormentors been more alert, properly doing their jobs, they might have seen the colonel coming.

Ken Rittenour was not a particularly big man, nor was he small by any stretch, but outsized or not—or outnumbered—just about every part of his body was a weapon he kept honed for lethal application. He could have announced himself, ordering the maltreatment to cease post haste, but his voice was tired. More than that, though, much more, he was gripped by an irrepressible need to vent. The altercation was over in seconds, brutally frank, and a moment later Rittenour was kneeling at the tormented conscript, shouting, "Medic!"

One was taking a smoke break behind the nearest tent. He glanced over curiously, not in any hurry, not until he spied Rittenour's eagles. They seemed to make all the difference. Ditching his smoke, he rushed over.

"Get this man to the base hospital on the double," the colonel barked.

"He's a conscript."

"Do you have a hearing problem, soldier?"

"No, sir." The medic turned and yelled for an ambulance.

A senior MP ran up and saluted. "We saw the whole thing, Colonel. It was the damnedest thing I've ever seen. They wouldn't listen. They've been trouble before, them two."

"Colonel, these men, they're ... they're dead, sir," the corpsman pronounced haltingly after checking on the two fallen MPs.

"This one's not, not yet," Rittenour said, cradling the head of the conscript. "He's your priority, corpsman. I will hold you personally responsible if that status changes between here and the hospital." The corpsman required no additional coaxing. The colonel had a way with words.

"*Where's that bus?*" the medic yelled, devoting his undivided attention to the conscript. Rittenour stayed at the conscript's side all the while.

"How does the colonel wish this written up?" the senior MP inquired. Then, to score points, he added, "Who would the colonel like punished?"

"Enter it as an unsupervised training accident," Rittenour said. "As for the other, have the base provost report to my office in one hour."

"Report, sir? The provost outranks the colonel, Colonel."

"He'll be there," Rittenour assured the MP without elaboration.

Just then, the ambulance rolled in. The medic gave the ambulance crew a quick heads-up, ever more desperate to keep his patient alive or suffer the colonel's wrath. Clearly, here was an officer who dealt with subordinates in an altogether summary fashion.

"Training, sir?" the senior MP asked as the ambulance rolled away. "What training?"

Rittenour turned to scan the MPs guarding the long line of conscripts. All were showing better restraint since the incident, all reluctant to look the colonel in the eye. "This your watch?" he asked the senior man.

"This is my section," the MP admitted.

"You be in my office, too."

"They're just Zone trash, sir."

Turned on him, the colonel's expression was wilting.

"I'll fetch the provost," the MP said. Faltering a salute, he made tracks to do just that.

Julian groaned out in unremitting agony, unable to defend against it as Nacho wrapped the Ace bandage ever tighter, pressuring the three cracked ribs of Julian's lower right lumbar. A rifle stock back at Barrington School had inflicted the damage. Savage baton strikes randomly delivered along the way had subsequently inflamed it. Nacho caught the eye of the nearest guard and winked. "You like it?" he taunted Julian. "Want more? Tell me you like it."

This was too much for even the MP to bear. Averting his face, he sidled a few more steps away—slowly, casually—trying not to look like a total pussy to his fellow guards. It was the opening Nacho had been waiting for.

"Sorry, B," he hissed in Julian's ear, unraveling the ace behind Julian's back, "but we gots to play the game, you dig? Answer me! You got peeps in the Zone?"

Julian merely groaned again, swaying on the table, chin on his chest.

"God damn it, can't you see I'm trying to help your ass, you dumb nigger?"

Julian could barely form words. "Why I should believe you?"

"You got no reason," Nacho said softly but rapidly. "And I ain't making no promises, hear? Straight up, your ass is goin' to the war. That's just the way it shakes out, B, no bull. But … gimme an address, names, get me even close, and maybe I can do for them you left behind, if you got 'em."

"How?"

"We got us what you call a network, savvy? We get folks *out*. Free, man. I can't say more. It's too dangerous, and it's now or never, dog, 'cause you're about outta here."

"Why me?"

"*Then fuck you!*" However, taking a breath, Nacho reconsidered. "Your number came up, OK? That's the way it works, how it *has* to work. Can't be everyone."

Blearily looking into his eyes, nose to nose, Julian reached a fateful, pain-racked, drug-addled decision, whispering a location.

Nacho was impressed. "Names now," he prompted, "at least one, and it better not be a whole fucking Mormon tribe."

"We're not … Mormons," Julian wheezed.

"No shit," Nacho scoffed humorously. "*Names!*"

"Wife, Jamyqua," Julian struggled to get out. "Jamyqua Quinn. Two boys … baby girl. I"—he broke down, inconsolable, his whole being shuddering—"just went out for some milk … for Baby Girl. Baby … dying … *my* baby." He wept out more, but it was incoherent, chalked up by the others in the tent to more of Angel's special barbarity. No one interfered, either, until ...

"*You!*" Colonel Rittenour's voice thundered across the tent like Mt. Etna blowing its top. "Step away from that man."

Nacho froze. Even Julian's sobs abated. "*Say nothing,*" Nacho whispered urgently. "*No matter what happens, if you love them, don't say a damn thing.*" Then he stepped back from the treatment table as ordered.

"Don't you move from there, mister, not a muscle," the colonel commanded in a tone that required minimal volume. "I'll get to you. The rest of you listen up," he addressed the others more broadly. "It all stops *now!*"

Those in attendance were bewildered, wide-eyed, sheepish. Rittenour tore the headphones off the doctor's ears and snapped the cord. Then, discarding the phones, he made a slow circuit through the tent—deliberately, expertly—surveying their faces, one man to the next, maximizing the intimidation factor. Had he raised so much as a finger to scratch an itch, anyone within striking distance would have flinched away or, more probably, ducked and been wise for it. In short, he had a way about him not seen in any command officer they'd recently had contact with, if ever.

"You don't know me," he continued more conversationally, albeit forebodingly. "Keep it that way. You'll like me better. Believe it. What's important is that I kill the enemy. This is my job. Sometimes it's clean, sometimes not, but clean or dirty, I have never known the enemy to treat us the way I've seen us treat our own countrymen here tonight."

"Zone trash?" someone blurted.

Rittenour whirled around. "Who said that?"

Another voice answered behind his back, this one authoritative. "The Evangelical High Council of North America," it said. Rittenour turned to find a Marine Corps two-star just inside the tent flap. He was the base CO. With him was Morty Parmister. "Squatters in the Zone were declared incorrigible more than three years ago," the general calmly informed Rittenour, "and therefore unsaved. If anything, we're doing them a favor, giving them a fighting chance—their *last* chance. Our methods are designed to bring them into the light, kicking and screaming if need be. Their alternative is soulless depravity, debauchery, and unclean living. This processing center follows the guidelines set forth by the conventions of Lynchburg and Virginia Beach."

And just like that the tables were turned. The church's authority was final, which the base commander had no compunction to wield like a club. For the rest of the country, the Zone had been painted as the last vestige of secular liberalism run amok. Perhaps it was maintained for no other purpose. The council owned the only paintbrush. Openly challenging its diktats was a ticket to the front. In Ken Rittenour's case, however, this meant little. He loved the front, its *clarity*. It was his home. Still, arguing with the church was tantamount to pushing string uphill. The general was holding out for an apology, publicly, in front of his men—demanding it. Rittenour had something else in mind.

"With all respect due the general," he said, "have the bishops ever been here to witness their guidelines in practice, up close and personal?"

The challenge caught the general short. His upper lip twitched malevolently. His voice, however, remained level as he promenaded a few steps further into the tent. "The colonel is new here," he told the men. "He won't be staying. Until then, this is his operation, so you will abide by and comply with his … way of doing things. He has and he will take full responsibility. Colonel, you have my complete support."

Outwardly, Rittenour was courteous. "Thank you, General."

"Thank Mr. Parmister." That said, the general unhappily turned on his heel and left. The base CO was a soft-around-the-middle bureaucrat who generally spent his days planning lavish dinner parties, his nights hosting them or playing canasta at the O Club. He represented everything martial law had wrought on the officer corps, both stateside and in occupied Canada.

"Colonel?" the supervising physician petitioned after no one knew what to do next.

"Carry on, men," Parmister spoke up for his friend. "*Nicely*. Keep to the schedule."

Rittenour grudgingly nodded, the previous pace gradually resumed, and Nacho was forgotten after the fixer from Washington, brooking no argument, hustled the colonel outside.

"I thought I told you to get some sleep," Parmister complained once they were out of earshot.

"I thought you'd left."

"Lucky for you, I had other business. I mean, gosh, Ken, you put two GIs in the morgue."

"It was my trade-off," Rittenour said.

"Bad trade," said Parmister, "all around. The grunt you saved was pronounced DOA. Then the provost marshal races in on my meeting with the BCO shaking in his boots. I don't know how, but I gathered he somehow knows your rep. The general wants your rear end in a sling. You saw him. He's darned near fit to chew glass. In his world, you're bad for business, Kenny-boy."

"I stepped over the line," Rittenour confessed. "I'll take my lumps."

"You'll do no such thing," Parmister overruled. "You're *paid* to step over the line, way over, but the where and when is of my choosing, not yours. What's up with this cowboy shit? Who made you Wyatt Earp?"

"'Shit'?" Rittenour tut-tutted. "Morty! That's worth what these days, twenty paddles?"

Parmister rolled his eyes. "It's all your fault. You went and got me all excited."

"Yeah, my bad. Are we done?" Rittenour had tired of the exchange, was tired in general.

Morty gave up a long-suffering sigh. "Know what I think? I think you've been in theater too long. We do things differently over here … now."

"Then I guess you'd better send me back."

Morty was legitimately perplexed. "What is it, Ken? This isn't like you. Tell me how I can help, and I will."

"You can't."

"Why?"

"Because you're part of it … and so am I."

Leaving it there, Rittenour trudged out to where he'd parked his Humvee. "Get some shut-eye, will you?" Morty called to him. "It'll all look better in the morning."

Chapter IV

It was dawn, two long days after the troop convoy had set sail from the port of Los Angeles. Its size and cargo hadn't been seen since shortly after the war began. All told, the armada numbered almost three hundred ships, loaded with enough fresh blood to keep the war percolating long into the foreseeable future

Here, however, the outermost boundary of the Zone was sixty miles away, the air light and crisp, the ground and tree branches dusted with frost. They had reached the Tejon Pass summit. Stretching to the north out to a far horizon was the San Joaquin Valley.

The two scouts, both women—that characteristic obscured by army surplus fatigues and grease paint—secured a small clearing in the woods off a ranch road of packed clay. Both carried rifles at the ready, their breath steaming in the frigid air. Satisfied that they were alone, one of the scouts gave a shrill bird call. Two black men stepped into the clearing. Each carried a small boy on his back. A woman with a tiny infant soon followed. Her name was Jamyqua Wilson Quinn. Prior to delivering her first child, she had been a Miss America finalist, the last Miss Maryland. You wouldn't know it to look at her now. Every day was an ordeal. The years of deprivation, combined with her last and very difficult pregnancy, had rewarded her with a list of health issues, not the least of which was chronic asthma. The elevation of the pass was only exacerbating it.

One of the scouts cleared away camouflaging brush off a derelict Subaru station wagon. Climbing inside, she inserted a key in the ignition. The engine sputtered, then stabilized. Everyone breathed a sigh of relief before the boys were transferred to the rear seat. Ages four and seven, they were blissfully asleep, despite the rugged going.

Shouldering her rifle, the second scout took the baby from Jamyqua to strap the infant into a cardboard box on the passenger seat. "It's got a full tank and a ten-gallon spare in back," she told Jamyqua. "There's grub enough for a week or more if you don't overdo it. Just keep heading north, and steer clear of small towns. You'll stand out like a sore thumb. Portland is your best bet, big enough so you can blend in. Even so, you won't stay put longer than a week or two in any one place if you're smart. And don't tell nobody you're from the Zone. That would be bad. The council has eyes and ears everywhere. It's the last one you suspect that'll finger you for a runaway."

Jamyqua's belated realization made her ill with dread. "You're not coming with us?"

The scout shook her head. "That's not the way it works."

"What about my husband?"

The scout sympathized, but only briefly. "You keep your mind on these kids. That's where *his* mind is, wherever he's off to."

Jamyqua's chin trembled. Her small voice came out an octave higher than normal. "I don't know if I can do this."

The scout shrugged, almost callously. "Wanna go back?"

Jamyqua immediately toughened up, her eyes hardening. "You gonna give me a gun?"

The scout tapped her own temple with a finger. "This is the best weapon you've got, sugar pie. Don't be afraid to use it. Good luck." She signaled to her compatriots. "We're back." And a moment later, Jamyqua's angels were gone, shadows merging with shadows, as the eastern sun cleared the treetops with blinding intensity.

On its forty-third day at sea, somewhere in the central Indian Ocean, still a day or more east of the Seychelles, the massive convoy of troop ships made a wide swing north into a U-turn, where it was abandoned by its warship task force, including a pair of attack submarines. The task force steamed on west, drawing down the colors, raising white flags. Aboard a former cruise liner refitted as a troop transport, Julian Quinn reported to Colonel Rittenour's cabin.

Quinn had added a few pounds since departing Long Beach, thanks to three hot squares a day. Regular workouts in the ship's weight room and twenty laps around the main deck every dawn and dusk had transformed him back closer to game shape. Cleanly shaved, his hair cut razor-close to the scalp, a number of years had also fallen away. He now filled out his fatigues like a proper soldier.

Indeed, he was considered a model conscript, had been given responsibilities, even granted his run of the ship without the usual armed escort.

Waiting at the cabin door, the colonel's adjutant, a major, accepted Quinn's salute and pushed the door open, remaining outside. Taking a breath, tugging down on his camos to smooth the shoulders, Julian went in, and the door closed behind him. Rittenour was at his desk, cleaning his sidearm. His quarters were otherwise spartan, with only a single bunk and a foot locker. There were no photographs, no personal mementos. The 9 mm Heckler & Koch on the desk was disassembled, indicating a thorough cleaning, indeed, though when it had last been fired was anyone's guess. Standing to attention, Julian crisply saluted.

"As you were," the colonel invited without looking up, continuing to clean his gun. "Quinn, isn't it?"

Julian stood at ease, hands behind his back. "Specialist J. Quinn, sir. The colonel wanted to see me, sir?"

"They tell me you've been leading the men in prayer, Quinn, among other things."

"No other things, sir. Does the colonel have a problem with prayer?"

"It's all wasted energy if you ask me," Rittenour staunchly replied, gradually softening. "Regardless, whatever you've got going on with the Almighty, Quinn, don't lose it."

"Sir?"

Rittenour began reassembling his weapon. "It's over, Quinn."

"Over, sir? I don't follow."

"The war. Don't tell me you didn't notice we've turned around."

"I noticed, Colonel—I just didn't know what it meant."

Rittenour glanced over. "And now you do. When the word gets out, the men will mutiny. I don't think wild horses could hold them back. The numbers are all on your side. Your challenge will be to keep it together until you make port—this ship, at any rate. I've ordered the regulars to stand down and disarm. Revenge is pointless. It's also inevitable. Curtailing the violence will increase your odds of making landfall in one piece, so make peace, especially with the sailors, as best you can. They're really your only hope, and they're not bad men. When all is said and done, you all want the same things. I'm counting on you, Quinn."

Julian narrowed his eyes. "Why me?"

"You're a natural leader, Quinn," Rittenour said, reattaching the pistol's slide before taking one last drag off the remnant of a cigarette that was curling up smoke from an ashtray. There was also a bottle of whisky on the desk beside a single glass, both empty. "The ranks look up to you," the colonel continued. "Be fair but firm. It's the best advice I can give you. Good luck. Dismissed."

Not sure whether a salute was in order, Julian didn't offer one, drifting to the door in a quandary as Rittenour loaded a single shell in the chamber. "Sir?" Julian asked in afterthought.

"What is it?"

"Who won?"

Rittenour massaged his neck. "Wars aren't won, Quinn. They're survived."

"Then who's in charge?"

"There's a new sheriff in Dodge. Someone new, from out of the blue. Reports are sketchy. They say it's a miracle."

Julian's brow furrowed hopefully. "I know who."

"Do you?" Rittenour asked skeptically.

"You don't believe in prophecy, then," Julian said.

Rittenour measured his reply. "I believe it's what got us here. The rest is up to you … all of you. FYI, we met once."

"Yes, sir, I remember. Seal Beach."

Rittenour shook his head. "Before that, way before, before you were traded to LA—a grocery store parking lot outside of DC when you were still with the 'Skins. It was raining. You gave me a jump." The colonel chuckled. "You were driving a Jag, brand new. I was out of uniform in an old beater of a Chevy pickup coming off a bender. Couldn't get the time of day out of anyone else. Ring any bells?"

Julian shook his head, then frowned angrily. "You knew me all along?"

"I knew," Rittenour said with sad finality. "Goodbye, Mighty."

"Goodbye, sir."

As Julian pulled the door shut, there was a single gunshot, making him jump. The major outside made no move to investigate. He merely handed over his sidearm. After a long moment, Julian took it and walked on.

"What happens now, Quinn?" the major called after him. He didn't get an answer, nor would he have liked the one Julian was mulling over. Forgiveness was always easier in concept than practice. It all depended on who needed it and who was in a position to grant it. "Quinn!" the major yelled. But Julian had already disappeared around the corner.

Chapter V

War's end, assuming the news was true, came with other startling changes—startling because they were beyond the grasp of scientific understanding, certainly at its present level.

An immediate shift in global weather patterns was detected, coinciding with a palpable re-intensification of the earth's magnetic field, diverting deadly solar winds into empty space. Heretofore silent communication satellites, thought irreparably damaged, came back online, mysteriously of their own accord. New rains fell where they hadn't for years. By what seemed the same stroke, precipitation subsided over flood-ravaged regions. Fresh cold snaps refroze the polar ice caps in a matter of weeks, restoring ocean currents to their previous tracks. Even the protective ozone layer reasserted itself for no convenient reason. The jet stream stabilized, normalizing, reverting back closer to its former predictability. The word *miracle* and its plural, long dropped from the lexicon of any language for all practical purposes, suddenly reintroduced itself with head-scratching rapidity on any number of fronts—all of them, in fact.

Disease vanished. Infections healed without treatment. The water table inexplicably purified itself. Blighted, dormant plants and trees greened, flowering anew. The healthy buzz of pollinating insects was everywhere, virtually overnight. The birds were again happy, the bullfrogs and the crickets. All wild fauna began its steady regeneration, marching toward a new age. Attitudes of the human sort, however, at least in some spheres, proved somewhat less adaptable.

A strong, fearless, unconventionally adept personality, historically and politically unprecedented in terms of both intellect and temperament, was required lest surviving humanity slide into an unrecoverable post-war anarchy of misanthropic revenge. For good or ill, just such a leader took center stage, immodestly crowning himself king of kings in Jerusalem to the popular acclaim of an exhausted world. Proclaimed the *Mahdi* by some, or the 12th Imam, Christ and Messiah by others, his name was Janus Philio, and his very first royal edict officially outlawed priestcraft in any form. Ultimately, the act would prove either a stroke of unmitigated brilliance or the hapless conceit of a ridiculously naïve iconoclast. Only time would tell, and there were far more pressing issues: feeding a starved world, for instance. The king got right to it, and with amazing results.

Concurrently, a sea and an ocean away from Jerusalem to the west, developments in the Holy Land and elsewhere were being assessed with considerable misgivings.

Years before, the three branches of constitutional government in the United States had all been homogenized into one under a joint resolution of the Congress, designed to reduce redundancy at the federal level and the bureaucratic inefficiencies inherent in a representative democracy. Considered vital to release the Unitary Executive from time-consuming oversight reporting relative to the exigencies of wartime, the measure was appropriately entitled the Government Unification Act, a logical expansion of the suspension of habeas corpus, as the war consumed more and more of the president's focus.

Temporary, and complete with a sunset clause, it effectively dissolved both houses of congress and the judiciary, which being dissolved were unable to meet officially to review the act, either for extension or repeal. Martial law further ensured that no such meetings took place, officially or otherwise. And, whereas the new law stipulated that the White House must always act in good faith given its broader, unchecked powers, the president dutifully affirmed that his personal faith was, in fact, quite good. To whatever extent this was true, the District of Columbia and its suburbs had been transformed into an armed camp, wherein paranoia was the overarching policy.

Now, of the many councils maintained under the current structure—National Security Council, Council of Economic Advisors, the Foreign Affairs Advisory Board, the President's Council on Physical Fitness, et al—the most potent of these was the Evangelical High Council of North America, an august body of respected clergymen delegated to monitor the moral health of the republic, each of whom did so with commendable vigor. The High Council did not grasp for power; no need for that. It *was* the power, retiring and appointing presidents at its whim—three in the span of the last eight years—to the point that it was said, not altogether facetiously, that the reigning president had had a rubber stamp surgically affixed to his right hand before taking the oath of office.

More commonly known simply as "the council," the EHCNA was headquartered with a staff of thousands in a marvelously modern, glass-and-steel complex—the bridge between church and state—at the center of the National Mall where the Washington Monument had towered before heathen terrorists toppled it. Precisely how the fiends had managed this was never fully explained, although no one doubted that the plan's mastermind was the Antichrist, whose identity had never quite been nailed down. There was no shortage of candidates, however, so that when one died or dropped out of sight, another took his place. At any rate, rather than rebuild the obelisk—no less than a pagan symbol from ancient Egypt, rife with Masonic undertones—the council had happily appropriated the acreage to erect its own sprawling headquarters, reminiscent of the medieval cathedral at Cluny. At a cost estimated to have exceeded one billion dollars, the construction project was a single line item buried in a budget supplemental for prosecuting the war overseas.

At the moment, the council was meeting in emergency session to consider the sudden cessation of hostilities half a globe away, news of which had taken this long to assemble with any clarity. Chairing, as always, was the Reverend Dr. Darius Block, a photogenic shepherd with sandy-gray hair, somewhat darker eyebrows, and perfectly bleached teeth. The rest of the council ranged from early middle age to advanced senility, some brooding. All were affluent and decidedly well fed.

Amid a mélange of regal and high-tech appurtenances in the chamber, a slide show was in progress, presenting the newly ascendant King Philio in a variety of oriental venues addressing huge, adoring crowds outdoors. Of some note was Philio's wardrobe—consistently rather plain, office casual, minus coat and tie. Indeed, he was unremarkably average-looking for the most part, a virtual everyman, hard to pick out of a group of any size had he not been the center of attention. Additional slides portrayed him with his sleeves rolled up, feeding the hungry, distributing staples, or with hammer and nails, building new housing in a dusty refugee camp.

"Quite the little populist, isn't he?" Chairman Block remarked off-handedly. His accent betrayed roots in New England. "Who are his handlers, I wonder?"

"Unknown," said a staff member. "The consensus is, what you see is what you get."

Darius Block cracked a grin. "Almost never," he scoffed, "which is why the consensus is almost always wrong. Besides, were we to rely on the consensus, we wouldn't need God, now would we?" Block pondered the situation for a moment. "How did this happen? I thought we made arrangements to, you know, take him out."

The staffer was loath to respond. A member of the council from Texas, paraphrasing from his briefing package, took the plunge. "Circumstances accelerated beyond our control. I mean, who knew? He was just another upstart feel-good do-gooder until he slicked his way into the troops on both sides of the front. All we know is that whatever he's peddling spread like a rash, infecting the field commands, friend and foe alike. There was an unauthorized powwow under white flags, both sides represented. By the end of it, both sides surrendered … to him. He declined, said he wasn't seeking surrender, only cooperation."

"How noble," Block inserted without inflection.

"Our frontline officers caved like dominoes, top down and bottom up, resigning their commissions," the Texan went on. "Theirs, too, evidently, mutually pledging their allegiance to him—a complete breakdown in discipline, not to mention loyalty. It's the damnedest thing anyone's ever heard of, but the long and the skinny of it is this: he now commands upwards of twelve million men under arms—that's boots on the ground, all tested in battle. He's got unquestioned air superiority, at least over there, along with both navies, giving him undisputed control of the seas and the oil reserves of the Middle East, and more are flocking to him in droves as we speak. It all happened so fast. They love him over there—no accounting for it. Competing cultures and doctrine have taken a backseat to everyone just getting along. The time to heal is now and forever, he says, and they believe him."

The chairman smirked. "Has he ordered them to beat their swords into plowshares?"

"Swords maybe," said the Texan, "not their tanks and artillery."

The others nervously shared the humor.

"They say he's got magic, that he *is* magic," the Texan concluded.

"I like magic," Block said. "Where's he headed?"

Another council member picked up the train. "For the time being? Asia. Tehran and New Delhi both signed treaties within the last week without a shot fired. He's now in talks with Beijing. Intel suggests a final deal with the chinks is strictly a formality. They've revolted in North Korea, a full-scale uprising against the party, long overdue. What's left of Europe is already demobilizing. Let's see, the Vatican-in-exile has expressed 'cautious optimism.' Russia is rapidly drawing down. He's sending food north."

"Where is this food coming from?" Reverend Block asked curiously.

"You got me. Thin air. It's being delivered in the millions of metric tons, though."

"I don't mean to pile on, but we're soft to the south," a third council member tossed in gravely, "leaving the border in imminent jeopardy. Central and South America were never really in the fight. Nonetheless, they've dispatched emissaries to Jerusalem. If the spics invade, our underbelly is defenseless, except for scattered vigilantes."

Block reclined in his chair, interlacing his fingers behind his head. "Sounds like he's on a roll."

"More of a juggernaut," someone else said. "It's only a matter of weeks, days, maybe hours, before he turns his attention on us."

The chairman absently regarded the vaulted, cathedral ceiling and its high, stained-glass windows, slanting in sunlight in a rainbow of vivid colors. "Hmm, leaving us for last. Interesting. What are our chances of speedily raising fresh forces to resist?"

Nobody answered. Block swiveled to the staffer tasked with this. She pressed her palms together prayerfully, fingers to her lips, her outlook bleak. "Nil. The public has no stomach for it. Daily food riots have spread from the cities into the heartland. Rationing is all fouled up. Massive corruption. Frankly, there's no one left to press. The last big batch put back into the LA Zone just a few days ago from almost three months at sea, on the scrap and on the march."

"We've been running a whole country," someone else griped, "two, actually—forget World War III. There's only so damned much we can do. Don't they understand? God willed it!"

The most wrinkled member of the council scowled, mildly twitching with Parkinson's. "Ingrates, reprobates the lot. They deserved everything they got. No faith."

Ignoring him, Block turned to the lady staffer. "On the march, you say?"

"Some nobody," she stammered, checking her notes, the paper trembling. "Um, a Julian Quinn, conscript, with a couple hundred thousand, on a beeline this way, picking up numbers."

Block's crystal eyes bored into her. She hesitantly amplified, fearing she'd be blamed.

"They say he's a true believer in Philio, a total convert. We're not sure if they're actually in contact, coordinating, but this Quinn's techies from Silicon Valley have pirated our broadcast satellites and relaunched a limited Internet, preaching the gospel of Philio, uncensored. Worse, he's a nig—um, what we used to call an African American. A whole bunch more's with him, mostly darkies, swelling by the mile." She swallowed painfully. "And, well, from all reports, this Quinn is no Martin Luther King, Jr."

"Meaning?" Chairman Block asked.

"They're armed to the teeth with all the latest weapons, are highly organized and motivated—our worst nightmare. Again, they seem to think they haven't been treated fairly."

"Zone trash," crowed Pruneface, twitching. "Unsaved muds, every one."

"Call them what you will, Minister," said the staffer, "but even whites like what they hear, especially about Philio's edict against organized religion. They're just, well, tired of it all."

Another council member spoke up. "My understanding is he's banned priests, not faith. Actually, priest*craft*, whatever that is."

"Has he now?" said the chairman. It was difficult to tell what he was thinking.

"And good riddance," seconded the prune-faced council member. "The papists have been dodgy on the war ever since the Dome fell, the Anglicans and Lutherans a close second ... no backbone, no stomach for extinguishing evil. They can all go to the devil along with the mullahs, muftis, imams, and ayatollahs; the brahmans, yogis, and lamas, too. Let them all burn. This Philio is doing us a favor." Wincing crankily, he shifted in his chair. "Aw, to hell with it. It's over, all of it. We gave it a run ... hell, almost won the whole kit and caboodle, and very nearly put things back the way they *ought* to be, the way the good Lord intended. Why he refuses to support us I will never know. We did it all for him, for God's sake! Nope, I'm afraid this dog just don't hunt. I say we order the dad-blame *president* to push the damn button. Kill 'em all, every last one. Let the Almighty sort it out." Twitching, Pruneface again shifted uncomfortably. "The whole subject is inflaming my piles."

Bemused, Chairman Block folded his lips. "Oh, don't be so gloom and doom, you old fart. A crisis is merely a fresh opportunity in disguise." He plunged into deep concentration.

No one intruded on his silence, repressing their panic, content to observe a strategic, spiritually incisive master at work. He'd brought them this far. Many were convinced he was the reincarnation of Moses himself, a fanciful presumption the Reverend Block did little to discourage. In under a minute, he had devised his new game plan.

"Issue a public statement," he ordered generally. "The administration criminally overreached, despite our continual and repeated warnings. Thus, this council has no choice but to intervene on behalf of the people, in the name of God.

Immediate and emergency steps are being undertaken to restore the shattered framework of our constitutional democracy."

There were outbursts of bewilderment around the council table.

"*Meanwhile*," Block had to shout above the fray, "send to Jerusalem. Sue for peace. Tell the 'king' we're behind him all the way. Indeed, our joy knows no bounds. Unmasked as an agent of the Antichrist, the president has been popularly overthrown, or will be." Pushing up to leave, Block muted all dissent with his matter-of-fact calm. "Send Morton Parmister. Whatever it takes, he's to get as close to the king as possible—our enlightened, freethinking envoy—and keep me informed. Lord knows Brother Morty has a unique talent for such things. In the meantime, we'll put the president and his entire cabinet on trial for crimes against humanity and high treason—*posthumously*, if you catch my drift. It must all be very public. Before that, burn this building to the ground, every scrap of paper and computer file in it. Charge the White House for that as well. On that score, the backlash, I expect us all to be arrested in no time flat as rebel sympathizers. Fill in the blanks. Some of us may very well be martyred. Welcome it. Embrace it. Or don't, at your peril. Either way, this meeting is adjourned, and this council is dissolved."

There was a flurry of wild speculation. A heretofore speechless member couldn't contain his alarm. "With all humility, Pastor Block, we're *endorsing* Philio's reign?"

"Check 2 Chronicles 10 and 11," Block was quick to reply, stretching out his shoulders. "What choice do we have except this? Solomon's successor was Rehoboam. We can be either the old men or the young men. Just remember, it was the old men who lost. Personally, I'm not ready to give into age quite yet. Too much of the Lord's work remains undone."

This merely created more confusion. Ever-ready Bibles materialized, their pages thumbed with alacrity, the passage scanned, minds stretching to mine from the text a contemporary parallel, if any, though no one doubted there had to be one. Pastor Block could inerrantly produce on the fly a scriptural argument for just about everything he did or thought. It was uncanny. "You're saying this Philio is the real deal?" someone asked him.

Chairman Block smiled. "Fiddlesticks; how could he be?" Block nodded to an inscription prominently chiseled in the marble wall of the chamber. It was the council's biblical charter, from Amos 3:7, and from which it drew its present "legal" authority, reading:

> *Surely the Lord God will do nothing,*
> *but he revealeth his secret unto his*
> *servants the prophets.*

"Besides," Block added, pausing malevolently before the larger-than-life image of Philio on the projection screen, "where's the glory? No, I see only flesh and blood with a weakness for flesh and blood. Has he declared himself the Second Coming, implied it in any way?"

Several at the table scoured the intelligence. "Not in so many words," one answered, "not personally, not yet. But he did enter Jerusalem through the Golden Gate after blasting it open with a howitzer. Rode in on a donkey, shofroth sounding from the parapets."

"Gimmicks," said Block. "Cheap theater. It only proves he can read—and not well."

"The Jews certainly seem to be giving him the benefit of the doubt," someone said.

Block gave a condescending roll of the eyes. He was about to leave but stopped again with an afterthought. "Oh, and dig up everything you can find on this rebel Quinn. He's more dangerous than anything coming out of Jerusalem, I can tell you that for free. He could also prove useful."

This said, the chairman departed the room and, shortly, the building for the last time, ending the session without the usual closing prayer, leaving the others beside themselves with apprehension. Old men or young, what would become of them when Quinn's rebel masses besieged the capital—uncouth barbarians at the gates? Had not everyone here served the will of the Most High to the extent of their capacities with great toil, only to be deprived of final victory over evil? Who was Janus Philio, this strange interloper, strangely named? What gave him the right to put on pretensions to the mantle of Jesus Christ, even if only inferred? *What was God thinking?*

Chapter VI

Portland's brick-paved Pioneer Place, at one time a hip shopping district, was today a drizzly mess, not that this was unusual. The people here were used to it, had learned to accept it, ultimately forced to accept a whole lot more than that. Still an open city, Portland had dodged the fates of Los Angeles and San Francisco by rounding up its most undesirable and vocal activists early on in the Apocalypse. They filled whole trains. The destination wasn't important, just that it be somewhere else. Better not to know; easier on the liver. Now, five years since the clear-out, the thunder of heavy artillery not ten miles upriver had Oregonians everywhere second-guessing.

Newly arrived in Portland, gratefully employed where so many were not, Jamyqua Quinn had the afternoon off. It hadn't come cheap, though it served no good purpose to dwell on such things. Her looks had gotten her the job right off. Keeping it, however, had quickly warped into a lesson in humility, then humiliation. It didn't qualify as harassment, though. Harassment implied resistance. Resistance suggested dignity. The scant little Jamyqua had left she reserved solely for the protection of her children.

Getting here had been one long nightmare that was far from over. On her own, things might have been different. But with three youngsters it was emotional suffocation—the hiding, playing the 'Quiet Game,' constantly on the lookout, afraid of her own shadow, always on the move, allowing herself to sleep for no more than thirty minutes at a stretch. These days, everyone was suspicious of everyone else—all religiously blessed. Council agents were everywhere. For all practical purposes, everyone was a council agent—on its payroll or not. Self-interest ruled supreme; or, rather, self-preservation. All in all, and to

Jamyqua's ceaseless wonder, the entire country was really just one big zone. She hadn't escaped, she soon realized. There was no escape. And then came her ultimate horror.

Weakened by stress and lack of nourishment—rations she appropriately deferred to her children—the telltale signs of plague had revealed themselves in ghoulishly rapid succession, numbering her days in single digits; fewer days, perhaps only hours, before the virus went airborne and infected her babies. Treatment would have been pointless, had it even been available. With the symptoms this advanced, her odds of recovery were statistically flat. Zero. Then, inexplicably, the nosebleeds stopped. The hemorrhagic discharge in her stool cleared up. The headaches, the painful swelling of her gums, in her joints and muscles, the conjunctivitis—all vanished. Somehow, she'd beaten it, and for no earthly reason, now barely resembling the woman who'd stared back at her in the mirror just a handful of days ago.

And so, venturing out with her brood like a mother duck to pick up a few essentials, calculating the risk an acceptable one, Jamyqua was here at Pioneer Place to reintroduce the kids to a forgotten treat—ice cream cones with sprinkles on top. She carried tiny Lana Sue in a baby sling, holding an umbrella in one hand, a grocery bag in the other. Sternly instructed not to let go of each other, the boys held hands. Her firstborn, Clinton, also helped with the grocery bag, since he was now the man of the family. Though she had been told there was an old-fashioned ice cream parlor still in business hereabouts, Jamyqua was having a devil of a time finding it among the mostly gutted-out storefronts. The looters had struck at the first news of rebel scouts in the area. There were other predators about, as well.

"*Mommy!*"

The child's pitch could have shattered glass.

Jamyqua's first impulse was to blink her eyes in disbelief. *What is up with the kid-friendly dude in the yellow rain slicker?* Ubiquitous in this weather, its hood concealed his face. And then he was running, Justin under his arm—*her* Justin!—a streak of yellow lost to countless other streaks. *Oh no you didn't!*—except he had. Not only had he, but he was getting away with it; no one up ahead so much as lifted a finger to slow him down.

Jamyqua's newest dilemma was a psychedelic miasma of complications. Like a Chinese finger trap, every maternal instinct she had was instantly in conflict with another. She had two other children to think of. Escapees from the Zone were still outlaws, legally shot on sight. They might tell stories. Children were no exception. It happened all the time. The Portland police, any that hadn't already skedaddled with as much loot as they could carry, remained ostensibly loyal to the district's military governor. Even should the rebels upriver ultimately prove victorious, they were miles away. Calling for help might lead to exposure. *Show me your papers.*

Out of options, Jamyqua chucked the umbrella and groceries and snatched Clinton's wrist to give chase. Just seven, her Clinton was already a speed demon, easily keeping up. Unfortunately, Jamyqua's shoes were all wrong for a run, failing to grip the rain-slick pavers. Slipping at a full-on sprint, she lost her center of gravity first, then her feet, nearly wrenching Clinton's arm out of its socket as she madly twisted her own hips and torso. Had she not, exactly when she did, Lana Sue would be a pancake. That was the miracle, even as the back of Jamyqua's head slammed the wet pavers like a ripe cantaloupe.

The last working hospital in Portland was right where Sam Goode needed it. Ironically, had he begun his search here, he would have saved himself a couple of days. Currently, the price for each passing hour was soaring exponentially. For some, mere minutes were a commodity in short supply. The last regular army units in this sector, a patchwork of light and mechanized infantry under ad hoc command, had fallen back to the city to make their final stand. The fighting was now street by street, block by block—a meat grinder of house-to-house combat.

The converted hanger stood a good couple of miles from the main terminal complex; the airport, officially closed. Sensing the inevitable, all of its air traffic controllers had called in sick or simply not shown up for work, joining the snarled flow of refugees backed up at the bridges and viaducts to all points away from the fighting. Using his sat phone, Sam ordered his plane brought closer, if only to speed his own departure should this last-ditch effort fail. He then entered the hanger's gaping aperture.

Designed for jumbo jet maintenance, the immensity of the makeshift triage center was staggering. There were countless hundreds, maybe thousands. Beds were at a premium. Even rudimentary blankets were in short supply. Most of the wounded, military and civilian alike, had only the cold comfort of varnished concrete beneath them. Keeping out the rain, the hanger's roof kept in the smell. Eye-watering as it was, Sam's team was prepared. He'd taught them well. From among them—four men and two women—a jar of Noxzema was produced for a quick dab directly under the nostrils. Only Sam declined. Any sign of weakness on his part now could prove deleterious to morale.

"Fan out," he told them, wiggling his fingers into latex gloves. The others did likewise, and the search commenced—bed by bed, stretcher by stretcher, broken soul after broken soul. The recently expired were no exception, their ragged shrouds pulled back for possible verification. Emotion served no good purpose. It was just a job. Success struck under twenty minutes into it, at least potentially.

Armed with a well-creased 5 × 7 glamour shot of a nineteen-year-old beauty queen, Sam rejected any match at first but quickly backtracked to hold the photograph directly beside her face. The bandaged-wrapped head hid the lush, auburn hair beneath. He tried to imagine her with foundation on, soft makeup to bring out her cheekbones, some eye shadow, liner, lash extensions, tasteful lip gloss. Even his most vivid imagination made it a stretch. He quickly checked her chart. *Doe, Jane #427.*

Sam purposefully cleared his throat. "Mrs. Quinn?" She didn't rouse. He checked her pulse, raising his voice just below a shout. "Jamyqua Quinn!" Nothing. Wait, scratch that. There was REM activity. Sam added volume. "Mrs. *Julian* Quinn!" It worked, opening her eyes—not much, but she was conscious. Her lips were as dry as a Saharan sandstorm. Sam quickly alerted the others, asking for water. Allowed just a drop, she revived a little more, and her vision seemed to clear. "Are you Jamyqua Wilson Quinn?" Sam asked her formally.

Her eyes weakly scanned him, drawn to the heavy-caliber magnum poking out of a shoulder holster under his open jacket, then to the badge on his belt. It bore the dreaded chi rho symbol. *Council.* Shutting her eyes, her chin quivered; tears streamed from the corners of her eyes. Her voice was barely audible. *"Don't hurt my children."*

The rebels overran the airport just as the sleek corporate jet reached takeoff speed. Climbing fast, it absorbed a few random potshots, the damage superficial. Even so, the pilot waited until he'd achieved his cruising altitude of 33,000 feet well out over the Pacific before correcting course into a wide swing back to the east.

Inside the cozy cabin, Jamyqua's reunion with her babies continued with uninhibited joy. Her own condition dramatically improved from just being with them and the knowledge that they were each still in one piece. She could swear Lana Sue felt a little heavier. Borderline anemic before their separation, Baby Girl had since received the best pediatric care money could buy. *But why?* And then there was Justin to consider as the horror of the abduction came flooding back. Soberly, Jamyqua probed the preschooler's eyes. "Justin, honey, listen to me. Did the bad man ... did he touch you, like we talked about no grownup ever should?"

Justin was unequivocal. "Uh-uh." The boy threw a tiny finger at the stuffy council agent. "*He* shot him."

Off-balance, Jamyqua glanced across to Sam, who was currently immersed in a newspaper. The younger members of his team were dozing in their seats, all needing the rest, too, after virtually ripping metro Portland apart, floorboards to rafters. Truth to tell, they'd scoured the entire Left Coast north of Los Angeles to connect the dots in search of their quarry.

"Mister?" Jamyqua pressed the dour council agent.

Peering over reading glasses, Sam wasn't expansive. "It seemed the prudent thing to do."

"Is he ..." Jamyqua resisted saying the obvious in front of the children, but she had to know. "I mean, did you ... you know ..."

"Lady, I don't draw my weapon for any other reason." He lowered his gaze to read on.

"Seems like an awful lot of trouble just to send us back to the Zone."

Sam didn't look up. "There are no more zones." But then his curiosity got the better of him. He covered it by stretching his shoulders and back. "It shouldn't have taken as long as it did, but you are good—damned good. I've seen your file, and there's no accounting for it. Who taught you evasion tactics?"

"You did," Jamyqua said pointedly. "All y'all. What I can't figure is what you want with a skinny war widow and three skinny kids."

"You're too modest," Sam returned, his direction hard to decipher.

Jamyqua snorted, almost amused. "Ain't much left," she said, referring to herself, "but if it'll keep my children alive ... take what you want."

Sam met her gaze head on, holding it. "It wasn't supposed to get where it did."

"What?"

"Are you a forgiving person, Mrs. Quinn?"

"Depends," she said. "For now, let's leave it at ... rusty."

"Understandable," Sam allowed. "How do you feel about favors? Do you return them?"

"Speak your mind, Agent Goode."

"Would common Zone trash be flying in a plane like this, ya think?"

"At least we've established how you think of me," Jamyqua said without animus.

For Sam, a tennis buff, her topspin backhand was unreturnable. He'd misjudged her reserve. Hammered hard by life, dented but not broken, the Quinn woman retained a crackerjack mind. He was the cagey professional, but it was *she* steering the conversation. He fast-forwarded to where he thought things could possibly go now, insincere apologies notwithstanding. Without a dramatic shift, all endings were unacceptable. Regrettably, the only tenable shift available was the truth. Thus, restoring his newspaper to its original shape, he adopted his approved fallback position. "Two wrongs don't make a right."

Jamyqua instinctively gathered her children closer around her on the opulent cabin's sofa. "Friend," she said levelly, "y'all been so wrong for so long, I can't do the math."

Sam tossed the newspaper on the cocktail table. "Judge not lest ye be judged."

The uncensored headlines made Jamyqua dizzy, not that her present condition required any help in that department. The headlines explained little and everything all at the same time.

> QUINN CRUSHES FEDERALS AT MEMPHIS
> ROAD TO WASHINGTON WIDE OPEN
> LENGTHY SIEGE ANTICIPATED

Chapter VII

As things turned out, there was no siege of the capital—none required. With the leading surge of the enormously popular rebellion still many days to the west, advance scouts arrived to offer terms. The only problem was finding someone in authority to give them to. Politically and militarily, the District was a ghost town. This was hardly surprising.

The rebellion had begun tacitly enough, with unification of the mutinous conscripts while still at sea, who were urged one and all to remember a time before the Zone, before there was a council. Even the regulars, soldiers and seamen alike, warmed to the memory, although the long years of indoctrination were an obstacle not easily overcome. Keeping them unified was the chore. Making landfall only reinvigorated their bloodlust, albeit in reverse. Marauding the countryside was the standard reaction; and because of this, approving summary execution orders for even those who were among the closest to him became a daily routine for the supreme rebel commander, who had been elected to the post by a simple voice vote. He soon learned that leadership is a cruel business, outdone in its cruelty only by the absence of strong leadership, rendering revolution a messy proposition at its best.

Now, having swept over purple mountain majesty and across the fruited plain in three fast-moving prongs—north, central, and southern—Julian Quinn's forces numbered more than one million and growing, liberating dozens upon dozens of forced labor camps and political detention centers. The prisons were emptied, wherein the great majority of the inmates were there for drug, alcohol, and alternative lifestyle violations, awaiting the noose. Needless to say, those freed were exceedingly grateful. Those that could joined the great march to the east by the tens of thousands. The degree of abuse suffered in confinement, the mortality rate, was mind-boggling by even the most conservative reckoning.

Curiously, the nearby townsfolk claimed no knowledge of the savage treatment of their fellow citizens. Then again, world history, confirmed or denied, was the history of confirmation and denials, undoubtedly the principal reason for its incessant repetition. As a partial remedy for this, the press were also freed to be completely unregulated. Politically detained journalists and others previously in hiding restarted their newspapers. Radio programming of a kind not heard in a long time was soon back on the air, along with television broadcasts in the larger cities. There was much to be documented.

Vast inland depots of fuel and portable power-generating equipment, massive stores of undistributed grain, and grossly overcrowded stockyards were discovered. Tremendous warehouses of canned and freeze-dried goods previously under military guard on rail lines literally out in the middle of nowhere were mainly gathering dust—all of it hoarded by the theocratic decree to nourish the surviving elect, however many or few that turned out to be, at the end of the "end of days." Intended or not, such foresight had only hastened, intensified, then prolonged the wartime misery of almost everyone, religious and not.

But, whatever the theologically anticipated outcome, the rebel advance also stumbled across incredible caches of factory-fresh armaments and ordnance. Had they been made available to the troops battling overseas when produced, these arms might have profoundly altered the war's denouement. It was arguable. What *wasn't* arguable, unworthy of any debate whatsoever, was that such arms now ensured the military supremacy of the rebellion.

As for its leader, he was an intensely private, if determined, revolutionary. Lonely. He gave no grousing speeches, offered no trite syllogisms or self-serving rhetoric. He spoke his mind, to be sure—off the cuff or from the hip—as it struck him, without dissembling or excusing his mistakes or those of anyone else in his inner circle, except for his admission, oft repeated, that "I'm new at this. We all are. Cut me some slack, jack." Most everyone found such candor enormously refreshing. Then again, Julian was still basically just a football player, thinking almost exclusively in terms of Xs and Os. Everyone had assignments. Blow an assignment, get benched. His world was no more complicated than that, not at present, nor did it need to be. To Julian Quinn's way of thinking, history itself was ended. More pertinently, he was a true believer that prophecy was history written in advance. Its interpretation was a matter of expediency rather than reflection. He gave it no deeper thought. This made him human. It also made him vulnerable.

Nonetheless, and despite his profound deficiencies in the military sciences, Quinn's victorious entrance into the capital came on a golden springtime afternoon when the cherry blossoms were in full bloom. The breeze-blown petals were his ticker-tape parade. Cheering locals turned out en masse all along the route. They were particularly thick along Constitution Avenue. There, a high school marching band in punctilious uniforms greeted Julian's armored column with "The Battle Hymn of the Republic." All in all, it was no less than an inauguration—their messiah and redeemer returned.

Julian wasn't inclined to dampen the outpouring. It felt good to be adored, the faulty premise notwithstanding, certainly to the extent that he was being identified as the Savior, whom he was yet to meet, at least in person. Plenty of time to set the record straight later. Let them party, let them worship his triumph. There was much to be thankful for, too much. In fact, it was amazing just how much booze and bubbly there was to be had, looted from the basements and wine cellars of the former Beltway elite, all top shelf. But, if hypocrisy had its rewards, it also had its downside, what King Philio called the "inevitability of eventuality." By royal decree, capital punishment had been abolished worldwide. For some, though, word arrived too late.

On the Mall, just off the charred ruins of the council headquarters, stood a large gallows, facing the South Lawn of the White House. From it, the rotting corpses of the president and a dozen members of his cabinet still swung by the neck, pecked at by cawing flocks of black birds. From his perch on the lead tank, Julian halted the column, requesting binoculars, focusing in on a large, hand-painted placard that proclaimed: "*NEVER AGAIN!!!*" The band stopped playing, and the crowds quieted.

Nacho Angel hustled in from a secondary vehicle. He was now Julian's trusted lieutenant, his second in command. "Why we stopped? What's the problem?"

Julian motioned out to the gallows. "What the fuck is this?"

Nacho looked. "Oh, yeah, *them*. Strung up a week, maybe a good ten days, 'fore we got here. It's not like they didn't have it coming."

"This is wrong," Julian said. "Cut 'em down."

"That won't be very popular," Nacho warned. Julian pasted him with a glare. Nacho raised his walkie-talkie and delegated the task accordingly.

"See that they get a proper burial," Julian ordained. "I mean it."

"What, like Arlington?" Nacho scoffed. "That ought to go over like a lead balloon."

"I didn't say that. Dig the holes right there for all I care." Julian then gazed out over the razed council HQ. "Who burned down the temple?"

Nacho shrugged. "Looks like their John Birch Utopia wasn't all that. My guess? With us breathing down their necks and e'erything, they got into it 'mongst themselves. Go figure. It'll all come out in the wash. Yo, *jefe*, it's getting late. Where you wanna put down, B? How 'bout that big ol' white house over there? I hear it's got a vacancy." Nacho smirked, testing.

Julian shook his head. "Ain't my speed. Any hotel with a bed and a shower'll do."

"I'm way ahead of you," Nacho said. "The Mayflower, across the way out yonder, presidential suite. E'erything's set. Don't settle in too fast, though. The local mucks wanna smoke the peace pipe."

"I'll bet," said Julian. "First, turn up the *holy men*, if they're still around. We got us a reckoning to be had with them what dreamed up the Zone and the rest of it."

"I'm on it," Nacho said.

"Take me to the Mayflower," Julian relayed to his tank driver, adding to Nacho, "No comeuppance, hear? Vengeance is mine, sayeth the Lord, so give regular folks a break, all colors and stripes. The son is on his way. We're just his pathfinders, humble and forthright."

"Word," said Nacho, raising a fist, before striding off to get a handle on the more mundane organizational aspects of the occupation, muttering, "It's all rock 'n' roll to me." He signaled the flamboyant drum major to strike up the band again. It did, with a brassy rendition of "I Need a Hero." The crowds went wild, dancing, cheering anew, chanting "Mighty-Mighty-Mighty!" as the parade resumed.

After cleaning up and grabbing a bite, Julian was set upon by the wonks late into the evening, soon learning that the difference between conquering and governing was as vast as the lands he'd just pacified, perhaps too rapidly. He personally avoided the term "liberated," smart enough to recognize that liberty was a perfectly nebulous concept with a host of qualifiers, the passage of time being chief among them. Having too much freedom tended to confuse and irritate people, he was counseled; too many choices. Structure was required, and structure meant rules and obedience to them—the *freedom* to conform. On the other hand, the central feature of a truly "free" society was also an oxymoron: popular disagreement, making an open democracy terribly inefficient and painful, especially in times of crisis and other hard transitions. Tight regulation was the ticket, some lectured. Absolutely not, thundered others.

Thus, presented with the raft of decisions to be made and/or mediated, large and small, crucial or trivial, Julian's idealism swiftly melted away. Anyone who loved politics or enjoyed this had to have a screw loose. Anyone actively seeking political office was a masochist. Too many voices demanded to be heard, voices rife with disparate agendas, some hidden, most of them obvious. Cooperation and compromise was for the other guy. All sides were equal believers that the squeaky wheel gets the grease, convinced that it was the volume of their argument, rather than its merit, that would ultimately hold sway. The shrill inanity of it all was overwhelming.

What form of government do you envision? Will all of your advisors continue to be minorities and women? What legal basis do you claim for assuming power? How liberal do you intend to be? Will conservatives be invited to share power? What about the faltering economy? What are your plans to jump-start it? Will you respect religious freedoms and the right to worship according to choice? Or will you revert to unrepentant secularism? How will you pay for it all?

Any administrative abilities Julian possessed were nascent, raw, and untested. Academically, insofar as his collegiate career at Georgia Tech was concerned, he'd majored in drinking beer and cognac, smoking the occasional joint, snorting the recreational line of coke, and chasing rich girls in Buckhead, greatly assisted in all of these pursuits by his cinematic good looks, a totally cut physique, and being his conference's leading rusher and scorer, a runaway media and alumni favorite, not to mention a Heisman Trophy also-ran for two consecutive years. Professionally, marriage put the brakes on chasing anything other than personal wealth, product endorsements, and the like. He'd accepted few responsibilities that didn't include a first-down marker or the end zone, picking up the blitz and Pro Bowl selection, until fatherhood, and then reluctantly. He was paid to run and shoot the shit with glib sports pundits, to be fast on his feet and fast at the mouth, the fastest, the quickest, always. For that matter, being elusive was what Mighty was all about, and, on that score, he was sorely tempted to run away from this, you can be sure, all of it, fully knowing he could not, not now. It was worse than a wall of three-hundred-pound linemen.

Who will be punished for the nation's slide into evangelical totalitarianism, its excesses, and how soon? Who will be prosecuted for the wasteful prosecution of perpetual war? For the abridgement of civil liberties? For the termination of all scientific research not serving a militaristic objective? So much time has been lost, so much social progress derailed! When, god damn it, when—with all due respect—when, when, when? You're in charge. Decide!

Julian put a stop to the hectoring by calmly declaring, "Except I'm not."

Then, who?

"These are all choices for His Majesty the king."

Monarchy? Surely you jest. This is America. We're to be ruled by a foreigner? A Jew? Preposterous. How do you know this Philio is not a myth, more propaganda from our enemies?

"Is the Bible a myth?" Julian asked levelly.

Get real! God will impose his will when the time is right, when it suits him. No man can. You can't dictate solely on the basis of your personal beliefs. That's what they did—*the council.*

"That's not going to happen," Julian promised. "You have my word on it, before God."

When they were all blessedly gone, Julian dismissed his bodyguards, leisurely helping himself to a crystalline decanter of Armagnac. This was more like it, what he was used to, had worked for, sacrificing his body endlessly and mercilessly, behind the scrimmage line and beyond, to enjoy. Its bite against his taste buds was so familiar—grand beyond words—both innervating and relaxing, the burn down his throat savored, welcomed. It made his eyes moist. Swirling the elixir in the glass, inhaling its bouquet deeply, generously, he also sensed the fragrant potpourri infusing the suite, its cleanliness, its innocence. It reminded him of Jamyqua, her loving attention to detail in their own home, everything in its place—lavender and vanilla with the perfect feminine touch of spice. Cinnamon, perhaps. *Was that it?* It had been so long.

It also made him think of everything else he missed, those *other* little things—now looming large—the things he'd so wantonly taken for granted, the simple pleasures and friendships so easily disregarded. Turning to a window overlooking the shimmering lights of the city, he drifted toward despair, wishing for what he could never reclaim—the unconditional love of his loved ones—ever. Empty. He had different responsibilities now—forced upon him—beyond anything he could have previously imagined, that *anyone* might have imagined, realistically, for a black man. He could trust no one, not anymore, not completely, of any color. Frankly, his life still sucked, all of it. Any change between surviving the Zone and now was cosmetic, merely a difference of degree and scenery. Julian tightly shut his eyes. *Who the fuck am I kidding?* He wasn't cut out for this. He was a jock, a football player, a professional athlete—a good one by all accounts, breaking records—but with no business being in this business. *Damn that dumb-ass colonel for giving me the confidence to try!* Rittenour had taken the easy way out, leaving stupid, naïve Julian holding the bag.

His sour musings were interrupted by a rap on the suite's front door. He was in a poor mood for company. "Come," he invited anyway.

Nacho Angel cracked the double doors. "You decent?"

Julian's weary reply was full of self-doubt. "Depends on who you talk to. Hell, B, you're looking at the leader of the free world."

Nacho made a sour face. "You ain't all that yet, homey. Nigger, straighten up and fly right, or I will bitch-slap you back to Africa."

He made Julian laugh. The banter helped to center him.

Nacho was the only one whom Julian allowed to take such liberties, and only in private. Angel had already launched the insurrection a few weeks before the conscript flotilla made port. He was leading a ragtag band of around fifty Latinos and Vietnamese, mostly former busboys and shopkeepers, that had been surrounded in Garden Grove by elite council storm troopers trucked in from Phoenix. The insurgents had all but run out of hope and ammunition when Julian arrived with the cavalry, and in overwhelming numbers. Even so, the fighting was fierce; the council force was fearless, battling to the last man. The women who'd spirited Julian's family out of the Zone were among those killed in action. Nacho himself was shot to pieces, and upon winning the day, he'd vowed his unquestioning fealty to the Mighty Quinn, come hell or high water—to the death. *"We can do this,"* Nacho had said. *"You can do this. We got to, B ... all the way to Washington."* The rest was history. Perhaps no two men alive enjoyed a tighter bond, differences of philosophy notwithstanding. Nacho still wasn't sold on Philio, encouraging Julian to personally step up and put things to right—with or without the new king's blessing.

"Sorry. *Whassup*, beaner?" Julian tossed back.

"I need you to get ahold of yourself. Take a breath. Pour yourself a drink."

Julian toasted Nacho with his snifter. "I'm way ahead of you."

"Now put on your fearless leader face. Stand tall. I like the sweater. It's a good look for us. Ralph Lauren, right? Dang, I wish you smoked a pipe. I'll make a note of it."

"Will you stop! What's up?"

"Call it providence. Ready?"

Sighting the glaring spotlight of a video cameraman behind Nacho in the corridor, Julian caught a glimpse of the sound man's boom mike. Nacho was big on squeezing out the most publicity he could, whenever and wherever he could. Fortunately, being on camera was second nature to Julian from his jock days. "Get on with it, Spielberg," he complained, "'fore I slap you back to Mexico. Difference is ... I can."

Framing Julian between his outstretched hands, satisfied, Nacho threw the doors open, respectfully retreating into the hallway. His jaw dropping, eyes widening incredulously, Julian's heart leapt into his throat, his respiration sprinting, his knees going weak. The brandy snifter dropped from his hand, staining the carpet. Beyond his wildest hopes and dreams, standing in the doorway, without blemish or visible physical hurt, was his never-more-lovely bride Jamyqua, holding their baby, with their two sons clutching at her skirts. *Alive! Healthy!* Julian's whole body went numb. His face burned, mainly from the camera's hot light. He felt faint. Free-flowing tears coursed down his cheeks as he covered his mouth. "Dear, sweet Jesus!" Clasping both hands to his head, he collapsed to his knees. "*Sweet, everlasting Jesus!*" Nacho was enormously pleased. He couldn't have scripted a better reaction.

They rushed to him there on the floor, Julian's family, hugging and kissing with abandon, no words, emotions unrestrained. Beautiful. Perfect. And there was more.

Waiting in the wings were Julian's mother and father and his six brothers and three sisters and their spouses and children, a huge contingent, making it an even sweeter reunion. And still more came—Jamyqua's parents, her three sisters and their husbands with their children. In short order, Julian's suite was bulging, stretching its walls and seams, all happily so, deliriously happy. Scrupulously supervised by Nacho and Julian's bodyguards, room service waiters carted in food and soft drinks, a smorgasbord. Someone put a Luther Vandross CD on the stereo, his voice praising heaven above with a rousing gospel choir backup—immeasurably inspiring.

Slipping free of his precious loves, Julian found Nacho. "How?" he wanted to know over the music, wiping his nose, the tears from his eyes. "How is this possible? Don't get me wrong—it's the greatest thing that's ever happened to me, to us, all of mine. Still, it might be good for me to be clear on, you know, *how?*"

But Nacho wasn't feeling chatty. "What do you say we talk about it in the morning?"

Julian caught his arm. "Whoa, hold up now. Hang with me a minute. Talk to me."

Taking him into the outer corridor, away from the camera, Nacho hesitated, then obliged. "That's what I'd like to know—more the *why* than the how. Wasn't me, any of our people, much as I wish it was."

"Then who?"

"According to yours inside, the high priest of the apocalypse hisself."

"Block? The council?" Julian took a moment to think. "Have him brought to me."

Sighing, Nacho scratched his head. "Maybe in a couple of days, if he makes it. The boys worked him over pretty good. They found him in a Secret Service holding cell under Treasury on a routine sweep. Like I said, there was some kind of a falling out with the prez. The mob took care of the ones on one side. They would have had at Block and the others, too, if they'd found him, if he hadn't been locked up. For what, exactly, nobody knows. Every last scrap of paper was burned up in the council fire, all the evidence. We figure it was the mountain of shredded files that touched off the blaze." Nacho waxed sarcastic. "You don't think they was trying to hide nothin', do ya?"

His emotions elsewhere, Julian wasn't even curious. "See that he gets the best doctors, whatever it takes. I said no comeuppance, so I'm holding you personally responsible."

"Yo, shit happens, man! Ain't nobody's fault. You can't change human nature, B."

"That's exactly what we have to change," Julian said firmly.

Nacho resisted, turning away. "I don't like it when the bad guys go good. Don't trust it."

Julian grinned. "Like you?"

Nacho whirled back. "*Especially* like me."

Julian put a hand on his shoulder. "Just get it done. You always do. And thanks for this, by the way." He moved off to rejoin the party. "It's real thoughtful. I owe ya."

Nacho grunted. "Damn straight. Go on, enjoy. I got your back, B."

Julian nodded. "I know you do." Then he slipped back inside the suite to the boisterous affections of his large, extended family, too overjoyed for words that they'd all survived.

Nacho had more general concerns. Closing the doors, shutting in the party, he beckoned one of his adjutants over. "Find me one of the holies that can still talk, that's still got a tongue. We'll need a nice, quiet, private place. And don't forget to fetch my tools."

Chapter VIII

Well after dark, now nearly three months since Julian's triumphant entry into Washington, Nacho breezed into the Oval Office looking like a million bucks. Underneath it all, however, he was not a happy camper. Behind the big executive desk, reviewing paperwork, Julian was dressed more for a round of golf, the one he'd taken in prior to the brief helicopter ride from Camp David. With him was his father, Merlin Quinn, an aging, heavier version of Julian himself, with horn-rimmed glasses and more white than not on his scalp. The elder Quinn was similarly dressed for the links. Shortly before the war he'd risen to the Council of Bishops of the AME Church Worldwide. The staunchly anti-war organization was soon banned as seditious, declared antithetical to Christian values and the American way of life. Consequently, Dr. Quinn had spent the balance of the apocalypse at Camp Delta in Guantanamo Bay, Cuba—in a largely bemused state ever since his release.

"Nice suit," Julian told Nacho, looking him over. "Very fly."

"Hey, gotta show proper respect for the office, huh?" Nacho said. "Anyway, screw my threads!" He shot a finger at the door. "Why are you doing this?"

Julian continued reading. "If you're worried he's gonna take your place, forget it. That ain't gonna happen, not as long as I'm in this chair."

Nacho clenched his teeth. "It ain't about me. I'm worried for *you*. I'm telling you, the dude is bad news!" Nacho fought to contain his frustration and lost. "Why we need some honey-tongued, sugar-mouth preacher telling us what to do?" He threw a sheepish glance to Merlin. "Sorry, Rev."

The elder Quinn let it go, wisely holding his peace.

"Come on, JQ," Nacho pleaded with Julian. "We're doing all right. We're getting it done."

"And we're gonna *keep* getting it done," Julian said patiently. "But there's nuances, the little stuff. We need his experience. Hell, he practically ran this town."

"Ran it into the *ground*," Nacho snarled, "and the rest of the country with it."

"It takes a team to win the big one."

"Yeah," Nacho agreed, "and only one to lose it."

"You can't lay it all off on one player," Julian argued.

Taking a breath, hands on his hips, Nacho grimly paced over to the fireplace. "This is about him digging up and ferrying in your peeps, ain't it? You been talkin' to Jamyqua."

"You leave her out of this," Julian said strongly. "She's been through enough. People change. He did what I should have done."

Nacho angrily spun around. "But what you couldn't! *We* needed you more—the movement. Don't let it slip away now. We've worked too hard."

Julian's look was frightening. "I *am* the movement." Losing interest, he softened. "Nothing's gonna slip. We'll keep an eye on him, keep it on the down-low."

Nacho huffed. "Till when?"

Julian snapped. "Till I say different! Now step off! I've made my decision. He's in, and so is my dad."

"And me?" Nacho asked dismally.

Julian grinned devilishly. "Well, now, lookin' so fine like you are, I *got* to keep you around. How else am I gonna get the name of your tailor?"

They laughed together and, for the time being, the issue was shelved. Julian then pressed the intercom button on his phone. "Send him in."

A moment later, a staffer ushered Darius Block inside, and closed the door. He was on crutches, one of his legs in a cast, and he wore a neck brace. Otherwise, Dr. Block was pretty much his old polished self. "Thank you for seeing me, Mr. Pre—" He caught himself. "I'm not sure what to call you."

"For now," Julian said, "you can just call me The Man, but I won't take it badly if you want to shorten that to just JQ."

Block frowned. "I thought it was MQ, the *Mighty* Quinn."

"In another life," Julian said.

"Fine." Block gingerly eased himself over to a seat on one of the opposing sofas. His mouth ran faster. "Well, JQ, we've got a lot on our plate. We need to schedule national elections for the earliest possible date to reseat the Congress and get back to square one, legislatively and, more importantly, to revamp and restart the tax code. I trust it hasn't escaped you that you have no revenue stream. Until you do, you're working up IOUs you have no hope of covering."

Nacho gave up a condescending snort. "We're the government. We'll print more money."

"That's not a solution," Block said. "The more you print, the less it's worth, until it's worthless, which it already is."

"So we raid Fort Knox," Nacho said.

Block resisted rolling his eyes. "Will you? That'll cover about, oh, three days' worth of expenditures at the current rate you're going."

Julian scowled out at Nacho. "Nuances, *see?*" He regarded Block more respectfully. "Leave all that for a minute. I need you to take a look at this, Dr. Block." He held out a sheet of paper across the desk. There was a pregnant pause as Block awkwardly started to push up from the sofa. Julian leered at Nacho, who begrudgingly came over to hand the paper to the cripple.

"A cable from Jerusalem," Block said with a tinge of conspiracy, settling in with it.

The missive was in two parts. By royal appointment, Julian was named provincial governor-general of the United States and Canada, with a commission to "USE BEST JUDGMENT." The second part ordered him to promptly disarm and dissolve all standing military forces. By royal proclamation, wars and warfare were now officially obsolete. The cable closed with the promise of more to follow at the king's pleasure.

"Congratulations on the first part, Governor," Block said, betraying little enthusiasm.

"And the second?"

Block grunted. "It's the worst idea I've ever heard of in my life. First of all, it's too soon by a long shot, and second, who the bloody hell does he think he is?"

"I'd say that's pretty obvious," Merlin Quinn remarked.

"Is it?" Block challenged darkly. "If he really *is* Jesus, why doesn't he call himself that?"

"He didn't call himself that the first time around," Merlin pointed out. "Jesus is Greek. He was rebelling *against* the Greco-Roman establishment. In the original Aramaic, *Yeshua* is the correct diminutive for Yehoshua, son of Yosef or Ioseph."

Block poorly masked his irritation. "Whatever. Fine. Does he call himself Yeshua—this Philio?"

"No."

Block looked at Julian. "Then I rest my case, with all due respect to the bishop."

"Dr. Quinn will do, thank you," Merlin corrected him. "Without a church, there's hardly any call for bishops."

Block jumped on this. "Good; I'm glad you brought it up. Because if he's the real deal, we're his loyal base, sticking with him through thick and thin. Why, then—*why* has he outlawed churches?"

"You did," said Nacho.

"Not all," said Block, perfectly content with the distinction.

"Perhaps he views the whole world as his church," Merlin suggested. There was a faraway, almost spacey cast to his face. "The open sky as his cathedral, without limits or boundaries. Universe." His spaced-out look faded. "I'm beginning to think it always was." He gave Block the snake eye. "And, believe me, I've had a lot of time to think about it."

"Again, with all respect, Dr. Quinn," Block complained, "spare me the New Age mysto-babble. Our churches are the center of American life, the glue that binds our communities together."

Merlin regarded him harshly. "The glue, Dr. Block, or the wedge that drives them apart?"

"Semantics. Word games won't get us anywhere. You know what I'm talking about."

Merlin engaged, somewhat cryptically. "I know exactly what you're talking about. Denial is not just a river in Egypt, *Reverend*."

Nacho was compelled to step in. "Break it up, the botha yuz, or I'll put you in a ring where you can beat it out of each other." He eyed Block. "Two'll get you ten who wins."

"That'll do, Nacho," Julian gently scolded.

"Nacho?" Block quizzed humorously, unfamiliar with the sobriquet. "Appropriate."

The Latino's glare bored into him. "That's right, preacher man, I'm *Nacho Angel*. Want me to prove it?"

Block ignored him, definitely preferring the company of the Quinns, which he was hard-pressed to weather as well, clumsily reaching for a water pitcher on the coffee table, groaning with the effort. "Speaking of proof—again, if Philio is biblically legitimate, why doesn't he step forward and show it … empirically?"

Merlin helped him out, filling a tumbler. "Since when does faith require proof?"

Block accepted the glass and took a drink. "Don't be tedious. There's no Janus Philio in *my* scriptures."

"Perhaps you place more value on words than substance," said Merlin. "I seem to recall another fellow of that sort. His name was Shylock. It worked out rather badly for him, as I remember."

Block harrumphed. "There's no Shylock in the Bible, either."

Nacho made a face. "What, are you kidding me? It's loaded with 'em. Take Luke 20:46, 47. 'Beware the scribes, which desireth to walk in long robes, and love greetings in the markets, and the highest seats in the synagogues, and the chief rooms at feasts; which devour widows' houses, and for a show make long prayers: the same shall receive greater damnation.'"

Dr. Quinn was thrilled. "Very good, Felix. Are you equally familiar with the Bard?"

Nacho snorted. "I'm familiar with sharks." He leered at Block. "Do you even have a clue how much evil you did?"

Block remained stoic. "You're welcome to question my results, young man, not my intentions. And I never acted alone. My entire being, all that I am, every bone in my body, was, is, and always will be devoted to glorifying God in heaven."

Nacho laughed, shaking his head. "What you call glorifying, old man, other people might call taking a wet squat right in the middle of his house."

Block appealed to Julian. Receiving no support, he turned again to Nacho with a condescending grin. "I'll not trade barbs or be besmirched by someone with the vocabulary of a cheap whore's bastard," he lashed out. "That's right, Mr. Angel—I know all about you."

"Apparently ... not," said Merlin, off Nacho's smoldering expression.

"Momma was never cheap," Nacho told Block, coldly level, "and you're a dead man."

Julian interceded. "That'll be difficult. Or haven't any y'all been paying attention?"

Merlin looked over to the desk. "What do you mean, son?"

"Heard about anyone dying lately? I haven't, not a peep." Julian nodded to Block. "Look how quickly *you* healed up. The docs tell me that cast can come off anytime. They also say there's not the least thing wrong with your neck."

Block hurried to object, but Julian cut him off.

"The hospitals are empty. Just this morning, busy intersection in Crystal City, there's a head-on crash at high speed. Both drivers walked away." Julian swiveled around for a newspaper piled with others on the credenza. "The papers are full of more. Like this one. A bandit robs a mini-mart, or tries, takes two shotgun blasts in the back at close range from the shopkeep. He shook it off, gave back what he took. Later, the shopkeeper bought him breakfast."

Julian's father clasped his hands together. "Praise God! So, if no one can die, there's no reason for war, making it truly obsolete."

"Maybe," Block ventured skeptically. "But if no one can die, then there's no reason to disarm." Somehow, it didn't quite have the same ring to it. "Look," he forged on, "let's be smart about this. I'll grant there may be more here than meets the eye. I'm not convinced, but I'm not unwilling to *be* convinced. If Philio is truly, legitimately the son of God, why won't he throw us a bone? What is he waiting for? The real Jesus performed documented miracles throughout the gospels, hands on. It's what gave him credibility."

"What do you have in mind?" Merlin asked dryly. "What would please you?"

Block shrugged. "Nothing too big or flashy. He could move a mountain. Part a sea. Remove the sun from the sky, the moon, and rearrange the stars, then put them back. Nothing permanent, just temporary. Just enough to let us know he has the power."

Nacho, still simmering, said, "Why don't you write him a letter and tell him about it?"

"Entirely my point," said Block. "I shouldn't have to. He should know. The people need a sign—anything, but something, and something nobody else could possibly come close to—because we must never forget his own warning, from the real Jesus, I mean." Block proceeded to quote from the Gospel of Mark. "'Then if any man shall say to you, lo, here is Christ; or, lo, he is there; believe him not. For false Christs and false prophets shall rise, and shall show signs and wonders to seduce, if it were possible, even the elect. But take ye heed: behold I have foretold you all things.'" Skipping a bit, Block resumed, slightly paraphrasing, "'Only *then* shall they see the son of man coming in the clouds with great power and glory.'"

Merlin was plainly moved by the passage, which pleased Block to no end. But then Dr. Quinn, a theologian's theologian, whispered verse from the same chapter. "'For in those days shall be affliction, such as was not from the beginning of the creation which God created unto this time, neither shall be. And except that the Lord had shortened those days, no flesh should be saved: but for the elect's sake, whom he hath chosen, he hath shortened the days.'"

Block applauded. "There, you see? We've got time. It hasn't gotten all that bad yet. Indeed, from all reports, things are only getting better and better, faster and faster."

The Quinns and Nacho stared back at him blankly. Merlin shook it off first. "What the fu—what in blazes do you want?"

Block shed his neck brace to massage his chafing throat. "Only what the Bible promises. I'll put my faith in the word of God, thank you, before I put it in some upstart charlatan from the backwoods of God knows where. In short, I want clouds. There have to be clouds. If he truly is the One, how hard can it be?" He turned to Julian. "Until then, it would be the height of madness to unilaterally disarm and leave ourselves defenseless. We must be prudent in the exercise of our faith. Satan remains ever on the prowl, lurking in the places we least suspect. I've made many mistakes in my time, JQ, as I know we all have. I pray you do not add to them. You look good behind that desk, by the way. It suits you."

After a long moment, Julian finally spoke. "My new job description tells me to use my best judgment. I plan to. We'll put together a committee to study on it, figure out the pros and cons, and make recommendations. Good work, everyone, good meeting. We make a good team."

Relishing this small victory, Reverend Block quickly extended the olive branch to Nacho. "Sorry for the crack about your mother, son. Uh, heat of the moment. It's really not like me."

Julian nudged Nacho with a look. "It's a fair apology, Nacho. You're bigger than that."

Nodding, even if with distaste, Nacho accepted Block's offered handshake. Block leveraged it to scoot off the couch to his feet, one foot anyway, as Merlin held out his crutches. "Excellent," said Block, shifting around as Julian came out from behind the desk. "Governor, I'd like to speak to you about my quarters, if I may," he requested, hobbling over. "Not to put too fine a point on it, but I'm getting the runaround from your people."

"Runaround?"

"Yes, unfortunately. Squatters have moved into my home in Chevy Chase."

Julian seemed genuinely surprised. "Squatters? No shit?"

"Yes, well, *they* claim to have negotiated with the bank to assume the paper," Block explained, "with a low-interest government subsidy to boot. Seems that while I was illegally jailed, the bank foreclosed my mortgage, seizing all my other assets. Lowlifes have taken the place over, helping themselves, leaving me basically homeless and penniless."

"Have they? That's terrible. I'll bet it's a really nice crib, too."

"It suits my needs," Block demurred. "Please know I wouldn't think of bothering you with this if there wasn't so blessed much red tape to cut through."

"Want me to throw them out?"

Block was ecstatic. "On their ears, if it's not too much trouble."

Julian nodded. "So *they* can be homeless and penniless."

Block was unfazed. "We all have our crosses to bear."

"I know," said Julian. "Doesn't it get your goat how some people think the government is the be-all, end-all for all their personal problems? Where's the pride, their sense of personal responsibility?"

Block was delighted, having given this speech many times. "Exactly. It's un-American. Do they think we're socialists? You'll help me out, then?"

Julian smiled. "Happy to." He delegated Nacho to look into it. Consequently, Block ended up spending a fretful night in a crowded street mission off Stanton Square, rank with some of the foulest body odor on record. But, if the cot was hard and lumpy, at least the soup was hot and the black coffee strong.

Nacho had insisted that the Watergate and the area's other fine hotels couldn't touch it for building character. It built something else as well—Darius Block's pitiless hatred for Julian Quinn and everything he represented. If there was one thing Block couldn't abide, it was ingratitude. Had he not rescued Quinn's dirt-poor clan from the jaws of their destiny at great personal expense and risk? It wasn't that Block was a racist; he simply felt that people should know their place. As the scripture instructed: *'Servants, be obedient to them that are your masters according to the flesh, with fear and trembling…'* Could the Bible *be* any clearer on the matter?

Chapter IX

The telephone awakened Morton Parmister. Only a crack of sunlight seeped through the tightly drawn curtains in his King David Hotel room. "Yeah?" he sleepily answered the call. "That soon? No, no, that's fine. I'll meet you in the lobby in thirty minutes."

Hanging up, he turned on the bedside lamp and rubbed the sand from his eyes. Someone moved under the covers next to him. His main squeeze for the past ten or twelve years, off and on, was Gwynn Reynolds, a former Broadway actress back when there was still a Great White Way. She'd also been a minor daytime soap star, still a dish. They'd first met at a Billy Graham Crusade at which they'd both been saved. For some reason, Morty had never gotten around to marrying her or even popping the question. Then again, nobody was perfect. Besides, things during the Tribulation were too unsettled, too up in the air. Frankly, Morty's duties, official and not, had kept him way too busy for a proper church wedding. Through it all, Gwynn had been a trooper, always there for him, behind him, which was why she was with him now.

At the moment, Jerusalem was a whole lot safer than Washington, certainly for Morton Parmister, now essentially an ambassador at large for a government that no longer existed. They'd basically been holed up in the King David since arriving months ago, ordering from the room service menu.

"Who was it? What is it?" she asked over a yawn.

"I've been granted an audience with the king."

Gwynn huffed. "Finally. How soon?"

"They're sending a car in half an hour."

"*Jesus!*" She literally sprang out of the bed. "Hit the shower," she commanded. "I'll dress you. The blue suit. No, the pinstripe. No, too sinister. We'll go with beige, powder blue button-down with a red power tie." She changed her mind again. "No, red's too ostentatious. A checkered bowtie. More intellectual."

"Too nerdy," Morty overruled, a toothbrush in his mouth at the bathroom sink. "How about my solid coral tie? Softer, less pushy, more angelic."

"Perfect," Gwynn agreed, "on a white shirt. Tasty. Fits with the desert motif."

Parmister rinsed and spat. "Wanna come?" he offered. "They didn't say you couldn't. How fast can you get ready?"

"Not that fast," Gwynn pooh-poohed the idea, laying out his clothes, "not for a king, pretend or not. Anyway, it'd be bad form. I'm a scarlet woman, remember?"

"They say he doesn't stand on protocol," Parmister replied.

"He may not," Gwynn said firmly, "but I do, and you *will*."

Morty had to smile. "What would I do without you?"

"God knows," she said, twice clapping her hands. "Shower, now! Time to be all that you can be. I'll order up a pot of coffee. And no spills or you'll ruin everything."

It was a glorious morning, weather-wise, nary a cloud in the sky. The drive from the high-rise, urban milieu of modern West Jerusalem to the ancient Old City was uneventful for the most part. The traffic was exceptionally polite. Drivers tooted their horns in friendly greeting rather than hostile impatience. Reconstruction was the order of the day, bombed-out side streets undergoing methodical repair. A forest of construction cranes dominated the skyline, virtually as far the eye could see. It all seemed to be coming together awfully fast. Parmister couldn't help wondering about where the funding was coming from. Who, precisely, was investing? What did they know that he didn't? Washington and Wall Street had always been Israel's sugar daddies, but no more, not for a long spell.

Morty had expected to take the trip in an official motorcade. Instead, he was picked up by a single car and driver. His escort introduced himself as Avi Mandelheimer. He was mid-thirties, Hasidim, British born and educated, an East Ender before immigrating, and evidently way, *way* down in the royal pecking order, if his wheels were any indication—a dated, knocking-diesel Mercedes wagon with squeaky shocks and singing brakes. The rear seat was half taken by a drooling toddler belted in a car seat, sucking on a pacifier in between catnaps and throwing fits. Parmister opted to ride shotgun after dubiously extricating a shrill squeeze toy from under his butt. Avi explained over one of the rug rat's tantrums that it was Dad's day to keep an eye on the little munchkin, saying little else. The child's lucky mother obviously had better things to do.

As they drew closer to the Holy City, Parmister noticed that conspicuously missing above its ramparts was its ageless, crowning set piece, the Dome of the Rock. Anything else was yet to fully take its place, although Parmister got brief glimpses of scaffolding on the site. "The new Temple," he guessed knowingly.

"In a pig's eye," Mandelheimer laughed. "Would you start the war all over again?"

"What, then?"

"A monument, in memoriam, compassionately understated. The king's personal design."

Parmister squinted out the window. "A monument to what?"

"Futility," said Avi without elaborating.

Morty shifted the subject. "Want to give me some pointers?" he requested. He was starting to get butterflies, something totally uncharacteristic of him since his days as a snot-nosed congressional aide. "How does the king prefer to be addressed?"

"Respectfully, cordially, pretty much like anyone would, really," Avi coached. "Mmm, nothing over the top. Just be yourself." Avi chuckled. "Dear me, old boy, if you try to be anything else, he'll know it."

"I meant the form of address," Parmister clarified uncomfortably. "You know, what's appropriate—Your Majesty, Highness, *Lord*? How about—I don't know—*Master*?"

Avi gave a shrug. "They all work. I suppose one's as good as the other. Nothing too pompous, though, or groveling. That bugs him."

It wasn't helping. "Like what, for instance?" Morty pressed.

"Oh, I don't know." Patiently slowing at the pedestrian-clogged Damascus Gate, easily the walled city's most impressive, built by the emperor Hadrian, Avi thought about it. "Let's see, uh, no 'O blah-blah-blah *Wondrous and Great One*,' no 'O *Terrible and Ever-Most Wise Sovereign Who Surpasseth Mortal Apprehension*,' none of that—no put-on fear and trembling; that's out. You'll find he despises affectation and anything that comes close—any sort of, you know, that showy, plastic bullshit, almost always directed at everyone but him. Besides, he has no interest in being feared."

Parmister looked askance. "No?"

"No"—Avi broke off to ease the car forward through the madding crowds before having to brake again, glancing over at his passenger—"only to be understood. And, I should add, *when* you understand him, even if it's only a glimmer ... well, the awe just sort of comes naturally. Of course, that's just one man's opinion. I can't claim to speak for everyone."

"What do you call him?" Parmister asked. "And I mean you, personally, when you're one-on-one, assuming that's ever happened. No offense."

"Quite regularly, as a matter of fact," Avi answered, none taken. "Me? I usually just call him Janus—Jan, when I'm in a rush, JP sometimes. He's never given me a problem about it. 'Hey you' will bring scorn. Oh, yeah, I once called him a crafty bastard—slip of the tongue, the bastard part—which I hastened to follow up with profuse apologies. 'Why?' says he. 'After all, it's in my official bio.'"

"He's put out a biography?" Parmister asked, intrigued. "I'd like to see it."

Avi shot him a long-suffering glance. Morty chose not to explore it, the butterflies in his stomach churning anew. It was all nonsense, of course, fantasy. It had to be, and it would only get stranger.

The uncredentialed ambassador's initial get-acquainted session with the self-proclaimed king of kings ended up more of a klatch than an official audience, held at an outdoor café on the perimeter of bustling Hurva Square in the heart of the Jewish Quarter. As it turned out, Morty had overdressed, certainly in comparison to the monarch, who showed up in jogging sweats and a red baseball cap worn backwards. If he had bodyguards, they were keeping an extremely low profile, virtually invisible. He also brought along no advisors, none that attended. His celebrity was no less for it; he was fawned over by literally everyone who passed by.

After parking, Avi Mandelheimer, bouncing baby in hand, had halted on foot a distance away from the café, citing a sour diaper in desperate need of changing. "Go on," Avi invited, "he's right there. Really, ambassador, no worries. You'll never meet anyone more approachable."

Parmister was basically in shock. "I had more in mind a palace."

The king's social secretary gave up a guffaw, then bolted with his smelly bundle of joy.

"Doesn't stand on protocol," Parmister muttered under his breath. "There's the understatement of the millennium." Nonetheless, straightening his tie, Morty made his approach, every political instinct he had soon humming in overdrive.

Up close, venue aside, the first thing that struck Parmister was equally off-putting. Janus Philio was just so distressingly, well, Semitic—sweat-oiled, jet black hair; dark, full eyebrows; and deeply olive skin tone. His eyes were a pale green. He was clean-shaven, but no more recently than the day before, and his bottom teeth, brightly white, were slightly crowded, though they were nothing an orthodontist couldn't remedy in short order. He wasn't repulsive or anything, not on this part of the planet—far from that. He was extremely fit and toned in the arms, chest, and belly, deceptively so under his loose-fitting sweats—all in all, a rugged stud, clearly in fantastic physical shape. He also had comely, matching dimples with a strong, square chin that made his smile radiate with disarming pleasantness. Indeed, it was hard not to be pulled in. Still, by any standard, the king took some getting used to, given the biblical oeuvre he had to live up to or play at doing. Otherwise, he was fashionably tall, between six-two and six-three, and chose to repose almost too casually, definitely not regally, with his long legs extended, crossed at the ankles, as if he had not a care in the world.

OK, so where's the glow, the supernatural spark, his divine aura? Morty detected none. No, he concluded early on, Philio was entirely terrestrial. Somewhere in the neglected recesses of his mind, way in deep, Parmister felt a twinge of disappointment. *Bummer.*

As soon as they got past the awkwardness of mutually identifying themselves—awkward for Morty—absent the convenience and formality of someone equipped to diplomatically smooth such things, they got right down to it over mocha frappes and a variety of Eastern Mediterranean breakfast treats, mostly salted fish and flaky pastries, attentively served and replenished without undue intrusion.

The king had a surprising grasp of foreign affairs and international relations, confidently plain spoken, almost disconcertingly so, wouldn't be dodged with euphemisms or abstractions, wouldn't be patronized, doing it in a way Parmister couldn't help but admire for its effortlessness. Morty also couldn't blunt, dilute, or divert the king's bottom line: the unconditional and total subjection of the American empire to absolute rule by the throne of Jerusalem.

Responding, Parmister trod delicately. "I understand and appreciate your concerns, Majesty. What you must try to understand, if I may be so bold, is that my countrymen will resist tyranny in any form. Dare I say it's become genetically ingrained in us to react this way."

"You can dare," Philio allowed. "Now let's look at the facts." He took a sip of orange juice before continuing. "It seems to me that somewhere between your temperance laws and your economic improvement zones the definition of tyranny got lost. All that was *after* your Patriot Act, detention without trial, tort reforms, and letting your voting and civil rights acts expire." The king's directness, mildly accented, was like a finger-thump between the eyes.

"We were at war," Morty asserted. The king was getting on his nerves.

Philio yawned. "Funny how it always seems to work that way, isn't it? Anyway," he resumed, "I can simply invade you and be done with it. But this is not what I want."

"What *do* you want?" Morty asked, almost afraid of the answer.

Philio got right to the point. "I want to give a well-deserved rest to all those who feel, however deeply or stubbornly, that it is their mission in life to bait the fear and guilt of the powerless. Then, while they're catching up on their sleep, I'm going to remove all of the other barriers to natural intelligence. With any luck, they'll wake up to a brand new world."

"Ambitious," said Morty. He could think of nothing else that wasn't overtly combative. Given the opening, he also couldn't resist throwing a jab. "Oscar Wilde said ambition is the last refuge of failure. Just a thought."

"He also said there are no good or bad people," said the king, lightning quick. "People are either charming or tedious. Which are you, Ambassador Parmister?"

"Realistic."

"It's overrated," said the king, gamely slapping his thighs. "You can be the candle or the mirror that reflects it. Everything else is just part of the darkness." He got up to leave.

Morty graciously stood to honor his departure. "Edith Wharton. I've always liked that one. Who wouldn't? The real world is rarely that simple."

But Philio was already on his way to somewhere else, calling back over his shoulder, almost chillingly, "What makes you think this is the real world?"

Staying put, Parmister watched him move out alone into the throngs of loving faces in Hurva Square, where the king glad-handed and shared himself without so much as a rope line. They cherished him like no one Morty had ever seen— not a god, exactly, more like everyone's best friend. Purely from a security standpoint it was ridiculously risky, incredibly foolish. *Does he think he's bulletproof?* Retaking his seat, Parmister smirked to himself. *What a rube.* No doubt about it, taking this one down would be like taking candy from a baby. When a muscular grip suddenly attached itself to his neck, Morty's smugness vanished. *Maybe not such a rube after all.* This was it, then, he sadly realized—the king's men come to arrest him. So, for all of Philio's sticky-sweet homily about forgiveness, he was just another double-talking despot. A mafia don had more class, more honestly come by. But then, releasing his grip on Morty, someone vaguely familiar came around the table. Parmister's heart suffered a painful arrhythmia.

"Good golly, Miss Molly. You look like you've seen a ghost."

"*Son of a bitch!*"

The newcomer straddled the opposing chair backwards, reaching in to help himself to the leftover noshes. Atop his second-hand street clothes, he had on sunglasses and a kaffiyeh, the traditional Bedouin head covering. "Yeah, it's good to see you, too, *Morty*."

Parmister checked for eavesdroppers. "We heard you were buried at sea."

"I was."

"Neat trick."

Ken Rittenour lowered his sunglasses. "You have *no* idea."

Chapter X

Stoked by a newly unfettered media striving to reclaim its lost relevance, the so-called swords-into-plowshares debate quickly caught fire—or, rather, the hair of opposing talking heads did—rapidly becoming more truculent than trenchant. A verbal Donnybrook broke out, international in scope. On the political level, the issue of single, globally integrated monarchy was recast as one of patriotism vs. appeasement, sovereignty vs. subjugation, self-determination vs. dictatorship. For religious purists and the theologically minded, it revitalized fundamentalist sensibilities and nagging suspicions that had been more or less sidelined, out of vogue.

Somehow, the apocalyptic schedule had gotten all screwed up. It wasn't supposed to be like this. Things that were supposed to happen hadn't; things that weren't, had. Any which way you wanted to look at it, something was rotten in Denmark—or, rather, Jerusalem. World peace, after all, was the prophesied deception of the Antichrist, a ploy to sucker the weak-willed—darkness and light, bitter and sweet, juxtaposed. Evil called good and good, evil. Less contumely but equally cocksure voices reminded anyone tuning in that the foretold Messiah, first go or encore, was *supposed* to be the "prince of peace." It all boiled down to who and/or what "King" Philio thought he was or claimed to be, and *he* was stonewalling.

During a gathering of sage and moneyed East Coast patricians at a cliff-top weekend getaway above the moonlit waters of Chesapeake Bay, one such prime-time rant fest was airing on one of the four U.S. cable news channels back in operation. The volume on the sixty-inch plasma TV screen was currently muted. As for the place, its design was post-modern Scandinavian, rustic stonework and cedar, airy and spacious, with broad, tinted windows reaching up to the vaulted, open-beam ceiling, giving it a ski lodge quality, topped off with the fragrant scent of evergreen. Gas flames in the fireplace were strictly for atmosphere. It was late June, summertime, still unpleasantly warm outside even at this hour, nicely air-conditioned inside. Soft, classic jazz was piped in to complete the sumptuous ambiance.

Casually mixing, catching up on small talk while enjoying after-dinner cocktails and cigars, they numbered right around twenty, all male, Ivy League. In many respects, they were all that was left of the old-boy network at their level—captains of industry, investment bankers, top-flight Washington lawyers, a former senator or two, a handful of pre-war cabinet secretaries several administrations removed, and so forth. They took no pains to keep the get-together a secret; no need to. None of the current rabble running the country could find their own ass with both hands and a flashlight. It would be laughable if it wasn't so tragically pathetic—the greatest, richest, most powerful nation in the history of the world crippled by a washed-out football player and his pack of gutter rats. It was only a matter of time before they were in over their heads and sank.

More pertinently, the hard-earned war profits of every man here meeting at the bayside hideaway were potentially in jeopardy. Jesus said, "Blessed are they which are persecuted for righteousness sake, for theirs is the kingdom of heaven." And, though they might not look like it at the moment—schmoozing and joking with their Grand Marnier, VSOP cognac, Chivas Royal Salute, and Havana stogies in hand—each of the men hobnobbing in the opulent cliff-top redoubt was feeling terribly oppressed and persecuted. Word had filtered in from overseas that Philio was moving to place paralyzing economic sanctions, excluding food and medicines, on the continental United States until it fully complied with his disarmament directives, including, but not limited to, all weapons of mass destruction. As part of this, all American assets abroad were being seized by the crown, all bank accounts and pending transactions now frozen. Between those gathered in the Chesapeake retreat and the clients and affiliates they represented, the sums in limbo totaled in the many tens of billions of dollars, notwithstanding the crown's recently adjusted and singularly generous foreign exchange rates. Months ago, when the lumbering West Coast uprising had turned from a comical farce into a political reality, the good men here had squirreled away huge sums offshore for safekeeping in protected, numbered accounts—clever maneuvers which were all backfiring now.

So, financially, except for a few spotty domestic reserves, they were all facing receivership, which was the reason for this meeting. It wasn't that they were hum-bled, nor were they in any particular panic—they were too seasoned for that, each a wily veteran of corporate trench warfare, each boasting decades of winner-take-all boardroom combat. No, to the contrary, caught with their britches down once already, they were here to proactively plan and begin whatever was required to take their country back, by any means necessary, followed by the rest of the empire—and, God willing, to expand it. To this end, they had christened themselves the *Guardians*, and the very first item on their planning agenda was the murder of Janus Philio.

One of the most senior among them capitalized on the sudden lull in the ebb and flow of the mixer to get things rolling. "Rumor has it the pope is finally going to give in to the bastard," he announced, languidly sucking to light his Cuban.

"I thought Philio had to walk on water first," remarked another.

"Evidently, for some people he does," someone else said.

"Yeah, and I got a real nice bridge in Alaska for sale," scoffed a third.

"You think it's funny?" a fourth scolded nervously. "We lose the Catholics, we can all kiss our Latin American portfolios bye-bye. I'm so heavy into spic futures it makes me sick."

"It's your own fault," said the one with the bridge. "I told you to diversify."

"Screw you."

"Our portfolios be damned," said a silver fox straddling the arm of a sofa, dunking the chewed end of his stogie in his cognac for flavor. "I'm here to save civilization as we know it."

"Question is, how?" said another Guardian.

"He's right," yet another chimed in. "Rub him out cold, and he's a martyr. The best scenario hoists him on his own petard."

"What's his petard?" another asked.

"The Lord Jesus wouldn't hide," he was told, "wouldn't mince words."

"What do you call a parable?"

"Scripture."

"It's a stretch to say he's hiding," a younger, trimmer, closer-to-fifty member injected. "He's a fucking media darling, on the tube practically 24-7. Plus, it's not what he says, it's the way he says it. He's got that thing with his voice … like Hitler … puts the crowd in a trance, but different, all lovey-dovey."

"Let's package it," said another Guardian. "The negative."

"Too done," someone objected. "All our enemies can't be like Hitler."

"Why not? Whatever works."

"They presumed he was a fool, but then he opened his mouth to prove it."

"Kiss my dribbling sphincter!"

"You'll have to remove your head first."

The tension, enough to bean a stray cat with a slingshot at long-range, was interrupted by sudden activity at the front door before a trusted member of the host's household staff admitted Pastor Darius Block into their midst.

"Sorry I'm late," he breathlessly apologized, winded. The cast was off his leg, so no crutches, and he otherwise appeared completely recovered. "Had a devil of a time shaking that overdressed mariachi." He was apparently referring to Nacho Angel. "The greasy lout is an absolute pest," Block went on. "Thinks he can discern the intricacies of governing just by asking infernal questions. Right about now I'd give my left testicle for one of the Bush brothers—better at the step-and-fetch-it, if you know what I mean. My God, those were the days."

"Did you hear from our man in Jerusalem?" someone asked.

"I did, and because of it, I bring good tidings of great joy."

"Do tell, Reverend."

"I could use a touch of the grape first, if I might," Block cheerily delayed, intentionally building the suspense. He was shortly given a large snifter of brandy, its bouquet intoxicating all by itself. "Exquisite," he said, swirling it under his nose. "Heavenly."

"Under council rules, you could be taken out and hanged for that," he was reminded.

"No," Block corrected. "Under council rules, anyone else would be taken out and hanged. The Bible is quite clear on the disjunction of shepherd and flock, even more so between high priest and laity."

"What about us?' someone asked with a snort.

Pastor Block was genuinely magnanimous. "You, I forgive. Frankly, without being free to draw such distinctions, there'd be no point to ordination. One should never cease to marvel at God's wisdom, brethren. Without it, the whole universe would blow apart in the blink of an eye."

The Guardian over-positioned in Latin America bluntly interjected, "Enough twaddle. What've you got?"

Block took his time. "Philio is ersatz, no question about it, not that that's news. What is pleasantly unexpected is that our secret weapon, Alecto, has been miraculously returned to us, almost as if he'd been, well, *resurrected*. There's no other way to put it."

"You're kidding."

"Clearly, there's an empirical explanation," Block chided. "What's important, gentlemen, is that we are not alone in the wilderness. Our people have already made contact."

"Speak plainly," he was prodded.

Block proceeded carefully. "There are those who want their religion back—its institutions—as much as we do. Theirs is clearly wrong-headed but, well, beggars can't be choosy. Either way, Philio is our common obstacle. Once the king is removed, we'll deal with our, shall we say, strange bedfellow accordingly, though it's not a bridge that need be crossed at this juncture. But I digress. Given the nature of the beast, ideally, Philio must be toppled from within by his own. Technically, *our* hands must be squeaky clean. I don't need to tell you how sticky things could get if this warps into a modern remake of the Passion. God forbid—" Block reflexively guzzled down his whole glass of brandy in one go before resuming.

"Damn you, preacher, *who?*" someone griped.

"And what do they bring to the party?" another joined skeptically.

"Enthusiasm, for openers," Block easily replied. "Let's just say they're willing to die for a cause greater than themselves, and we're willing to let them. When you think about it, it doesn't get any better than that. We'll do the oppo research and provide the brains. In return, they'll furnish a limitless supply of warm bodies."

"Everything has its limits," someone said.

Dr. Block looked down his nose. "Not my faith."

Grabbing a bottle off the bar, the silver fox came over to liberally refill the pastor's snifter. "Enough suspense," he said. "Who's our new best friend?"

Dr. Block took a moment to savor the irony with his brandy. "Al Qaeda."

Chapter XI

The following Tuesday was a scorcher. A band of high pressure hovering over the Atlantic seaboard had temperatures soaring well into the nineties before midday. The humidity in the capital stung the face like a hot towel in a barbershop. But, if the weather was nobody's fault, the same could not be said for holding Governor-General Quinn's first televised press conference outdoors in the White House Rose Garden. Its purpose was to address mounting concerns related to who, exactly, was calling the shots—Jerusalem or Washington, Philio or Quinn? What point was there to successfully revolting if everything fought for was being handed over to a foreign power—literally lock, stock, and barrel? Why had new elections not been scheduled? *Did public opinion matter even one iota?* Then there was the issue of the upcoming Fourth of July holiday. Would it still be celebrated with cookouts, fireworks, Main Street parades, and brass bands in the town square? Where was the sense in observing Independence Day if the country was no longer independent? Did the Stars and Stripes still carry any meaning?

As he took the Rose Garden podium in a conservative gray suit, Julian was studiously prepared to answer, at least for himself. Well-rested, he possessed that indefinable quality called poise, his bearing impressive, his demeanor calmly reassuring. After thanking everyone for coming, singling out dignitaries for praise, he opened with an unforgivably bold statement: "Welcome to the future."

Foregoing notes and a teleprompter, he then delivered from memory the dry tally of seven long years of global bloodletting, lest anyone forget: eighty million war dead, millions more maimed and crippled, half a billion people displaced, families and communities ripped apart, whole cities leveled to the ground, plague and famine, on and on. A few short steps away from the podium, locked in the

West Wing, were graphic photographs never seen by the public. Perhaps Julian hadn't seen them, either. Either way, he hadn't brought them along, content to let the numbers speak for themselves, which they never do. A whole bunch of dead folks certainly couldn't. Clearly, though, it had been bad, real bad—wrath-of-God bad.

"Someone had to stop it," Julian declared in no uncertain terms. "Someone did. And, because he did, he has my unqualified respect and admiration."

Polite applause broke out, more earnest from some than others, then died down.

"Unqualified," Julian went on, "not unconditional, and not blind. This nation will not go gentle into the night for any tyrant."

Like an erupting volcano, his approval rating rocketed off the scale. The speech was seen in homes across the country, in resurgent neighborhood bars and restaurants, even on Times Square's newly restored JumboTron, bringing cheers. The bottom caption on one TV broadcast quickly abbreviated precisely what had *not* been said: "MIGHTY TO KING: COOL IT." On another channel the caption read, "QUINN TELLS PHILIO TO BACK OFF." The standing ovation in the Rose Garden was deafening.

Under twenty minutes later, Julian stormed into the Oval Office and tore off his suit coat. His shirt was soaked. His brow and face were dripping. Dr. Block was holding a fresh towel. Nacho quickly took it from him to give to Julian, who snatched it away, furious. "Whose big idea was it to do this outside in the heat of the day?" he demanded, toweling off.

Nacho shrank back with a glance at Block. "What's the problem? The light was great; *you* were great. Did you get a load of that applause?"

"I've heard better. Look at me, you nitwit!" Julian bellowed. "I'm sweating like a pig!"

"So? Everyone was."

"Everyone didn't just throw down on the King of kings! *Fuck!*"

Only then did it dawn on Nacho—the trap he'd fallen into. Block's hint of a smirk confirmed it. Nacho took it like a man, though. "OK, my bad," he said. "Sorry, B."

Something entered Julian's eyes Nacho had never seen before, and it wasn't good. It went away as Julian turned to Block. "You write a good speech, preach."

"More of a statement," Block said drolly. "In both, less is more. What you don't say is almost always more telling than what you do."

Julian nodded. "I'm learning that." Now more comfortably dry and cooled off, he threw the sweat-sodden towel at Nacho as if he were the towel boy and little else. Then, plopping down behind the desk, he lazily propped his feet up. "Do something useful, will ya? Bring us something cold to drink." Nacho bristled but obeyed, leaving his friend alone with the reverend against his better judgment. Julian watched him until he closed the door. "Actually, no small thanks to you, Rev, I've learned a whole lot more'n that."

"And you're one of my better students," Block returned the compliment.

"Grab a seat, doc," Julian offered. "Take a load off."

Block accepted, taking a chair across the desk. "To be completely honest, I didn't think so at first—far from it—but you surprised me."

"I've still got a few moves in me," Julian said.

Block eyed him curiously. "You're talking about football."

Julian met his gaze directly. "Any game you wanna play."

Block played it coy. "I'm not sure I follow, Governor."

"Oh, I think you do," Julian said. "I like it on top. Like you said, this desk suits me."

Block remained cautious. "I see."

"Then let's stop working at cross purposes. You need me as much as I need you. Your house is yours again, by the way." Julian opened the top desk drawer and jangled a set of keys.

Block was genuinely surprised.

"Get settled in, then come to the residence tonight for dinner," Julian invited, sliding the keys across to him. "We'll talk."

Still a bit unsettled, Block put up token resistance. "What's on the agenda?"

Reclining his head back on the big executive chair, Julian absently regarded the ceiling. "How does it go ...? Oh, yeah ... we'll sit on the ground—something a little more comfortable in our case—and tell sad stories of the death of kings."

Picking up the keys, Block was pleasantly stunned. "Clearly, Governor, there's more to you than meets the eye. You, sir, are proving to be a diamond in the rough."

Julian put a finger to his lips. "*Shh.* It's our secret."

Just then, Nacho reentered the Oval Office with a tray of iced teas, setting it on the desk. "Done up just the way you like it, JQ," he said, craving approval. "So what's our next move?"

Sliding his feet off the desk, Julian stood up, completely ignoring the beverages. "I'm gonna take a swim." To Nacho's dismay, he walked away without another word.

Chapter XII

Haneviim Street, one of the oldest streets outside the Old City, separated the ultra-Orthodox district of Mea Shearim and its jumble of narrow byways and keeps in the north from the drinking and dining scene of the Russian Compound to the south. Once one of the city's most prestigious addresses, Haneviim was still lined with grand, nineteenth-century residences, and an observer might well imagine the echo of regal, horse-drawn carriages from the Victorian era clattering over its cobblestones, the red-lined silk cloaks and black top hats of refined gentry. Nowadays, the larger homes were subdivided into apartments that nevertheless retained much of the elegance and splendor of old. It was to one of these flats that Morton Parmister and Gwynn Reynolds had recently moved.

Among the half dozen or so languages Morty had mastered, he spoke Russian like a commissar from Riga, negotiating better lease terms than most Israelis could have bargained for, and for the past few days, Gwynn had busied herself setting up house. The new place was a welcome departure from the confines of their King David Hotel room. The vibrant, open-air market in Makhane Yehuda was but a brisk walk away, and the neighbors were exceptionally pleasant and helpful. Even the crowds on the street seemed to be in a sort of fantastical dream state, conducting themselves in an utterly well-behaved fashion, as if they knew such good times must eventually end, eager to squeeze the most out of them until they did. For Gwynn Reynolds, the abrasiveness of New York and Washington, the dog-eat-dog competition over the simplest things, seemed a lifetime ago, another world. She couldn't imagine a happier place, which made it all the more confounding—no soldiers, no checkpoints, no fear. This was, after all, Jerusalem.

Morty came home at sunset. Gwynn had been decorating and tidying up all day. Through the windows, their new digs were washed in golden light, creating pastel hues. As for her handiwork, she'd outdone herself. Though it was quite small, the apartment, their cozy, Middle Eastern pied-à-terre, was now comfortably livable, with everything in its place. But Morty was oblivious.

Days ago he'd gone into what Gwynn called his "dark mode." It wasn't so much a mood shift as a calculating process, like an overtaxed supercomputer crunching enormous amounts of data, unresponsive to any inputs external to its current algorithm. Morty did his best work in dark mode, or so the people he reported to liked to believe. Then again, it was how Morty made his living—he was the best there was at whatever it was he did. And, although a part of Gwynn admired his dedication and passion, dark mode could also be irritatingly tiresome.

"What do you think?" she asked, greeting him with a loving smile and a chilled martini. He wordlessly passed on both.

"I've got to change," he said in a monotone, shedding his shirt on the way to the bedroom. Pouting, Gwynn helped herself to a gulp of the bone-dry cocktail.

"Then you know," she said. "How'd you find out?"

"Find out what?"

"That we're having supper with the king."

Morty reappeared in the bedroom doorway, buttoning a khaki short-sleeve shirt. "Come again?"

Gwynn fetched an envelope from a sofa table. "It came by royal messenger," she explained. "Kicks off at eight sharp. We're both invited. Doesn't specify attire, but that shirt'll never do."

Parmister rolled his eyes. "You might be surprised." He disappeared back into the bedroom, calling, "Supper, you say? Not state dinner, no royal feast? How pedestrian. What kind of a king does he think he is? Better yet, king of what?"

Gwynn followed him into their boudoir. "I take it we're not going." She said it with more than a tinge of disappointment. Deep down she was a terribly social animal.

"*Au contraire*," Morty corrected. "I expect you to be there right on time."

"And you?"

"Extend my regrets," Parmister said, taking a seat on the bed to lace up his desert boots. "Still, it's the perfect entrée for you. Lord knows it's high time we put those tits and ass to work. Snuggle in as close as you can. Work it. Mind you, just a taste. You can give me a complete rundown later."

Gwynn turned sullen. "You're pimping me out?"

"Don't get your panties in a twist, darling," Parmister cajoled. "In fact, don't wear any. It'll be good to finally know where he lines up on the fairer sex. If you can't push his buttons, he's either gay or inhuman. Either way, knowledge is power."

"And if he goes for it?" Gwynn asked.

"Then I'll have him right where I want him."

"You're forgetting just one thing," Gwynn said tartly. "What if I like him?"

Parmister laughed. "Trust me, the devil has a better shot." Morty became deadly serious. "Just remember, my love, whatever we do—according to our God-given capacities—we're doing it to preserve our faith as we know it. Our reward will be in heaven, not on earth." Tying off his second boot, he got up to pocket his wallet, comb, and other accessories. "So gussy up, girlfriend, and do that method acting you're so famous for." He turned to tenderly smooch her forehead, adding softly, "With any luck, it'll all pay off in the end. You'll see." Then, donning sunglasses despite the hour, he headed out. "By the way, don't wait up." This said, he left in somewhat of a hurry.

Hugging herself, Gwynn moved to the front windows. Down on the street, Morty got into a BMW sedan with a man who'd been idly smoking a cigarette on the sidewalk. Morty's partner's disguise, at least from the shoulders up, poorly hid the fact that he was another Occidental. Something else was poorly hidden as well. He carried a gun—a definite no-no in King Philio's new Jerusalem.

The host of the royal shindig was the king's social secretary, Avi Mandelheimer. He lived at Batei Makhase Square in the Jewish Quarter of the Old City. Named for the so-called Shelter Houses built by Jews from Germany and Holland in 1862 for destitute émigrés from central Europe, the Batei Makhase had incurred significant damage during the 1948 and 1967 wars. It had since been restored, though not to the extent of the palatial splendor of the adjacent Rothschild House. Arriving fashionably late, Gwynn wondered if the king was now lodged in the Rothschild complex. She would find out that he wasn't but little else.

A Mrs. Mandelheimer greeted her at the home's unpretentious entrance. The unspoken message flaming in her imperious eyes was inescapable. Staci Mandelheimer was an alpha female. Somehow, Gwynn also knew she'd been raised within earshot of the Bethnel Green or Shoreditch, the Bow Bells. Her dropped *H*s, intrusive *R*s, glottal stops, and diphthong shifts told Gwynn it was authentic Cockney, not the Mockney Gwynn had once tried to master for a role in *Sweeney Todd*. Locked in a room in Charing Cross with a perfectionist vocal coach, they'd gone at it for days: *Faw'y fahsan' frushes frew ova fawn'n 'eaf*—Forty thousand thrushes flew over Thornton Heath. Had Gwynn skipped the training, communicating with her hostess now would have been nearly impossible.

"Do you need to see this?" Gwynn asked, proffering her invitation. Whatever the actual reply, Gwynn gathered it meant this wasn't the kind of party someone would cheerily crash. What Mrs. Mandelheimer said next was a bit clearer.

"Mind your shoes, Septic. On my knees all day."

Allowed inside, Gwynn took that to mean scrubbing the floors. Seeing them, however, left this an open question. *Septic* was slang for Yank. Conversely, Gwynn remembered, *Listerine* was someone not enthralled with Americans. With stone walls and floors with scattered area rugs, the place had the feel of a keep in a medieval castle. Everything else was up to date, postmodern.

"Ambassador Parmister extends his regrets," Gwynn said. "Matters of state."

The mention of Morty only heightened the woman's hostility. "He won't be missed."

Gwynn debated leaving immediately but checked the impulse. Politically, there was too much riding on her performance. She'd just have to gut it out. The show must go on.

"We're on the roof," said Mrs. Mandelheimer. Along the way, she stopped in the kitchen to check on the progress of one too many cooks—all women, all guests, like Gwynn herself. It might as well have been an Amish barn-raising. Blessedly, Gwynn wasn't asked to participate. There simply wasn't room for another. Here, the Mandelheimer woman switched to Yiddish, leaving Gwynn clueless, though not altogether. The glances from the other women were not warm. *Ouch*. Turning away, Gwynn wandered a few steps to an open doorway, drawn by the voices inside. Men. Wondering if Mata Hari had felt as creepy as she did now, Gwynn risked looking inside.

The dining room table, surrounded by half a dozen men, all standing, was spread with charts, blueprints, and engineering diagrams—some rolled, others stretched out. Only one of the planners was seated. His back was to her, and positive identification was made more impossible by the two huddling over his shoulders. The men noticed her presence a second later. Coming over, Avi Mandelheimer quickly blocked a closer view of the table. "Lost?" he asked.

Gwynn batted her eyes. "The loo?"

Avi smiled knowingly, half-turning back to the planning meeting. "As soon as we lick the water problem," he told her freely, "the whole of the Sahara and Gobi will see the greatest, most environmentally advanced cities ever built—housing for millions, billions even."

Gwynn was floored. Surely, there weren't that many people left in the world. A bothersome possibility bedeviled her mind, but it was too far-fetched. Or was it? She said it aloud before she could stop herself. "*Resurrection?*"

Avi smiled at her again, this time patronizingly. "In a manner of speaking." Informing her that the others were on the roof, he pulled the doors closed, shutting her out.

"Roof's this way, *love*," Avi's wife beckoned tersely, even less inviting than before.

They wordlessly climbed several flights up to a flat rooftop where a long table was set, al fresco, for a big dinner party. Oil lamps and candles provided the lighting, soft enough not to blot out the stars. Gwynn absently imagined what the night of the Nativity must have been like. The hostess with the mostest disingenuously muttered something approaching "enjoy," before trotting back downstairs to oversee the meal preparation. The invitees, and there were many, had separated into cliques. Finally, one gallant soul came to Gwynn's rescue, offering her a glass of chilled white wine, introducing himself as the Swedish ambassador.

"I had the pleasure of seeing you on the London stage," he said. "You were captivating."

"You date yourself, sir," she parried, eating the attention like candy. It had been so long. More guests came over, extending similar accolades. Soon she was the center of attention. Gwynn felt reborn. Then the ambassador lowered his voice ominously.

"May I extend a word of advice, young lady?"

"By all means, Ambassador," she invited, relishing the "young" part.

"Be very careful ... extremely."

Glancing at the others, Gwynn's guard shot up. "I'm sure I don't know what you mean."

"And *we* can't be sure, any of us, what we're dealing with here. There's something ... unnatural in it. I'm sure Mr. Parmister would agree."

"You know my Morty?"

"By reputation only," said the ambassador. "It would be unhealthy to speak on it further. However, if you would be so kind, please give him a message."

"Of course. Shoot."

"Slow down," the ambassador said gravely.

"Excuse me?"

Just then, a gregarious group mounted the rooftop from below, tallest among them His Royal Majesty, carrying a Herringbone sport coat over his shoulder.

Otherwise, he wore dark, pleated slacks under an open collar sans necktie, all plainly store-bought.

The ambassador cleared his throat, telegraphing that the previous conversation was closed. "Your Majesty," he announced, turning to the entourage, "may I present the lovely and talented Ms. Gwynneth Reynolds of New York."

As the king approached her, Gwynn performed a perfect curtsy in the finest Elizabethan tradition, keeping her eyes averted until she could no longer resist. Glancing up, her heart fluttered. His effervescent smile was intoxicating, clean white teeth contrasting with the perfect Mediterranean tan. *And those dimples!* His full, luxuriant head of wavy, dark hair practically demanded to have fingers run through it, especially when compared to Morty Parmister's. Saying Morty was thin on top was like saying an egg was. The king's physique was nothing short of dreamy—tall and broad shouldered, his torso sculpted down to no more than a thirty-one-inch waist. She couldn't wait to get a look at him from behind. *My God!* He was right off the pages of a *GQ* spread.

"A royal pleasure, Miss Reynolds," said King Philio, kissing her hand before taking a step back to coax her erect. He then pulled her in to alternately brush each cheek in the Continental style, whispering so that only she could hear, "An even happier one to meet Ruth Ann Khoury." Keeping her hand, he stepped back, glancing down. "I like your shoes."

Gwynn's jaw dropped, her alarm too great to even fix upon. *How could he know?*

"Kid, you've got something," the casting agent told her privately at her umpteenth Broadway cattle call. Her career wasn't stalled; it hadn't started, making these the first positive words she'd heard from someone who mattered since she'd been in New York. Everything else had been slinging suds and kamikazes at a club joint for spaced-out, oversexed debutantes with eating disorders. Keeping up a good front spelled the difference between making rent and being on the street. At the end of the day, it was really all that good acting was about.

More meetings followed.

She'd have to change her whole approach to hair and makeup. A boob job could only help. "You have to want this," she was told. "Talent is optional. Now, what did you say your name was?"

"Khoury."

"Lose it. Sounds foreign."

"My father is Lebanese."

"You don't look it."

"My mother is Scots-Irish."

"Her name?"

"Reynolds."

"We'll go with that, but Ruth Reynolds sucks big-time. No sizzle, no pop. No, you look like a Gwyneth. Gwyneth is hot, but with a double N. We want to keep you unique. Religious?"

"Not particularly."

"You are now. I'll make the arrangements."

A shady lawyer, a smarmy publicist later, and it was all legal. Ruth Ann was no more.

The roles poured in.

Even Morty didn't know. But if he ever found out she was Semitic—even half…

"Serious actors are the most honest people I know," the king's voice gently intruded, softly enough for only her to hear. Gwynn's eyes met his. They were devoid of deceit, cunning of any kind. "The honest portrayal of a fiction is the hardest job in the world," Philio added. "Believe me, I know." A noisy train of servers bringing hot dishes and salads to the rooftop from below put an end to the moment.

Gwynn was seated next to the monarch on his right, a place of honor, she supposed, however undeserved, her mind still reeling. Then everyone joined hands, quieting, with heads bowed, as the king said grace.

"To the degree that I may presume to speak for those here gathered," he began, "we are thankful for the bounty provided by our own hands. Reciprocating, we pledge ourselves to good works. Where there is need, we promise to address it. Where there is hopelessness, we will offer hope. Where there is inequity, we will not turn a blind eye. Where there is hate and suffering, we will offer compassion and healing. To the extent that we honor these promises in clear conscience, we ask for our sustenance and good fortune to continue. All this we pray in the name of Eternal Love."

"*Amen*" was sounded in solemn chorus around the table.

Gwynn had never heard a blessing quite like it. Nor was there any commentary or discussion afterwards. Gwynn certainly didn't push it. Still, there was something blasphemous about it, something evil—not in what was said, but in what wasn't—the complete absence of God, all dangerous. There was something … *unnatural*, as the ambassador had portended. It would have been better, less off-putting, if he'd offered no prayer at all. *Who thanks themselves?*

As she'd already guessed it would be, the meal was conducted informally, family style, without servants, the dishes passed hand to hand around the table, all a bit underwhelming for a royal soiree. The king even served her!

Quite soon, the conversation turned to international economics, highly technical. At the crux, the diplomats were anxious to discern the throne's trade policies, if any. From what Gwynn could glean, the king was being given a series of Hobson's choices, all of which he patiently rejected; he was definitely not one to be swayed by high-toned jargon. When he finally spoke up, he did so for the benefit of everyone at the table.

"There is nothing wrong with competition that leads to mutual improvement. What must end is conflating competition with conflict and, more specifically, with conquest."

"Yet does not the natural balance dictate there be winners and losers, sire?" one of the diplomatic guests ventured.

"Only where scarcity and exclusivity are imposed," said Philio.

"Imposed, sire?"

"Profit is and should be the reward for risk," the king continued, "unless the risk is illusory, intentionally so. Thus, the paradigm will be adjusted."

"How so?" more than one guest piped up.

"With information," said the king.

"No more secrets, Lord?" someone ventured.

"Let us just say that as the advantages of deception diminish, the disadvantages of disclosure will likewise vanish."

"What about privacy?" Gwynn blurted out without meaning to.

"If you want to preserve it, don't abuse it," Philio said too easily.

"Who judges that?" she asked rather tartly.

"Good question," he allowed, "very wise, very poignant." Sipping wine, he gave it extended thought. "What is a private truth? Is there such a thing? Do we hold it closely to refrain from harming others, or simply to preserve ourselves, our personal options? Are they options we deserve, have merely appropriated from the ignorance of others, or stolen outright? Can a private truth serve multiple purposes simultaneously? Perhaps, all of the above, yeah? And perhaps the energy wasted to conceal it is better spent on other things. In the end, Miss Reynolds, it is the honesty we afford ourselves that shapes our destiny."

Gwynn was bowled over. Her face went flush; she was tremendously affected. She prayed it didn't show. It wasn't the words, it was the delivery. It was so ... *not* Christian—firm but not fixed, without pedantic strictures and grasping sophistry, without unfeeling judgment; simple, yet immeasurably deep, logic and empathy combined. Divine. She shivered involuntarily. *Who are you, Janus Philio? Who are you ... really?* She couldn't let it go. "Do *you* have secrets, Majesty?" she blurted anew.

Having already re-engaged the original topic, he patiently broke off again, smiling at her, a smile she felt in an unwelcome region. "Absolutely," he granted.

"Then aren't you imposing a double standard?"

"Clearly," said he.

"Is that fair?"

Biting his lower lip, he sighed, shaking his head. "On the other hand, let me put it to you this way: it's good to be king." He appended this with a wink, causing Gwynn to surmise he felt more the opposite, much more, verging on profound melancholy. Her intuition, something she'd always relied on, told her that, underneath it all, Philio was perilously close to emotional exhaustion. "In time," he resumed with the others, "both econometrically and spiritually, cooperation and coalescence must, and will, replace domination and surrender. The status quo simply cannot withstand strong inquiry in the light of day, at any level, no matter how stubbornly it chooses to resist."

"That sounds suspiciously like an ultimatum, Your Majesty," said a diplomat.

"It is," Philio said wanly, "the inevitably of eventuality." Heard before and often, it was swiftly becoming the slogan of his reign. Only a beat later, he added a total non sequitur. "I'm going to end poverty forever without diminishing existing personal wealth." He wasn't joking.

Indefensibly outrageous, the statement begged more and immediately in a torrent of "*How?*"—not all of it pleasantly. After a moment of quiet, the king responded.

"The poor happen to be sitting on an untapped reserve of infinite power," he said. If he hadn't before, he now had everybody's undivided attention.

"Do they know it?" a startled voice asked.

"They will shortly," Philio said. "And when I tell them, it's going to change ... everything." His gaze landed on Gwynn. "Do you dance, Miss Reynolds?"

Staci Mandelheimer almost spit up. "She's a *nafke*."

"*Shtumm!*" Avi thundered, cutting her off. Theirs was a curious match, Avi and his wife. Physically, she outweighed him by a good fifty pounds. Nonetheless humiliated, she promptly fled downstairs. Several of the women followed to console her. Avi turned to Gwynn, his apology on behalf of his spouse implicit. To the king, he said, "A spot of music then, Jan?"

"Don't bother," said the king, his eyes never leaving Gwynn's. "We'll make our own."

Nafke was a Yiddish word for prostitute.

Chapter XIII

Thirty million years ago in what would become southwestern Jordan, the earth heaved and shook, throwing up huge walls of rock just to the east of the river Jordan. Carved by time into fantastic shapes, these mountains formed a formidable—but hardly the only—barrier between the fertile lands of Palestine and the vast deserts of Arabia. For thousands of years, this stark and unforgiving landscape had been the playground of the jinn. The jinn were the bogeymen of desert folklore, demons that haunt deserted places, pestering unwary travelers, sometimes to death. Here, the jinn relentlessly taunted a man's idle mind with questions and temptation. The only defense against such tricksters was not to think, for thoughts are corruptible, whereas faith is eternal.

On horseback, now shortly after midnight, Morton Parmister and Ken Rittenour rode through a rugged, twisting gorge so narrow in places that it shut out the stars. With them was a single Bedouin guide. Not so very long ago, members of his Bedul tribe would have killed on sight any foreigner trespassing in these parts to protect a great secret, and this particular towelhead didn't look the least bit averse to upholding that tradition. In fact, the whole escapade was giving Morty a bad case of the willies.

Rittenour, on the other hand, seemed right at home. It was, perhaps, the terminal affliction of warriors who'd been too long in enemy territory. They forgot who they were and, all too often, what they were fighting for. Fully aware of the syndrome, Parmister nevertheless harbored no doubts about his old friend. In a dicey situation, there was no one he'd rather be with. It didn't make the ride any less creepy. This place, like nowhere Morty had ever been or even imagined, was utterly forsaken by God—cold, bone-dry, lifeless.

Startled when Rittenour broke the eerie silence save for the clop of hooves, the snorts of their mounts, Parmister was also relieved. Ken wouldn't risk talking unless it was completely safe to do so. Riding side by side, they were keeping their guide in sight but not too close. Eyes in the back of his head, Ken wisely wanted to maintain the option of wheeling around on a dime should the tribesman prove untrustworthy.

"I've been doing some checking," he said.

"Have you? What on?"

"Turns out Janus was an ancient Italian deity," Rittenour said. "In Roman mythology, he was the god of gateways, doors, and beginnings, typically depicted with two faces, one looking forward, the other back, making him also the god of time. The month of January is named after him—the start of the new year, but also the middle of winter. The name Philio is a derivation of the Greek word *philos*, for love."

Morty grunted. "And all pagan, but what's in a name? Anyway, I already knew all that."

"Did you?" said Rittenour. "I didn't."

Given their surroundings and primitive mode of travel, the topic only made Parmister more uncomfortable than he already was. "Wanna tell me what brought this up?" he asked. "It's not like you to go all to pieces over some jack-off's made-up name."

"I don't go all to pieces," Rittenour said quite calmly. "It's called intelligence, something we can all use more of, I think."

"What's that supposed to mean?"

Rittenour sighed wearily. "Look, man, I'm just telling you."

"Yeah, well, do me a favor," Parmister replied tartly. "When there's something I don't know, *I'll* tell *you*. Otherwise, keep it to yourself. It'll save time."

"Your funeral," Rittenour mumbled.

Morty sniggered. "You black-ops types always have to get in the last word, don't you?"

"That's because we know it could very well be our very last."

"Cue the violins," Parmister mocked him. "You love every minute of it, and you know it. You guys live for the adrenalin rush and not much else."

"There's never been much else," Rittenour said sadly.

"Has anything changed?"

"I'm still trying to work that out."

"Well, don't work too hard," said Parmister. "I need you focused."

"Don't worry about me. I've never been more focused in my life."

"Glad to hear it," Parmister said, welcoming the ensuing silence as they rode on. Being morbidly cryptic had been part and parcel of Ken's personality for as long as they'd known each other. Rittenour liked to think it made him inscrutable. It didn't. Morty had always been able to read him like a book. At bottom, the only code Ken followed was the code of the warrior. All it asked for was a black-and-white reason to kill, and Morty had always been able to come up with plenty of those. It wasn't even hard.

"Almost there," Rittenour whispered, urging his horse in front of Morty's. He had to. The gorge here narrowed to under a meter's width, its sheer, red-rock walls rising seven hundred feet straight up on either side. Though geologically fascinating, it was a claustrophobe's nightmare.

This snaking, otherworldly chasm known as the Siq, about a klick and a half long in total, the wog had said earlier, followed the Wadi Musa, or the wadi of Moses. According to Bedouin legend, it was created when Moses struck a boulder with his staff to get at water for his people. Then, around the next bend, dead ahead, softly effervescing under a brilliant crescent moon, Morty beheld something he was completely unprepared for, more enchanted than anything he'd ever seen, the Khasneb el-Faroun—the Treasury at Petra.

Carved out of the living rock, its dramatic, multi-level porticos towered some fifteen stories high, deliberately positioned at the end of the Siq for maximum visual impact. Bedouin lore held that it was built by Pharaoh in the course of pursuing the Israelites through the wilderness. Curiously, this would place him a bit far afield of the Red Sea, where his six thousand charioteers drowned before making it across, which the Bible and the Koran adamantly say was the case. Hence, the Bedouin story was just plain wrong. Then again, factually, Ramses the Great did indeed live to a ripe old age, overrunning Canaan at the same time the Israelites were roaming Sinai. His tomb in the Valley of the Kings proved it. The historical stumper was that they never crossed paths. Perhaps someone was fibbing. Actually, they all were; the Treasury carbon-dated to no earlier than the first century BC.

Beyond it lay the ruins of a once vital city, painstakingly hewn by hand into the mountainsides, making it one of the most mysterious places on Earth. While Jesus was walking the hills of Galilee, under two hundred miles away, Petra was a cosmopolitan center of classical art and commerce, thirty thousand strong, whose urban technology, inexplicably set on some of the most desolate acreage conceivable, dwarfed that of the next nearest city of any size, Jerusalem. Its temples rivaled anything in Egypt, the Acropolis, even the Pantheon. Fiercely independent, Petra wasn't fully annexed by Rome until AD 106, whereupon it died a quick death, virtually overnight, and was abandoned. The few inscriptions and ancient texts remaining to posterity speak of mighty kings who were great lovers of democracy, of powerful gods and sumptuous feasts, and of the right of women to own property and vote. Little else is known about the builders of Petra, except their name: the Nabataeans.

As an archeological site and tourist attraction in more modern times, Petra was again abandoned early on in the apocalypse, when the far western strip of Jordan paralleling the river once again reverted to a no man's land. Now, Morty was pleased to see, his new allies had converted it into a secret base of operations. He could hear the distant hum of portable generators, and there were scattered electric lights. Military-surplus trucks rumbled in and out, their cargo unloaded by forklifts. It wasn't hard to guess what they were moving. There was even a short airfield with runway beacons, capable of accommodating multi-engine prop planes up to the size of medium-payload cargo craft, of which there were several vintage models chocked at one end—restored B-25s and a DC-3. An old Piper Cub in pristine condition was ready to ferry out VIPs at a moment's notice. There was even an old Huey helicopter painted in desert camouflage.

"What's with taking the snail's route?" Parmister complained. "We could've flown in."

"Shut up!" Ken snapped at him. "We're not out of the woods yet."

Incensed, Morty was forced to put off a royal ass-chewing for the insubordination when, up ahead, paramilitary Arab sentries, armed to the teeth, halted the three riders under torchlight. They were a humorless, battle-hardened bunch, which Morty found encouraging. It would take men like this to do what had to be done.

"How should I your true love know?" the lead sentry asked, or thereabouts, in Arabic, waiting for the countersign.

"I must be cruel only to be kind," Rittenour replied, also in Arabic.

The sentry looked at Parmister, sizing him up. "He is the one?"

"He is the one," Rittenour confirmed.

"Let them through," the lead sentry ordered his men.

Without warning, his delivery complete, their Bedouin guide reined his horse around and galloped away back toward the Siq, crying, "*Allahu akbar!*"

A couple dozen shrill voices, their owners unseen on the dark cliff-tops of the gorge on both sides, war-whooped his departure, firing rifles into the air, making Parmister's stomach turn a flip. Had the Americans made one false move in the narrow confines of the Siq, instant death would have rained down from above. Yet, in a weird way, it was also heartening, for it meant none of Philio's spies had followed. *This is going to work*, Morty thought happily, marveling at the irony, at the fathomless depths of God's supreme wisdom.

Lit outside by hanging pan fires, the interior of the cavernous Palace Tomb had the benefit of good ol' incandescent light bulbs, albeit drooping naked from wires crisscrossing overhead. Aside from its rustic antiquity, though, as a command center it was none too shabby. All things considered, the new global headquarters of al-Qaeda was nothing short of a Pentagon-slick field operation. They had the latest in Wi-Fi notebook computers, marvelously detailed Plexiglas maps marked up in multi-colored grease pencil, and a bank of satellite radio consoles powerful enough to reach every corner of the globe. Even better, an array of hi-def LCD flat screen TVs was pulling in every international news broadcast you could think of. Somewhere in the Petra complex was a motherfucker of a dish antenna, more than one. Truth be told, had Morty been interested in anyone else's truth, the around-the-clock operation was devoted to getting relief supplies to remote desert enclaves throughout the Arabian peninsula, east across the Strait of Hormuz, and west across the lower Red Sea into East Africa.

"Jesus! Who's paying for all this?"

"You are," said Rittenour. Nudging him by the elbow, he brought Morty down the interior steps and onto the operational floor of the terrorist nerve center.

At the central worktable, a round job thirty feet in diameter that was spread with more maps, a grizzly-bearded Muslim holy man in traditional robes and a turban looked over. There was more gray than not in his whiskers, and he had round, wire-frame spectacles riding down his nose. To Morty, he looked about as lethal as Mohandas Gandhi with a dirty diaper.

"Showtime, Morty," Rittenour said under his breath, quickly explaining that this was Sheik Nidal, an alias meaning the "the teacher of struggle."

Parmister frowned. "I thought *jihad* meant struggle."

"Wanna argue?"

In truth, Parmister's fluency in Arabic made Rittenour's look average. He'd never let on that such was the case and wasn't about to now. A level playing field only helped the losers. As the sheik stood upright, Morty made a grand show of playing the stumbling, bumbling bureaucrat, beginning with an ungainly bow, more Japanese than Near-Eastern. "Um, salaam aleichem?" he butchered the expected greeting.

"*Aleichem salaam,*" the sheik replied tersely, dismissing him to concentrate on Rittenour, continuing to converse in Arabic. "Have you prepared him for what must be done?"

More than the words themselves, it was the sheik's inflection that raised Morty's hackles. Suddenly, something wasn't right. There were advantages in playing the village idiot—much of Morty's career had been built on it—but this wasn't one of those times. "I speak for myself," he asserted to the sheik flawlessly. Nidal was pleasantly amused. Ken Rittenour wasn't, not remotely. Parmister stepped out in front of him to steal the sheik's focus. Ken's usefulness as a tool, at least for the moment, was finished, kaput. He'd just have to get over it. There were bigger issues.

"Yes, good idea; let us drop tiresome pretense," the sheik said affably, switching to English. "I, quite frankly, prefer your tongue when talking business," he went on. "No pregnant pauses to reflect upon and savor subtle symbolism. Straight down the gut, as it were—slam, bam, thank you, ma'am."

"Helps keep us honest," Parmister replied, his impatience showing.

The sheik's expression wasn't kind. Then, whatever he was thinking, he let it go. "I must say you're taking this all remarkably well."

"Neither of us was born yesterday, sheik," Morty replied. "Sometimes you just gotta go with the flow."

The sheik's brow furrowed ever so briefly. "One day we shall look back with great wonder on all this, I expect."

"I expect so," Morty agreed.

"Shall we skip to the end game?"

"By all means," Morty concurred, eager for a look-see at the planning maps, whereupon the sheik twice clapped his hands, the staccato noise of it resounding off the vaulted stone chamber with a sharp echo, bringing a column of guards from a side archway at the quickstep. They surrounded Parmister in a semicircle, cutting off any escape, but not Rittenour, who swung around in front to join Sheik Nidal. Morty gamely figured it was some sort of initiation rite. He could not have been more wrong.

The sheik officiously cleared his throat, proclaiming clearly: "In the name of the Mahdi, King of Jerusalem, master of the world, I arrest you for high treason."

Morty found it all very funny, some kind of test. Unfortunately, no one was laughing.

"That is all," said the sheik, rather perfunctorily signaling the guards to take him away.

As he was grabbed firmly by the arms, Morty shot his eyes to Rittenour. "What the fuck is this?"

Rittenour shrugged. "I tried to give you a heads-up, Morty. You weren't listening."

"*You set me up?*"

"Hey, he didn't raise me from the dead for nothing."

"Huh? Are you out of your mind?"

"I was."

"Wait!" Morty tried to reason it out, appealing to the sheik. "Why lure me all the way out here? You could have picked me up anytime, on any city street." Jerking free, he jabbed a finger at Rittenour. "Hell, I've been with *this* traitor almost every waking hour for weeks."

"Only the king knows his own mind," said the sheik, "but there is a reason for everything."

Morty's mind raced, not having to sprint far. *Gwynn?* He instinctively knew the question was the answer, sending him ballistic. "*Why, that philandering son of a bitch!*"

He was immediately punished by a leather truncheon that caught him behind the ear, blurring his vision. Suddenly, Rittenour was mixing it up with the Arabs, trying to get to him, but there were too many of them. Morty was hit again and then a third time before everything faded to black.

Chapter XIV

A full week after Morton Parmister had failed to report in, the first slivers of daybreak in Washington found Darius Block on the National Mall taking in a casual stroll along the Lincoln Memorial reflecting pool with the newly elected grand master of the Guardians. He was the silver fox from the Chesapeake Bay promontory, the one whose financial concerns were outweighed by more altruistic instincts, starting with rescuing civilization from the runaway train wreck of Janus Philio's soul-stealing nihilism. Other than an early-rising jogger heading the other way with her dog off leash, Block and the Guardian were pretty much alone. The frolicking mutt seemed to focus the Guardian's thoughts, none of them especially positive.

"How's your new White House pet coming along?"

"Surprisingly well," said Block, "both precocious and hungry." The reverend couldn't resist a chuckle. "Who would've guessed? Truly, God moves in mysterious ways."

"Well, tell him to speed it up," the Guardian said sharply. "These sanctions are killing everyone's shareholder guidance. Worse, the natives are getting restless. The whole union thing is rearing its ugly head again. Organizers are popping up all over the place. There's talk of a general strike. It's not about benefits. It's not even about pay. They want us to close down all our goddamn weapons factories! They want Philio, the rank and file—they think they do."

"At least universal healthcare is off the table," Block said. "That's got to be a plus."

"No, that's the *other* problem," said the Guardian. "The medical establishment's gone belly-up. Physicians and surgeons can't afford to pay their country club dues. The insurance business hasn't written more than a handful of new policies in weeks, and, like a spreading rash, folks are skipping out on their premiums, especially on their mandatory auto casualty. Actuaries are walking around with their thumb up their ass. The big drug outfits are radically scaling back production. Overstocked pharmacies are closing their prescription counters for lack of traffic. All this wellness is wrecking lives! The mortuary industry is in the toilet." The Guardian smacked a fist against his palm. "*Damn it*, something's gotta give! Somehow we've got to get people back to the fundamentals."

"Market fundamentals?" Block posed. "Or my kind?"

The Guardian rather boorishly gargled up phlegm from the back of his throat and hocked a loogie. "One man's religion is another man's bread and butter, and *your* bread and butter, Reverend, is being cut off at the knees right along with the rest of us. Enough dicking around! Where are the fireworks you promised?"

Block tried not to blanch but failed. "Our asset in Jerusalem is ... off the air," he relayed reluctantly. "I don't have an explanation. With any luck, it's only temporary."

Fortunately, they'd reached the base of the Lincoln shrine. The Guardian's limousine was waiting in the parking lot, and he had other places to be, so he lingered only a moment longer, becoming more objective, certainly softer spoken. "It's not," he decided. "We have to assume he's been compromised and that he's compromised you."

Block vigorously shook his head. "He wouldn't do that."

"Everyone has a breaking point," said the Guardian. "On top of being almost completely cut off from the rest of the world, it seems we're up against something—I don't know—mythical. I've worked every international source, every contact I've got, and I still can't get a handle on who this Philio is or even *what* he is."

"I know what he is," Block said with undisguised loathing, "and he's no avatar."

The Guardian sighed dubiously. "Just how many antichrists are there going to be before we get to the real one, Dar?"

"That's not fair," Block objected, though not strongly. "God brought down the Dome—Daniel's abomination of desolation. Only a dope needed to read the tea leaves to know what had to come next. I only delivered what you asked for. Give them a kick in the pants, you said, get the juices flowing. *Make* them believe. From there it kind of took on a life of its own."

"Can you do it again? You haven't pounded a pulpit in awhile."

"Do I have a choice?"

Shoving his hands in his pockets, the Guardian moseyed on to his car. An answer would have been superfluous. But then he had a sudden epiphany. "Don't take this the wrong way, but what do you do when a competitor blindsides you with a superior product?"

Block frowned.

"You rebrand and repackage," the Guardian submitted, waiting for his chauffeur to come around and open the door. "Just a thought," he tossed out before sliding in. "Clock's ticking."

As the limo drove off into the now vivid sunrise breaking over the Potomac estuary, Darius Block absently took the steps up to the Lincoln Memorial to steal a few quiet moments to himself, his mind working feverishly with little result. He was just so tired anymore, dangerously close to burn-out—at a total loss, the walls closing in. How do you sell God's loving destruction of the world to save it when a cad like Philio was out there mucking it all up with other options and getting traction? How do you pitch divine mercy when God's wrath no longer carries any particular dread? *Rebrand. Repackage. But how?* It was like trying to squeeze blood out of a stone, and it was giving Block a headache. His swelling, grinding, now molten hatred of Janus Philio was only making it worse. Back when it was not only legal but praiseworthy, there'd been an *a posteriori* dividend in burning a Liebnizian smart-ass like Philio at the stake: sweet release—for the inquisitor! *Good God, I hate that guy!*

Darius—Dar to close friends, the rare few equipped to ascend to such heights—had been summoned into the Lord's service at the age of twelve; actually, before that, before he was ten. The Divine Plan had been crystal clear to him ever since. How did he know? Because most everyone else was so blind to it. It wasn't like it was rocket science or anything; no, it was all black and white on the pages of the Bible, staring everyone right in the face. And yet, being so clear on it, so in tune with God's genius, was also Block's burden, a heavy one, weighing him down, *slowing* him down. They just didn't get it, anyone else, not its full impact. Oh, sure, they paid it lip service, but that was just to get on the reverend's good side, to butter him up for handouts—all wannabes of shallow faith, *so* disingenuous, *so* transparent. His only real solace lay in Luke 8:10–12, which his personal savior spoke aloud to him, quite frequently as a matter of fact. "*Unto you it is given to know the mysteries of the kingdom of God: but to others in parables; that seeing they might not see, and hearing they might not understand ... then cometh the devil, and taketh away the word out of their hearts, lest they should believe and be saved.*" Generally, it was all the encouragement Block needed. That was the beauty of the reverend's savior. He always came through loud and clear in a pinch, the power and the glory: strength, pure, raw, and unadulterated—no wimpy, bleeding-heart pussyfooting allowed.

"Hey, man," a sleepy voice intruded on his thoughts. "Can you help a brother out?"

It came from the shadows behind him. Block spun to it, angry at being caught unawares, unnerved by the surprise so soon after his sensitive rendezvous with the Guardian. A yawning, filthy tramp on the ground propped himself upright at the waist against a pillar just this side of the steps. He was wrapped in fetid horse blankets and had a gold tooth in front. Otherwise, if not for that alone, he looked like he'd time-warped in from the French Revolution, the reincarnation of just about any ne'er-do-well Charles Dickens ever penned. Block's reflex was wholly devoid of pity. "Get a job," he recommended, making tracks out of the memorial. "I gave at the office."

"Yeah, I bet you're a real saint."

Block halted cold. The sarcasm genuinely hurt. Digging into his pocket, he pulled out his money clip and peeled off a generous bill. Pivoting back, he held it out to the bum, whose eyes, alcohol glazed or drug addled, and likely both, lit up instantly. "It's yours," the reverend confirmed. He then tore the bill to pieces and tossed it like confetti before adding, "just as soon as you get off your lazy butt and chase it down."

Carried on a wisp of breeze, most of the fragments ended their flight on the waters of the reflecting pool, turning to mush, which Block found vaguely satisfying. Tough love was the only way to deal with these people. Indeed, he took the stairs down to the Mall with a little extra zip in his step, only to hear the tramp's defiant comeback in a rolling echo from inside the memorial.

"*God save King Philio!*"

As he picked up his pace, Block's spirits took a nosedive, if that was possible. Unchecked, Philio's celebrity among the underclasses was continuing to mushroom, stoked by the newly renascent and still godless gay-liberal-feminist agenda. Any further proof of the Antichrist's unholy alliance with Satan was redundant, *de trop*, prolix. The reverend had also zeroed in on his only practicable strategy— no repackaging, no rebranding. The Roman Church had gone that route with Vatican II and inflicted unrecoverable damage on itself. No, the only sure-fire way to defeat a myth was with a counter myth, and nobody was better at the propaganda game than Dr. Darius Block. *Welcome to the big leagues, Philio. Your free ride is over.*

Meanwhile, back at his perch against the column, the vagrant produced a camera phone from under his blankets and flipped it open, hitting a number on speed dial that connected him to the White House switchboard. "Chief of Staff Felix Angel, please," he requested. "Code Pink." He was on hold only briefly. Unfortunately, he landed in Nacho's voice mail, but perhaps it was just as well. The message he left was in Spanish, translating roughly to: "It's Rojas, chief. I'll be on the move when you get this, but we got him. Contact is positive. Repeat, subject made contact with the last of them, probably their leader. I'm sending over his picture now. *¡Viva el Reino!*"

Chapter XV

Like opening an overstuffed closet crammed with household junk, the word on Philio spilled out, unleashed, scrubbing the disciples of virtue into a righteous lather. Attributed to anonymous victims of conscience who could no longer sit idly by, it was disseminated in no particular or logical order. Had it been, the merchants of verity might have detected premeditation. The gusher of truth was finally tapped by the sheer weight of "evidence." Blogged to death on the Internet, its veracity was a technicality. The illegal regime in Jerusalem obstructed independent verification. Even so, a religiously informed person could not escape the cumulative feel of a *fait accompli*, answering a long list of nagging doubts. Capping it all, and genetically indisputable, the so-called king was a Jew. From there it was a grab bag, although the subtext was clear.

Philio was a creation-denying, ransom-ridiculing, science-loving atheist. One World Government and religious persecution were at the top of his anti-social agenda. Faithful, unsuspecting Christians, secretly classified as useless and unsalvageable, were being singled out for ghettos, slave camps, and systematic annihilation. There could be no other explanation for Philio's massive, unparalleled construction projects in the most Godforsaken, previously uninhabitable places. *Damn it all, people, how much plainer can it be? Philio will do and say anything to protect and extend his power! At first, he was only laughing at us! Now he plans to kill us all because we're in his way! Think of your children! Be afraid! Be very afraid!*

As right-wing commentators and churchmen fanned the flames of myopic panic, the White House trotted out none other than Dr. Darius Block for a series of press interviews. Totally in the dark as to the source of the leaks, Dr. Block cautioned against what he termed "excessive overreaction." He said the governor-general was investigating, concerned but hopeful, suggesting that the king could allay burning doubts about his rule by relaxing the sanctions against America, a good-faith gesture that could not but be looked upon favorably.

Jerusalem's response was an unreserved "No." Its terms remained unchanged—unilateral disarmament, complete and total, including the verifiable dismantling of any and all war-making capacities—no exceptions, no latitude. The throne otherwise expressed no reaction to the stateside proliferation of scurrilous rumors and innuendo, except to quote the king in passing. "Motes and beams," he was reported to have said off the cuff, evidently referring to the scriptural lesson about hypocrisy, wherein Jesus railed against plucking a sliver out of your brother's eye when you've got a whole plank in your own. And therein lay the rub.

Philio was no pushover. As the Guardian had more than implied, the Reverend Block had cried wolf a little too often, one antichrist to the next—if anything, erring on the side of caution. Still, Block's intentions were pure. He'd gotten crossed up by the Rapture, or lack thereof. It was an honest mistake. He'd jumped the gun, a misstep Philio had masterfully capitalized on. More infuriating still, the king refused to bite back. And, because he ignored the smears, his popularity only rose in some national polls. Thus, to step up the pressure, Block had Julian Quinn hit the stump for a campaign-style *tour de force*.

His schedule jam-packed, the governor-general appeared at a series of red, white, and blue rallies across the country, presented as a national godsend, the only ready counterweight to Philio's boundless tyranny. Physically, it was a role for which Julian came perfectly equipped. Big, handsome, and impeccably groomed, he was a former sports superstar with good name recognition, solely motivated by democratic ideals wrought from unbending piety: a devoted family man. As wholesome agitprops, Jamyqua and their three kids completed a Rockwellian portrait of domestic bliss and divine intention.

Behind-the-scenes handlers, mostly former council operatives plucked from political exile by Dr. Block, carefully screened each invitation-only event to maximize its nationally televised impact. Peace activists and proponents of disarmament were kept at bay by a heavy police presence. Julian crisply delivered narrowly scripted speeches, long on nostalgia, short on details. Impromptu questions, randomly fielded from the audience, were leading and implicitly supportive. With honorable abandon, Quinn hurled the labels "appeasers" and "patriots" and "evil-doers." The long years of unprecedented carnage on the apocalyptic battlefields of the Near East were declared "inflated." The Zone, plague, the labor camps, the press squads, the hoarding—all were blamed on the late president or his predecessors and their out-of-control administrations. Block's council was magically rehabilitated, turned into powerless spectators who had been sidelined from the start and whose dire warnings had gone unheeded. School textbooks were ordered rewritten to better reflect "the truth."

More than the East's decadent and debauched excesses, it was Jerusalem's intransigence on the trade embargo that made for Julian Quinn's biggest applause line. "Make no mistake about it," he thundered from the lectern at every stop, "the world needs us more than we need it," typically followed by the durably obtuse refrain, "America is best when America leads." Nevertheless, whether the sanctions were minimized as a temporary setback on the one hand or condemned as an act of unprovoked aggression on the other, just about everyone who had anything was starting to feel the sanctions' bite. Those that didn't were ignored, having no more to gripe about than normal—whiny have-nots and losers, the bunch.

The rural heartland and suburbs of Middle America, propelled into action by Washington's media blitz, became hotbeds of antiroyalist incitement. Churches were reopened to theologically validate the outcry and kick sand at Philio's moratorium on priestcraft. Angry street marchers egged on by council agitators waved banners emblazoned with *"Death to Philio!"* and *"Death to the Antichrist!"* The king was serially burned in effigy, occasioned by much shooting. Though they hadn't been seen for some time, brave men in hooded masks and white bedsheets once again convened midnight vigils around flaming crosses. Mob attacks on royalist sympathizers declaimed as "Janusians" and "Philioists" became commonplace; their shops were looted, their homes vandalized and burned while law enforcement turned a blind eye. Largely because there were never any fatalities, the violence was chalked up to "condign exuberance." The growing evidence that mortality was now a biological impossibility seemed to faze no one. Other than calling it a persisting anomaly, the medical community, in general, was mum. Theories to the contrary were dismissed as reckless speculation.

"Yea, though I give all my earthly goods to feed the poor and have not ...? *Help me out here, people!*" Julian baited an especially enthusiastic crowd in Greenville, South Carolina.

"FAITH!" they shouted back, for the most part sincerely, even tearfully, raising the chant: *"Might-y, Might-y, Might-y,"* with tomahawk motions, picking up steam until there was no point in Julian continuing, if indeed there'd been a point to his saying it to begin with. A squad of lily-white high school cheerleaders on the gymnasium floor, each a potential Magnolia Queen, encouraged the roar with pom-poms and drum-tight booties:

Who'll fight the beast?
Mighty's our man
If he can't do it
No one can

One two three four
Kick that beast right out the door
Five six seven eight
Who do we appreciate?

High kicks and more shrieks of "*Mighty!*" turned a deadly international standoff into a popcorn-and-cotton-candy pep rally.

As the schoolgirl cheer suggested, Julian was hailed as the champion of all things pure and noble, the new icon of Yankee know-how and steely resolve in the face of adversity. His race was trumpeted as proof of the country's unhindered social progress. Inevitable comparisons were drawn with the "great communicator" and "Morning in America."

This time, however, there was a slight wrinkle. The new Evil Empire showed no signs of imploding, and quite the reverse. Beyond contiguous U.S.–Canadian boundaries, the world had entered a post-war economic boom unrivaled in the annals of history. Consequently, a burgeoning exodus of asylum seekers was stacked up on the northern side of the two-thousand-mile wall demarking the Mexican border, creating a humanitarian crisis. Floundering boat lifts out of Miami and the Florida Keys bound for the Bahamas and Cuba were overwhelming the Coast Guard.

Undeterred by this or other cumbersome minutiae, Quinn delivered his closing zinger. "You know, folks, and correct me if I'm wrong, but I seem to remember another king that put our backs to the wall once. Remember how that worked out?"

As the decibel level red-lined, he was handed a replica of a Revolutionary War–era flintlock musket. Raising it high overhead, his sleeves rolled up, his face contorted with umbrage, he uttered his most brazen challenge to Jerusalem yet, one that made his own wife cringe.

"*From my cold, dead hands, Philio!*"

Pandemonium. Julian had never felt so much love.

Finally, it was time for a well-deserved, if short, break from the rhetorical grind. Jamyqua Quinn insisted and would brook no argument, promising to have her husband back in twenty-four hours, despite Dr. Block's objections, due in no small part to the fact that he was not invited, nor were any of Julian's "handlers." She chose a place Julian knew well but that was otherwise off the radar of anyone outside the family—a rugged enclave of cabins for no-frills sportsmen in the mountains of northeastern Tennessee, well off the beaten path. Julian's father had brought him here often as a youngster. Merlin was here now. Keeping the children back, Jamyqua pointed Julian down the trail armed with a fly rod, catch basket, net, fishing vest, and waders, commanding him to "Go." When she chose to, a blessedly rare occurrence, she could be intolerably bossy. But the sky was blue, the sun comfortably warming, the summer woods naturally fragrant—and the alternative was a bedtime snub. And so Julian set off to make the best of it, shadowed by a protective escort of Nacho Angel's hand-picked security troops.

Quinn, Sr. was already fly casting for trout midway across the sun-shimmering crystal shoals of the river when Julian came upon him. The setting befitted a painting. A six-pack of canned beer was chilling at water's edge. Helping himself to one, breathing in the woodsy scent, belatedly praising his wife's wisdom, Julian pulled on his waders before expertly rigging his own line. "Sure brings back the memories, don't it? I should've brought the boys."

"This one's for us," Merlin said, recasting without looking over. "Better if they don't know what they'll never have."

Julian waded out into the stream and made his first cast. "Never know'd you to be so gloomy. Wake up on the wrong side of the bed or something?"

They fished in tranquil silence for the better part of a quarter hour before Merlin replied. "Call it none of my business, but just how comfortable do you intend to get in that White House? And why, in God's name, are you so hell-bent to set the clock back?"

"What are you talking about?"

"Didn't nobody vote for you that I know of ... not that they wouldn't. Not now."

"Maybe that's the plan. Maybe you should try showing up for a meeting, earn your keep." Julian's tone was abrasive, belittling, one he'd never before used with his father.

"Maybe it's time to stop meeting and planning and start living, start ... *thinking*," Merlin said. "Me, I had a lot of time to think in that cell at Gitmo."

His back to Merlin, Julian made an awesome cast, pleasing himself to no end. "Maybe too much," he said. "Know this, though. I will never forgive them that put you there."

Merlin's shoulders slouched. "Why not? I have." His line suddenly snapped taut, bending the rod. "Looks like I got me a fighter." Mindful of the slippery rocks underfoot in the fast-moving stream, Julian came over to assist.

"Give it some play," he coached excitedly. "That's it. Not too much, now. Don't give it any ideas." He was preaching to the choir. His father was a veteran angler who'd forgotten more about fishing than Julian would ever know. Reeling it in, giving and taking, it turned out to be a good eighteen-incher, a monster steelhead, easily four pounds, bigger by a far cry than anything recently fished out of this shallow stretch. Julian was ready with his net as his father lifted the trout by the gills, methodically extricated the hook, then knelt to gently reintroduce the fish to the water and let its shock subside. Then, inexplicably, he let it dart away, rendering Julian speechless. Staring blithely at the streaking trail of sediment underwater, Merlin waxed philosophical.

"Sometimes, son, as good as it feels, you just gotta let it go."

"What's on your mind, Pop?"

Merlin rose up to face him, nose to nose. "I want you to stop beating the war drums."

"It's no big deal," Julian said, turning away dismissively. "It's just politics."

But Merlin wasn't buying it. "Boy, what do *you* know from politics?"

"Cool down. I know what I'm doing."

Sloshing for the riverbank, Merlin was short. "You don't know shit. Nobody does. Only an honest man admits it, and first to himself. Everything else is smoke and mirrors."

Standing put in the stream, Julian put a hand on his hip. "What about faith?"

"In what?" Merlin shot back, popping the tab on a beer. "It's not a totem or a golden calf, Julian. No words can contain it. True faith is experienced in here." He thumped his breast. "It's not a garment you wear. Nor is it a weapon, not true faith. True faith is a solemn pact between you and your maker. No one else is involved. Break that bond with cheap theatrics, and you're no longer faithful, you're just a … performer, a hack salesman peddling a bill of goods."

Julian waded closer to shore. "The Bible says spread the word."

"The Bible says a lot of things."

"And one of those things it says quite clearly. Or maybe you've forgotten." Julian's voice cut, truculent, enough to bring his bodyguards to the edge of the woods. "And I quote: 'Think not that I am come to bring peace on earth: I came not to bring peace, but a sword. For I am come to set a man at variance against his father, and the daughter against her mother, and the daughter-in-law against her mother-in-law. And a man's foes shall be they of his own household. He that loveth father or mother more than me is not worthy of me: and he that loveth son or daughter more than me is not worthy of me.'" Julian paused to let the scripture sink in. "Go on, I'm waiting. Argue with that ... *Dad.*" His tone was downright venomous.

Merlin was hushed for a long time, his brow furrowed. More than incredulous, he was ashamed—a father's regret over his own parenting gone awry. Still, he was unwilling to accept all the blame. "I guess I was wrong," he said. "Darius Block doesn't have a gift. The man's a goddamn sorcerer."

"Leave him out of this," Julian said strongly. "And I'll thank you not to take the Lord's name in vain." Then he threw down the gauntlet, his eyes like daggers, his voice like doom itself. "Tell me straight up, old man, now and forevermore. Do you stand against me and the ransom sacrifice of our lord Jesus Christ?"

Merlin was understandably affronted, but his resentment quickly softened into profound hurt. "Oh, son," he said with unbounded sadness, his throat tightening, his heart racing. "I'm your father. You're my blood, my essence. If I have to say more, then we are truly lost to each other."

Julian didn't appear to be listening. Instead, he was staring at his watch, counting off the seconds. Then, for some reason, he perked right up, happy as a clam. "Dang, I'm getting pretty good at this, huh? Had you goin' there, didn't I?" He chuckled wickedly. "And don't worry about Dr. B. He don't know it, but I got that little ass-fucker right where I want him."

Appalled by the saucy language, Merlin nervously licked his bottom lip. Hesitating, he then took the plunge. "Son, I need you to listen to me carefully and take this the right way. I've always only wanted what's best for you. Block and his people ... they're professionals. They and their ilk have been at this since before you were a twinkle in my eye. You don't play people like that. You either stab a wooden stake through their heart and deep-six 'em from the get-go, or you run away from their kind as far and as fast as you can, singing 'Feets don't fail me now' all the way, because if you don't, they will suck the marrow right out of your bones. Boiled down, their game plan is simple: to keep the striped shirts—us, all of us—scared shitless, too knock-kneed covering our own gonads to throw a flag. Eventually, they win by attrition, when the opposing team is too beat up, too shocked and awed by their savage, unpenalized cheap shots to retake the field."

Julian shrugged it off. "Yeah, and I wasn't born yesterday, Pop. As for the hackneyed sports metaphors, this may come as a huge surprise, but I actually understand four-dollar words like polarization, protectionism, isolationism, and brinkmanship, although there's many a day I wish I didn't. I guess the genie's out of the bottle now, though. Who knew? Then again, I *am* a college graduate, little as I've used it." Then, betraying the first telltale signs of creeping mania, Julian suspiciously checked for eavesdroppers, lowering his voice to a whisper. "Don't go blabbing it, but you and Nacho are the only ones I trust."

Emotionally off balance, Merlin covered it with a grateful guzzle of beer, wishing it were something stronger, as Julian impatiently waved his now conspicuous bodyguards back out of sight. He then concentrated on working out an imaginary knot in his line.

"Speaking of Felix," Merlin ventured, "where is he? Haven't seen him around lately."

"He's over there," Julian said without looking up.

Confused, a bit dazed even, Merlin glanced all around, seeing neither hide nor hair of him.

"I meant *way* over there," Julian softly amplified. "Keep it under your helmet, huh?"

"You mean—"

"A little diplomacy on the down-low, Pop, *way* down low." Julian drew a finger to his lips. "*Shhh*. They've got eyes and ears everywhere. Up top, too. Spy satellites. I've seen."

Ever more troubled, Merlin took his fly rod back into the calf-deep water to where the gurgling stream better covered their voices. Smoothly whisking his rod from ten o'clock to two o'clock, he patiently paid out line under the brilliant sunshine as if he had no other care in the world. Julian did likewise. The glare off the swift water was nearly blinding from the shoreline, virtually blotting them from view. Then, with a snap of his wrist, Merlin made a perfect cast, slowly retreating backwards until Julian was right behind his shoulder, back to back, picking up where they'd left off, impossible to be overheard from the riverbank, or even a few feet away. "It's the right play, son," Merlin said. "Wrong personnel. God bless him, Julian, but … Felix Angel has all the diplomatic skills of a bouncer in a crack house."

"Afraid it was you or him," Julian said. "That's how deep the bench is. No offense, Dad, but had it been you, you wouldn't have made it back to the line of scrimmage. They're keyed on you all the way. Nacho they think is on my shit list. And, like you say, grace is definitely not his forte. But he has two things going for him: he's tough as nails and honest as the day is long—granted, sometimes brutally."

Merlin shook his head. "It's *you* that needs to be over there, Julian. Talk to the king, man to man. Work it out."

"Why?" Julian said a little too flippantly. "The king is doing exactly what I want him to do, what *needs* to be done."

"Huh?" Merlin was genuinely nonplussed.

"I'm gonna smoke the bastards out, Dad, once and for all, every last one of 'em," Julian declared softly. "Philio may be what you'd like him to be, and maybe not. Either way, God put me where I am for a reason, and I aim to take full advantage of it ... to put things to right."

Briefly closing his eyes, Merlin moaned. "I want you to take a step back and think very hard about this, Julian, maybe deeper than you've ever allowed yourself to think before, because right here, right at this moment, it's never been more crucial to your eternal spirit. Do you know what happens to a man, any person, who makes the leap from humble worship and intentional goodness to presuming he represents the will of Heaven? He *becomes* a Darius Block."

"That's not gonna happen to me," Julian said.

"Fool everyone else, Julian, but don't fool yourself," Merlin implored him. "What makes you think you can avoid the pitfalls no one else has escaped ... ever?"

Julian scoffed coldly. "Because I don't give a flying fuck about the will of Heaven. Any god that would stand idly by while people suffer the way they have deserves nothing but my contempt—deserves it and has it—just like any one of us caught guilty of the same."

"Easy, boy, easy," Merlin soothed. "You've had it rough; we all have." He suddenly frowned quizzically. "Hold on. You said you believe it's *God* that put you where you are."

"That's right," said Julian. "And that's *his* mistake." Reeling in his line, he smoothly, even pleasantly, switched gears. "I think I'll try that patch over there."

Without further ado, he waded away to do just that, leaving his father with serious and painful concerns about his son's deteriorating mental health.

Chapter XVI

Though somewhat less adventurous than the Quinns, the Reverend Block had likewise cleared his calendar to spend his first free weekend in months with family, delighting in his grandchildren. His stately home in Chevy Chase, Maryland, recently reoccupied and scrubbed top to bottom inside, played host to the full brood and featured a backyard cookout and pool party.

His happily married sons Parker and Timothy came with five small fry between them, the oldest not yet twelve. Sadly, Block's eldest, Ezra Isaiah, had been taken from them. He'd been a war hero, sacrificed to freedom's march by an improvised explosive device while patrolling the streets of Baghdad. Much of the home's interior was a photographic shrine to his memory. He'd only just turned nineteen on the fateful day. Block's daughter, Caroline, his youngest child, had married well but was still childless, though at only twenty-three, there was little cause for alarm. Nonetheless embarrassed, she and David Chillicothe were "working on it." Among other things, Papa Block was a stickler for the commandment "be fruitful and multiply." In that regard, albeit behind his back, his two daughters-in-law, Patricia and Deborah, referred to him, and not always unkindly, as "the Pope," little appreciating that the patriarch was hardly insulted by the comparison. The main thing was that the family remained intact and closely knit, blessedly normal and healthy—all branches fully functioning models of nuclear stability, exemplars of faith-based values—due in no small part to Block's lifelong helpmate, Nettie.

His teenage sweetheart, now partner of nearly forty years, and the mother of Darius's children, Nettie Block was a *de rigueur* dynamo, a doyenne of domesticity, a walking shibboleth of tireless devotion to her man and his ideals. Nettie reveled in her role as the preacher's wife, going to pains, it seemed, to epitomize self-effacing dowdiness. This was slightly misleading.

Though she was demure and sweetly disposed on the surface, Nettie had a nasty habit of pulling rank on other women, especially those whose men sought the orbit of her husband's influence, much like a military officer's better half who believes her husband's rank extends to her, to be wielded over subordinates' spouses in social settings, if not everyday life. As a mother-in-law she was no less presumptuous, usurping parenting rights over her grandchildren, doting on them with little regard for their mothers' wishes. Consequently, to avoid internecine strife, Patricia and Deborah Block, when visiting the matriarch or being visited by her, basically punted, giving Nettie free rein. Anything less was a recipe for bad blood, not to mention a lengthy sermon from "the Pope" on honoring thy mother and father. As with all control freaks, not being allowed to win an argument was tantamount to persecution—sanctification by victimization; feckless bullying, really, posing as hurt feelings. All too often in such cases, one-sided accommodation merely stoked the pressure-cooker of petty disaffection, so that when it blows, and it always does, it can be an ugly mess.

At any rate, it was an absolutely sparkling afternoon as the grandkids frolicked in the kidney-shaped pool under a scorching summer sun. The youngest was equipped with water wings, and all were under the watchful supervision of Grandma Nettie, who was weeding and pruning her flower bushes with loving care nearby under a sunhat. Grandpa Dar, in a dapper tweed cap, cleaned and prepped his built-in barbeque grill for a feast of hamburgers and hot dogs. He'd not used it since the previous summer. An inspirational Christian rock CD played on a boom box at a tasteful volume. David Chillicothe, Caroline's hubby, was snoozing in his Speedos on a poolside chase lounger, under a strategically placed copy of *The Purpose-Driven Life*.

A treadmill marathoner, already surgically improved several times over at age twenty-six, heir to the fortune of a DC-area cosmetic dentist, Chillicothe was yet to put in a full day's work in his life, dabbling in all sorts of things, none of which had met with much success, if any at all, and all leading to his present ambition, politics, another career move yet to bear fruit. Whether or not his twenty-month-old nuptials with Caroline carried an ulterior agenda was anyone's guess, although before her wedding, Caroline's outstanding attributes were best summarized to a blind date as "she has a really good heart." Suffice it to say, David's subsequent conversion and baptism in her church had made his relationship with his father-in-law extremely positive.

Regardless, ice-cold lemonade, the aroma of freshly mown grass, the shimmering reflection off the pool as the children splashed and played Marco Polo—all of it combined to create a portrait of multi-generational suburban bliss, a snapshot of a nation at peace, war free—a whole world, in fact, arguably for the first time ever, persistent ideological tensions notwithstanding.

On the other side of the upscale house, "the boys," Park and Tim, ages thirty-four and thirty-one, respectively, and both amateur grease monkeys were changing the points and plugs on Timmy's dual-cab Ford pickup in the driveway in front of the four-car garage. The two were both strapping lads who favored their mother more than their father, each beginning to show signs of middle-age spread at the beltline. Both men were racing enthusiasts, so it was no surprise that the truck's radio aired coverage of a round of NASCAR trials underway at Laguna Seca Speedway in California. Though they had been long suspended under the threat of terrorism and wartime rationing, mass spectator sports were finally on the rebound, underscoring Jerusalem's nascent control over the international situation, a development generally overlooked in popular commentary. Regardless, the boys were having a blast, courtesy of an eight ball of Colombia's finest in a neatly folded bindle. A secret pint of peppermint schnapps stashed in the truck's toolbox rounded things out nicely.

At the same time, staying cool indoors, ensconced in the basement bonus room, the girls—Patricia, Deborah, and Caroline—were on their second bottle of Pinot Noir, getting pleasantly smashed, intermittently giggling up a storm. Patty had smuggled in the wine, and she had two more bottles to help take the edge off these always overlong stays with her husband's sainted parents. Debbie was being particularly wicked. She lit a scented candle, then fired up a half-smoked doobie, fanning away the smoke, and exhaled out the cracked window. She offered the roach to the other two, who declined while not objecting, at least not strenuously.

Meanwhile, natural male enhancement via a magic pill was the girl-talk topic, vis-à-vis who was getting the short end of the stick, as it were. All agreed that their husbands could each stand some extra oomph in that department. Still, how much was too much? It bore discussion. The semidrunken one they entered into had clinical overtones, assuming a garden hose had clinical significance. Abruptly realizing their drift, they laughed so hard it hurt.

Through it all, Caroline veritably basked in the sorority-like gaiety, the conspiracy of it. Because she battled a weight problem and had an overabundance of beauty marks, her self-image was a cruel one, and yet she'd somehow managed to land the best-looking mate of them all, as well as the richest one. In contrast, her sisters-in-law, both drop-dead gorgeous, had gotten stuck with Caroline's brothers, neither of whom was worth spit—chronically underemployed and financially overextended, not to mention the biggest macho assholes in the world.

The downstairs television was on—the kids had earlier been watching cartoons—with the volume muted. Narrowing her eyes, Patty saw that the channel was now airing an al fresco event live from Jerusalem. "You know *he* don't need no pill," she remarked lustily, her diction a bit slurred. "Mm, mm, *mmm*. Check out those dimples, that hair."

"Still single, too," Debbie said, more than slightly stoned.

Followed by the camera as he was smothered by an outdoor crowd of ecstatic fans, the swarthy center of attention stood a head taller than anyone close by. The current close-up showed him to have vibrant hazel eyes, almost green but not quite. The hint of a beard, unshaved chic, only added to his rakish good looks. Patty and Debbie went totally gaga. Romantic fairy tales of put-upon maidens swept off their feet by handsome royalty were among the few girlish fantasies that had made puberty bearable. Though yielding to the torpid practicalities of adulthood, such fantasies never really went away. All the same, this king didn't come close to fitting the mold. He certainly wasn't glamorous, wasn't trying to be. Wasn't much of a politician, either, not the way he was dressed, not even bothering to shave; he was more of an everyman—a poor one at that.

Even Caroline was absorbed. "What's he doing?"

"Looks like some kind of sermon-on-the-mount deal," Debbie surmised.

"Turn it up," Patty said.

"Don't," Caroline nervously objected. "Daddy'll hit the roof."

"Girlfriend," Patty pooh-poohed her caution, "that's all the reason I need." Scrounging up the TV's remote, she motioned to Debbie with her head. "Block the door with that chair."

The last glimmer of dusk was waning on the Mount of Olives, painting the horizon mauve. Towering arc lamps had been erected to flood a temporary stage situated just down the hill from the old Carmelite monastery and Church of the Paternoster. In addition to the event staff and the television and sat-radio crews, somewhere in the neighborhood of five thousand people had come to listen, bringing their own lawn chairs, some with blankets to cover the rocky earth where they sat, some without. It was a culturally variegated multitude of both male and female, Jews and Arabs, Ethiopians and Eritreans, Greeks and Turks, Russians and Chechens, Scandinavians and Slavs, Tartars and Uygurs from the Steppe; Persians, Indians, and Pakistanis; Malays, Filipinos, Koreans, and Okinawans; sub-Saharan Africans and Pacific Islanders. They came from as far away as Brazil and Argentina. There was even an Aussie contingent and Kiwis from New Zealand with a number of Maoris. Most were here, all expenses paid, at the invitation of the crown. The majority was under thirty years of age but no younger than eighteen or so. Not pilgrims per se, they had been selected from out of millions more who'd responded to an essay contest with a daunting theme: "*Describe the future you want and why you want it.*"

Geared up with a wireless microphone looped behind one ear, Philio had the run of the stage platform. There was no podium, no cheesy backdrop with a glib slogan. In a raised array behind the stage, giant plasma screens kept the king in tight close-up with captioned translations in Arabic, Russian, Hebrew, French, Farsi, Spanish, Italian, Thai, German, and Mandarin. Dressed in working-class hip, he was nothing short of a rock superstar, taking full advantage of the stage, his movements unrestrained, nothing to hide behind. Heck, he was positively evangelical.

Down in the midst of the hillside gathering, dressed plain, wearing no makeup and blending right in, Gwynn Reynolds sat on the cushion she'd brought, hugging her knees; she was clearly entranced. Not far away, Nacho Angel, there incognito as well, drifted closer, as if pulled by a magnet, a spacey cast to his face. He carried a backpack slung over one shoulder. Neither betrayed any hint of recognition, one for the other, nor should they have, being complete strangers. Even so, Gwynn beckoned him over with a "*Psst,*" offering to share her cushion. Standing, he was blocking the people behind. Nacho wordlessly accepted.

Meanwhile, the translations stayed in perfect sync, and with good cause. Philio's initial spiel had been prepared and written down long ago in ancient times, and he recited it flawlessly by heart, *with* heart, in English, leaving little doubt as to the true audience he was targeting. Gwynn could only marvel. Nacho, too, was bemused. The king was *on*, and he was hot—sizzling hot! And while nothing he said was anywhere close to new, he wasn't relying on the Bible or the Koran or the Vedas or any other holy book. Instead, his rap was nothing more than a loose compendium of the sayings of Socrates right out of the dialogues in Plato's *Republic*—no incantational or antiphonal lobotomy attempted, no liturgical hammer and tongs required. His amplified voice was pleasantly engaging, sweeping down the mount and across the Valley of Jehosophat, his delivery magical, surreal.

"He who is the real tyrant, whatever men may think, is the slave, and is obliged to practice the greatest adulation and servility, and to be the flatterer of the vilest of mankind. He has desires which he is utterly unable to satisfy, and has more wants than anyone, and is truly poor, *if* you know how to inspect the whole soul of him. All his life long he is beset with fear and is full of convulsions and distractions, even as the State he resembles: and surely the resemblance holds.

"And is not this the sort of prison in which the tyrant will be bound—he who by nature is full of all sorts of fears and lusts? His soul is fragile and greedy, and yet alone, of all men in the city, he is never allowed to go on a journey, or to see the things which other freemen desire to see, but he lives in a hole like a woman hidden in the house, and is jealous of any other citizen who goes into foreign parts and sees anything of interest."

Centered in the dazzling spotlight, Philio quick-stepped to the other end of the stage, roping them in. "Young people and old souls," he said energetically, "*be* the future by *wanting* a future, then create that future by creating a better present. Stop waiting. The age of parables and mythology has run its course. We have serious problems, requiring serious solutions by serious thinkers. Some will say to you be *in* the moment, but I say unto you, *be* the moment—*do*, then for heaven's sake move on.

"*Extend* yourselves, consciously, then *expand* your consciousness, willingly, *willfully*, and eagerly. *Explore* your own energies, *investigate* your passions. When you do, you will find some of them positive, some negative. *Appreciate* the difference, but accept the electromagnetic facts, because unlike subjunctive ritual, *they* are incontrovertible. Any completed circuit—every synapse in your brain—requires the presence of a positive charge and a negative charge. Without both, there is no *potential*. The key is *balance*, and for good or ill, everything you are and everything around you, visible and invisible, ineluctably shifts *whenever* that balance shifts.

"Universe is dynamic; it *never* stands still," he powered on, adding mysteriously, "so is *the* universe—this one and all the others. Things change; *quarks* change—up, down, charm, strange, top, and bottom—the heavier ones decaying into the lighter types; via this process of decay *building* all matter as we know it; that which we can see, that which we cannot, even antimatter. *Transformation.* Energy is merely transformed matter. Matter is transformed energy. *Learning* is a transformation. When you discover something new, it changes you. No matter how slight the change, you are *not*—no, nor ever will be—exactly the same as you were. *This* is the benefit of learning," he submitted. "It is also its price."

He paused at a simple stool, his only prop, for a quick swig from a bottle of water, the gesture all too human. It was quite warm out, hovering in the high eighties, Fahrenheit. He was perspiring normally. The sweat glistened under the bright lights on his face and neck, on his arms, soaking his shirt under the armpits and in a V down his front. His scalp line was damp. The king seemed to think nothing of it. He was enjoying himself, teaching rather than ruling.

"Learning can be additive or subtractive," he said, capping the bottle. "It can invigorate or emasculate. It can ennoble or abuse. It can *dis*abuse. It can open you to unconsidered possibilities or blind you to them. You can learn anything, but you can't *know* everything. You may *think* you do. You don't. You may think someone else does. *They* don't. No one does. No one does, because it never stays the same. It changes. *It* doesn't have a choice. You do."

On that note, he requested a towel, pausing to mop the sweat on his brow and dry his neck and arms before tossing the towel off stage. It would be prized as a relic.

"You can believe," he went on. "You can choose *not* to believe. You can profess. You can *con*fess. You can opt not to give it any thought at all. The frustration in wanting to know more is that you will never be satisfied, but the penalty for ignorance is a cage."

Arching his back to ease out a kink, he walked the stage with his hands on his hips, continuing. "In all cases, we tend to believe whatever it is we *think* is acceptable. The question is, of course, to whom. The *why*, however, is easy. Benefit. We are attracted to beliefs that benefit us, rejecting beliefs that do not. All too often, we say we were *led* to believe something. If it proves false, we say we were *mis*led. In actuality, neither has occurred, because, led or misled, *you* haven't actually *gone* anywhere." The king stopped, center stage, facing the multitude directly. "*You* are still in your cage, there feeling safe—waiting, yielding to reflexive dread of the unknown and the promise that the zookeeper, at his leisure, will provide for your needs." The king's tone was cutting. "*You* ... are livestock."

The pronouncement was not well received. Minds shut down, some angrily, predictably indignant. Shown on TV, his live audience shifted uncomfortably, talking amongst themselves. He let them. Indeed, he seemed pleased.

Then, down the hill, off to the side, a spirited demonstration broke out. Evidently, more than a few party crashers had snuck in. A bedsheet unfurled between two sticks was spray painted with 'PHILIO IS ANTICHRIST!' "You are fooling no one, devil!" a bellicose voice screamed. The commotion spread. Members of the event staff closed in.

"Hold fast," the king commanded. "You, step forward," he invited the protest leader. The rants from the group quieted. The leader hesitated. "No worries," said Philio. "I don't bite. Besides, it's all on TV, yeah?"

Puffing up his chest, clearly apprehensive, the protestor reluctantly made his way closer to the stage, picked up by a second spotlight. Seen in blow-up on the big plasma screens, he was a black African, decked out in colorful tribal robes. When he reached a vacant spot, Philio said, and not unreasonably, "That's far enough. Sit. Listen. Quietly. We can't both talk at the same time. It is your right to disagree with anything I have to say *after* I've said it. I'll even give you this microphone. We'll switch places, and I will listen to you. Fair enough?"

Glancing back to his cohorts, who were at a loss without his generalship, the protestor grunted in the affirmative and sat down cross-legged, conspicuously taking out prepared notes, apparently a ready-to-go speech he wanted to review.

"There, you see?" the king resumed to one and all. "As long as there are strongly held beliefs, perhaps there will always *be* rancor, but a tiny bit of effort, a small dose of patience, and the sky need not fall. If we can learn *that* without coming to blows, I, for one, am very hopeful."

There was confusion. The mood shifted. Minds reopened. Beginning slowly with a few claps, then spreading, building to a roar, the applause brought the house down. And then they were on their feet, deliriously appreciative. Some were openly weeping. Gwynn and Nacho were up too, the energy incredible. Nacho fought a lump in his throat. Gwynn tapped him to hand him a lacy, monogrammed hanky. Nacho didn't hesitate, blowing his nose into it, which was slightly beyond what she had in mind. She told him to keep it.

Televised commentary, reaching all points of the planet, was equally affected. If a *king* could do *this*—no arrests, no recrimination—after being so vilely slandered ... et cetera, et cetera.

Eventually, the outpouring abated as Philio stole another swig from his water bottle. "Control," he resumed conversationally. "Socially speaking, the very word stimulates in each of us two conflicting emotions: desire and fear—the selfish desire to have more of it, *fear* of someone else having too much of it. Some souls are obsequious by nature, others more domineering, aggressively on guard lest control be taken from them. In all cases, control comes in three flavors: constructive, *de*constructive, and destructive—enabling, disabling, or destroying. All control is temporary. *Limited* control is an oxymoron. You either have it or you don't. Political control is either gained or lost. Maintaining control is merely the interlude between getting it and squandering it. Hence, always dissembled, control is a transaction. Control is *purchased.* The *quid pro quo* can be money or privileges; it can be letting you *keep* your money and privileges. It can be food and shelter; it can be letting you *keep* your food and shelter. It can be affection or the withholding of affection. It can be the threat of ostracism and exile from the group. All too often it is extorted by violence or the threat of violence, the price paid in blood or capitulating to the threat of bloodshed. Conversely, it can be extracted on the promise of protection and security."

Once again pacing the stage, hands clasped behind his back, the king seemed to debate the wisdom of continuing down the same track. Caution lost, and he forged ahead, submitting darkly: "But by far the most resilient form of sociopathic control is and always has centered on 'the end;' *id est*, when all is said and done in the here and now, what happens *after*?"

Logically calculated or not, he'd arrived at that place over which rulers are elevated or ruined. He'd referenced eschatology, but everyone knew what he meant. *Theology*. As well, no one could possibly misinterpret his disdain for priestcraft, although he'd never actually defined it. His other radical policies aside, *this* was the global showstopper, and he was yet to show any willingness to bend. Regally robed emissaries, nuncios of the cloth of every conceivable sect, had talked themselves blue in the face to the crown, but the king would not budge. And yet it would be so easy to give, even a little, on this one small point. He wasn't being asked to endorse ecclesiasticism, per se, only to tolerate it. In fact, he'd been privately assured, desperately, of free wheel and free reign, no official religious opposition whatsoever, not a peep, if he just *would*.

The people needed their shepherds, were lost without them. Perhaps more at issue, the shepherds were starving without their flocks. Well, not quite, but it sounded dire. Suffice it to say, institutionally approved spiritual self-esteem had hit an all-time nadir. Was not Philio's stubbornness something only an antichrist would have the temerity to risk, tampering with eternity itself? Shockingly, *this* king wasn't just tampering. He was bulldozing. And, in his case, there was no éminence grise, no gray cardinal, no Sanhedrin, no cabal of long-bearded muftis or sin-hating presbyters lurking behind the throne to pull him to his senses. A religiously ambivalent autocrat content to expand his personal wealth and holdings was divinely appointed, perhaps even isometrically celestial. A free-thinking one who put the common good above church, temple, and mosque was something else entirely, dangerously anathema, economically devastating to the clergy of any cloth.

"Hear me!" King Philio shouted to the multitude. "There is no end! There is only *transformation*. Transform *yourselves*. Do not be led; *go* to that place you want to be. Do not wait to be taught; *learn*. Do not dwell in confusion; *ask*. Do not idly imagine; *manifest*. Do not be afraid; *trust* … yourself. You have power. And yet you relinquish it so easily. You *are* power. But you needn't hurt another to experience that power. Ergo, inflicting pain on any living thing is the poorest expression of power—fruitless, loveless, destructive … *always* to yourself.

"Do not compete; *achieve*. Do not dominate; *cooperate*. Do not blindly obey; seek *accommodation*. Be thoughtful. Consider the needs of others. You are not an island. You are part of an eternal quantum field. You can deny it, but you will never escape it.

"Neither be a slave ... to any fashion or doctrine. Judge with understanding and compassion. Do not forsake; *forgive* ... yourself, first. Anger is a reflex. Hate is a calculation. Love is not a compromise. Do not cheat; *innovate*. Demand, graciously, what is fair, then *reciprocate*. Do not worship; *wonder*, then *wander*, intelligently—guilt free. Henceforth, the only deadline is the one you impose on yourself. Be curious. The cage you are in is of your own making. *Free* yourselves." Then he contradicted himself, or seemed to.

"Finally," he said gravely, dolefully, almost angrily, "let no man speak of knowing God until first he knows himself. And when he knows himself, the God he hears will no longer speak to him from the pages of some book, but in the echoes of his own heart, for the Kingdom of Heaven is in *you!* I mean, how many times must I repeat myself? *Rule* yourselves! The enemy—and there is only one—is *intentional* ignorance. Emotionally elevate yourselves, and the answers will be plain. I can't stay forever, and in the interim there's only so much I can do. There is no panacea. But for many, there will be a final conclusion. We have halted, for the time being, the distractions and impediments to earthly survival. Take advantage of it. Universe is infinite, but time dilates relative to gravity. Only *it* has duration. *Pull* free. Life is a gift, but consciousness is a responsibility. There is no middle ground—not any longer—not on this planet, not on any other. Spiritually evolve, or forfeit existence."

Wow! On that direst of presages, he stepped to the very edge of the stage to verbally confront the protest leader. "The microphone is yours. Still want it?"

All the cameras zoomed to the colorfully robed African. Agog, hesitating, understandably timid, he shook his head as he tore his speech in half. *Who could follow that?*

"I want to know more," he declared.

"Go for it," Philio encouraged, weary but serene, "*do*, with our blessing." And bowing his head prayerfully, palms together, he took a deep, cleansing breath. Then, opening his eyes, he softly uttered, "*Namaste*," and left the stage without saying *how* to go for it. Or had he?

The women in the suburban Maryland basement stood slack-jawed in front of the television set. None of the three had ever given significant thought to their own mortality, much less what lay beyond, not intrinsically. They'd done the hard part. They'd been saved, and they went to church, always tithing ten percent … well, almost always. They said grace before meals. They'd each voted a straight Republican ticket when there'd still been voting. They condemned gay marriage and earned income tax credits, loathed Planned Parenthood, supported the death penalty, never used contraception, hated the ACLU with a venom, despised the French, and were convinced that PETA and Greenpeace were communist-atheist fronts. Their husbands were card-carrying members of the National Rifle Association. They took their children to G-rated movies only, or rented Focus on the Family–approved DVDs. They only read racy novels in private and didn't pretend to understand foreign films. With rare exceptions, they confined their predictable sex lives to their husbands or mechanical substitutions. They drove American-made cars with "Support the Troops" stickers and a Jesus fish and shopped at Wal-Mart whenever possible. They only cursed when they were really, *really* ticked off.

Switching off the set, Caroline broke the spell. "I told you he was the Antichrist."

"Thank God," Debbie gushed with relief. "Who wants to think that hard?"

Patty suddenly felt a deep-seated need to be closer to the Pope and the umbrella of his unswerving certitude. "We should help with lunch," she said, removing the chair from the door, glad it hadn't been needed. "Ditch the empty bottles. This never happened, right?" And she left.

Back on the Mount of Olives the multitude was dispersing, many in shock, stumped; others skeptical, certainly wary. There was lots of debate, a lot *to* debate. As reported fairly consistently before, Philio's presence itself was his most compelling feature—the timbre of his voice, the piercing directness of his gaze, eyeball to eyeball; his open, at-ease body language, the very fact that he was monarch, an odd one, granted; even more so that he took the time, extemporaneously, risking misinterpretation. All of it somehow transcended words. It was a good thing, too. The words were … *unharness*-able, at least in the short run. The feeling they conveyed, however, was something else altogether. Enchanting. Mesmerizing. Hypnotic. *Liberating?* Perhaps, but if so, from what exactly? For that matter, from what generally? Was it actually contrary to scripture or merely to stale exegesis? Lots to debate, lots to think about. The inns and cafés of Jerusalem would be busy tonight.

Nacho got to his feet and offered Gwynn a hand up. "Thanks for the sit," he said.

"American?" she inquired.

"Don't spread it around."

Gwynn nodded. "I know what you mean."

Expelling a sigh, Nacho glanced across to the empty stage. "Well, that was different."

"How do you mean?"

Nacho shrugged. "No promises. No ... guarantees."

"He wasn't selling," Gwynn said. "He was notifying."

Nacho chewed on that, then shook it off. "It'd be nice if he'd just come out and say it."

"What?"

"Whatever he's trying to get across."

"Didn't he?"

Nacho regarded her strangely. "Then it's like ... we're all on our own."

Gwynn didn't disagree. "We're responsible ... for ourselves ... together." The very next instant she seemed irked. "I wish he wouldn't lean so hard on Socrates, though."

Nacho squinted. "Who?"

"Four hundred years before Jesus, Socrates was big on self-examination," Gwynn explained. "Got a little too big for his *chlamys*, citing his *daemonion*, or mystical inner self, as his source, more than hinting that we are, each of us, innately divine. He was executed for blasphemy, treason to the gods of the state, and corrupting Athenian youth. Athens," Gwynn added bleakly, "was a democracy."

Nacho regarded her oddly. "I'll take your word for it. Schoolteacher?"

Smiling, Gwynn shook her head. "But I played one once. It was a commercial for ..." She sighed. "Would you believe I don't even remember?"

"It's not a test," said Nacho. "What's a chlamys?"

"Think Hercules, one shoulder bare."

"Got it. See, you *are* a teacher."

Gwynn scooped up her cushion. "Want to meet him?"

"Hercules?"

"No, silly. Janus."

Nacho's guard went up. "The king? The two of you are tight?"

Gwynn toggled her hand and headed off. "Come on; we can probably still catch him."

Bowled over, Nacho tarried, trying to think up an excuse. He'd just gotten into town, hadn't even checked into a hotel yet. Plus, the chance encounter was most irregular. He didn't even know her name. More than that, though, he'd arrived in the Holy Land illegally, with phony papers. Curiously, not once had he been asked to show them. That couldn't last.

Halting, Gwynn turned back to him. She seemed to understand. "Don't sweat it. It's no big deal. I mean it is, but not like that. Like he said, he doesn't bite. If he tries, I'll protect you. Trust me."

"Why?" Nacho replied uneasily.

She batted her eyes. "Because we're dating. He's my fella."

Chapter XVII

A misforecast squall, prematurely blown in north by northwest up from the Carolina coast, hurried the Blocks' backyard affair indoors, to the grandkids' waterlogged disappointment. Everyone pitched in to clear the outside tables, and not a minute too soon. Portended by a few heavy drops, an angry thunderclap preceded a thorough drenching, the rain falling in sheets. Grandpa Dar alone braved the elements under his wind-buffeted umbrella to rescue the main course off the patio grill, getting soaked down to his BVDs. Small surprise, a little wrath of God was no match for a minister on a mission. The burgers were a tad soggy, and the BBQ sauce on a rack of baby-back ribs got drowned, but those were the breaks. After drying off and changing, he rejoined his loved ones in the dining room, taking his place at the head of the table. Clearing his throat—the cue for everyone to ritually hold hands—he offered up thanks.

Not untypical of pious windbags, it was more hectoring than homily, less praise and honor than lecturing the Lord on what was required of him in these dark times. Of course, "the times" were always dark, always inexorably tragic, which was the whole point of prayer. In all practicality, the Deity, if he actually bothered to abide the harangue, was an overlooked bystander, at best a condoned eavesdropper. On and on it went—dreary, self-pitying, self-indulgent affectation. Close attention, which nobody ever paid, not willingly, revealed it to be less of a petition than a commodious extolment of the prayer-givers' attainments over a catalog of real or fabricated trials and tribulations, overcoming endless oppressions and persecutions—yet again, sanctification through victimization. With the little ones fidgeting, eventually boring himself, Block drew on the Lord's Prayer, always a good closer.

"And so," he labored on, eyes tightly shut, "our Father who art in heaven, hallowed be thy name; thy kingdom come—your *true* kingdom—thy will be done on earth as it is in heaven—your *true* will as it is revealed unto your loyal servants. We thank you for this meager repast, nourishment for our corruptible flesh, for as it is written, man shall not be sustained by bread alone, but by every word that proceedeth out of the mouth of God. We ask only that you keep your rich blessings flowing our way to show your approval as we bear up against the temptations of wickedness and iniquitous thinking. Keep us faithful, Lord, ever mindful of our shortcomings and deficiencies. In his name, your one and *only* son, our savior, amen."

"Amen," the others chorused with a yada-yada quality. And they dug in.

Conversation had never been a mealtime imperative in the Block house. Even so, Darius was in his glory, providing for his family, his emotions completely genuine and deeply felt. Everyone should know such joy. Not often, but sometimes, in moments of weakness or travail, he privately wondered why God had singled him out for high service, to the neglect of his family. His was a heavy cross to bear. He saw so little of them these days.

"How is it done in heaven?" Patricia idly tossed out, passing a dish of potato salad.

Block smiled at her. "What's that?"

"His will," she said. "We pray for it to be done on earth as it is in heaven. How is it done in heaven?"

"What a stupid question," her husband Parker belittled her.

"Do you know?" she challenged him.

"Of course. It's in the Bible."

"Where?"

"I don't know, somewhere." He gave her a nasty look. "What's gotten into you?"

"Do you know?" she asked her father-in-law.

Nettie cut in sharply. "Stop arguing. We don't do that at the table."

"I'm not arguing," Patty said. "I'm asking."

Timothy couldn't resist razzing his older brother. "You let her act this way?"

"Act what way?" Patty objected. "And what do you mean, *let* me?"

"I said, stop arguing!" Nettie exclaimed shrilly. "Think of the children!"

Patty blew a gasket. "Butt out, Nettie! In case you forgot, they happen to be *my* children."

The Pope put his foot down. "Be civil." He confronted Patricia squarely. "Where did this come from?"

"What?"

"All of these questions, all this sudden doubt."

Patty made a face. "It's one question!"

Block got his back up. "Don't use that tone with me, young lady. You're in *my* house."

Patty glanced from Debbie to Caroline. Both cowered. She threw up her arms. "Fine. Come on, kids. We're outta here."

"Sit down!" Parker barked. "You're not going anywhere. How can you diss my mom and dad like that after everything they've done for us?"

Lightning flashes lit up the yard beyond the window, followed by booming thunder. The lights flickered. Trembling pitiably over this and the harsh words, the youngest child broke out crying, the other small fry not far behind her. Nettie was out of her chair in a flash to console them, leering accusingly at Patty. "What kind of a mother *are* you?"

David Chillicothe decided to weigh in. "If you want my opinion—"

Patty cut him off at the pass. "Stuff it, Silicone Boy. Everyone knows those Arnold pecs are a boob job. Is even your pecker real?"

For Caroline, them were fighting words. "Oh, Patty, that is so un-Christian. Maybe my brother should know you've been using the morning-after pill."

Patty's mouth dropped. "You bitch."

Caroline looked at Parker. "It's why you haven't knocked her up again."

"He can't knock her up anyway," Timothy threw in.

"Shut up, Timmy!" Debbie hissed, too late.

"Hoo-hoo!" Tim laughed at Park. "Dude! You didn't tell her you went and got fixed?"

"Course I did, ya mook. *We* don't keep secrets from each other, not like some people."

Debbie cocked her head at Timothy. "What secrets would those be?"

Meanwhile, Parker's eyes went big at Patty. "Why would you be on the pill?"

Patty blanched, at a loss. "Those snip jobs don't always hold." It came out as a question.

The rapidly deteriorating situation was literally saved by the bell—the front doorbell. Pastor Block held up his hands, commanding silence. It wouldn't do for outsiders to witness any part of this. "Everyone take a deep breath, *please*," he begged them, suddenly the paragon of rationality, "then ask yourselves: what would Jesus do? We'll hash this out when I get back."

Leaving to answer the door, he was immeasurably pleased to overhear his son say, "What have you got against God and his holy word? Have you ... have you been drinking?" The reverend mentally logged it. It would be the coup de grâce when he lovingly set Patricia straight. Block was a master at leveraging highly private, undisclosed foibles into teary-eyed genuflection, just one of his many God-given talents. Moreover, he had no qualms about using a sledgehammer when a squeeze of WD-40 would do. Besides, pain and the memory of it was a more effective deterrent to relapses. It was certainly nothing that wasn't in Patricia's best interests.

A moment later he opened the front door, totally mystified to find a dripping wet Morton Parmister on his front stoop clad in a trench coat. He had a set of luggage with him. A taxi lingered in the driveway, its wipers raging in a full-tilt boogie. Parmister signaled to the driver, releasing him. Gobsmacked, Block folded his arms, extending no offer to come in out of the rain. "Where the hell have you been? Better yet, what are you doing here?"

"It's a long story," Morty said. Looking exhausted, he was chilled to the bone. "I got deported." His bloodshot eyes pleaded with the reverend. "I had nowhere else to turn."

Backstage on the Mount of Olives, a white marquee was set up to host a reception for the king. The event staff was on guard against unruly interlopers, but their caution was generally non-confrontational. Still, not just anyone was granted access to the royal presence. Frankly, anyone more than those officially invited would have overwhelmed the tent, as big as it was. A string ensemble inside played Mozart. All in all, the mood was highly medieval, but in a festive sort of way, highly international. Buoyant laughter spilled from the tent. The king's sense of humor was already legendary.

Gwynn halted far from the well-lit entrance. "Wait here," she told Nacho. "I'll get you a pass."

As she stepped out of earshot to talk to a senior member of the event staff, Nacho took stock of his surroundings. He was hardly dressed for a soiree. On the other hand, neither was Gwynn, whose name he now knew. For that matter, neither was anyone else—everyone was comfortably informal, like an Oregon grunge festival he'd once attended. Then, out of the corner of his eye, he spied the African protestor, easily spotted due to his colorful robes, chatting up a group of crown officials noticeably affably. Rolled together on its sticks, the ad hoc bedsheet banner was leaned up against the tent. Nacho allowed himself a cynical grin. Then an older gent in a conservative sport coat worn over faded jeans, shirt collar open, stole out of the air-conditioned tent for a smoke, tapping a Dunhill on a silver cigarette case. Seen closer, he had shoulder-length gray hair fastened into a ponytail. Apparently, the interior was a non-smoking environment. Spotting Nacho, his expression non-threatening, he came over, cracking open his cigarette case, offering it up to the lonely loiterer. Nacho merely shook his head.

"Do you mind?" the gent asked after he'd lit up. He was an Englishman.

"They're your lungs," Nacho said, becoming agitated. Gwynn had disappeared inside the tent without so much as a glance back his way. Alarm bells went off in his head.

"Derrick Arbogaste," the smoker introduced himself, "Viscount of Chelmsford. Most people just leave it at Chelmsford. The king seems to prefer it. All strictly hereditary, mind you. No, those days are long gone. Imagine it, a crown without an aristocracy."

Nacho was surveying for the best egress, if he had to make a break for it. "Chelmsford? Never heard of it."

"It's not there anymore," Chelmsford said woefully. "Plague. And you are …?"

"Sorry, Alberto Gonzales. Most people just call me *twerp*."

Chelmsford eyed him wryly. "Then I suspect they don't know you very well."

Changing the subject, Nacho nodded in the direction of the robed African. "That was a nice touch, totally convincing. *Totally*."

"But not to you," Chelmsford said.

"That's just me. *No problema*. I've taken a dive in my time."

"You really think it was faked?"

Nacho shrugged. "It got the point across. What's a little healthy deception among friends? Look at the payoff."

Chelmsford was intrigued. "You sound remarkably knowledgeable in such matters."

Nacho reslung his backpack. It was getting heavy. "I was tutored by a master."

"Oh? What school?"

Nacho met Chelmsford's eyes. "The school of hard knocks … the hardest."

Just then, Gwynn reappeared at the marquee entrance with another man, too far away to be clearly made out. Gwynn was pointing at Nacho, raising his hackles. *This couldn't be good.*

Chelmsford stubbed out his cigarette underfoot, then stooped to recover the butt. "My friend," he said in parting, "some things are not what they seem, but *all* things are exactly what they are, if you bother to look close enough, listen closely enough."

The suddenly strident volume of the black African's voice drifted over. He was not happy, upbraiding the crown officials. "You fools, we already have a god! Let *yours* show himself to my people and perform miracles. Everything else is just words. Let the king *show* himself to be more powerful than Great God Almighty. Then and only then will we bow down in worship." This said, he indignantly grabbed his furled banner and stalked away into the night, unhindered.

Forced to reassess, Nacho turned back to Chelmsford, but he was gone, nowhere in sight, had literally vanished. The whole encounter gave Nacho the heebie-jeebies.

Gwynn's voice intruded. "This is Al. Al, this is Ken. He works for the king."

Girding himself for an official inspection, Nacho slowly turned their way. It took great effort to keep his eyes from bugging out. Old instincts borne of rigorous drilling and strict military discipline started to kick in. Nacho very nearly saluted.

"Ms. Reynolds tells me you don't have a place to stay," Rittenour said, betraying no familiarity. The expected demand for Nacho to produce his papers, a passport and visa, never came. "You're welcome to bunk in with me," the colonel offered, his tone unbelievably disarming, considering. "Don't worry—I'm straight," he appended. "Rigidly. I just figured it'd be fun to talk to someone from back home, catch up on the box scores, stuff like that. Whaddaya say?"

"Sounds ... good," Nacho replied. Declining might rouse suspicions. "I can pay, though."

"Your money's no good with me," Rittenour refused. Nacho's masquerade as a penniless Bohemian wanderer, a student, was apparently working overtime.

Gwynn was anxious to get back to the party. "Great, then it's settled. I'll leave you two to get acquainted. Nice meeting you, Al. You couldn't be in better hands." She returned to the reception tent. The way she did it, intentional or not, drew all male eyes to her derriere. No doubt about it: plain or painted up, she was a stunner.

"Check that, mister," Rittenour chided Nacho. "You will never tap that. It's spoke for."

"Yeah, I already got that," Nacho said. "Not a problem. A little long in the tooth for me."

Appraising him closely, Rittenour was troubled by something, but he let it go. "They're never too old, amigo. Ask any of 'em." Winking, he straightaway became all business, and Nacho knew the jig was up. "Now that the lady's gone, let's walk to where we can put our cards on the table."

There was no ducking this sneaky uppercut, despite which Nacho swiftly regrouped to tally his options, finding them severely limited. Maybe one on one, distanced from reinforcements, he stood a chance. Otherwise, none. For someone utterly out of his depth, undereducated, and without any formal training to speak of in these pursuits, he was amazingly sanguine. Then again, his personal mantra had always been *Tu necesitas a quedarse allá y continue a golpear*. Basically, you just gotta stay in there and keep punching.

Rittenour led the way beyond the exterior tent lights to a spectacular overlook. From here, the lights of the Holy City twinkled like precious gems on a blanket of velvet, reaching as far as the eye could see. There was a quiet here unlike any urban place on earth. Taking out a pint flask, the colonel uncapped it, wiped the rim, and politely offered it to Nacho. "Care for a bracer? It's mescal."

Nacho wasn't interested. He was instead trying to decide how to take the older man in hand-to-hand combat, now sure it was coming to that. Realistic enough to realize his odds weren't strong—the colonel was a soldier's soldier—Nacho wasn't afraid, merely resigned. No, he had to be honest with himself, he *was* scared. Either way, he wouldn't be taken alive. Too much time would be lost. He'd personally deliver his message to Philio or die trying. This was his pact with Julian, and, for Nacho, it was a blood oath. Regrettably, Mighty had put himself on ridiculously lousy footing with the king—too many hasty words, too much red-faced saber-rattling. Nacho couldn't fault the king. Philio would be a fool to accept anyone or anything from America at face value, not with the Bible-thumpers all screaming for his head.

Meanwhile, Rittenour took a long, leisurely hit off the flask, then put it away with an uninhibited belch. "Look, son, I know you're from Washington, traveling under an assumed identity. I'm even pretty sure why. Hell, I've been expecting you. And, while your caution isn't entirely misplaced, do yourself a favor, and give it a rest. You made it. You're here. Rejoice."

Nacho didn't bite. "I don't know what you're talking about, *Ken*. Expecting me?"

Rittenour was surprisingly forthcoming. "We've been on you since you came ashore in Jaffa. Weren't quite sure what to make of it or who was who. I'm guessing you didn't know it, but you had a lot of company waiting. I decided to roll the dice and see what developed. It didn't take long. They have that look about them." Rittenour lit a cigarette. "It's all in the eyes."

Nacho knitted his brow. "A look? Who?"

"Council," Rittenour said, still exhaling. His distaste was unvarnished.

Stunned, Nacho angrily ground his jaw. "*Block.*" It came out like acid.

Rittenour scoffed. "Darius Block is nothing more than a front, an errand boy. He may not even know, too busy being superior to wonder, too sanctified to risk questioning himself."

Nacho unshouldered his backpack and sank to one knee, the stress finally catching up with him. "My homey Julian guessed as much," he finally confessed. A palm to his forehead, shaking his head, he glanced up. "I guess I'd like that drink now." Rittenour obliged. "But we were so careful," Nacho went on, squinting past a gullet-burning belt of the potent elixir. "It's *why* we were so careful." He handed the flask back with unspoken thanks.

"Quinn's a good man," Rittenour said. "I saw it right off. But he's overmatched. Philio says where money is useful, justice is useless."

Nacho pushed back up to his feet. "Those council goons'll report back."

With a sly grin, Rittenour shook his head. "Nope." He didn't amplify. "The king can help," he said. "Smartest SOB I've ever known. It's why he's here. Come on, I'll hook you up."

"Just to get it off my chest," Nacho called after him, "I know you."

Pausing, half turning, Rittenour nodded. "You know what? I think you do."

"But you're like … dead."

The ex-pat colonel smirked. "Yeah, I get that all the time." He motioned Nacho onward with his head. "Let's not keep the king waiting."

Despite all the funky weirdness of late, Rittenour possessed in buckets the one thing Nacho Angel understood and valued: street cred, something no amount of money could buy. Back in the Zone, what now seemed a lifetime ago, the stories whispered about *el dardo*, the dart, had taken on almost mythological proportions, all rich with the same leitmotif: he didn't fuck around. You could trust a man like Rittenour, because he didn't give a shit whether you did or not.

Catching him up, Nacho felt strangely at ease. Safe. *Hopeful.* Nacho had never known his own father, had never met him. How bizarre, he mused, that it would be the gringo colonel who came closest to the image of his childhood longings.

Announcing himself with a soft tap on the door, Block entered his private study with a plate of food. The first-floor room, just off the entry foyer, was equipped with its own half bath. Parmister was at the sink freshening up, his wet clothes in a pile on the floor. He'd changed into dry loaner duds, chinos and a polo shirt, courtesy of the reverend, since just about everything in his soft-shell luggage was damp. Block's sanctum sanctorum showed him to be a remarkably broadly read bookworm. In fact, his library was of some note and not what one might expect. He seemed to have a keen interest in Nietzsche and Marx. An original Tocqueville was prominent, along with Darwin's *Origin* and *The Descent of Man.* Immanuel Kant's collected works, Descartes' *Principles of Philosophy,* and Newton's *Principia* were in there. He even had a soft spot for Howard Zinn, the

Holy Qur'an, and the Bhagavad Gita. Everything else, though, was conservatively down-the-line—biblical commentaries and concordances and close to everything in print on end-times prophecy, including affectionately signed first editions by Jenkins and LaHaye of their *Left Behind* and its follow-ups.

Feeling better, wiping the excess Visene from his cheeks, Parmister stepped out of the bathroom, smiling warmly. He motioned to the off-canon texts on the shelves. "You surprise me," he told Block.

"Better the devil you know." It was all Block had to say on the matter as he set the plate on the desk and gestured his guest into a facing chair, taking his own. "There's cold soda in the ice box," he invited, putting on his reading glasses. He was referring to a small cube refrigerator tucked off to the side. Parmister helped himself.

Grateful for the home-cooked chow, Morty wolfed it down as Block read over his hand-written report. It pretty much filled a quarter-inch-thick spiral notebook, the edges of which were water-damaged, the ink running and smeared in places, but decipherable. Couched in legalese to obscure context in case it fell into the wrong hands, it nevertheless contained quite an adventure, much of it self-absorbed, both self-congratulating and self-forgiving insofar as Parmister's role was concerned. Indeed, forced to rely on his quick-witted strength of character alone, he was lucky to have survived at all, overcoming a litany of danger-fraught obstacles and close calls. Underpinning the libretto throughout, it was solely his unshakable faith in service to a cause greater than his own self-interest that had safely delivered Morty from the clutches of evil.

Seated at his desk, only getting about halfway through it, Block peeled off his reading glasses to wipe the lenses. "I like it," he said. "With a few touch-ups, it'll make good copy."

"Just trying to get down the essentials while they were still fresh," Morty said.

"Of course," said Block. "Now tell me, what really happened?"

So, for the better part of the next hour, Morty did, Block interrupting only occasionally for clarification. Parmister could only offer speculation on Jerusalem's long-term objectives. The only thing perfectly clear was that it all added up to a stunning setback for the Divine Plan.

Cunningly abstaining from hypocrisy, the king had terminated weapons production and research throughout the realm, closing armaments plants or converting them to non-lethal, green technologies with the emphasis on sustainable/renewable energy sources and bio-remediation. Water management and cutting-edge irrigation systems were another priority. Reforestation of depleted woodlands and restoration of coastal wetlands ranked right up there. He was pulling out all the stops in astronomy and space exploration, too, diverting the creative energies of weapons designers and war planners, throwing gobs of money at interstellar travel and the required propulsion, navigation, and life-support systems, even if they were only theoretical.

In concert with these heady initiatives, the crown was rapidly disbanding all standing defense forces, gainfully reintroducing military personnel to civilian life with an ambitious menu of reorientation and retraining programs. The peace dividend was being poured into free and accessible civilian education at all levels across the board for all royal subjects, with dramatic increases in teachers' salaries, improved facilities, and reduced class sizes.

Automotive factories were already pumping out the first generation of clean-burning, hydrogen-powered cars and trucks. Larger industrial fuel-cell applications were in the works. Non-toxic, zero-radiation, cold fusion reactors called "water-engines" were a small-scale-prototype reality. Post-war reconstruction and infrastructure renewal was humming. Agricultural advances were creating a food surplus. The arts and humanities were flourishing like at no time in recent memory. Religiously policed taboos on myth-busting scientific investigation had been officially erased. Going jobless was suddenly and in every respect inexcusable indolence, justifiably ridiculed. If anything, there was a labor shortage. Octogenarians were gleefully coming out of retirement and going back to school. Empty entertainments were giving way to reading, or being read to, just for fun. Print and audio book sales of formerly frowned-upon and forbidden works, classical and contemporary, were skyrocketing, the more ribald and boundary-testing the better. Worse, religious humor—make that irreligious—was all the rage: big laughs.

Most exasperating of all, petty crime had fallen way off, took more effort than it was worth—too many legitimate opportunities paid better—which, by extension, largely eviscerated organized crime, now that death and the threat of it had, quite literally, lost its sting. And, while vice hadn't completely disappeared off the map, with much of it now morally redefined, it was hard to find anyone who had time for it—no allure. Similarly deprived of its channels to government and authoritarian corruption, corporate and industrial malfeasance saw its smoky back-room profitability melt away. Slick lawyers beware: anything less than straight shooting, in any language, earned the royal displeasure where it hurt the most—smack dab in the pocketbook. Even the most artfully worded bluffing was a potentially disastrous gambit, financially, and cooking the books got one's own goose cooked. Enforcement was diabolical—a listing in the *Royal Registry of Fraud*, available to anyone just fingertips away on its own Web site with a robust search engine. A public apology accompanied by a heavy fine got your name and/or the name of your organization removed from the RROF and Pariah City, with the proceeds *in toto* going straightaway into the king's educational fund to build new schools and centers of learning in developing regions. Arguing or dissembling with the RROF was wasted breath. Somehow the king always had the goods, all spelled out in layman's terms. It was downright spooky.

Added to this and underscoring his madness, he'd ordered the secret archives, every last crypt and vault, of all the former nations comprising the kingdom, including Vatican City, opened to public scrutiny—all of them! Everything was declassified. Nothing was off limits. Scholars were having a field day, some an embarrassing one. Accepted histories and official accounts were under siege, sacred cows slaughtered left and right. Day by day, more and more was coming to light with appalling objectivity. The past was literally being rewritten!

Taken on the whole, though still embryonic, Philio's global kingdom sans its provincial holdouts in North America was on the fast track to becoming one big integrated, socially cytoplasmic *force majeure* with Jerusalem as its nucleus. Unchecked, the point of no return was right around the corner. He had to be stopped!

Block wasn't sure how much of Brother Morton's report was a knee-jerk reaction or to what degree it might even be sneaky disinformation planted by crown agents, but he agreed that it was all bad, patently ungodly. He continued to puzzle over Jerusalem as Philio's base of operations, since Babylon, the mother of harlots, was in what had been southern Iraq. What was left had been bombed back into the stone age years ago and wouldn't be rebuilt any time soon. Still, such a detail was a glitch, not a showstopper. God would resolve the confusion in due time. Hadn't he always?

"And our rogue colonel?" Block asked Parmister.

Morty shook his head. "He suckered me good, had me totally snookered. I'm not sure at what point he sold his soul to Satan. Upon reflection, it might have occurred back here. It's conceivable he was in league with Philio before that. He was acting strangely in LA before he set sail for the war zone. Murdered two innocent men in cold blood with his bare hands. At the time, I chalked it up to blowing off a little steam; you know, keeping his skills honed. He didn't want the final Zone roundup assignment, was anxious to get back to the front. Now I know why." Morty paused, narrowing his eyes contemptuously. "It's funny. He keeps trying to say he really *was* raised from the dead."

"After committing suicide," Block remembered, plainly disturbed by it.

Morty scowled. "He wanted to, was going to, he says, to honorably save himself from a messy war crimes tribunal. Apparently, it was Quinn who pulled him back from the brink. Quinn was so dead certain about Philio that Ken decided he had to stick around and see for himself."

"Then he *wasn't* buried at sea."

Morty shrugged. "You don't get to be top gun in Special Forces without learning to dodge a few landmines."

Block was relieved. As ridiculous as it was, the idea that Philio could go around resurrecting the dead would have been hard to compete with. "So the whole thing was a hoax," he said. "I'll wager Quinn was in on it from the start."

Parmister wasn't so sure. "The way Rittenour sees it, he was brain-dead for forty years, that it was a few snappy one-liners from Philio that opened his eyes. That's the trouble with unbelievers; they live in a fantasy world." Morty scoffed acidly. "Peace at any price."

Block shared his sentiments. "Everyone knows the Antichrist will be a wolf in sheep's clothing. I'll bet Philio even wears wool underpants. What about his nukes?"

"Done deal," Parmister said. "They were the first things he scrapped; couldn't get it done fast enough. Russian, Chinese, French, British, the Paks, India, Tehran, North Korea—all arsenals, every last kiloton. That's gospel, by the way. He made a big show of it, lotsa media."

"Israel's?" Block pressed.

"Officially, they never had any," Parmister said. "It's all small stuff, anyway. As soon as we retarget ours, we can blow any part of the kingdom off the map at will. He'll cave. He won't have a choice."

"Except we can't do that," Block said. "Not a first strike."

Morty made a sarcastic face. "Why?"

"Because we're the good guys." Block said it with a tinge of regret.

Morty crushed his empty soda can in his fist. "Then we'll have to figure out a way to make him attack us. The Bible says so."

"And it's never wrong," Block agreed, locking Morty's report in a desk drawer. "What about that hussy you took over there with you? Sorry—her name escapes me."

Morty glowered. "She betrayed me. I think she has a thing for Philio."

"Physical?" Block inquired, suddenly eager to know more.

Morty hissed. "For him, what else could it be?"

"And for you?"

Morty was gripped by depression. "She was always just a Christian in name only. Paid it lip service, put on a good show. Hell, she's an actress. But she never really got it—the truth, the holy spirit. To her, church was just another social club, a chance to flash her wares, never willing to go the distance, to do what it takes to *prove* her faith, to show her obedience to God's will."

"I know what you mean," Block commiserated. "There are so many like her."

"Twelve years," Morty rued. "That's how long we were together."

"In sin," the reverend pointed out.

Morty sadly nodded. "I paid the price. She really hurt me. But to dump me for a Jew … I mean, Jesus. It shows she took me completely for granted. I was just an object."

"With the king now, this … whatever her name is?" Block asked.

Morty shrugged. "Hard to say. He's probably got a whole harem, the prick. All she would say while I was packing up was that she wanted the three of us to be friends." He allowed himself a hollow laugh. "Can you imagine? I suppose I got a little rough with her, language-wise. I told her she was sleeping with the enemy."

"What did she say to that?" Block asked.

Morty grunted. "She said, 'Not anymore.'" Burying his face in his hands, he rubbed his eyes. He quickly shook it off, recomposing himself. "Pardon my French, Pastor, but she was a really, *really* good lay, great arm candy to take to parties. I'll miss that part. The rest can go to hell with all the other whores."

"I want to know more about her relationship with the king," Block decided. "It could be important. Prurience sells. Also, given the right push, what are the odds of turning her back in our favor, back onto the path of righteousness?"

Parmister gave it not a thought. "I'd rather just wring her neck."

"Work on it," Block ordered. "Now, then, I'm a little confused. You say you were deported. You even mentioned that you were allowed to pack your things. And yet you were arrested for espionage. You're obviously in full body. Surely you were interrogated, questioned. Were you tortured, and how brutally? How much did you reveal? Be honest."

Morty's mind was miles away. "I wasn't."

"Wasn't what?"

"Questioned," Morty said, regathering his wits. "Not at all. I was provided medical treatment, released, and given twenty-four hours to leave the kingdom. They even gave me money for the trip. All charges were forgiven. To be perfectly honest, it was insulting."

"All right, let's leave it there for the moment and back up," Block said. "You say in your report that al Qaeda is on friendly terms with the king."

"More than friendly," Parmister said, "but not integrated. From what I gathered, the king has asked for a seven-year armistice to demonstrate his good will. At the rate he's going, seven years won't be required. They already think he's the Mahdi. Apparently, he had a long talk with the Wahabists. Dunno what was said, but it worked. They say he has the gift of eloquence. I think much of it boils down to fatigue. We hammered the Arabs pretty good during the war. The most conservative estimates place their casualties at somewhere around forty percent—professional military and irregulars, but mostly civilian women and children. Religiously, maybe even culturally, they're done in, that's all. No more fight left."

Block was enthused. "Praise God! The seven year period *was* prophesied."

Morty squinted one eye. "The war just ended was seven years, give or take."

Block darkened, offended. "That was different, a false start. It's all in *Left Behind*."

"That's what you said the first time," Morty reminded him.

"I'm even more sure *this* time," Block replied chidingly. "It was a test, preparation. God has always tested his people to keep them on their toes. We'll call it the *pre*-Tribulation. The real one is now on. Oh, yes!"

"I'm just playing devil's advocate here," Parmister said respectfully. "Still, what makes you so much more sure this time?"

"Because it was just revealed to me by God this very instant," Block asserted humbly. "That's the way it works sometimes. I wasn't wrong before. How could I be? Him only do I serve. The transmission got a little garbled, that's all. This time it's coming in loud and clear."

"It's not my place to doubt you," Morty said. "I only live to pursue the greater glory of God. Anyway, I'm thinking tomorrow I should check into the Watergate, a furnished apartment or suite, something with a view, but I'm a little shy on cash. How soon can you reinstate me on the payroll?"

Block wasn't sympathetic. "No savings?"

Morty frowned. "I blew it all in Jerusalem … for you."

"The Bible says neither a borrower nor a lender be," Block pointed out.

"No," Morty hotly disagreed. "Shakespeare did. He was a fag. You owe me."

Block matched his tone. "I owe you nothing. All for the glory of God, remember?" He got up from his desk. "There's public assistance. I suggest you look into it. Try a little place off Stanton Square. For tonight, you can sleep on the couch there. There's a blanket and pillow in the closet."

Morty was beside himself. "I want what's coming to me, god damn it!"

"We'll talk about it in the morning," Block postponed, moving to the door. "Right now, I have some family business that needs taking care of." Opening the door, he paused. "Oh, don't look so down, will you? I was just teasing."

"Then you'll stake me for a check-in at the Watergate?"

Block laughed. "Good heavens, no! I meant there really *is* excellent public assistance. Haven't you heard? The country's been taken over by liberals." And, laughing again, he shut Morty in.

Chapter XVIII

A few days later, on his way in to work, Block agreed to rendezvous with the grand master of the Guardians. Block arrived first, locating himself in the designated pew. The venue was apropos—the cavernous nave of the National Cathedral. The rising sun, beamed in through stained glass, formed a kaleidoscope of colors on the floor. Block had the whole place to himself. Indeed, because no one else was about for the moment, he allowed his mind to wander a bit, much of his thoughts centered on his daughter-in-law Patricia—her willful betrayal of her faith. Over the weekend, she'd insisted on pressing him on the single issue of how God's will is done in heaven. *What a question!*

Never particularly perspicacious on matters of doctrine, she kept pushing the conundrum that if we don't know definitively how the Almighty rules his own domains, how can we know if and when his will is actually being done here on earth or being thwarted? The post-modern understanding suggested that, rather than statically ordered and fixed, the heavens were actually chaotic—perhaps wholly predictable, mathematically, over great spans of time—but nonetheless profusely dynamic. If so, does this not evidence God's own adaptability to change? After all, even rocks change given the time to do so. What makes the Rock of Ages an exception? And, whereas for eons the visible cosmos had remained reliably stable, was this not more a function of delayed information taking light years to travel, rather than an inflexibly rigid design?

Such pseudo-intellectual drivel was, of course, biblically imponderable. The scribes of the divine explication weren't astrophysicists. Furthermore, the Bible wasn't a technical manual. Or was it? Clearly, it was highly technical on matters of law and punishment, sacrifice, priestly duties, and commemorative ritual. It was quite specific on issues of genealogy and chronology. By any stretch, however, it couldn't be illustrative fable or allegory and indisputable fact at the same time, but where to draw the line?

Block had explained in his own inimical way that these types of curiosities were entirely Luciferian in origin, preposterous sophistries intended to deride God for endowing Adam with an immortal soul—to test the divine mettle. Maybe, Patricia had wondered aloud, or *maybe* it's the other way round. Maybe it's God testing *us*—to see just how much bullshit we're willing to put up with. Darius was caught flatfooted, uncharacteristically speechless. Patricia obdurately felt it was worthy of contemplation. At what point does empirically reproducible discovery supersede quaint superstition and dogged attachment to archaic tradition? *Who gains from our fear of the unknown and, more specifically, the religious strictures that promote it?* She didn't phrase it that way, being an imbecile, but that was her drift, at which point her father-in-law laid down the law, denouncing her disgraceful guesswork as unforgivable blasphemy, condemning her to eternal damnation. Whereupon she took his grandchildren and left, adamant about never returning, to never again darken his doorstep, presenting Parker with a painful choice.

Sadly, leaving his father and mother desolate, Parker chose wrong, condemning himself, such a miserably unnecessary blunder. The rest of the family sided with the patriarch. Parker was being pussy-whipped into blindness. *Vanity, thy name is woman!*

Even now, Block felt indescribably low, verging on nausea. To save his son and restore his grandchildren to the bosom of the Lord, Patricia would have to go. Permanently. He could conceive of no alternative. The chafe of it was that he remained terribly, terribly fond of her—in many ways, continuing to admire her spirit, as misguided as it was now proving. *Where had such notions come from?* There was only one answer: the wretched and despised Philio. Moreover, how many others were falling under his spell, falling prey to his bedevilments? The time was nigh to move and move decisively, lest the virus of godless self-empowerment spread.

"It is the hard decisions that take the measure of a man," the Guardian's voice intruded on Block's mournful thoughts. He'd soundlessly slipped into the pew directly behind. "I'll keep this short," the grand master went on to say. "We are, to put it politely, disenchanted with your headway. Were we wrong to expect more ... sooner? Do not turn around."

"Not wrong," Block replied. "Irrationally exuberant, perhaps. After all, Rome wasn't built in a day."

The Guardian lost patience. "Oh, wake up! Someone else is doing all the building. There is strong consensus that you've reached the point of diminishing returns. The numbers are not encouraging. These unimaginative attacks on the king's character have entrenched your base, achieving little else."

"Polls," Block scoffed. "Reeds in the wind."

"But a stiff wind," the Guardian said. "He's got them clamoring for fresh ideas, which only *he* seems to have any of. Unfortunately, they're working. Who knew globalization would play right into his hands? No, the winds of change are upon us, old friend. Time to fold, other hands to be dealt, so be of good cheer. Your efforts will be richly rewarded."

He piqued Block's curiosity. "How richly?"

"Harp, cloud, a fast set of wings—you know what's in store for you better than I."

"You mock me."

"Sorry; you had your chance," said the Guardian. "You didn't deliver. Nothing personal. Additional research suggests Philio's a bit more down to earth. His economic philosophy is already paying dividends to our peers overseas. His new rules are different but workable on closer examination. We feel it's time to give him his shot."

Block shook his head vigorously. "It's a mistake. Don't give in to him! It will end horribly for you; it must!"

"We gave in to you," the grand master pointed out. "That's turned out to be pretty horrible all on its own—for us, financially; for others ..." He didn't finish the thought, didn't have to. After a moment, the Guardian's equanimity returned. "Come now—it's not the end of the world."

Block shifted around to look at him. "But it is!"

The Guardian sternly gestured for him to face back around. He had intimidating bodyguards with him. Block felt patronized, and it was driving him nuts. He willed his blood pressure under better control.

"Am I not your spiritual advisor?" he reminded the Guardian.

"Very well, then. Advise me."

"Don't you see?" Block submitted ardently. "The trouble with widely known prophecy is that any villain worth his salt knows it, too. And, because he knows, he can skirt it, avoiding the more obvious pointers and pitfalls, eluding what's expected of him, manipulating it—changing up the sequence, making substitutions to deflect suspicion. If the prophecy is highly symbolic, it gives him a tremendous amount of wiggle room. If it's fundamentally literal, well, he simply need not go there. The fortress of faith is our only sanctuary from the predations of Lucifer."

"Still, it *has* to happen, right?" the Guardian queried. "This prophecy."

"Absolutely," Block said. "It *is* happening. No power on earth can stop it."

"Then there's no point in losing any more sleep over it," the Guardian replied, adding soberly, "or any more money." He leaned forward, closer to Block's ear. "The decision has been made. You are … disengaged—as spiritual advisor, as anything else. Arrangements are already in the works, *overtures*, to soften the king's bad humor."

"Bad humor?" Block railed. "His whole message—his lie—is love!"

"And this is a bad thing?"

"It is *blasphemy*!"

The Guardian lost interest. "Against whom? When you get right down to it, all Philio is saying is that God may have a slightly bigger heart than you give him credit for—more understanding, more … reasonable. At any rate, we feel there's room for cautious optimism. That said, you will be wise to adopt a low profile. You are not unknown to Jerusalem."

"Don't do this to me!" Block objected. "God's patience is wearing incredibly thin. His mercy is not without its limits. Come back to him, or I fear for you in an *eternal* way."

The Guardian rolled his eyes. "Christ, you're like a broken record. Take a vacation, Dar. Get out to the islands. Regain some perspective. Find some sweet young thing and get yourself laid. You're becoming … tedious." The Guardian then added a warning. "But whatever you do, do not attempt to make contact again. That would be bad for you. You're … tainted goods."

"You *used* me!" Block assailed the grand master. "And now you cast me aside."

The Guardian laughed. "Oh, grow up, will you?" He was abruptly somber. "My best to your wife and family." The wish carried an unambiguous threat.

As the grand master's echoing footsteps trailed away with his entourage, Block knelt in prayer, unctuously petitioning his god for needed guidance. Within moments, he received a divine revelation transmitted with unmistakable clarity, although he already had more than an inkling of what it would be.

"Thy will be done," he closed with votive serenity. "We'll see who laughs last."

Meanwhile, the unsuspecting Guardian never made it to his car. Emergency lights flashing, a dozen unmarked sedans and SUVs swooped into the cathedral parking lot, tires squealing, cutting off all escape. It was but one of many such arrests taking place nationwide, all tightly coordinated. Handcuffed, the grand master was stuffed none too gently into the vehicle that would take him away, his protests falling on deaf ears.

Morton Parmister was overseeing the operation as the Reverend Block appeared on the church steps. "Status elsewhere?" Block inquired.

"No glitches," Parmister reported, his cell phone in hand. "Fish in a barrel, spooked coveys on a quail farm."

"Well done," Block pronounced, checking his watch. "The White House?"

"All yours," said Morty. "They don't have a clue. All outside communications have been cut. We now control all the major military bases and National Guard armories. The new joint staff has occupied the Pentagon and are well into cleaning out the barn. Quinn's loyalists never saw what hit 'em. Come on, I'll drive you." He called to a council agent. "You, see to the ... *president's* car."

"Keys are in it," Block said helpfully, unused to his new title, though not unhappy with it.

Technically, this wasn't America's first coup d'état, wasn't its second. Regardless, a recomposed Supreme Court of justices drawn from loyal council elders would bless the sudden regime change, legally or extra-legally, as the case might be, but all retroactively consistent with the new constitution already drafted and based squarely on the Priestly and Deuteronomic Codes of the Pentateuch. Under it, tiresome recourse to habeas corpus and equal protection under the law would apply only to "Christians" baptized in the new, state-controlled Church of America. The country, including Canada, would be officially renamed the United States of Jesus Christ the Savior; *Jesusland* for short. A massive chiseling of the Ten Commandments, already commissioned, would be housed in its own Greco-Roman memorial on the National Mall, replicas to be placed in all courthouses and government buildings, far and wide. Let there be no mistake. The long-awaited *Christian Revolution* was on, soon to go global.

In planning ever since the Council Headquarters was set ablaze, the revolution had merely been awaiting the appropriate apocalyptic sign. Block read that to be Philio's sacrilegious sermon on the mount, heard by a billion or more, replayed in excerpts to, or available in transcripts by, twice as many more, one of the seven vials poured out in the Book of Revelation. Block wasn't precisely sure which one and didn't much care. *But really, did Satan and his Antichrist think the Lord's people would just roll over and play dead?* At any rate, Brother Parmister's unexpected return from the Holy Land with his dire new intelligences could not be viewed as anything less than auspicious. By God's grace, Block had easily predicted the spineless recidivism of the Guardians right off. The wisdom of the scripture would never again be underrated. One simply cannot serve God and mammon both. Case closed.

President Block was exceedingly pleased with himself, though still a humble man, eschewing the pretensions of high office for the present. He joined Parmister in the front seat of the latter's new government wheels and adjusted the air conditioning vent. Flushed, he was sweating with relief. "How's the Watergate?"

Morty had to chuckle. "You really enjoy jerking my chain, don't you?"

"I was teaching you a valuable lesson," Block said. "Never take providence for granted. Good river view?"

"Best suite in the house," Parmister confirmed, shifting into drive to join the motorcade. "And, thanks. I mean that from the bottom of my heart."

"I'm sure you do, but don't thank me," Block demurred. "Thank our Heavenly Father … for bringing me into this world."

Julian Quinn was meeting in closed session with his father, Merlin, and members of his security staff when Block barged into the Oval Office unannounced. Parmister was right behind him with several heavily armed council agents in SWAT gear.

"My, my, your ears must have been burning," Merlin said, hinting at the interrupted meeting topic. Regrettably, it was taking place at least a day late.

Julian took belated umbrage at the intrusion. "What the fuck is this?"

"I have a confession to make," Block said with undisguised hauteur. "I lied—about everything—strictly with the Lord's blessing, mind you. Consider yourself a prisoner of the revolution. *Mine*. Now get out of my chair."

"For now, confine them to the residence under house arrest," Parmister instructed his men. "No visitors."

There was token resistance from the deposed governor-general's security team; little point to much else. The executive mansion was crawling with council thugs. Through the windows, more could be seen rappelling down from black helicopters, swarming.

As the prisoners were shuffled out, Block couldn't resist a parting shot. "Just so you know, *Mighty*"—he scoffed out the sobriquet—"this was going to happen one way or another. Sending the Mexican away in shame only made it that much easier, which was my plan all along. You were never really anything more than a muscle-headed jock, you know. Him, though? He spelled trouble from the word go. You did me an enormous favor."

Looking severely ill, Julian came close to vomiting, his shock total. "You're a real piece of work, you know that, Parson?"

Block regarded him smugly. "I accept the compliment. Have a nice day."

When the room cleared, the reverend got acquainted with his new executive desk. Only Parmister stayed behind. "Man, that was sweet," Morty said. "You were right, dumb as a turnip. Just more Zone trash taking up space."

Block didn't disagree; he was too busy playfully swiveling around in the big chair.

"What's your pleasure, Mr. President?" Morty asked wryly.

Stopping the chair, Block reclined back with his hands behind his head. "Stick to the dusk-to-dawn curfew, martial law coast to coast, violators to be shot on sight. As soon as all sectors report in A-OK, I'll go live with a prime-time national address. See to it."

"We'll be ready," Morty assured him, pausing at the door. "It'll be good to finally get things back to normal."

"Oh, they'll be normal," Block promised. "Normal and then some."

Chapter XIX

It was unfit for man or beast out of doors; yet another in a series of unseasonable late-summer monsoons was ravaging the national capital region. Flash flood warnings were in effect until the wee hours of the morning. Doppler radar was tracking a band of violent thunderstorm cells stretching all the way into Kentucky and southern Indiana, all eastward bound.

For Morton Parmister and the coup leadership, the foul weather was a godsend, keeping folks off the streets, forestalling a panicked exodus from the capital and elsewhere nearby as news of the overthrow spread. As well, it nicely covered continuing raids on potential dissidents, the roundup of likely subversives, and the annexation of all broadcast media centers in proximity, with the additional benefit of keeping the populace glued to their radios and televisions.

At present, now shortly before nine o'clock in the evening, Morty was back in the Oval Office, a bustling hive of activity as the freshly ascendant president was prepped for his national address. Block was being fawned over by a makeup artist and hair stylist. Half sitting on the desk, Parmister read over Block's speech copy betwixt final light and sound checks. The TelePrompTer on the big floor camera was already loaded, and bottles of soon-to-be-contraband bubbly were chilling for the aftermath—a toast to usher in a "new" age of American democracy.

"Powerful stuff," Parmister remarked after he finished the last page of the copy.

"So happy it meets with your approval," Block said caustically, appraising his reflection in a hand mirror. The protective tissue stuffed under his collar was giving him a rash. The reverend had particularly sensitive skin.

"We're live in five, Mr. President," the floor director cued, rather effeminately clapping his hands for attention. "Listen up, people. Unless you're essential, make like a hockey stick and get the puck out of here, or these very large men with their very big guns will shoot you."

"Speaking of pucks," Block said to Parmister, "I expect to be out of here like a shot for Camp David immediately after my close."

Setting the speech aside, Morty nodded. "Command central is already up and humming, perimeter secured out to five miles by two whole battalions, nothing in or out."

"These first seventy-two hours are crucial," Block said. "If there's a counter-rising, I'm the most vulnerable between now and then." A rumble of thunder rattled the windows. Block looked uneasy. "What is *up* with this weather? The forecast missed like Dick Cheney on *Meet the Press*."

Parmister shrugged. "What can I say? There's minor flooding along the most direct route, so if it doesn't let up, we may have to take the long way around."

"Overland is no good," Block complained. "Too many opportunities for an ambush."

Yawning, Morty languidly stretched his arms. "Marine One is here and primed. All we need is Mother Nature's cooperation. It's that … or a pilot fit for a straightjacket."

"Then get me one," Block commanded, looking to a military officer toting a lot of brass on his epaulets. A newly promoted admiral—just today, in fact—he was obediently on the horn, tout de suite. "There can be no slips in the schedule," Block reiterated to Parmister. "Until all opposition is smashed, I'm a sitting duck."

"Concentrate on your speech, Mr. President," Morty reassured him. "Everything's under control. Have a little faith." The president was hardly mollified. He knew all about faith.

Needing to escape Block's negativity, Parmister smoothly eased himself over to the French doors for a look outside. From what he could tell, there was no letup in the rain. If anything, it was coming down harder, continuing to overflow the gutters, creating a steady curtain of water off the eaves. He let himself onto the portico as if it would help, greeted by the contingent of council sentries spaced twenty feet apart all along the covered walkway. As Morty unwrapped a stick of chewing gum, another roll of thunder underscored the storm's wrath, centered miles away. It had to be. No lightning flashes preceded it. And yet it persisted, vibrating up through the ground into his legs. He was about to put the gum in his mouth when his stomach did a flip-flop. No thunder could be that close and the lightning that far away. Then it was gone, and so was Morty.

Squeezing his way back through the crowded Oval Office, he waited until he cleared the interior doorway to pull his walkie-talkie, ordering the watch commander to double the guard around the president without disturbing the telecast, lest the switchover betray any sort of forlorn hope the opposition might latch onto. Unfortunately, there were no reserves; every available man was on duty, so Morty pulled all but a skeleton crew off those guarding the upstairs residence. Quinn and family were scheduled to be publicly hung as soon as a proper gallows could be built—they weren't going anywhere, not in this weather. The president's well-being was Parmister's only concern.

Next, marching on through the West Wing, he radioed all other guard posts and security patrols to report in. Each did, one after the other, indicating nothing out of the ordinary. The main security hub reported nothing on radar, no trips of motion detectors, nothing on their closed-circuit video monitors, all entrances and exits locked down tight, even as more than a dozen council agents raced past Morty to reinforce the Oval Office. Still, something nagged at him, though nothing he could put his finger on, just a hunch, and a very vague one at that. Then the watch commander rang him on his private cell number to talk offline.

Morty was at the foot of the red-carpeted stairs up to the residence when he paused to take the call. The security honcho wanted to know, specifically, what was up Morty's butt, reminding him that there were tanks and sandbagged machine gun nests all along Pennsylvania Avenue. More troops were all over Lafayette Park. Indeed, at this very moment, no single address on the planet was more secure. The security chief became gruff, saying that, with all due respect, Parmister would be wise to leave this to the professionals. Actually, he put it this way: "We do this for a fucking living, jackass! My people are under enough goddamn—"

Hanging up on him, Morty became aware of the now deserted East Room's solitude. Not even rattles from the kitchens downstairs broke the quiet. Earlier in the day, among others, the White House chef and culinary staff had been unceremoniously sacked and sent home—better safe than sorry. Pending new blood, President Block was plagued by fears of poisoning. His paranoia was infectious. *Was that it?* Morty questioned himself. He'd been up since three in the morning. Maybe the long day, its tremulous excitement, was catching up with him. He checked his trusty Rolex. Any minute now, Block would crystallize the changeover with his stellar speech to the nation, brilliant in its Spartan simplicity, its irresistible return to good, clean, traditional evangelical faith and charity—*values*. Yup, it all came down to values, something neither Philio nor the upstart Quinn knew anything about. They'd made history today—Morty and his pastor—and would make more tomorrow. Thus, giving his worries the rest of the night off, Parmister trudged back up the corridor for the nearest men's room to freshen up.

The Oval Office became hushed as the president peered into the camera, adopting an aura of world-weary gravitas. Off camera, teleprompter rolling, the floor director launched the countdown with his fingers. "And ... five, four ..." finishing it silently.

Block's talking head lit up televisions coast to coast, even the JumboTron on Times Square.

"My fellow Americans and our Canadian friends, brothers and sisters all, these are the times that try men's souls. But I come before you tonight with good news and glad tidings of great joy. My message is one of hope and prosperity to all who would believe. The past is prologue. Let us put it behind us, for as *before*, when in the course of human events, it becomes necessary for one people to dissolve the political bands which have connected them with another, and to assume among the powers of the earth the separate and equal station to which the Laws of Nature and of Nature's God entitle them, a decent respect to the opinions of mankind requires that they should declare the causes which impel them to the separation ..."

Dousing his face and neck at the men's room sink, Morty turned off the faucet, blindly grabbing a handful of paper towels as he listened with delight to Block's resonant voice piped in over the public address system. Patently unoriginal, its grandiloquence was nevertheless timeless.

"*But when a long train of abuses and usurpations pursuing invariably the same object evinces a design to reduce them under absolute despotism ...*"

A toilet flushed, startling him. Morty could have sworn he was alone. In the mirror, he watched one of the stall doors open, and his eyes bugged out. *Impossible!*

"Hey, at my age, when you gotta go, you gotta go, ya know?"

Morty lurched for his radio on the sink counter, but a silenced slug blasted it out of reach, knocking it out of commission. He whirled around from the sink just as Rittenour jabbed two rigid fingers into his windpipe, disabling Parmister's larynx, buckling his knees. Smoothly returning his suppressed sidearm to its thigh holster, Rittenour delivered a short uppercut to Morty's solar plexus, putting the kibosh on any fight Morty had left, even as the colonel caught him by his lapels and dragged him to a sitting position on the commode he'd just vacated. Heck, the seat was still warm. Patiently allowing Morty to regain his wind, he then, with expert if brutal care, put just enough of a whammy on Parmister to keep him out of the game for the next hour or so, thoughtfully arranging him on the toilet so that he wouldn't fall off. If longer was required, Rittenour would already be history. Such realities were part and parcel of the colonel's vocation, the occupational hazards of his kind of soldiering.

Shutting the stall door, he gave his own reflection a once-over in the mirror. Geared up in damp, jet-black commando fatigues and a watch cap, his face was dulled with grease paint. A tiny microphone on a hair-thin filament extending from a recessed earpiece could only indicate that he was in close communication with others. Leaning over the sink, he pumped out copious amounts of hand soap to clean his face before stripping off his tearaway fatigues.

Throughout it all, Block's voice droned over the PA system. "*The history of the present and* false *King of Jerusalem is a history of repeated injuries and usurpations, all having in direct object the establishment of an absolute tyranny over these United States. My friends, fellow patriots, and lovers of freedom, such* cannot *be allowed to stand.*"

Confined to their bedroom with the children and Merlin, Julian and Jamyqua were watching the broadcast with sinking spirits. At present, the new president was outlining the varied crimes of the overturned governor-general's administration—the violent riots of late, rampant crime in the streets, and before that, the closeting of the clergy; the country's porous borders, allowing the unchecked outflux of intellectual capital; Marxist liberalism run amok with its gay rights, stem cells, abortion on demand, suspension of capital punishment, legalizing the private use of marijuana and cocaine, glorifying the (non-prescription) drug culture, imperiling employer profits by increasing the minimum wage, raising taxes on the hard-working rich while emptying the prisons and labor farms; raiding the defense budget for handouts to slackers, wastrels, and unwed mothers; Julian's refusal to reinstate national elections, and so on and so forth.

"The motherfucker told you it was too soon for elections!" Jamyqua railed.

Julian draped his arms around her, nuzzling her neck. "Language, woman." He glanced at his father. "Don't say it."

"Say what?"

"That you told me so."

Merlin had his sleeping grandsons on his lap in a wing chair. "You did nothing to be ashamed of, son," he told Julian. "You were being set up. I kick only myself."

The bedroom door was rudely kicked in. "Nobody kick nobody." Nacho quickly put a finger to his lips. Only his voice was familiar. Otherwise, he came straight out of a testosterone-pulsing war flick. He motioned Julian and Jamyqua off the bed, touching his earpiece. "Clear."

A pop no louder than a staple gun sounded just before a piece of the ceiling six feet in diameter bounced onto the bed, and a rope ladder was lowered.

Merlin was the first to gather his wits. "My wife?"

"*My baby?*" Jamyqua shrieked. Both were in the Lincoln bedroom.

Nacho was brusque, motioning them to climb. "Safe," he said. "Got 'em both."

"My other sons and—"

Nacho kept it terse. "Not here, not goin'. Unless you wanna be hanged in the morning, up you go." He turned to cover the door with his machine gun. It had a serious clip and was extended with a powerful suppressor. "*Move!*" he hissed.

At the same time, on the executive mansion's roof, an elite foursome drawn from the former Israeli Defense Forces was erecting a strange apparatus. Assembled, it was a simple framework reaching quite high, nearly twenty feet. On a catch-wire at the top was a florescent green ribbon attached to a transponder with a flashing red diode. Farther afield on the rooftop, half a dozen council sentries lay prone and unmoving where they'd fallen in their hooded rain ponchos under the relentless downpour. Helped up by two additional Israelis, Julian and his family surfaced into the rain through the hole left by a displaced HVAC unit. The unit itself continued to operate. Helped by the deluge, its noisy fan and compressor masked all other sound.

"Halt! State your business," a burly jarhead challenged Rittenour as he brazenly approached Marine One on the South Lawn.

Shielded overhead by an unthreatening umbrella, the colonel was dressed in the flight suit of a USMC aviator. Multiple flashlight beams picked him out of the rain. Both sentries promptly saluted. "Stand easy," Rittenour said, stopping under his umbrella with a lazy return of salute. "I'm here to fly this thing, ferry the CNC wherever he wants to go. Camp David, they tell me."

"Begging the general's pardon, but that would make the general insane."

"As it happens, Gunny, that's my middle name," Rittenour replied easily.

"Yes, sir, we were told to expect you, sir."

"Shitcan the lights, then," Rittenour ordered.

The beams were diverted, and a moment later the mammoth helicopter's hatch popped open, its stairs lowered. A seasoned marine officer in a flight suit identical to Rittenour's remained under cover, using his own flashlight to check out the newcomer, fixing on the two sparkling stars along Rittenour's collar on either side, despite which he didn't salute. Furthermore, what he said wasn't helpful. "I know every qualified jockey for this bird in the Corps, but I don't know you. Besides, going anywhere tonight is suicide."

"Don't wet your pants, Captain," Rittenour said. "Sit right seat and learn a thing or two, but until I say otherwise, it's *sir* or General. Got me? With everything that's going down, you really do not want to piss me off, not tonight. This wasn't my idea."

But the helo captain didn't lower his beam. Talking the talk and walking the walk were two different things. "I like the umbrella, *sir*, but I don't scratch my balls without written or voice say-so from my chain of command." Snapping his fingers, he put out his hand. "If you've got the goods, cough 'em up, *General.*"

In his way, Rittenour loved this marine, felt a bond with him. It didn't stop him from unzipping his flight suit and shooting the captain in the face. Left with little choice, he promptly dropped the two on the ground, point-blank.

Back on the White House roof, a package was being readied for an insanely dangerous pickup. Julian and Jamyqua, Merlin, and Julian's white-haired mom—the children sandwiched between the adults—were all strapped tightly together under the apex of the ungainly apparatus, told to hug each other for dear life. In fact, it was best to keep their eyes closed. Had they been told more, they might have literally died on the spot from fright, even as the storm continued to drown out the women and children's whimpers. When all was set, jellied gasoline, better known as napalm, was poured in a circle around them. They could smell it. Anticipation of being burned alive at the stake could not have been worse. Their fervent trust in Nacho was taking a beating, but the alternative was Darius Block, so in a word—two, actually—no contest.

Stepping clear, Nacho struck a phosphorous stick flare, his eyes glued to the luminescent face of his chronometer—waiting, waiting. Over the rain, a low-altitude rumble was heard approaching, descending, its roar steadily building.

Downstairs at the end of the West Wing, Block had reached a televised crescendo, righteously hammering away at godlessness and un-Americanism. As he did, the council watch commander popped his head up from the HVAC aperture in the roof. Spotting the flare, he guessed it wasn't supposed to be there, among everything else that shouldn't have been, but the flare was his only clear target. So, awkwardly lifting his machine pistol over the lip of the opening, he fired a strafing burst that ripped into Nacho's legs, mere inches below his body armor. The IDF team returned fire, spot on, literally taking off the watch commander's head even as Nacho crumpled. Down but not out, he stretched out the flare to light the signal fire. *Whoof*—the flames ran the circle, blazing brightly in spite of the deluge.

Julian was mortified. "Raise your arms!" he ordered everyone in the package over the deafening roar that was still growing. They did without thinking it through. Unclipping the line to his seat harness, Julian slipped the noose, instinctively yanking on the straps, retightening them to compensate for his absence—and not a second too soon, as a huge plane thundered in overhead, lights out, dragging a hook. "Hug!" Julian shouted, unheard over the roar of the engines. The belly of the beast was so close he could almost reach up and touch it. Electronically zeroing in on the transponder, a trailing hook caught the overhead transom wire of the apparatus, whisking his shrieking family airborne like a weightless feather into the pouring rain, soon lost to the night.

One of the Israelis pressed the hot muzzle of his machine gun to Julian's neck. "Lose your ticket? That was your ride."

Julian slapped the barrel away. Rushing to Nacho, he rolled him over. The rain and Nacho's black fatigues made it all but impossible to see where the worst damage had been done. Then Julian felt a warm gusher of blood just below the groin inside the thigh. "Medic!" he yelled to the Israelis, who kept to their defensive postures, night vision gear in place.

"Keep it down!" Nacho scolded him. "You're looking at him."

It took a moment to register with Julian. It's how they'd met, he and Nacho—the hapless, beaten-down conscript and the crazed army corpsman. It seemed so long ago. There was no time to dwell on it. *He had to stem the bleeding.* He was fumbling with his belt buckle in hopes of applying a tourniquet when Nacho caught his wrist, peering into Julian's eyes with resignation.

"It's the femoral ... artery," Nacho coughed out weakly, receding into shock. His teeth were red. "I'll bleed out in ten, no more than fifteen minutes."

"You *can't* die," Julian insisted, meaning not just that it was unthinkable, but somehow medically impossible. A ferocious gun battle ensued as more White House troops attempted to breach the roof from a maintenance door thirty yards away. For the moment, the Israelis had them pinned inside. Nacho tried to smile.

"When someone kills you, B, you die," he wheezed out. "Even God can't change them physics, only ... minds." He closed his eyes.

Julian shook them open. "Oh no you don't! Stay with me, brother." His mind raced. *Physics?*

The flaming napalm ring was already dying out. The flare stick, however, was still pulsing red fifteen feet away. Julian went for it. A burst of lead from the maintenance door narrowly missed him as he dove into a roll. Snatching the flare, he launched himself back the other way, hard pressed to hold it clear of a standing puddle as he sprawled through it on his belly. Crawling back to Nacho, he felt with the fingers of his free hand for the gushing wound. Then, without warning, he stabbed the hot end of the flare into Nacho's thigh as far as it would go. The scream produced came straight out of hell, ceasing when Nacho blacked out, but the artery was cauterized. *Physics.*

By this time, one of the Israelis had flanked the maintenance door. The next time it opened, he lobbed a grenade inside and hit the deck. The explosion blew the door off its hinges, silencing the remaining threats inside, at least for the time being. Then, like a flying whale, whipping the rain into stinging pellets, Marine One was on top of them, hovering before touching down, but not really, its landing gear merely skimming the roof, holding, its cabin hatch open.

Julian didn't wait. Scooping Nacho into a cradle, he single-handedly lifted him through the hatch, pushing him in and rolling him over, climbing in after him. The commandos followed him in, the hatch was secured, and the chopper lifted off, banking away back over the South Lawn, zinged by gunfire from more of Block's council goons on the ground. Still more were pouring out of the West Wing, almost immediately fleeing back inside under a fifty-caliber spray from the flank gunner on a Blackhawk. The second chopper swooped in under Marine One, their rotor blades missing by what seemed no more than a few feet in an absurdly perilous maneuver. Spent shell casings streaming, the gunner savaged the southwestern exposure of the White House with an unrelenting hail of lead, blasting windows, desks, and furniture to kindling, exploding lighting fixtures and computers, riddling interior walls and cubicles, disintegrating a water cooler.

When the mayhem began, President Block had been no more than a few scant lines from victoriously concluding his televised speech, calmly reassuring the nation that everything was under control. He now cowered in the well of the Oval Office desk. Diving for cover himself, the cameraman had left the tape rolling, terrified screams and shrieks punctuating the gunplay, all of it captured live. Indeed, the camera was one of the few appurtenances that went untouched.

In under fifteen seconds, the Blackhawk rose and veered away, vanishing into dark skies as though it had never been there. Antiaircraft batteries in Lafayette Park blindly pounded the roiling cloud cover in mostly the wrong direction as the storm reached its full fury.

When the senior council agent in the Oval Office gave the all-clear moments later, the president was helped out from under his desk, urgently asked if he was all right, if he'd been hit. Visibly shell shocked, he shook free of his aides' concern, refusing to sit so he could be checked over, muttering something about having to change his drawers. Then he noticed that the camera light was still on, the teleprompter still running. "Is that still hot?" he demanded in horror, staring directly into the lens. A second later, his image blinked out, but not before being indelibly imprinted on the national psyche.

The Russian-built equivalent of a C-130 Hercules, its rear loading bay partially lowered, hugged the treetops to stay below radar as it skirted Baltimore. By power wrench, it reeled in its dangling, slipstream-buffeted cargo. Its flight crew was Saudi. Hypothermia was the chief concern regarding its unconventionally boarded passengers, so blankets were plentiful, along with urns of piping hot Earl Grey tea, hot cocoa for the children. Dry changes of clothing were also awaiting. An onboard physician from Cairo assisted by two nurses was already tending her new patients even before the aft transom sealed, shutting out the howling wind. As soon as the pilot was alerted by intercom that the pickup was complete, all present and accounted for but one, he throttled up into a climb with a gentle easterly turn, more than happy to put U.S. shores behind him, fully aware that they weren't out of harm's way yet, not by any stretch.

Aboard Marine One, Julian finished tucking Nacho in blankets the Israelis had scared up, along with a first aid kit, oxygen canister, and mask. Unless circulation was surgically restored to Nacho's right leg, and soon, he would probably lose it. Otherwise, he appeared stable—decent pulse, respiration steady. He was still out cold and running a fever. One of the commandos had alertly drawn an IV saline drip to keep him hydrated. On that score, the executive helo was stocked with just about everything you could think of, except a real doctor.

Having done for his friend all that could be done, Julian blindly stumbled to the flight deck. Other than the glow from the cockpit displays, they continued to fly dark. Much of the console was all hi-tech Greek to Julian. Even so, he knew a compass when he saw one, and this one told him they were heading due east. He pulled a spare headset off a hook. "I'm no pilot," he said, adjusting the mike, "but you're gonna run out of a place to land pretty soon, aren't ya?"

The pilot didn't respond. The co-pilot's seat was vacant.

Julian squinted to see beyond the beating windshield wipers. They were skimming along close enough to the storm-tossed swells below for him to tell they were already out to sea. "It's not like I'm worried or nothin'," he said, "but how much fuel does this thing hold?"

The answer wasn't encouraging. "Not enough."

Julian didn't pursue it, except indirectly. "What was with the crazy high-wire act? Everybody would have fit in here with room to spare."

"Who would you rather have 'em take pot shots at?"

The voice was vaguely familiar, though it was not that of his regular pilot. This one was older, cagier. "Look, we're in for a bumpy ride," the pilot advised, "so if we're gonna chat, I suggest you plant your ass in that seat beside me and strap in."

Julian did as requested, buckling up. Turning for a better look, he jerked back so fast that he banged his head. "I buried you, man."

Rittenour found it funny. "It didn't take." A cockpit alarm sounded. Abruptly checking his various scopes, the colonel tensed. "Showtime. Bogeys on our six, closing fast." He relayed the news to the passenger cabin, telling its occupants to secure for combat. "They've got tone," he said, yanking back on the stick to pull into a steep climb, ejecting chaff. The first two sidewinders, heat-seeking, fell for it, detonating harmlessly in brilliant fireballs. As well, the chopper's abrupt vertical ascent forced the pursuit to radically trim up speed or overshoot their target, which they invariably did anyway. As Rittenour poured on throttle, so steep was the chopper's climb that it was shaken to its rivets. Rittenour madly pushed the machine to the limit and then some—it was a hairbreadth from stalling—before easing out of the climb upon reaching the clouds, not that they meant anything in the era of electronic warfare.

Zoom, zoom, zoom—blurs of sound more than sight; three high-performance jet fighters, one below, the other two on either side, shot past the chopper and vanished ahead.

"F/A-22 Raptors," Rittenour identified them.

Julian, slumped in his seat as if his ducking had helped, instantly lurched back. "*Jesus!*" Dead ahead, five inbound fast-movers streaked past just shy of supersonic going the other way. "How'd they turn around so fast?"

But Rittenour was too disciplined to be distracted; he was on the radio transmitting something incomprehensible, something that sounded French. Over his headset, Julian caught another voice, calmly mechanical. "*Engagement.*"

"It's out of our hands," the colonel said. "If you're still a praying man, now's the time."

Nauseated, airsick, Julian closed his eyes. "No good. Kinda burned my bridge with God."

"Apparently not," said Rittenour. "You're still here."

Meanwhile, and for most of the next hour, the chopper barreled on to the east without further incident, save for expected, weather-related turbulence, eventually outpacing the storm cover to achieve a star-studded horizon. Not quite sleeping, not quite awake, Julian had drifted off when the cockpit door swung wide, spilling in light from the cabin. Saying nothing, one of the Israelis leaned in between the two cockpit chairs. Rittenour motioned Julian to look out the window. All around the helo, flying in tight formation, were five Mirage warplanes. "Bad guys bugged out awhile ago," the colonel informed him. "No stomach for it."

Just then, the chopper's fuel-critical alarm sounded, flashing bright red on the display.

Rittenour automatically tapped the fuel gauge as if it would do any good. It didn't. "Talk about cutting it close," he said dryly as their escort peeled away. The lumbering chopper was too high to bail out, too low for parachutes to adequately deploy. The wave-tossed seas below were running fifteen to twenty feet. "Crash positions," he ordered. "Brace for impact."

Out ahead, the runway lights on a French aircraft carrier were still several miles off, right at the cusp of U.S. territorial waters. The lights from a number of support vessels indicated a good-sized task force.

"Will we make it, sir?" Julian asked hopefully.

The main turbine sputtered, bucking the craft, its forward momentum stalling. It took everything Rittenour had to hold her steady, but he was losing. A moment later, the stick went dead in his hands as the engine died and the overhead rotor ground to a stop.

The helo briefly floated, or seemed to. Only the gusting wind outside was heard. "*They* did," Rittenour said, almost too casually, "all of 'em—wife, kids, mom, and pop."

Julian glanced over gratefully. "Who do I thank?"

"Who do you think?" And they dropped like a stone.

"*Was it bad, sir?*" Julian yelled over the roaring slipstream.

"*What?*"
"*Being dead!*"

Nose-diving ever faster, the end hurtling up to greet them, Marine One took a header into the mountainous Atlantic swells, crashing hard just under a kilometer shy of the carrier task force. Bobbing there like a cork, it slowly but surely slipped under the surface, tail up.

Coming in low and slow, an air-sea rescue scout plane deployed a buoy with a homing beacon on the spot and continued to circle even as a pair of rescue choppers charged in from the carrier support flotilla with powerful searchlights. The first to reach the beacon slowed to a stationary hover not ten feet above the churning waves before disgorging three frogmen. Under its spotlight, the cable on a power wench was quickly played down to the divers. Fifteen seconds later, the wench reeled in the slack, and Marine One's tail rotor cut the waves. It could be lifted no higher, but its descent into Davy Jones's locker had, for the moment, been halted. At the same time, more frogmen splashed into the sea from the second chopper.

Miracles aside, that higher power Rittenour alluded to had arrived. Whether or not it was too late remained to be seen.

Chapter XX

Within a week of the coup, followed by the surprise raid on the White House, the executive mansion was almost back to normal—its bullet holes patched, its shattered windows replaced, all good as new. Praise God, the attempted counter-coup was handily routed, sending the Antichrist's cowardly governor-general packing with his tail between his legs.

Nonetheless, to blunt unavoidable speculation, Morton Parmister arranged a free-wheeling interview of the newly unelected president by a neutral, faith-based correspondent. If the goal was to solidly establish the entrenchment of the new rulership, Parmister succeeded magnificently. To believers and not alike, this came as welcome relief. Quinn's post-war reforms had been terribly confusing, unanchored to any particular ideology—unfocused—a little of this, a little of that, none of it fast enough—to the point where no one was sure where he stood or what he stood for. Politically unqualified, he'd quickly become an embarrassing joke. He gave rousing speeches to be sure, which everyone was quite certain had been scripted by others, but then he didn't follow through, leaving no one quite sure in what direction the country was headed, pro or con. *Who the hell did he have advising him?* Whoever it was, they should have been fired a long time ago.

Darius Block, on the other hand, left absolutely no doubt about where he would take the country. For the quiescent majority, it was comforting to have a strong leader again. For the doctrinaire minority on the right, it meant a return to police-state stability. For everyone else, it was the beginning of their worst nightmare. The long-awaited marriage of church and state could now be consummated without pretension; there was no going back.

The exclusive interview was conducted in the residence, where the First Lady was quietly entertaining redecorating ideas from a trio of swishy interior design consultants.

"How many changes will you make, Mr. President?" the reporter asked Block. "How extensive? I mean, constitutionally."

The president was personably evasive. Staying on message, he gave one of his patented smirks, nicely framed by the cameraman. "This wasn't my idea, you know, but I could no longer ignore the voice of the people. I didn't ask to be commander in chief. It just sort of got dumped in my lap. But the bottom line is this: I don't question Almighty God. And, because I don't, I see no call for people to question me." Block chuckled, "I mean give me half a chance already. There's a lot to fix."

"What's at the top of the list?"

"Without question, I will defend our faith and protect our way of life to my last breath. No energy and no expense will be spared. And you can take *that* to the bank."

"Mr. President, with all due respect, not all Americans, er Jesuslanders, share—"

"For too long have we drifted from our core values," Block interrupted. "Let us once again be one nation under God. To get there, certain sacrifices are required. The times we live in have never been more dangerous, nor more fraught with peril. Vice and depravity will be rooted out. Lawbreakers will be punished. Our children will be properly schooled. Those who continue to hate this country and hate God are invited to leave or shut up. Most importantly, it is imperative that decent, law-abiding citizens stand up for their right to live their beliefs."

The interviewer nodded, clearly in support. "Yet, as I was saying, Mr. President, there are Americans who love this country but who don't necessarily believe—"

Interrupting anew, Block was splendidly magnanimous. "Then we'll just have to teach them, won't we, assuming they're teachable. We have a culture founded on biblical principles, which I believe is unique in all the world, and which I believe is the best ever devised. If you don't like it, if you want to hate us for our freedom, hate the Bible, then, sorry, get lost. Go be heathen or atheist or whatever, go be pagan somewhere else. As for *this* country, we will serve the Lord of Hosts. As for Philio, his loyalties—his values, if you can call them that—clearly lie elsewhere. To him, Jesusland is just another insurrectionist province. Well, Mr. Philio, I say: and *proud* to be. Bring it on. Let our goodness be measured by the hate coming from our enemies."

"Actually, Mr. President," the interviewer said bashfully, "Jesusland is the *only* insurrectionist province. The rest of the world has accepted Philio."

"Then the rest of the world is wrong. It's certainly not the first time. Look, if I wanted to be French, I'd learn French; or, if a Jew, Hebrew. Unfortunately for Philio and his supporters, I'm an Evangelical Christian—one who strongly believes we stand at the gateway to Christ's kingdom on earth."

"Some might say literally," said the questioner.

The president smoldered. "Any thinking person of faith *knows* what *he* is. I'll let history judge my actions."

The interviewer trod delicately. "The thing is, Mr. President, a lot of people could get hurt while history is making up its mind."

"No one who's been saved. We who have, know the Rapture is right around the corner."

"How soon?"

"Anytime now," Block predicted. "So, to any unrepentant holdouts I say, wake up! Catch the spirit or be left behind." Block looked directly into the camera lens. "'For it is written, I will destroy the wisdom of the wise, and will bring to nothing the understanding of the prudent.' 'Because the foolishness of God is wiser than men; and the weakness of God is stronger than men.' My friends, countrymen, brethren, the threat of that madman who would call himself king to our way of life, all our hopes and dreams, has never been more terrifyingly real. Resist him! Resist the beast! And everything the Bible foretold will come true. I guarantee it."

Across the Oval Office, First Lady Nettie was having difficulty with the new upholstery swatches. "Dar, honey, stop all that and get over here. I need an executive decision."

The president found her timing both politically and theologically perfect. "My dear, I believe you just made one. Your voice is my command. Gentlemen, if you'll excuse me …"

"Cut," the reporter told his photographer.

Watching from the wings, Morton Parmister stepped over. His busted nose was bandaged. Purple circles ringed his eyes. "That'll have to do, boys."

The reporter nodded. "I expect you'll want final cut."

Parmister grinned. "You're psychic. Good job—fair and balanced."

"Let's just say I don't fancy speaking French for the rest of my life. Or worse."

"*Qua?*" Morty joked. "Go on, get out of here and make me happy."

As soon as they were gone, Block lost all interest in upholstery, shooing his wife and her decorators out a separate door. "I thought that went well," he told Morty when they were alone.

Parmister wasn't as optimistic. "Salve for the base," he said. "Buys us time, but not much, not without some dead bodies to lay at Philio's doorstep. Nice work maneuvering clear of that horseplay the other day. Still, if it gets out that a dozen of our men walked away from kill shots while Quinn waltzed out of here lickety-split, imaginations are sure to run wild."

Block sloughed it off. "Quinn means nothing to me—a means to an end."

"The end—that there's an alternative—is the problem," said Morty. "You can't effectively govern people who aren't afraid, either of their own government or what their government is protecting them from. Those are the rules. If Philio is allowed to rewrite them, he might as well *be* Jesus Christ."

Block turned grim. "I see what you mean. What do you suggest?"

"Those wounded during Rittenour's terrorist raid cannot be allowed to recover."

"Each of those men is loyal to me," Block complained. "They put their lives on the line."

"And they'll be honored for it with a showy state funeral—twenty-one gun salute, folded flags, the works," said Parmister. "Heroes of Jesusland, martyred for their abiding faith in service to a cause greater than their own self-interest. I'll personally draft the eulogy, citing clear proof that the Antichrist is on the warpath, that no one of faith is safe, that Quinn was about to capitulate to the demonic fiend in Jerusalem."

"I still don't get what made Quinn so blessedly important to the king," Block said. "All he ever did was bad-mouth Philio."

"Maybe the king is a sports fan," Morty suggested. "Or maybe he's got a soft spot for abandoned kitty cats. My guess is it was just to embarrass us—to show that he can reach in here and do whatever he wants, *when* he wants—that his imperium recognizes no borders. What did you expect out of the Antichrist?"

Block nodded. "For a minute there, trapped under my desk, he even had me believing it."

Parmister put a comforting hand on the president's shoulder, saying, "And then God came to the rescue." Checking his watch, Morty headed out. "Busy day. Good luck with the airheads, boss. Give 'em hell."

Block's lips thinned. "The truth is self-evident," he said woefully. "Why can't they see it?"

At the same time, a convoy of chauffeur-driven limousines and big-engine SUVs arrived at the White House. Moments later, Parmister hosted a coffee klatch in the Map Room. Among his guests were the heads of the country's major Protestant denominations, filling the room with a mélange of competing colognes. Politically melding the still vast congregations devoted to this vaunted clergy into one, unified, monolithic Church of America was Morty's morning challenge.

Small talk was generally favorable to the new regime in Washington, especially concerning the new dress code, decreed by President Block under his aphorism: *"Power underdressed is power redressed."* The Heavenly Father was a well-known aficionado of fine tailoring with a special fondness for gold jewelry and multi-carat diamonds. If not in so many words, the scriptures more than implied it. Certainly when Jesus next appeared, it would be in a power suit and tie, a six-figure timepiece on his wrist. Indeed, if nothing else, it was Janus Philio's wearisomely peasant wardrobe that exposed him for the fraud that he was. At any rate, Parmister opened the broader discussion with the only question of any practical pertinence. "Gentlemen, given our mutual circumstance, does anyone here doubt we're stronger together than apart?"

The presiding magnate of the LDS Church from Salt Lake City was first to respond. "I think I safely speak for us all when I say that recent developments have infused our movements with a much-needed second wind. Nonetheless, any answer to your question must be predicated on the extent to which strength and independence are, shall we say, mutually exclusive constructs."

"Shrewdly put, Prophet," Parmister dolloped out the compliment. "The sacrifices we propose are small, while our common enemy is great. I've met him, personally. He could sell an icebox to an Eskimo. When you get past the effete platitudes, when all is said and done, his agenda is to put each of you out of business. Permanently. A faith-centered alliance is the only defense that makes any sense."

"These sacrifices ... how small?" queried the grand poobah of the Southern Baptists.

Morty's smile was benign. "Ask not what your country can do for you, but what you can do for your country."

On that note, the Mormon spoke for them all. "We're listening."

Among the initiatives Parmister briefly articulated was a major voting rights reform bill guaranteed to pass the soon-to-be-seated interim Congress, guaranteed because its members would no longer be elected on the basis of demographic census or gerrymandering, but by the member institutions forming the Church of America. On the basis of certified headcount, each sect would be assured a proportionate number of seats, clean and simple. Instead of legislated redistricting, church membership rolls would determine official representation. What could be more fair?

Along with election reform would be a major overhaul of the tax code, since tax cuts were as near and dear to the clergy's heart as ever. Under President Block's new scheme, virtually all government social relief programs would be eliminated, paving the way for the church to pick up the slack—slack which carried unlimited recruitment and conversion potential. The savings in entitlements would be passed on to the taxpayer with a fifteen percent, across-the-board cut to be balanced by a mandatory tithe of ten percent of gross income to the Church of America levied on members and non-members without distinction, these funds to be equitably distributed among its member institutions on the basis of average, documented Sunday morning attendance—Saturday for Adventists. If a sect wanted more say, translating into more federal dollars, it would need to get busy in its missionary efforts.

By extension, the public education system would be abolished, fully privatized under the auspices of the church, which would lend its religious imprimatur to all curricula, K–12. Colleges and universities would likewise be religionized, acceptance hinging on church membership. Only students from two-parent households of opposite gender, legally married, would be allowed to attend classes, discouraging divorce and recriminalizing homosexuality. Illegitimate offspring would be turned away from any formal education to give incentive for proper, monogamous marriages and the prescribed wholesome upbringing. Legal adoption would remain an option for infertile churchgoers in good standing, but in-vitro sorcery was now dead as an option. Widows and widowers would thus be encouraged to remarry for the sake of their school-age children. Chronic orphans would be SOL. Then again, what more obvious manifestation of the loss of God's grace was there than being unwanted?

Still, as draconian as these measures might at first appear, they would renew the vitality of acceptable Christendom for centuries to come, proportionately growing its flocks. The nation had had its fling with Quinn's quasi-liberal jabberwocky and Philio's pseudo-spiritual edicts. For the good of all, for the sake of their souls, it must be done. And there was more.

Under the new revenue scheme, the federal government's role would be limited to physical infrastructure, law enforcement, the spread and maintenance of prisons and correctional facilities, tax collection, and, of course, national security.

The newly combined Church of America would be the sole authority on issues of a moral or ethical nature. Consequently, a network of religious courts would be shortly established as the arbiter of alleged sinfulness and wrong thinking, all crimes against God. Also, though a ridiculously small detail, the right to vote would be limited to landowning church members of good repute, strongly suggesting that a wrong vote might tend to put one's good repute in jeopardy. Elections would commence just as soon as each of these measures was in place and smoothly functioning.

All in all, it was a good plan, the best anyone had heard in a long time, for surely a methodically controlled, spiritually obedient democracy, efficiently monitored for emotional purity, was better than no democracy at all.

As for any doctrinal differences among the recognized clergy, an all-encompassing conference would be convened in Colorado Springs to find a middle ground and adopt the new church's creed, wherein bipartisanship would be a presidentially rewarded virtue. Being bipartisan meant you agreed with the president.

Hence, after Parmister finished up with the salient points of the president's reforms, the only sticking point was Block's role as both head of state and head of the church. Morty assured them that the latter office was strictly symbolic, wholly titular, and while Block would responsibly seek to influence religious affairs for the good of the state, the permanent council of ten bishops would always have the final say. They had the president's word on it. On the other hand, since he could replace the church authorities at his whim, such assurances were transparent. Nevertheless, after pockets of discussion, the Baptist raised his final concern.

"I hate like hell to bring this up," he said, "but what about the Catholics? They're everywhere, in every walk of life. It won't work without the Catholics. There's too many of them. And the Jews still control all the big money."

"I'm glad you brought that up," Morty responded easily. "We've privately extended an offer of sanctuary to the pope-in-exile here in the states, pending his endorsement of what we've just discussed. One seat on the COA council of bishops is his—if he wants it. Think of it, brethren—official Christian unity not seen since before the Reformation."

"How is the pope leaning?" Everyone was interested in the answer.

"It's come down to us or Philio," Parmister said. "What choice does he have?"

The Lutheran was bothered. "The pope and Darius Block can't both be infallible at the same time. One of 'em'll have to give, or we'll have us a full-blown religious war on our hands."

"All in good time," Parmister said. "For now, the priority has to be Philio."

"And the Jews?" the Baptist pressed.

"Convert or be dispossessed," said Morty. "Shit or get off the pot—if you'll pardon the French. They've had two thousand years to get with the program. It's now or never."

"That'll just send them over to Philio's camp by the droves," someone said unhappily, "ratcheting up the nonsense that Philio *is* the messiah, forget creating economic panic here, not that it hasn't already started."

"Relax," said Morty. "Their money's not going anywhere. And if *it's* not, *they're* not. Besides, St. Paul said we're the true children of Israel, and we reject Philio."

The Mormon stroked his chin. "To put him down, this Philio, we're looking at a war like never before, the whole world against us."

"Fulfilling the prophecy," Morty said. "Does anyone here doubt that it hasn't come to that—Armageddon?"

"So what was the last war?" someone asked.

Morty shrugged. "Practice."

"From everything I've heard, the kingdom has disarmed, all but the French, and they've only kept a small reserve," said the Presbyterian.

"What do you expect? They're French," said Morty. "Technically, we're still the only superpower. *We* haven't disarmed, and that's all the edge we need. The president has ordered a quiet mobilization to begin immediately."

"That's not going to win us any friends," an Anglican bishop threw in.

"Friends like that we don't need," Morty said resolutely. "Peace, peace, and there was no peace. Remember? This is America. We never go to war unless it's absolutely necessary."

"But we haven't been attacked," someone pointed out.

"What do you call Jerusalem's infernal sanctions?" Morty said. "Read the signs."

"Abolish the priesthood, will he?" softly muttered a feeble Pentecostal minister with oversized dentures. Truth be told, he was looking much better of late, even a little younger. Using his cane, he stood to his feet, surprisingly without help. "A world-cleansing war of faith," he managed in stronger voice, an ever angrier one. "As it is written, so let it begin. God wills it."

Meanwhile, President Block was meeting in conference with delegates from an opposition group calling itself the League of Spiritual Progressives. Dubbed "the airheads" by the religious establishment, they were fence-sitting Janusians, so showing up at the White House under the present circumstances took a huge dose of guts. Very like their conservative counterparts, they looked like investment bankers, not that looking like one is especially revealing. Acting like one, however, in the context of spiritual husbandry, remains the world's second oldest profession. On the flipside, were they to expend half as much effort dressing the inner man as the outer, haberdasheries would go broke. But, alas, it's veneer and a well-kept lawn that sells—the best reason going for covering up the plumbing.

"No president *wants* war," Block assured them. "Still, if it's forced upon me, I won't turn tail and run from it. Don't forget, all the pressure is coming from Jerusalem. I've done everything I know how to seek a parlay, but the king won't hear of it, won't relent on his impossible demands. If you have a problem, gentlemen, it's with him. Given what we know—and I'm not completely sold on the idea, will do everything in my power to avert it, to avoid jumping the gun—but it could be that what we face here is a prophetic inevitability."

"Prophecy can be misread," a member of the league spoke up. "It can be twisted."

"That cuts both ways," said Block.

"His miracles can't be denied."

"Can't they? Define a miracle."

"You know what I'm talking about."

"Results can be manipulated," President Block said affably. "For instance, my scientists tell me ecosystem regeneration is entirely cyclical. No, gentlemen, while there has been a blessing, there's no supernatural phenomena here. We have the charts and graphs to prove it."

"Charts and graphs don't tell the whole story," another league rep complained.

Block's calm rejoinder stung. "And neither does Philio."

"Maybe not, but people aren't dying. How do your scientists explain that?"

"Play it," Block requested of no one present. The lights dimmed, and a multimedia presentation was remotely launched on the conference room's large plasma viewing screen.

Soberly devoid of any religious connotations, slick computer animation purported the existence of a naturally occurring antigen way up high in the planet's atmosphere, its molecular matrix dramatically reproduced in the billions of particles per trillion by a methane catalyst attributed to global warming. The methane gas was promptly neutralized by the reaction, rendering it inert. The antigen, in turn, was then chemically altered by the sudden introduction of a germ warfare agent, resulting in a heretofore unknown compound, the properties of which induced self-healing in a plethora of damaged and diseased biological tissue, halting the aging process. Filmed endorsements of the theory, incomprehensibly technical, by a cadre of respected molecular biologists persuasively bucked up Block's "proof."

"Well, what do you know?" he remarked sarcastically as the lights were raised. "Without greenhouse gases and biological warfare agents, none of this would have been possible—no magic wand or abracadabra required. No, gentlemen—good, wholesome, *American* capitalism played a far bigger role in this than any half-baked snake oil salesman in Jerusalem."

The members of the league were stupefied. "You need to be medicated," one said.

Blocked shrugged away the remark. "And you need to stop living in denial. This is hard science about little more than an ecological coincidence. Sorry, fellas, but there's nothing deeper going on here, except maybe in the king's tortured psyche. They say insulin-shock therapy can do wonders for this kind of messianic megalomania."

There was complete silence.

"Now, now," Block consoled them, "try not to take it so hard. To be perfectly candid, even I was almost taken in at the beginning, which just goes to show you when something sounds too good to be true, it usually is." Getting up to adjourn the meeting, he added, "No, gentlemen, when the true Christ returns, and he will, I have a feeling he'll demonstrate something a little more stupendous than potions and nostrums that can be cooked up with any grade-school chemistry set."

"Such as?" someone asked.

"Casting out demons for starters. And, believe me, gentlemen, *that* takes real talent."

"May we have a copy of the research, Mr. President?" another league member requested.

"So your own scientists can rip it to shreds?" Block needled him.

"If it's independently verified, then we'll all know the truth."

"Except I'm already satisfied," Block said. "In fact, I've never been more convinced of anything in my life."

"Except you're not scientifically qualified to draw that conclusion."

"I'm talking about Philio being the greatest hoax ever perpetrated on the world," Block switched up. "I mean, come on, guys—get real. Do you honestly believe he just dropped out of the sky, clapped his hands, and the world was healed?"

"Isn't that how it was supposed to happen?"

"Only after a lot more *has* to happen," Block corrected the questioner.

"Can we have the research data?" someone else repeated.

"I'm afraid that's out of my hands," Block refused. "National security."

"Of course."

"Oh, don't be so cynical," Block said. "If there was even one molecule of holiness in Philio's whole body, I'd be the first one on my knees to anoint his feet with oil. It's just not logical. Furthermore, I'm sworn to protect the people of this great nation from all enemies, foreign *and* domestic. I'm eager to think that doesn't include you people. Never forget, we live in perilous times."

The league got the message, loud and clear.

"I still don't like your politics," a brave one said.

"Be thankful we still have the political freedom we do over here," Block countered. "Along with religion, I hear Philio has banned all political parties."

"He banned religion as a weapon," someone lobbed back, "not religious faith. As for parties, he merely issued a moratorium on negative campaigning."

"Same difference," Block muttered. "Thanks for coming. I may not have Philio's charisma, gentlemen, but I'm always open to spirited debate."

As the league representatives filed out, politely if unenthusiastically thanking the president for his time, they passed Morton Parmister coming in. After he was alone with Block, Morty gave up a chuckle. "Something tells me they just lost their best friend."

Block didn't share the humor. "How can reasonably intelligent people be so blind?"

"Want them to disappear?" Morty inquired.

Block shook his head. "They're harmless—kooks and fruitcakes, but harmless." He swiftly put them out of his mind. "Now, where do we stand on monetary reform?"

Appreciating the president's urgency, Parmister opened the door to admit a team of economists. This next meeting entailed the abolishment of the hard currency Julian Quinn had reintroduced. In its place, monetary policy would revert back to a national debit card, the reason paper money and coins had been worthless in the wartime Zone. Reinstitution of exclusively electronic transactions countrywide was about to make the banks extremely happy and skyrocket the price of gold. The old-cum-new debit card scheme, together with credit card records, would allow the administration to data mine every transaction of everyone in Jesusland—who bought what, when, and where—making it easier to track down the purveyors and consumers of contraband like pornography and alcohol, condoms and feminine prophylactics, but especially illegal reading material and uncensored films, not to leave out forbidden donations to seditious organizations and payments to outlawed abortion clinics. However, the biggest benefit by far would be in invisibly salting the offering plate from tight-fisted parishioners and the jobless, since, in the case of the latter, there would be no paycheck from which to deduct their contribution. Still, everyone had to do his part.

To this end, the economists produced an oversized mock-up of the new card on poster board, which held the flattering image of Darius Block across from a crucifix holographically superimposed over the Stars and Stripes with the bridging slogan between: "IN GOD WE TRUST." This created an unmistakable if subliminal link—President Block *was* God, at least in the latter's absence.

Appraising it critically, Block wanted some changes. "Shorten the nose a bit and give me a better chin, more square, firm yet dignified. Otherwise, I like it." He went on to complain about a blemish here and there that could be airbrushed out. Copious notes were taken. The new president was very serious about his image. Throughout the review, an operative passage of scripture was completely overlooked.

> *And that no man might buy or sell,*
> *save he that had the mark,*
> *or the name of the beast,*
> *or the number of his name.*

Chapter XXI

Julian had lost all sense of time, not a hard thing to do in this timeless sliver of geography that had exercised such an oversized influence on the rest of the world for so long. Perhaps too long. One thing was for certain: people over here knew a helluva lot more about what was going on back home than those back home were being told about what was going on here.

While the former televangelist now ruling from Washington continued to consolidate his power, backed by nearly a third of the country, King Philio was giving his away in spades, presiding over the inaugural session of a new global parliament, officially known as the *Oikoumene*. The word itself was ancient Greek for the inhabited world, or less broadly, the People of Earth. It was also the root from which the Latin concept of *Oecumenicus*—or unifying principle—and the English word ecumenical were originally derived.

At the invitation of the king, though he was still yet to meet him, Julian was en route to Gaza with Merlin just in time to enjoy an unbelievably beautiful sunset—vivid striations of purple, red, and orange over brilliant gold reflecting off the shimmering Mediterranean for as far as the eye could see. Avi Mandelheimer did the driving down the coast from Tel Aviv, during which he did his best to answer the Quinns' questions.

Avi explained that the king was transferring the day-to-day chores of government to the Oikoumene in order to concentrate on his passion, ending poverty throughout the realm. As for parliament, it was basically a reconstituted United Nations with a few changes. For example, there would be no Security Council—no need—and, hence, no unilateral veto power, except that reserved by the king, which could not be overridden. Nor would there be separate houses of parliament but rather just one big General Assembly, each royal province wielding a single vote. A super majority of two-thirds was required to enact legislation. If such a consensus could not be achieved, it was back to the drawing board. Otherwise, it was *Robert's Rules of Order* unabridged, under which the Oikoumene was tasked to organize itself and draft a constitution subject to the blessing of the king, who was on record as saying simply, "Surprise me."

At all events, Avi said, parliament was charged to uphold four inalienable liberties, the four cornerstones of the new kingdom: freedom of expression, freedom of choice, freedom of movement, and freedom from physical violence. Avi didn't elaborate, except to say that the king anticipated a spirited debate.

"To say the least," Merlin remarked dubiously. "The devil's always in the details."

Avi disagreed. "The devil is in the premise. Fix the premise, and the devil has no home."

"Will the king, too, be subject to the law?" Merlin asked as they reached the outskirts of Gaza. He couldn't help noticing that all the former checkpoints had been removed.

"No," Avi said, "not subject. The king *is* the law."

Taking off his glasses, Merlin rubbed his eyes despondently. *It was always the same.* "Then what's to stop him from becoming a despot?" he followed up. "Even Robespierre started out with the best intentions."

"Maximilien Robespierre was a lawyer who forgot that reasonable laws must first protect the people, not slaughter them," Avi said.

"And Janus Philio?" Merlin pressed.

"He's not a lawyer," Avi replied glibly. "Besides, he's only planning to stick around long enough to get things off to a running start."

"And after?" Merlin asked.

"Universe is a big place," Avi said obliquely, "and the king has many interests."

"But if he's the One," Julian objected, "his reign is supposed to last a thousand years."

"Yeah?" said Avi. "Then we'd better all keep our fingers crossed."

Merlin switched gears. "Where does God figure in all this?"

"First Epistle General of John, chapter four, verse eight," Avi replied. "God is love."

Just then, Julian went stiff. "Jesus!"

Avi had turned onto the ramp of a brand new elevated expressway. The distant skyline of Gaza City towered into the clouds. Like an inlaid jewel on the shores of the Eastern Mediterranean, the new metropolis rivaled Honolulu and Cape Town, even surpassing the seaside resorts of the French Riviera. She was breathtaking and still growing, and clean—enough to make the most anal German green with envy.

Julian was mystified. "Why Gaza?"

Avi took the next exit into the city center. "Why not? Turns out a modicum of dignity and respect goes a long way. And, with the Oikoumene headquartered here, Gaza's per capita income has rocketed into the ranks of the kingdom's top cities. Her beaches are world class; her hotels, restaurants, and nightlife are out of this world." Avi smiled wanly. "The king made a promise and kept it. The Pals did the rest. The results speak for themselves."

"Still, it must have been a bitter pill to swallow for some," Merlin said.

Avi grunted. "You have no idea."

Merlin furrowed his brow. "Four thousand years of bad blood takes a mighty big transfusion. Any guarantee it'll stick?"

Avi shrugged. "JP says time heals all wounds, if you stop picking at the scabs."

Ten minutes later, they were admitted into the Oikoumene complex, beholding a technological marvel. Completely solar powered, it was a sprawling campus set on fifty acres of meticulously landscaped oceanfront parkland with a super-conducting monorail system to speed getting to meetings on time. Its centerpiece, housing the floor of the General Assembly, was a stepped pyramid rising a hundred meters that recalled legends of the Tower of Babel, at the pinnacle of which was a huge satellite dish aimed into the heavens. Twinkling red lights said it was active. Truly, the rest of the world had not been standing still during Julian's joust with Darius Block. Realizing it, Julian felt shame. Here was something huge he could have been a part of from the outset. Instead, he'd walled his country off behind the opaque veil of righteous backwardness. Still, there was something missing he couldn't quite put his finger on. And then he had it—no flags. He mentioned their absence to Avi.

Mandelheimer informed him that the king refused to adopt even a royal standard, heraldry of any kind. Philio's logic was simple. If you stand for something, you *are* the symbol. Why hide behind a device? Julian chose not to push the point but had to ask why Philio was so gung-ho about tearing down the world's time-honored traditions in general. Avi answered that wrapping yourself in any tradition before fully researching its origin and meaning was tantamount to "borrowing" money from dead relatives. To wit, since they're dead, they can hardly accuse you of stealing. "There are many honorable traditions," Avi said sarcastically, "like honor killings and hunting defenseless animals for sport. His Majesty thinks it best to wipe the slate clean and take a fresh approach to everything with fresh eyes."

Julian was annoyed. "What's *that* supposed to mean?"

Avi shrugged. "Adding clean water to a fusty pool is a waste of good water."

"Do you really think people can change that fast?" Julian argued.

Avi was direct. "That all depends on who's holding them back ... and what."

"And why," Merlin added soberly.

Moments later, they entered the pyramid, instantly struck by its crushing anachronisms. Although it was equipped with every modern convenience conceivable, carpeted and climate-controlled under soft directional lighting, the vast lobby level paid homage to the world's ancient civilizations—Egyptian, Mesopotamian, Medo-Persian, Phoenician, Hellenic, Indus, and Chinese—with intricate wall tapestries and splendid mosaics, Ming Dynasty vases, sculpted pillars, friezes and statuary, along with marvelously detailed scale models under glass of the Temple at Karnak, the Parthenon on the Acropolis, Nineveh, the Hanging Gardens of Babylon, Angkor Wat, the Colossus of Rhodes, the Treasury at Petra, Solomon's Temple, Machu Picchu, Tenochtitlan, the Baths of Caracalla, and the great libraries at Alexandria, Pergamum, and Ashurbanipal.

"So much for the subtle reminder," Merlin remarked, no less awed by it all.

Julian squinted. "Reminder of what?"

"That nothing lasts forever."

Avi returned from the big reception desk with their visitor's badges. "This way, gentlemen," he prodded them, leading the way to a bay of inclinators, in the middle of which was a bust of Socrates, another not-so-subtle reminder of the price for free thinking.

Taking an inclinator up several levels, they were met by an usher and seated in the observation gallery, an open mezzanine overlooking the assembly floor, where proceedings were already in progress. Here, the interior of the pyramid was a soaring atrium reaching clear up to the top. Across from the observation gallery was a broadcast control center behind glass. On another level, also behind glass, were the translators. Down below, Janus Philio occupied a lone, upholstered wingchair beside the podium, as the master of ceremonies, familiar to the Quinns as the last Secretary General of the UN before the war, read the roll call of provinces, those that had pledged allegiance to the throne, a prerequisite for representation in the Oikoumene. A hanging vertical banner directly behind and above the dais, comprising a hundred feet of satin, read, "*UN MONDE, UN BUT, UN JUSTICE POUR TOUS*," meaning "One World, One Goal, One Justice for All." There were numerous similar banners in a rainbow of colors around the great hall that translated the phrase into the other major languages represented.

Julian leaned forward in his seat for a better look. "Why so many?" he wondered in a whisper, losing visual count of the delegates, easily in the many hundreds, and easily far more than the number of countries that had existed before the war.

Whispering, Avi explained that, with a notable exception, the world had been transformed into a global kingdom of cooperative provinces, all pledged to peacefully coexist and mutually support each other, rather than the strong exploiting the weak. Avi said the new structure impinged on self-determination only to the degree that bullying and conquest—violent aggression of any kind as a political tool—was off the table for any reason. Disputes, one province with another, would be resolved openly in the Oikoumene, or the king would step in. If that happened, Avi assured the Quinns, both disputants stood to lose. Far better to make nice and work it out. And so to obviate sheer size and wealth as an intimidation factor, large countries had been broken up and contiguous tiny countries combined, all with an ear to cultural and ethnic sensitivities, though not exclusively driven by them. The artifice of tribalism and nationalism as a power and control vehicle—racially, religiously, or geographically motivated—was dead as a weapon, as were all weapons of violent aggression. The utter futility and meaninglessness of the last war had finally brought the world to its senses, Avi said, "albeit with that one stubborn holdout I mentioned."

Sadly sighing, Julian nodded. "Eighty million dead."

Avi did a double-take, staring incredulously. "Come again, Governor?"

"The Pentagon's estimate," Julian said. "Too high?"

Avi flashed with anger. "Try two and a half billion with a capital B, Gov, more than a third of the world's population—whole races, entire cultures bombed into extinction. Christ Almighty, where the bloody hell have you been?"

Swallowing hard, Julian glanced helplessly at his father.

Avi was seething. "But I suppose it's no skin off your nose. After all, you had Star Wars or—what did you call it?—your *national umbrella*. It's how you talked the conservatives in Canada into annexation under the ruse of unification to get at their huge reserves of tar sands. But being shielded yourselves wasn't enough, was it? No, you had to go biological." Looking away, Avi hissed under his breath.

"Back off, friend," Merlin warned. "I spent the war in prison. My boy was trapped in—"

But Avi wasn't listening. "Nuclear incineration would have been a godsend," he hammered on. "My wife hopelessly watched every member of her family succumb. Only she was spared for some unearthly reason. She still hasn't recovered from the psychological trauma, so her abiding hatred—and that's putting it gently—for you *Septics* isn't completely without foundation." Avi took a breath, though it did little to calm him. "Imagine your bowels slowly liquefying, the pain unspeakable. If you could get up, you'd happily throw yourself from the tallest building or bridge; or, if a knife was handy, eagerly slit your own throat and the throat of every loved one you could reach, all of them suffering equally. But you couldn't get up, couldn't move a muscle, because every muscle in your body was jelly. As one by one they disengaged from your gums in your sleep, you'd swallow your teeth. If you were lucky, they'd puncture your stomach or colon or rectum, and you'd that much more quickly bleed to death, internally. No, it wasn't war you waged, gentlemen, it was pest extermination. So you got some blowback, did you? The thing is, even when you did, you kept launching. What were you thinking? For the love of God, *where did you think it would end?*"

Frustrated, Julian blurted, "It was supposed to end with the second coming of—"

"Quiet, please, in the gallery," the speaker at the podium chastised them before forging ahead with the roll call. "Lake District, Langoria, Latvia, Liberia, Lille, Lithuania, Lombardy ..."

"Did it?" Merlin softly asked with a glance down at Philio. "Is he ...?"

It took a moment for Avi to simmer down. "Do you want him to be?"

Merlin was vexed, fighting it, fighting himself. "When did it become up to us?"

"Who would you rather it be up to?" Avi asked, back to his usual self. "Before you decide, consider their track record."

"... Lugash, Luxembourg, Macedonia, Malta, Mexico City ..."

Merlin was distressed. "Then why doesn't he just come out and say it?"

"If you believe, *truly* believe," Avi said, "he shouldn't have to. Isaiah 52:7. 'How beautiful upon the mountains are the feet of him that bringeth good tidings, that publisheth peace.' 'For where your treasure is, there will your heart be also.' Matthew 6:21."

"You're a Jew," Julian said, as if it wasn't right for Avi to quote the New Testament.

"Truth is truth," Avi replied, "but not all truth is clarifying, just as not all lies are intended to hurt. And we are all—every last one of us, living or dead—guilty of both."

The speaker's voice droned on. "... Montenegro, Monte Carlo-Nice, Moskva, Mozambique ..."

Julian was eager to change the subject. "The provinces—how many total?"

"Six hundred and sixty-five," Avi said matter-of-factly, "not including—"

The number hit Julian like a punch in the gut. "No way!"

Merlin was just as cynical. "Convenient."

"Sometimes things just work out," Avi said, doing little to dissuade their skepticism, "and sometimes," he went on, "they need a little push. It's true it didn't have to be that number. It may also be true it couldn't have been anything else. Either way, by hook or crook, all prophecies are ultimately self-fulfilling. Even the staunchest absolutism is subject to the law of unintended consequences. Why? Because the fundamental duality in the universe isn't quite as comfortable as good versus evil. It's greed vs. generosity, and only a greedy person requires that it be any simpler than that, or any more complex. That said, were the holdouts here, the former states and its territories would comprise sixty-four voting provinces; Canada, another twenty-three."

The Quinns were speechless.

"I'll tell you this for nothing," Avi said after a moment. "There are not a few of us, and the number is swelling, who feel it's time to write off that part of the world and be done with it. You people just aren't ... lovable."

Julian's migraine did its best to split his skull. "The mark. We know the number. What's the mark?"

"Maybe the same thing it's always been," Avi said. "Maybe having it in your forehead or in your right hand is a long way of telling us where it's not—in your heart."

Above Times Square, now at the height of lunch hour in Manhattan, a new billboard was unveiled, the kind with alternating panels, like vertical blinds, automatically changing every ten seconds. On one side was a cross, backlit by a sunburst with the bold lettering: "JESUS IS LORD." On the other side was a huge portrait of Darius Block and the bolder caption: "TRUST YOUR PRESIDENT." Smaller print advised: "BE A PATRIOT. APPLY FOR YOUR NATIONAL DEBIT/ID CARD TODAY. IT'S MONEY IN THE BANK." A digital timer at the base of the billboard counted down the days, hours, and minutes remaining to convert hard cash to electronic funds. The clock's digits were blood red. From a flagpole atop the billboard, a gargantuan American flag waved.

Down below, the crawler on the Times Building read, "ALL THE NEWS THAT'S FIT TO PRINT ... UNDER NEW MANAGEMENT ... NO MORE LIBERAL BIAS," followed by "JESUS DIED FOR YOUR SINS. GOD BLESS JESUSLAND." There was nothing else forthcoming, the same crawler merely recycling, over and over.

Meanwhile, a resurgent FOX NEWS CHANNEL had cornered the cable news business due to an indecency crackdown by the FCC on its competitors. Most had been dropped by cable operators nationwide. Huge chunks of the cable system were now owned by FNC's parent. Other than vintage reruns of family programming not including *Seinfeld* and *Will and Grace* or *Rosanne*, every other channel blared government-approved inspirational programming focused on the end of days, much of it disturbing, 24-7. Hot blondes and rawboned men in pricey suits heaped unending praise on President Block, extolling virtuous living and its reward, salvation; interrupted only by late-night infomercials on how to get rich quick. On broadly censored talk shows, recovering homosexuals testified to the arrant nonsense of anything smacking of genetic predisposition, while telegenic preachers with bleached smiles thundered on about chosen-ness and predestination. The JumboTron in Times Square interspersed images of Hitler and Stalin, Mao, the Ayatollah Khomeini, and Saddam Hussein with more recent stock footage of Janus Philio, constantly cutting to classic Hollywood black-and-white clips of debauched Roman orgies and the horrific savagery of Christian martyrdom in the arena. These images then tastefully dissolved to crummy-quality silent films showing the French Revolution as it had occurred on a backlot in Burbank, blood dripping from Madame Guillotine, before cutting back to Philio at a ghastly, distorted zoom level and his out-of-context sound bite, "There is no end!" Film clips of the death factory at Auschwitz followed.

"Man, that is just cold," Julian said glumly, running his fingers over his scalp. The roll call of provinces on the floor of the Oikoumene was nearing its alphabetic end.

"Believe what you will," Avi said, keeping his voice barely above a whisper, which only made the words more ominous, "but whoever actually penned the Book of Revelation starts out chastising the seven churches of Asia Minor for doctoring the true faith and sliding back into idolatry. To any pious Jew of the time, which scholars agree he undoubtedly was—Jews being the first Christians—bowing down before graven images, *chi-rho* or any other, was blasphemy from the word go. Obviously, the author's original codex or scroll or wax tablets couldn't be allowed to survive, not the tiniest fragment, though even a mildly objective paleographer will tell you that all the blood libel hooey and Synagogue of Satan claptrap was inserted much later and not especially artfully—clearly forced, actually, syntactically—into the surviving Greek. How much more was added or changed? And why would any Jew except Saul of Tarsus, whom the Church of Jerusalem reviled, write down sacred thoughts in Greek?"

"We don't know that he did," Merlin said.

"Precisely," said Avi. "We don't *know* a lot of things—too many. Regardless, the book's graphic warnings about a beastly antichrist falsely usurping the mantle of the lamb of God, set in the context of when first written—the serial plundering of Anatolia and the Levant by monstrous Parthian horsemen, for instance—points to something far more imminently dangerous in the writer's mind, which is not to say he got the timeline right or that the rest of it wasn't desperate hyperbole intended to scare his readers back into line."

"As you're doing now?" Merlin suggested.

"Like I'm doing now," Avi admitted. "But," he quickly qualified, "whilst hyperbole has its place in discourse to underscore and illustrate a particular argument, it clearly has no actionable basis in fact or reality, nor should it ever form the core of a belief system, even though it always does. Gentlemen, I submit to you that we find ourselves where we are today, in part if not in whole, solely because the boundary between alliteration and literality became blurred—was allowed to *become* blurred; indeed, was actively manipulated *to* become blurred."

"That's an undisguised indictment of every chapter in history," Merlin said.

"Just so," Avi agreed, "editorial control appropriated by the victors. But, win or lose, both sides have only their point of view. The truth, if there is one, may better exist not in what *is* written, but in what was scrapped. Why were certain accounts banned and others blessed? If it's tomfoolery, expose it. Why burn it? If it's patently ludicrous, why not enjoy the humor? What is it that underpins religious insecurities? For that matter, what really constitutes religious 'authority'? Why is 'authority' required, and why is it so troubled by alternative hypotheses, many having only to do with realms unseen, dimensions unvisited? Could it be the perceived loss of prestige? Income? Control? Exposure of the 'authority' for what it really is: a—"

"Mind fuck?" said Julian.

Just then, King Philio took the podium amid a standing ovation on the assembly floor. The Quinns and Avi were compelled to stand, as well. Applauding mechanically, Julian glanced down at the diminutive Mandelheimer. "Just a social secretary, huh?"

"Discover the caliber of the people the king has chosen to surround himself with," Avi demurred, "and you'll know why I'm fortunate to be exactly where I am."

Eschewing the outpouring, the king motioned for it to end, no false modesty in evidence. If he had an ego, this wasn't serving it. He certainly wasn't a slave to fashion, not in any conventional political sense; he looked as if he'd just walked in off the street—no cufflinks, no tie, a store-bought tweed jacket over a common white dress shirt and faded blue jeans. Nor had he bothered to shave in days. It made him rugged, unremarkable otherwise. Nor did he seem to care in the least. But what Julian picked up on, could totally empathize with, was the king's utter fatigue. No matter how different their roads taken, they at least shared *that* in common.

In a way, Julian was relieved. Philio *wasn't* Superman. The realization was equally depressing because, without a superhero of comic-book proportions, none of this, no matter how good it sounded, stood a snowball's chance in hell of lasting. But then, as the ovation subsided and his audience settled in to don translation earpieces, the king spoke, without the benefit of either notes or a teleprompter. It may not have been so to everyone, but for Julian, Philio's lyrical delivery, spoken in his native Aramaic, was pure magic. Meanwhile, Nacho Angel limped into the gallery with Colonel Rittenour. Catching Julian's eye, Nacho gave him a thumbs up.

"He that governs best governs least." Philio's translated words, conveying so much more, resounded through the pyramid atrium.

The delegates automatically applauded. The king wasn't gratified. He wanted to be heard, not revered and honored. He waved down the applause as if time was of the essence.

"A wise opinion does not punish; it clarifies," he told parliament, continuing at a steady pace. "Listen closely to *all* of your constituents, not just the ones you like the most or that like you best. Seek out the quiet ones. Just because they're meek doesn't mean they don't have something to say. Examine your convictions daily. If you find everyone agreeing with you, you're probably wrong. Measure your success by the good you do for those who need it most, not the ones who demand it loudest. Loud people are loudest when they're afraid. Demonstrate that their fears are misplaced, and their fears will flee. It may take awhile, so don't be in a rush. Haste makes waste. It also makes bad policy. You will never fulfill everyone's expectations, so don't add to them with idle promises. Map out achievable objectives, and then achieve them. Failure simply means you guessed wrong, so don't blame; reassess and rectify. But, above all, you will keep *no* official secrets—none." The king was adamant about this. "Even for people who may not *wish* to be informed, it is a wish that *mustn't* come true ... or we shall be right back where we started."

A split second after his last remark was translated, the full Oikoumene was on its feet with a thunderous ovation, everyone in the gallery joining in, even the army of interpreters and members of the press, especially the press. Caught up in the moment with an ecstatic shiver up his spine, hungry for more, Julian fought a lump in his throat, never more convinced that Philio *was* the real deal, had to be … *if* he followed through or, more critically, was allowed to. And then disaster struck.

The king's balance faltered. He gripped the podium, holding on, but only momentarily, his lips losing color even as his larger-than-life image on the dual, elevated big screens on either side of the podium showed his eyes rolling up in his head just before he collapsed. The General Assembly fell silent, frozen in shock. Barking into a handheld radio, Rittenour bolted out of the gallery. Pandemonium ensued.

"*Yes!*" a West Wing staffer ballyhooed, trading a high five. "That's what I'm talking about! All talk and no holy." The entire White House staff was glued to the telecast. Indeed, all of official Washington was. For the rest of the country, the feed was electronically jammed.

Behind closed doors in the Oval Office, a more subdued celebration was in progress. "It's the opening we've been waiting for," Morty Parmister said. "You see? He's *not* invincible, just flesh and blood like the rest of us."

Stroking his chin, President Block was less ebullient. "Before you gloat, try changing the whole world all by yourself. That could've been me up there."

Morty shook his head. "You're smarter. You'd have paced yourself better."

"All the same, find out if there's anything more to this than meets the eye," Block decreed.

Morty scowled. "If so, whoever's behind it deserves a medal."

"Damn you, you'll do what I tell you!" Block exploded. "If there's a plot I don't know about, I want to know about it!"

The presidential outburst caught Morty by surprise.

Then, holding up his hands, Block imposed a calm over himself he clearly didn't feel, adding, "This has to go down the right way."

Morty eyed the president strangely. "What do you mean, the *right* way?"

Block sighed almost painfully, swiveling away. "I can't go through another antichrist. I'm too old. I need closure. I *need* Philio. If he's out of commission, God forbid people actually feel sympathy for him, it'll steal from the glory of the Lord's final victory. I damn sure can't allow him to out-good me. Unless this ends head to head, total good versus total evil, me against him, there will always be doubts."

Hiding it well, Morty belatedly came to the conclusion that his pastor was certifiably insane. "So what do you want me to do, send him a basket of flowers with a get-well card?"

"A big basket," Block said. "While you're at it, press for talks. Temporarily cool down the rhetoric. Let's give him a chance to catch his breath and get back to full form. To demonstrate our sincerity, draft an executive order granting amnesty to all dissidents, no questions asked. If nothing else, it'll get the opposition off my back for a few months. We can crack down later. At the same time, I want our invasion plans accelerated. Let's also go ahead and launch our covert destabilization plans, kingdom wide. Presuming he recovers, I want him coming back politically weakened."

Making mental notes, Morty was in awe. Insane or not, Block was a political genius without parallel, totally free of scruples. And, in Morty's world, there was nothing more godlike.

Chapter XXII

Post-reconstruction Gaza City's main hospital barely qualified as a clinic. Quite frankly, until now, there'd been no need for anything more substantial. Disease was a thing of the past. Infrequently, there was still a call for setting accidentally broken bones, suturing bloodier mishaps and the like, but all typically on an out-patient basis. Conditions requiring any more serious attention hadn't been seen since ... well, since Philio took the throne.

A swelling crowd now in the hundreds and terribly nervous had been gathering outside the modest facility since shortly after the king's ambulance arrived, accompanied by an inflated motorcade of worried courtiers and Oikoumene tag-alongs. Gwynn Reynolds was choppered in from Jerusalem almost immediately after seeing the drama unfold on television. She was at the king's bedside now. Otherwise, assuming firm command, Ken Rittenour was keeping everyone else, official and not, at arm's length, backed by an ad hoc company of ex-IDF specialists with a take-no-prisoners approach to crisis management and crowd control.

Eager to keep a lid on wild speculation, Rittenour cornered the king's attending physician, a Dr. Nabil Kadir, in the hallway as the latter was annotating the patient's chart. Hustling him clear of all the buzz and hoopla, Rittenour began with the doctor in Arabic, impressing him with a crude fluency geared more to surviving on the streets of Fallujah or Ramadi than intelligently discussing the nuances of medical science.

"I speak English if you prefer," the Cairo-educated Kadir interrupted with only a slight accent. "I certainly would."

"Good," Rittenour obliged. "I want answers, doc, and I want it straight."

Kadir nodded. "His Majesty's condition is stable. Beyond that, I'm at a loss."

said it, or, more germanely, what it meant. In no time at all, really, the discussion deteriorated into sectarian bickering.

Curiously, people who'd never met the king, many who'd never even been in his presence, proclaimed mystical insights concerning his character and nature, albeit in the most adoring terms, much of it downright shocking to the people who knew him best. An unemployed lawyer in Prague claimed to be communing with the sleeping king telepathically, shortly thereafter declaring himself the master's psychically appointed successor. Astoundingly, he quickly developed a growing following committed to installing him on the throne—by force, if necessary.

Meanwhile, without the king's guiding hand, the Oikoumene got off to a rocky start, passing a law that declared it high treason to speak ill of the king or to use his name in vain for any reason. Neighbors were encouraged to inform on each other. Even a patently deceitful accusation was grounds for detention and the confiscation of all personal property and assets. Then, further seizing upon the unsettled public mood, a bill was introduced in parliament to rearm the kingdom in righteous defense against all enemies, without *and* within, but the measure got bogged down in committee. Despite diminishing numbers, there were not a few in parliament who kept reminding the others that the king, while indisposed, was still alive. Upon his recovery, God willing, there would be hell to pay for so brazenly overturning his central tenet that war for any reason was obsolete.

Nonetheless, a growing multitude was convinced that the king's affliction was hardly happenstance, and that the enemies of the kingdom must be dealt with handily, despite a recent cooling of tensions with the belligerents in North America. Conspiracy theories flourished, leading to massive anti-Jesusland demonstrations in a slew of provincial capitals. As the pacifists lost ground, their jobs were threatened and their homes vandalized. Barring the speedy return of the king, everything he had worked for and accomplished was in danger of blowing apart, perhaps irreparably.

Throughout it all, Gwynn Reynolds devoted herself to Philio's bedside, each passing day no different than the last, it seemed. He'd been fitted with a feeding tube to keep him nourished, making the greatest fear muscular atrophy, so twice daily a physical therapist came to his hospital room to manually work out his limbs and joints, followed by a massage therapist to promote good circulation. These stimulations notwithstanding, Philio's eyes never opened, never once flickered. It was as though he weren't even there.

The medical staff remained baffled. Periodic scans showed nothing amiss neurologically, and Philio's autonomic processes were functioning normally with the

"Talk to me."

"There's nothing wrong with him, not physically," Kadir explained. "Mentally, *emotionally*, is another story. As near as I can determine, he's suffering, if it can be called that, from total nervous exhaustion. I won't speculate beyond that. I can describe the symptoms, colonel, but I can't explain them. It's like he's slipped into a coma."

The news wasn't welcomed. Rittenour lit a cigarette. The doctor didn't object. The second-hand smoke might be annoying, but it was no longer a killer. "All right, he's comatose," Rittenour exhaled. "Any idea for how long?"

"I said *like* a coma," Dr. Kadir corrected. "There's no neurological dysfunction, no embolism, no indication of a stroke, not even a mild one. His cognitive centers have simply shut down, although there's healthy REM activity, an enormous level, if you must know."

Rittenour's expression prodded him for more.

"The king is *dreaming*, Colonel," Kadir said. "Everything else is at rest. There's certainly no pain or discomfort. It's as if his conscious mind, as opposed to his brain, is hibernating—sleep, only deeper; much, *much* deeper. Still, I may be guilty of flying false colors here, colonel. I'm not a board-certified neurologist, not even close. Like it or not, the top experts in the field are all in America … what *was* America."

Rittenour regarded him cruelly. "Yeah, like *that's* gonna happen." He took a moment to think. "All right, have him ready to be transferred to Jerusalem at a moment's notice. I'll work out the logistics and security." Closing his eyes, Rittenour sighed heavily. "And God help us all."

"I'll have to give the media *something*, Colonel," Kadir called out as he walked away.

"Tell 'em the truth," Rittenour slung back. "It's the one thing no one ever believes."

With the king's condition unchanged, it was only a matter of days before the first cracks appeared in the nascent kingdom's unity. Soon, crafty opportunists far and wide were jockeying to fill the power vacuum, each laying claim to Philio's "true" vision. The only thing amazing about it was how many differing interpretations there were this soon. Although he was a prolific speaker, Philio had never committed his deepest personal thoughts to writing. It was small wonder, then, that the tapes and transcripts of his more expansive addresses and lectures should begin mysteriously disappearing. Even respected scholars who'd attended the same event disagreed on what the king had actually said, how he'd aid of catheters. Otherwise, as Dr. Kadir first diagnosed, it appeared to be no more and no less than the deepest sleep on medical record. Indeed, the person suffering the most wasn't Philio but Gwynn—reading to him, talking to him, *pleading* with him, never with a response of any kind, not so much as a twitch or the contraction of a finger—and yet she refused to give up hope even as the stress of it all wore her to a frazzle, day after day, week after week, month after month, threatening to steal her looks. It hadn't, yet, not by a long shot. The damage was all inside.

Beyond this one room, Mission Hospital in the Armenian Quarter of the Old City had been turned into an armed camp, so there were few visits not of an official nature to visually verify the king's continuing duress. At first, Ken Rittenour had been here almost as much as Gwynn, ever vigilant and scrupulous about every aspect of the king's safety, but that was before he fell under suspicion solely because he was an American, and a lethal one to boot. A resolution of the Oikoumene relieved him of command and put him on a watch list of potential enemy agents. As official kingdom paranoia escalated, Ken had barely eluded arrest, escaping to the forbidding mountains on the shores of the Dead Sea, where he was said to be holed up in a secret cave with a handful of anti-government insurgents now classified as terrorists. Among them, Gwynn had heard rumor, were Felix Angel and Julian Quinn, all with hefty bounties on their heads. Gwynn knew she was being watched closely as well, but because her romantic relationship with the king was widely known, and, added to the fact that she was a mere female, no moves had as yet been made against her. If, eternal love forbid, her beloved Philio expired, her life would be less than worthless, although in this continuing era of immortality, getting rid of her permanently presented certain problems, which was not to say she couldn't vanish. Already, quite a few had. These were generally the most outspoken proponents of nonviolence, and their whereabouts remained a closely guarded official secret. Given the looming threat from Jesusland, being opposed to fighting and bloodshed was considered a character flaw.

How had things reverted so rapidly back to barbarity? Gwynn questioned herself endlessly. What amazed her was that she was surprised. After all, for every action, there must be an equal and opposite reaction. It was a simple matter of kinetics and natural law. This was what made Janus Philio so *un*natural. He taught that, if you keep turning the other cheek, the person hitting you will eventually run out of gas. It may take awhile, and you will absorb a lot of pain, but if you hit back, the process merely starts all over again. Loving your neighbor as you love yourself was the problem. Deep down, most people can't stand themselves. Narcissism was merely empty compensation. Fear posing as hate was merely projection. Prevention and preemption strictly meant doing unto others before they got around to doing it unto you. At the end of the day, the Golden Rule was all about gold.

As night fell, per her long-established routine, Gwynn kissed her true love on the forehead and left him to go home for a bite to eat, maybe a hot bath, and a few hours of fitful sleep, always returning before the next day's dawn.

Ever her shadows outside, the team of government men stayed right behind her as she walked the meandering streets of the Holy City back to her apartment. She didn't deviate from her usual route and never did, tempted though she was, if only to put a scare in her uninvited entourage. Tonight, like every night, she was simply too tired for such horseplay. If Janus ever awoke—correction, *when* Janus awoke, she scolded herself—a lot of folks were in for their own rude awakening. Only then did it hit her, like a brick falling on her head. They didn't *want* him coming back, couldn't *afford* to let him back into people's hearts the way he truly was and had been. There were too many spoils up for grabs in the confusion. No, the king was just fine right where he was, and were his condition to ever change for the better … Gwynn shuddered, hearing it clearly in her head. "*Thanks for ending death. It's a royal pain in the ass, but what the heck. We'll deal with it. Now go back to sleep.*"

Tempted to race back to the hospital, Gwynn caught herself. She had no power to save him. Moreover, to presume that he needed saving violated the deepest lessons he'd tried so hard to get across. *There is no end. There is only transformation.* No, all she could do was believe in him and keep the things he'd taught her alive and pure. And hope.

Then, passing a newsstand, her heart jumped anew, her stomach sinking, battering that hope. She paused only long enough to briefly check out the cover story in tomorrow's *Jerusalem Post*. It said Avi Mandelheimer had been arrested on unspecified charges. A surprise search of his residence based on an informant's tip had turned up a trove of the king's personal papers. The confiscated documents had been removed to the Royal Archives for "study and analysis," obviously never again to see the light of day. *Poor Avi.* There was no one more loyal to the king and, next to Gwynn herself, nobody closer to Philio. With a heavy heart, Gwynn resumed her trek.

Coming down the home stretch, as she neared her cozy little apartment, the same one she'd acquired with Morty Parmister, a neighbor was taking out the trash. The dimly lit street was otherwise deserted. Throughout the city, perhaps the whole kingdom, few folks now ventured out after dark. Old ethnic tensions were on the rise. Once again it was every man for himself. Gwynn, however, had little worry on that score. She always had company, seen or not, and never more than a few meters behind her. She waved to the neighbor. The gesture wasn't returned, nor did she expect it would be. People just didn't do things like that anymore. Guilt by association had become a potent control tool as the various political factions vied for supremacy in the king's absence, and everyone, even your best friend, was a potential informant. Philio's happy kingdom, as it had been, now seemed like nothing more than a dreamy interlude in a dark symphony of despair.

Watching her neighbor skedaddle, trudging up the steps to her front door, Gwynn turned to wave goodnight to her unseen shadows as she did every night, mostly just to piss them off. Then, going inside, she was about to turn on the lights when a large hand clamped over her mouth from behind just before the door was kicked shut.

Summoned to the patient monitoring station on the floor outside the king's hospital room, the on-duty physician for the night shift warily accepted the document proffered by a no-nonsense government official. "Orders of the Oikoumene," the official tersely informed the doctor, "specifically, the Committee for Kingdom Security." The official had intimidating reinforcements with him, including the watch commander of the King's Guard.

Casually perusing the single page, the doctor's eyes were brought up short. "Whose medical opinion is this?"

"It's a legal order, doctor, requiring immediate execution. Do your duty."

The doctor frowned almost humorously. "Do you have any idea what this drug is, much less the ramifications of this dosage? Do you want to induce *permanent* coma?"

The official's expression remained flat.

Trying to stare him down, the doctor lost, then shook his head. "I won't do it. I refuse."

The official didn't appear particularly concerned, rather as if expecting it. He turned his deadly gaze on the duty nurse manning the station, daring her to disobey. "Young lady, do you have a family?"

Moments later, equipped with a vial and syringe, she led the way to the patient's very private and heavily guarded room. Seeing their watch commander, the men outside snapped to attention. Inside, there was only one small problem. The bed was empty.

Over a blaring alarm klaxon, the hospital was ordered sealed tight, not that it already wasn't, as a desperate room-by-room, floor-by-floor search commenced. Suddenly, the no-nonsense government official was sweating bullets.

Catching her breath in the dark, Gwynn was delirious. "*How?*" she gasped. "*Why?*"

Janus reached out to touch her face with tender affection. "We can't just go around short-changing prophecy willy-nilly, now can we? Well, not altogether. They've had their little season. It's my turn again. And this time—how do they say?—it's for all the marbles."

Chapter XXIII

Within the week it was official.

Morton Parmister broke in on an Oval Office photo op. Catching the president's eye, he held his peace. No need to alarm the youngsters. They were delegates from a COA youth group that had lobbied hard to replace "The Star-Spangled Banner" with "Onward Christian Soldiers" as the national anthem. Just moments ago the president had signed the measure into law. Now, flashbulbs popping, tears streaming, the teen leader of the group formally told Block, "Jesus loves you, Mr. President. Thank you for saving our country." Her voice cracking with emotion, she almost didn't get through it. Block opened his arms and gave her a grandfatherly embrace, basking in the moment, but for only a moment, before sending his young visitors on their way with souvenirs and a few choice words of pastoral encouragement. As soon as the room cleared, his affability vanished.

"Never put me off stride like that," Block chastised his most senior aide. "Image is everything, especially when it comes to impressionable children. What in blazes is so urgent?"

"He's back," Morty announced, switching on an office flat screen with a remote control. Tuned to a kingdom satellite network, the live coverage showed a massive celebration underway in Jerusalem. The Via Dolorosa was mobbed under a blizzard of flower petals. As King Philio walked the stations of the cross, his triumphal reappearance combined all the elements of an old Hollywood spectacular—*shofroth* sounding jubilantly in the background, the crowds ecstatic. Evidently back to his old self again, the king was in fine form, looking fit and trim and never healthier. "Check out his retinue," Morty said.

Block moved closer to the screen. "Hmm, the Mexican has grown a beard. How positively apostolic."

"Ahead on the right," Morty pointed out. "That's Ken Rittenour."

"You were right," Block said. "He's gone native. Who's the woman?"

Morty soured. "Guess."

Block toyed with him. "Looks like she's got a bun in the oven."

Grinding his jaw, Morty pointed. "There. It's Quinn."

Block's expression turned icy cold. "Traitor."

"You were set to rub him out, his whole family," Morty reminded the president.

Annoyed by the rejoicing crowd, this unrestrained worship of the son of Satan, Block snatched up the remote to mute the volume. "I meant to his Christian values. The man has no principles." Thundering softly, he added, "Behold, O Israel, how thou art deceived. Thy treachery shall not go unpunished."

Morty cocked his head like a curious puppy. "What verse is that?"

Block killed the power altogether, blanking out the screen. "Don't be impudent."

Morty followed him over to the desk. "So what's our next move?"

Block reclined back with his hands on top of his head. "We're going to give him just enough rope to hang himself."

Morty remained standing. "How do you figure?"

"He can stage all the Hosannas he wants," Block said, "but at the end of the day, his rosy little experiment is broken. The provincial governors and regional strongmen who grabbed power while he was off in Neverland aren't about to give it back voluntarily."

Morty briefly mulled this over. "Except those bully boys only had the gumption to jump in and go for it with our needling and financial support, not to mention a ton of U.S.–made arms."

"And they're going to continue to get it," Block said, "forcing a crackdown, and then the whole world will see what he's made of."

"In other words, we're going to prove how vile and corrupt he is by encouraging his opposition to be vile and corrupt. Nifty. He'll know where it's coming from, you know."

"That's the beauty of it," said Block. "To keep his subjects from looking too deeply into the contradictions and hypocrisies of his reign, he'll project all the ills of the kingdom outward, riling 'em up good until they scream for *our* blood, and when they do, even the marginally faithful and fence-sitting agnostics here will come to more fully appreciate why they need us. The external threat to peace and tranquility here at home will make war abroad not only a justifiable necessity, it will ardently resonate with the biblical inevitability the Lord's people know it to be ... given the right push."

Morty sighed with admiration. "Machiavelli 101. I like it. It all works ... almost."

"If there's a hole in my reasoning, Brother Morty, I'm happy to hear it." The president's tone suggested quite the opposite.

"It's just ..." Morty hesitated. "What if he doesn't *know* he's the Antichrist?"

"He knows," Block said without reservation, busying himself with paperwork. "He'd have to be in complete psychosis, totally detached from reality, not to see it."

Morty nodded. "Ezekiel 13:3. 'Woe unto the foolish prophets, that follow their own spirit, and have seen nothing.'"

The passage discomfited Block, but only for a split second. "Exactly," he concurred.

Just then, the press secretary and White House chief of staff barged in. "Mr. President, we need to craft your position on the king's recovery."

"As a matter of fact, we've just been discussing it," Block informed them cheerily, pushing up from the desk. "Brother Morty will fill you in. I've got a date with a treadmill."

Moving out, the president shot Morty a cautionary glance unseen by the others. Outside, the corners of his mouth curled into the beginning of a satisfied grin as Parmister's voice faded behind him.

"Take this down," Morty was saying. "The government of the United States of Jesus Christ Savior is pleased and relieved by news reports of King Philio's return to good health. The president strongly believes the prayers of the American people played no small part in the king's recovery. We therefore take this opportunity to renew our calls for a resumption of diplomatic ties and immediate talks aimed at reducing tensions. Furthermore, the people of Jesusland bear no grudge for the outrages and contumacious bigotry perpetrated against all peoples of faith and strong religious conviction, and we urge the King of Jerusalem to halt the slanderous persecution of God-fearing believers worldwide."

Pausing her pen, the press secretary was befuddled. "What persecution?"

Morty didn't blink. "Stay tuned."

Weeks passed, then a month, then another. A new Oikoumene was reseated in Gaza. Prior offenders submitting themselves to the king's forgiveness were pardoned, no questions asked, not so much as a harsh word spoken in punishment.

Thus, more popular than ever among the underclass, the king resumed where he'd left off, arguably with even more alacrity, once again the steady altruist, preaching prosperity through cooperation, opportunity through education, disabusing superstition and demagoguery with empirical observation and an avalanche of uncensored, reproducible results. Scientific advances marched on at an accelerating pace. The arts enjoyed an unprecedented renaissance. Economically, the king's policies were making a mockery of the old-school, market-driven orthodoxy. Throughout the kingdom, publicly distributed profits were soaring even as prices plunged to all-time lows. Monopolies withered like sun-scorched wheat without the subsidies to artificially sustain them. Corporate-influenced government curbs on independent innovation were erased. Interest-free barter of goods and services hampered the cocktail-hour caprice of central bankers. Classism took a beating. Exclusivity took a bath. Established wealth and dynastic affluence lost its cachet as the gap narrowed unchecked between the privileged and not, thereby realizing the worst fears of plutocratic hyperbole. For those of a recidivist persuasion, if Philio *wasn't* the Antichrist, he was doing a damned fine job of acting it!

And so the *haut monde* left the kingdom in droves. As the contrails of their private jets were endlessly rewritten high above the Atlantic and Pacific alike, they were welcomed in Jesusland with open arms and pious kisses, vowing to return once the plebian madness wrought by a populist king of dubious ancestry ran its course or God Almighty came back to his senses. Barring something extraordinary, neither seemed likely for the foreseeable future. Calls for the Block administration to do something, *anything*, were beginning to threaten domestic tranquility. Moneyed kingdom exiles began pounding the timbrels for decisive action or a regime change … in Jesusland! In certain quarters, Block was even excoriated as a moderate, this despite the increasing number of tumbrels rolling daily to the work farms and zones with unmasked leftist undesirables, all of it shoving the ideological center ever farther right.

Amid this growing insurrectionist milieu, one fine day found the president on the links at Camp David enjoying a round of golf under gorgeous skies. He was playing alone, grateful for the solitude. Officially, he was a scratch golfer. Unofficially, he was yet to ever break a hundred, one of the reasons he preferred to play alone. His Secret Service caddy kept his scorecard, removing the burden from the president, who never had any quibbles about signing them. He was already several strokes over on a par three green when he finally sank the putt.

"Nice birdie, Mr. President," said the caddy, noting it on the scorecard accordingly before pressing a finger to his earpiece. "Expecting company, sir? It's Mr. Parmister."

"No, but let him on," Block said, wishing he didn't have to. Moments later another agent delivered Morty by golf cart to the top of the next fairway. "Is it too much to ask for an afternoon to myself?" Block complained.

"Kind of goes with the job, Mr. President," Morty said. He was still dressed for work in a suit and tie.

Block shanked the drive into the trees, not the least embarrassed for doing so. He simply held out his hand for a fresh ball.

"I'm no student of the game, sir," Morty teased, "but is that what they call a mulligan?"

Ignoring the remark, Block teed up again. "Cut to the quick, son. What's on your mind?"

Morty sighed heavily. "It's not working."

"I want you to watch how I strike this ball," Block said, concentrating on his stance, "because your head is next if you make me play twenty questions."

Morty took the hint. "I'm talking about the kingdom insurgency, if you can call it that. It's not inflicting enough damage fast enough. We cripple the power grid, he fixes it. We blow up a market, it's back in business in a couple of days. I could go on. Plenty of casualties, never a fatality—"

"'And in those days,'" Block patiently recited, "'shall men seek death, and shall not find it; and shall desire to die, and death shall flee from them.' It's all explainable, son. All you need is a small dose of the holy spirit."

"—and no change in the king's intransigence," Morty finished his thought. "Earlier today I took a meeting with the kingpins of the kingdom expats. Needless to say, it wasn't pleasant. People are saying you're too disengaged, that you're going soft, too willing to give Philio a pass for his blasphemies and economic heresies. Even the church is starting to grumble. If this keeps up for a thousand years, it's going to be a long millennium."

Feigning disinterest, Block squibbed his do-over, butchering the drive, though missing the trees this time. Dismally watching the ball flop to a stop maybe sixty yards out, he shouldered his club. "Maybe you didn't get the memo," he said. "This isn't the millennium."

"Fine. When? How much longer are you going to let this evil bastard ignore us?"

Block extended his driver to the caddy. "I need a *casus belli*. Since Philio's not cooperating, I'm forced to await the next best thing ... a sign from God."

Morty perked up. "What sign?"

"The voice of the seven thunders," Block said academically, "'that there should be time no longer. Then seal up those things which the seven thunders uttered and write them not.'"

Morty experienced a flash of apprehension, in that instant seeing with complete clarity where the president's genius would lead. Block regarded him with a measure of pride, the pride all in himself, though the less said the better. Besides, it was all in the tenth chapter of the Revelation and beyond if anyone bothered to look. Clearly, Morty Parmister had.

A hard moment of decision later, Morty snapped his fingers at the caddy, requesting a three-wood and a new ball, teeing up like a pro. "Cinched grip, wrists locked, knees loose, eyes on the ball …" he coached the president. Then swinging fluidly, he looped a sailing, textbook-perfect 250-yard drive that dropped onto the fairway dead-center and well over halfway to the par-five green. "… and it'll always go where your package points," Morty added, handing the club to the president.

Block eyed him suspiciously. "No student of the game, eh?"

"I don't like to lose," Morty replied coldly, "at anything. I'll need an indefinite leave of absence, Mr. President."

"By all means," Block granted, "take all the time you need. If not before, God willing, I'll see in you in Jerusalem." Shaking hands, Block pulled him into a back-patting brotherly hug, and then Morty loped off for the main compound with a little extra spring in his step. Block indulged a small smile. It turned out you could lead a horse to water *and* make it drink. He was also not a little sad. Successful or not, Brother Morty was now a loose end that would have to be tied off, all to the greater glory of God.

Chapter XXIV

Chalking up a thinking assignment on the blackboard, the king was just adjourning class in a lecture hall on the Mount Scopus campus of Hebrew University when Ken Rittenour, Nacho Angel, and Julian Quinn surged in against the grain of departing students. The night course was entitled, "Critical Diacritics: Mishnah Before the Masorites."

That His Majesty loved to teach was no great surprise. That he insisted on making time for it despite his other duties was a chafing sore spot among royal court insiders, not to mention Hebraic traditionalists, ruffling the feathers of the rabbinical esprit de corps, but he knew his stuff. Where he came up with all his loopy ideas was the only mystery. He had a knack for making the arcane seem common, certainly less forbidding; rendering the unthinkable approachable, if not eminently plausible; turning conventional wisdom on its head.

"Sorry to bother you, Highness, but Quinn here has been studying," Rittenour said, less than happy about it.

"Always a good sign," said the king, packing up hand-ins for grading.

Rittenour remained surly. "Waste of time. Thinks he found something in his Bible."

"Oh?" the king asked without looking up. "Must be about the ten horns being the ten kings that give their power to the beast—these being remarkably consonant with the permanent conference of the ten bishops running the fledgling Church of America."

Julian was flummoxed. "How'd you know?"

Philio glanced over with amusement. "I'm a mystic. It's what I do."

"And you're not worried? You have no armies! No defenses to speak of."

"It's scripture, Julian, not a script."
"Tell that to Darius Block."

Deep in the bowels of the Pentagon, footsteps echoing, Morton Parmister was wordlessly escorted through a series of checkpoints to the antechamber of a nuclear-hardened vault. Left there alone, enjoying a security clearance second only to the president's, Morty underwent a retinal scan, after which the computer spun the tumblers, and the eighteen-inch-thick tungsten hatch cracked open with a *whoosh* of vacuum-sealed air. When he stepped inside, a pressure sensor in the floor activated the life-support system, after which the vault door automatically closed behind him, eerily relocking into place.

To Rittenour's dismay, Julian and Nacho's, too, the king relocated their discussion to the campus cafeteria and pub at the student union, nakedly conducting it out in the open. Before long, there were any number of students gathered about the king's table along with a sprinkling of faculty, all eager to listen in over pitchers of draft beer. Repressing his instinctive safety concerns for the king's person, Rittenour grudgingly borrowed Quinn's red-letter King James Bible to pass the time and conceal his anxiety. He'd never had much use for it or the people who did. Thumbing its onionskin pages now did nothing to change that impression. Meanwhile, the king was on a roll, his listeners entranced.

"Read uncritically, all fatidic soothsaying is a recursive trap," Philio was saying. "A test, if you will. Until you break the cycle—break out of it—its subjunctive elements continue to repeat. This is because the authoritarian impulse to inculcate submission through terror is the product not of too much imagination but too little, and it's completely understandable. What parent with impressionable children hesitates to threaten dire consequences in lieu of a cogent argument against unacceptable behavior? Why? Because it's easier, certainly less time-consuming. Plus, there's no guarantee a more rational deterrent will work. Consistently reinforced, the *sine qua non* is that the reactionary aversion to punishment suspends natural curiosity, relegating the vast majority to either credulous serfs or venal vassals of the prevailing status quo. The perceived upshot is stability and sustainability. There's only one problem: it's all illusion."

"How *does* it end, Lord?" a student at the back asked timorously.

"It doesn't," said the king. "It just becomes something else."

"Better?"

Slurping beer suds, the king summoned a smile. "Define better."

Continuing to randomly thumb Quinn's Bible with pretended interest, Rittenour rolled his eyes. The king loved to get them talking. Sometimes it got fairly spirited. When it did, it could go on all night. To Ken's chagrin, this had all the makings for one of those times.

Seated under a red hue at the vault's computer workstation with its triple-screen array, Morty got beyond each successive firewall and authorization challenge with flying colors, reaching that place in government cyberspace where angels fear to tread. No angel had the password. Somewhere far removed, a robotic arm was retrieving the optical disk with the requested files. God only knew how many more there were. *So many secrets*, Morty mused to himself. Loosening his tie, he languidly cracked his knuckles. "Talk to me."

Lighting up with a DUNS number, the center monitor displayed: "PROJECT SEVEN THUNDERS//EYES ONLY."

Ken Rittenour had totally lost the thread of the king's forum. His eyes were locked on a verse in the tenth chapter of the Book of Revelation. It made his blood run cold.

The king was saying, "All I meant is that when you change the way you look at things, the things you look at ... change."

But Rittenour's mind had already rocketed years into the past.

A watering hole in Crystal City. Alexandria, Virginia. Lots of sailors and marines. This was Navy territory. Ken felt out of place and outnumbered until Morty Parmister sidled up to the bar next to him. Morty had hair. The chatter cover was good, the jukebox nice and loud. Morty was all over the bar nuts. "Got a quickie," he said, chomping. "Down and dirty, in and out."

Ken wasn't interested. "Bad timing. I'm back to Baghdad."

"Not for another thirty-six hours. I checked. You're the only one I trust."

Ken got up to go, leaving money. "I don't do dirty."

"Since when?"

"Bite me."

"Could be there's a set of eagles in it for you, Major."

Ken scoffed, but stayed. "Like you've got that kind of pull."

"Call it a spiritual matter."

Ken wagged a finger. "That is fucked up, man, and you know it. Sleep with those people, and they steal everything you are. They don't give a shit about right and wrong. They only care about winning the argument. God is a plaything. They fling him around like they wave the flag."

"You're drunk."

"It's a bar and you're late. Sue me."

"Do you want the bump or not? How long do you plan to sit on your ass and watch a bunch of shave-tail Pointers get all the pickings?"

It was a clean kill, Rittenour remembered, he just couldn't remember where. Detroit, maybe. Cleveland? St. Louis? In for a penny, in for a pound—an assistant secretary of energy, some nobody with a mortgage, a wife and kids, and a missed rendezvous with a muckraking newspaper reporter who left town empty-handed.

"This it?" Morty asked when Ken turned over the goods, most of it stamped classified.

"What do you think?"

"Did you look?"

"Does the pope shit in the woods?"

"You are the worst liar on God's earth."

"I can live with that," Ken said. "But hear me, and hear me good. I don't get my eagles, I'm coming after you ... no matter how long it takes, no matter how lonely it gets."

"Ouch, I may not survive the fear."

"I have *honor!*" Ken blurted before Morty escaped.

Morty turned, cupping his genitals. "Brother, I got all the honor you got left right here. Go shoot bad guys in Baghdad. I got your back."

But Ken *had* looked. It meant nothing at the time, just another cheeky government code-phrase, more coy than obscurant, as forgettable as the man who'd dared to leak it. Now, with Quinn's Bible opened to the tenth chapter of the last book of the New Testament, the scripture was literally screaming at him:

Seal up those things which the seven thunders uttered, and write them not.

Rittenour whipped out his cell phone. "I need a chopper on the pad with fuel for Yaffo, now! Then any available bird for a jump to Europe, pre-flighted and juiced." Flapping the phone shut, he was out of his chair. "Angel," he barked at Nacho with command authority, "hold down the fort. Quinn, you're with me." Without awaiting the king's permission, he was already halfway out of the commissary. Julian looked at Philio.

"Best not to keep him waiting," said the king. "Colonel," he calmly called to Rittenour, pausing him, "chance favors the prepared mind. Infallibility clouds it. Hate kills it. Be open."

"Oh, I'm open," Rittenour shot back, "to all kinds of things. Quinn!"

"He's not a pleasant man," someone near the king remarked, watching them race out.

"Beset by a host of demons, I expect," said the king.

"Can you cast them out?"

"Who's to say they're not, in fact, the better angels of our nature?" Philio sighed. "When you cleanse a man's soul, care must be taken not to erase it."

"He's violent," someone judged.

"He's learning," said the king.

"What?"

"Not to take anything for granted—most of all, himself." Then, pouring refills all around, Philio signaled for another pitcher. "Now, where were we? Ah, yes. As I was saying, moribund prophecy has always been the didactic playground of moral authoritarians who've misplaced their moral compass—the more furtive and abstruse the better—making it the perfect hiding place for ulterior agendas. Ergo, vouchsafing venerable vicars the verdant vicissitudes of vox populi."

"Dang!" Nacho exclaimed. "Man, you got a way with words."

"Precisely," said the king. "I got away with words. The question is: why do you let me?"

Like peeling back the layers of a pungent onion, Parmister finally accessed what he was looking for. Marked with the official seal of the Department of Energy and the universal symbol for radioactivity, the center screen held the rotating, 3-D CAD image of a small but highly sophisticated munition. Beside it, the computer was scrolling specifications and statistics on size and yield. Another screen showed a map of the continental United States with seven blinking lights—Austin, Duluth, Denver, Helena, Knoxville, Oklahoma City, and Phoenix. At first blush, the distribution appeared random. Connecting the five outer dots, however, which Morty clicked a command icon to do, produced a giant, inverse pentacle, considered by some an abstraction of the devil's horns. This one was slightly skewed though plainly centered over the American heartland with Denver and Oklahoma City on the transverse. It sent an involuntary shiver up Morty's spine.

Dismissing it, he swiveled to the workstation's third monitor and clicked the help menu to bring up an online technical manual, taking a moment to rub his eyes and mentally regroup. He'd never been particularly mechanical or technically savvy, so there was a lot to learn. Happily, he wouldn't have to memorize it all. Stretching his arms and putting on his thinking cap, he skipped to the most important part. It showed a picture of what appeared to be a large briefcase—quite common looking, actually—under the section entitled, "*Activation.*"

Chapter XXV

Under the Tuscan sun on the outskirts of the sleepy village of Vorno, nestled in the gentle green hills of the Lucca district, Ernest Delvecchio doffed his straw hat to mop his brow as the helicopter roared in overhead at treetop level from Pisa, disturbing his manicured vineyard with gale-force disregard. In his early sixties, the old man was neither unduly alarmed nor at all pleased, merely resigned. Replacing his hat, he hiked without haste to his tool shed.

A retired two-star general with a doctorate in nuclear engineering in another life, Delvecchio had once headed DOE's fissile research lab at Oak Ridge, Tennessee, and was widely considered the father of tactical miniaturization. He'd since abandoned the brainy pursuit of better contained and more efficient mass annihilation for the less creative legerdemain of a gentleman planter.

The modest villa and winery had been in his wife's family since the Medici wars against the Lucchese going back five centuries. Lucca never fell. His beloved Francesca wasn't so lucky, taken by plague blowback at the height of the apocalypse. Notwithstanding his strategically sensitive position, Delvecchio was granted permission by a sympathetic superior to come to Italy to inter his late wife's remains. Her "Ernesto" never went back. The Armistice of Jerusalem, followed by the lynching of the last "elected" president at the hands of the all-powerful council, assured that he would never again have to ... or so he thought. Technically, he was a deserter lost in the post-war paper shuffle. *Why couldn't they just leave him alone?*

The rambling headquarters of the Tennessee Valley Authority was responsible for providing clean, hydroelectric power to millions from Virginia to Mississippi.

Morty took a rental car from the Knoxville Airport—his reputation, even more than his government ID, got him an unscheduled meeting with the board of the TVA. He timed his arrival so that all three board members were out to lunch, no doubt huddled together over sweet tea and chitlins, wondering what "credible terrorist threat" meant. The term hadn't been heard in ages, not since the war. Until they got back, Morty had the run of the place, insisting that he be unescorted, much to the consternation of the deputy security chief, who called it "most irregular." No one had said anything about any spot inspection, she said. Morty took her name. She never said another word.

Circling back around, the chopper touched down on the broad lawn fronting the Tuscan villa, surrounded by sculpted hedgerows of rosemary and thyme. The gravel driveway leading from the locked main gate was straight as an arrow and lined with dual colonnades of soaring junipers, the descendants of sentries that had stood a silent vigil since Etruscan times. Amid such classical, pristine splendor, the loud and grating flying machine was an uncouth trespasser.

As the rotor died, Julian Quinn was the first out, coming around to Rittenour's side. There was still no activity from the house. "Are you sure you've got the right place?"

A shotgun blast zinged the fuselage. Ricocheted pellets shredded the colonel's sleeve, even as he tugged Julian to the grass. "I am now," he said, yelling, "Hold your fire, General! We're here from Jerusalem on the king's business!"

"Don't move!" Delvecchio's voice called back from the unseen distance. It was even difficult to pinpoint in which direction it came from. The pump action of his weapon finally gave him away, the barrel pointed at their heads from less than five feet away. "I have no regard for the king," he said, "and even less for that devil in Washington."

Holding up his hands, Rittenour didn't mince words. "What are the seven thunders?"

The general's shoulders sank. "Oh, God, no."

Austin was Morty Parmister's next stop. The University of Texas housed the largest academic library in the post-war world, more than ten million volumes. Its Perry-Castañeda collection alone, covering the social sciences and humanities, was a national treasure—nay, *international*—and it was completely open to the public. Under a sub-floor panel in the deserted dead languages stacks, Morty had no trouble locating the next PST briefcase.

Clink. Another bloody pellet dropped into the terra cotta bowl. Leaving the tweezers in the bowl as well, General Delvecchio sponged off Rittenour's raw arm, then helped himself to an eye-watering gulp of his private-label grappa before drenching the wound in more of the same. "I admire your pluckiness," he told Rittenour. "Not a sound out of you."

"Habit," Rittenour said.

"It doesn't hurt?"

"Hurts like a bitch. The time to worry is when it doesn't."

They were in the villa's brick *cucina* on the lowest level. The rustic, naked beams holding up the ceiling threatened collapse at any minute but never did. The table was laden with ripe olives, unsalted Florentine bread, and skewers of tomato, leafy fresh basil, and balls of mozzarella. A fragrant wood fire was crackling in the open hearth. It was dusk now; the only other light was by candle. Julian was half gone on a chilled bottle of pinot grigio. He'd overstuffed on the general's leftover osso buco. "I love Italy," he slurred with drunken whimsy, patting his belly.

"Yeah, yeah," said Rittenour, "we heard you the first time." He was more frank with Delvecchio. "The thunders, General. Are they real, and if they are, am I too late?"

Delvecchio sank back with his glass of grappa, staring dolefully into the fire. "Yes is the first answer. And, since you're here, probably is the second. God forgive me."

Rittenour tied off his own linen field dressing with his teeth and helped himself to the grappa. "They were strange times, General. We all did things we're not proud of."

"I don't know where they are," Delvecchio said after a long moment, "or *if* they are. That was the whole point; everything was tightly compartmentalized. We each had a piece, never all of it."

"But you knew. A scarred old warhorse like you?"

Delvecchio feigned umbrage. "I followed orders."

"Believe me," said Rittenour, "I'm the last person on earth in a position to judge you."

The general met him eyeball to eyeball. "Which one of the Eumenides were you?"

Rittenour absently put a hand on the bandage that now covered the tattoo.

The Eumenides, also known as the Furies, had been the elite of the elite, drawn from throughout the Special Forces. Operating the world over under the doctrine of preemption, its original mission was to terrorize the terrorists using similar tactics. Given its stunning successes early on, however, mission creep was inevitable, especially after the Furies were placed under the control of the council. Eventually, to "send in a U" meant to "disappear" antiwar activists, religious dissidents, unreasonable journalists, and the whistle-blowers who fed them.

Delvecchio looked away. "You have the look of an Alecto, I think, first among equals. A man like you must have a lot on his conscience, if you have a conscience at all."

"Then we share at least that much in common," said Rittenour. "Talk to me."

His tongue loosened by the potent grappa, Delvecchio gave an account that was all the more chilling because of its matter-of-factness. Indeed, it was devoid of polemics, passion of any kind, really. Rittenour, a seasoned interrogator, refrained from interrupting. It didn't all have to be true to be the truth. A practiced listener learns far more from the *way* something is said than what.

They weren't getting through, the terrorists weren't. The post–9/11 precautions and safeguards, so expensively maintained, were working, it seemed, and it was election season. The party's grip on power was in danger of slipping. Wolf had been cried one too many times. On the most visceral level, budgets and turf were threatened by any change. Despite the merciless excoriation of the opposition for its weakness on national security, the public mood had shifted, so Delvecchio was only mildly surprised to be summoned to Washington along with others in the unconventional weapons design community. The meeting was extremely low key.

The only real surprise was the attendance of the president's spiritual advisor. Higher-ups vouched for him, and that was that. His celebrity in party circles, particularly his genius for fundraising, was easily his most compelling attribute. His turgid sermons had monopolized the radio waves for decades. His face was a mainstay on cable TV news shows. He had an answer for everything, always scripturally based. He never hesitated and shouted down all alternatives. The Israeli lobby had awarded him "best friend" status.

He took control of the meeting without effort, commanding, Delvecchio recalled, almost hypnotic obeisance. To question him was to question Almighty God himself.

Sensing the spiritual advisor's urgency, for some unaccountable reason craving his approval, Delvecchio and his colleagues suggested an off-the-shelf solution, making it really just a matter of parts acquisition and assembly, an exercise in catalog engineering. In fact, given the modest yield specified, albeit hypothetically, the paltry amount of fissionable material required was available in existing research stocks.

The spiritual advisor was extremely pleased. "Could a terrorist design such a device?" he asked. Terrorists just had, Delvecchio ultimately realized, far too late.

Seven of the devices were produced and delivered, allegedly for defusing techniques training. Only after, with an October surprise looming as the party's only salvation, did several of those involved get cold feet, threatening to spill the beans. A number of the most nervous were "removed," sending an indelible message to all the others.

"Fortunately, they 'won' the election by other means," Delvecchio finished, making inverted commas with his fingers. "Then the Dome fell. Everything else, as they say, is history."

"What was the yield?" Rittenour asked.

"Twenty kilotons each," the general said clinically. "Times seven, about what was dropped on Nagasaki; tidier package, limited but focused with far faster-dispersing tritium rads; depending on where deployed, enough to get people's attention. More than enough," he added drolly, "so that it wouldn't matter who was responsible."

"And you have no idea where they were placed?" Rittenour restated the obvious.

Lost in the flickering flames of the hearth, Delvecchio glumly shook his head. "Needles in a haystack, Colonel, hardly bigger than a lunchbox and about as visually threatening."

"You stupid bastards!" Julian hissed, fighting to sober up.

Delvecchio snorted. "Now there's the pot calling the kettle black, pardon the pun. Did you think I wouldn't recognize you, son, the Mighty Quinn? For a moment, for a supremely restful moment, you were the hope of a tormented nation, the happy mindspring of a hate-exhausted world. Those of us abroad, we expats, watched you with singular admiration. '*Finally!*' we wanted to shout. Darius Block was politically and morally dead. *You* brought him back to life. As a black man, as a *thinking* man, what did you *possibly* find redeeming in him?"

Burying his face in his hands, Julian wanted to die. "I was afraid ... afraid to be ... weak."

"Water over the damn," Rittenour interceded. "The king will know what to do."

Julian recomposed himself, more confidently asserting, "The king is Lord."

"Spare me, son," said Delvecchio. "I was a believer once, in all sorts of deific things. It was fun, mostly because it didn't have to make sense. Hell, it's what dreams are made of, bouncing between grace and retribution as the mood suits. Get real. Since the dawn of time, gods have come and gone with the frequency of the common cold. The only constant is the priests who use them, all of whom manage with uncanny regularity to turn it all to shit."

"My Lord Philio ain't got no priests!" Julian hurled back.
"Give it time, boy," Delvecchio laughed, "give it time."

Toasting those closest with forbidden bubbly, President Block was in his element, relaxed and self-assured. The invitation-only, black-tie fundraiser was closed to the press. He could speak freely here, safely, amongst his most die-hard supporters. The niceties dispensed with, they got down to business. Everyone wanted something. Heck, they'd paid for it. Patience was wearing thin. It soon became a pile-on, hammering him left and right. Block heard the voices, laboring to place the faces. It just wasn't fair.

"Jerusalem's continuing sanctions are crippling profits," he was told.
"So what the bleep are you waiting for?"
"Are we or are we not the world's only military superpower?"
"The only military power period."
"Yeah, use it or lose it."
"Gentlemen, gentlemen," Block objected smoothly, wishing Morty Parmister was here to run interference, "and ladies. Prudence, please. All is not as it seems. Call it the calm before the storm. The Antichrist is overdue to commit a major misstep. Our duty is to be ready."
"Are we?"
"Never more so. Has the nation ever been more unified, sharing the common goal of liberty? Will we be intimidated by tyranny? Have we ever allowed the forces of evil to sway us from our God-given destiny? Where's the faith?"

More than a few weren't taken in. Had his all-purpose rhetorical magic lost its punch? More telling still, they were engagingly disrespectful.

"The law of commerce is expand or die. You've done all the good at home you can."
"You broke the unions and guilds."
"Sealed the borders, filled the zones and prisons."
"Cut taxes, raised the poverty line, repealed entitlements. All commendable."
"But repudiating the national debt has made us a bankrupt pariah."
"There's no one left to borrow from."
"Our only option is military conquest. It's now a *fait accompli*."
"What, pray tell, are you waiting for?"

Block fought the urge to righteously lash out. His position was delicate. These were the owners of the country, old money and arriviste. "You exaggerate," he said. "Nor are the Lord's people naked aggressors. Neither are they cowards. No just and wholesome cause to war against their enemies will ever stop them, not as long as *I'm* their president!"

"So give it to them!"

"You can be replaced."

Do you think I've been sitting on my hands? Don't you know this is hard work?

Find a way or make a way, but make it happen, those gathered told Block in no uncertain terms. "And for heaven's sake get them back into church. Idle minds are the devil's playground—Philio's playground. He's making a mockery of old-fashioned values. I mean, how the bloody hell do you keep them on the farm once they've seen Paris?"

"Forget Paris. The new Jerusalem."

"Too many have left the reservation."

"He's a disease, is what Philio is, and it's ruining our quality of life."

"Enough!" Block thundered coldly, finding himself, reclaiming his center, his nostrils flaring. The gala hushed. "Don't you understand? Can't you see that this was all foretold, history written in advance? *'Woe unto the inhabiters of the earth and of the sea, for the devil is come down unto you having great wrath, because he knoweth that he hath but a short time.'*" The recitation carried with it a wilting power.

"How short?" a brave soul ventured from somewhere in the crowd.

"His faithful do not tempt the Lord their God!" Block lectured strongly. "But in fear and trembling do they await his pleasure. The Word tells us to prepare for a thief in the night, that the day and the hour no man knoweth. We can only *believe* and be ready to receive his grace when the sign is come." Block softened, his long-suffering smile ever so pious. "It will, because it must, at the appointed hour, with great power and glory. Trust, and he will show the way. Pray, and your prayers shall be answered. Let freedom ring! This nation and its people are the last best hope for a lasting peace. Our highest calling is to keep that hope alive! The richness of our reward will be commensurate with our faith. What God hath wrought, let no man put asunder!"

Prolix twaddle, patriotically sacred, it still sold. Their contrite, embarrassed faces made that plain. Money aside, the fundraiser was a total success, a grand-slam, cover-your-ass home run. When the seven thunders sounded, Block could safely be as surprised and outraged as everyone else—taking as long as, say, seven minutes to react—his stubborn reluctance to promote aggression personally attested to by these upstanding pillars of the community, leaders of unimpeachable character all. For a prophet, it just didn't get any better than this. God might have reservations, but Darius's faith in Morton Parmister was unshakable.

Nor was it misplaced. Now winging his way south on a King Air charter, Morty finished a dry shave with his battery-powered razor. He was whipped. He checked off Duluth, Minnesota, on his mental image of an upside-down star. One to go. Leaning around in the cockpit's right seat, the copilot advised him to strap in for final approach into Oklahoma City.

Morty reclined his head back to rest his eyes and tried to imagine the shock and awe to come. The usual suspects were already being rounded up in a nationwide sweep. An anonymous tip had helped to expose a sophisticated network of Janusian sleeper cells. The accusation was sufficient to make the morning papers. Mostly, it was intended to alert the president that everything was on schedule.

Chapter XXVI

Twilight was waning when Rittenour motored alongside the curb in what could best be described as a bullet on wheels. Though it was quite spacious inside, the chug of combustion propulsion was absent. The only mechanical noise it made was more of an airy whistle. The sleekly aerodynamic contraption might have seemed weirdly anachronistic on the ancient residential streets of the Old City if there weren't so many others out and about—different models and colors but sharing the same basic design. The colonel and Julian Quinn jumped out first. Julian was in a tizzy.

"Something is messed up," he complained fearfully. "What do you mean, *it's over?*"

"*Been* over," said Rittenour. "I'm just telling you what he told me on the phone."

General Delvecchio was having a devil of a time figuring out how to get out of the back seat. Rittenour aimed his remote, and the rear door slid open. Still marveling over the vehicle's emissionless "water engine," Delvecchio was yet to fully grasp the implications of cold fusion, just one of the kingdom's recent innovations now entering production across the realm. Visually taking stock of his surroundings, this being his first visit to the New Jerusalem, the general wasn't quite sure what to make of it. "I thought we were going to the palace?"

Rittenour was nonplussed. "Whose palace?"

"Uh, the king's?"

"Wrong king," said Julian.

Delvecchio dawdled at the curb. "Mind if I pop the hood?"

"Knock yourself out," said Rittenour, heading past the single sentry armed with a non-lethal stun gun based on compressed, ultrasonic pulse energy, another royal innovation.

Nacho Angel answered the apartment door. Wearing a ribbed tank top, he was cradling a newborn infant, one that was fascinated by the shiny silver crucifix on the chain around Nacho's neck. The heir apparent was a baby girl.

"What are you doing here?" Julian asked.

"What's it look like? Babysitting." Nor was Nacho overjoyed to be stuck with the duty.

Gwynn hurried up behind him, fastening an earring. She was dressed for a night on the town, one apparently long in coming, and her perfume was intoxicating. "Good, you're here. Traffic?"

Rittenour was put out. "Where's the king?"

"He's on Mount Moriah making a sacrifice, and we're late. There's formula in the fridge, Felix," she told Nacho, scrounging in her purse to make sure she had her cell phone. "You've got my number." Then, kissing the baby, she pushed out past Julian and Rittenour, tying off a scarf under her chin. "Well, don't just stand there. Come on. It'll be faster walking. I know a shortcut." Exchanging a glance, the other two were left with little choice but to tag along, picking up General Delvecchio on the way.

The Noble Sanctuary, née the Temple Mount, now a memorial park, was temporarily closed to the public for the ceremony. Al Aqsa was now a shrine to Islamic science, boasting a planetarium. The madrasas at the other end had been converted to a museum housing the storied history of Palestine with interactive exhibits dating back to the Phoenicians and the Jebusites and covering all the serial upheavals since. The wide-open center of the plateau's thirty-odd acres, where the Dome of the Rock was no more, where Herod's Temple had stood before it, was broken only by a modest monument, remarkable for its simplicity—a travertine marble obelisk of Egyptian origin, capped with a pyramid and polished to a reflective gloss, rising thirty meters high.

Anathema to staunch traditionalists on both sides of the Judeo-Islamic divide, it was now spotlighted by directional floods that accentuated its gleaming whiteness. In daylight, the sun made it positively radiant, visible for miles in all directions. Rancor over its blasphemous presence continued to ebb with time, having more to do with its neutrality than anything else, given the king's rare ability to persuasively argue against both extremes of the theological spectrum. It was mostly a question of going back or moving forward and the utter futility of staying put. Perhaps even more than that, though, the most viciously recalcitrant of the long-beards had killed each other off during the war, hapless victims of their own certitude.

As they came through the tunnel and up the steps from the Western Wall, Gwynn, Rittenour, Julian, and Delvecchio were halted by guards. What they beheld was astounding.

Under a full moon, wearing the Levitically prescribed vestments of an Aaronic high priest, out in the distance, squarely in the Herodian holy of holies or anyone's best approximation thereof, Philio was performing some sacred rite at a knee-level altar covered with a military-issue canvas tarp. Exactly what he was saying couldn't be heard, nor was there any livestock at hand for a blood sacrifice. It was nonetheless terribly mystical and holy. You could just feel it, the energy—a face-to-face communion with an invisible force of awesome, incalculable power.

Then, bowing his head, Philio prayed, palms upraised. During the lull, Avi Mandelheimer waved the group over, beckoning them to come on ahead to where he and Merlin were, still well on this side of the spectacle. Julian duly noted that his dad was in a trance, transfixed on Philio, making it hard to tell whether he was aghast or attuned. As they approached, Avi signaled them to keep it down and observe the solemnity of the occasion, but Julian's curiosity as much as his growing frustration with the king's pithy, pie-in-the-sky evasions got the better of him.

"What's he doing?" he demanded in a whisper.

"It's Yom Kippur," Avi said. "The last. You will not see this again."

"The Day of Atonement," Merlin said, adding with emphasis, "*At-one-ment.*"

Julian made a face. "There's no temple."

"That's the whole point," said Avi. "*We* are the new temple, each of us, together."

"Why's he all duded up like a priest? I thought he had it in for priests."

"Priest*craft*," Avi said.

Irritated, Julian huffed. "We've been over this before. What is it, priestcraft?"

"It's *using* God," Merlin said, "rather than serving him."

"What's the difference?"

"It starts with believing there *is* a difference," Avi said. "Shh, it's almost over."

And then it was.

As the king stepped back from the makeshift altar, an attendant brought a basin of water for ritual washing. Another had the king's street clothes. Two more stretched out a bedsheet, like a veil, to shield the king from view. Moments later, the sheet was lowered, and Philio was in blue jeans and a sport coat over a simple

T-shirt, handing over the neatly folded priestly garments. "Put these in a museum," he instructed in Hebrew. "They shan't again be required. Ever." As the attendants went on their way, Philio spied the others. "Hello, all."

Julian strode forth without leave, before anyone could hold him back. "Homily and ritual won't get it done," he said angrily. "I was right. Block thinks the Bible holds all the answers."

"I'm inclined to agree with him," the king said patiently.

Julian halted dead. "But earlier you said—"

"I said it's not a script," the king interrupted. "By the same token, many are convinced it's an acrostic puzzle, to be taken apart and refitted according to whatever worldview they embrace at a given moment. Or a code to be deciphered for hidden messages. In all cases, the answers are there. Far more relevant are the questions asked in *pursuit* of its answers. And more telling than the questions are the motivations of the people asking them—the few bold enough to ask at all."

It wasn't helpful, not to Julian. "Don't you get it, King? Block ain't *asking*; he's engineering. The shit's about to hit the fan, man! Tell him!" he urged General Delvecchio. "Tell him just how hot it's gonna get."

"Tens of millions of degrees," Delvecchio said, unsure of his standing. "Organic vaporization in the blink of an eye out to a half-mile radius."

"Times seven," Rittenour told the king. "No one'll much give a damn who's responsible. A targeted response carrying even bigger yields will be automatic, and they've got all the WMD."

Julian stared furiously at the king. "Heal *that*."

King Philio merely shrugged. "I like to think there's always possibilities."

If possible, Julian was even more exasperated.

Gwynn spoke up, her voice softly reassuring or attempting to be. "He's saying, Governor Quinn, that until we change the way we look at things—"

"Bullshit!" Julian swore. "Darius Block will *never* change!"

"He may not," said the king, "but you can. Even God can … and has."

"Say *what?*"

"Just so," said the king. "It is one of those questions that cannot be asked for a host of underlying reasons. To begin with, if God is unchangeable, what possessed him to create the heavens and the earth and all that has followed? However you choose to view it, creation *is* a change—especially if not least of all creating something from nothing. And if *God* can change his mind, then truly all things with him are possible."

Letting it sink in ever so briefly, Philio stepped over to the odd altar and yanked away the canvas tarp—*presto*—to reveal seven pieces of luggage, each identical.

"I'll be damned!" Delvecchio softly exclaimed. "It's them."

Without permission, he lurched past the king, dropping to his knees to spin the combination lock on the first case. It was an easy guess. 666. Opening the case, he made a quick inspection, moving to the next and the next.

"Defused," he announced, "all seven. The tritium fuel cores have been removed."

"Thrown into the proverbial pit, as it were," Philio said. "Still, for all our sakes, let's not let it warp into something it's not. For, you see, I had almost nothing to do with it."

Whereupon a lone figure stepped out of the shadows cast by the floodlights. It was Morton Parmister. Gwynn gasped, covering her mouth. Rittenour pulled her back, stepping between them to assume a battle stance. Morty wisely halted at a safe distance. "All my life," he said, weary and over-traveled, "I knew … there were *times* I knew I was capable of just about anything to advance my beliefs." He looked fondly at Gwynn. "And I truly do, you know—believe. At least I want to. But you have to draw the line somewhere, I guess. Go figure."

Rittenour was unconvinced. "How'd you clear U.S. airspace with this kind of cargo?"

Exhausted, Morty mustered a smile. "Who was going to stop me?"

"What made you see the light?"

"I didn't," Morty confessed, with a glance to the king. "I saw the darkness."

Meanwhile, Julian was caught somewhere between wobbly disbelief and pathetic shame, still terribly upset with the king. "You could've just come out and told us, saved me the embarrassment."

"Could have done," said Philio, "but passions, unlike bombs, are not so easily diffused. Situations are never hopeless, Julian, only the people that occupy them are. The only wrong belief is believing you can't be wrong."

"Can you be wrong, Lord?"

"The day I can't is the day I am. It is also the day I stop learning."

Delvecchio stood up from the luggage, strangely affected. "Now *that's* what I call a king."

"You're still learning?" Julian asked Philio.

"Good heavens, man! I haven't scratched the surface of what's out there. The simple fact that there's always more to consider and always will be, always a better way awaiting discovery, is the only thing that gives existence any meaning. Nay, what higher purpose, consciousness, than to consciously explore alternatives?"

Hands in his pockets, Julian toed the mount's ancient flagstones. "Kind of makes a set of wings with a harp on a cloud seem dull."

"But restful, I suppose," said the king. "All depends on what turns you on."

Something inside Julian snapped. He had to know, reaching out to whirl Philio around by the arm. "*Are you the second coming of Jesus Christ—Messiah, the Imam?*" he blurted, putting everyone on edge. They all wanted to know, had flirted with it, afraid to be disappointed.

The king took no offense; he was more amused than threatened. "Please, it's hard enough being the first coming of Janus Philio."

"Damn it, yes or no!" Julian pressed him. "Be straight with me."

"Do you want me to be?"

"I want the truth!"

The king's humor was sorely tried. "Whose truth? There are so many."

"Why can't you just say it?"

"Because just *saying* it isn't the same thing as *being* it, and never was."

"That's not an answer!"

"No, Julian," argued the king, "it is the *only* answer, and it will continue to be inconvenient until you stop looking for validation and start seeking illumination. When you do, you will find it in the most surprising place of all and where it's been hiding all along: *within yourself.*" Wilting Julian, the king then restored him. "What is *reasonable*?" he asked serenely. "There is no pat answer, because it will continue to change with more and better information, evolving, developing into a clearer picture as *you* evolve and develop. You must never stop asking, asking it honestly, or sheepishly allow anyone else to decide its answer for you, no matter how many accolades or privileges they heap upon you for agreeing with them in reward for your compliance, no matter what form of punishment they threaten for your heresy. Heresy means *choice*. What *is* reasonable? Warning: tomorrow's answer may not be the same as today's or yesterday's. That just happens to be the way Universe works. *It* grants you the freedom to correct yourself, to adapt. All you have to do is accept that freedom."

Julian pouted. "Why do you have to make it so complicated?"

"You find the static alternative simpler?" the king asked.

"A people need to know their boundaries, the rules."

"The sidelines and end zones clearly demarcated, is that it?"

"Something like that," Julian allowed.

"Except this game is slightly longer than four quarters," said the king.

"How long?"

"Forever."

"Then how do you know if you've won or lost?"

With a twinkle in his eye, the king smiled. "What is reasonable?"

"Will you teach me?"

"We'll learn together," the king promised. "It's the only reason we're here." He turned to the others, clapping his hands and rubbing them together. "I'm hungry; been fasting all day. Anyone else? Dinner and drinks on me, yeah? Dr. Delvecchio, have you ever considered the possibilities of time compression on an interstellar scale? Dimension-hopping, I guess you'd have to call it. I sketched out some formulas the other night, consistent with M-Phasing. All still strictly theoretical, mind you. Couldn't sleep. Love to have you take a crack …"

As the royal entourage moved out of earshot for the exit back down to the city, Julian dallied at the monument, the devil playing in his thoughts until his eyes drifted onto the marble inscription at the base of the obelisk. It was chiseled in Hebrew, Greek, Arabic, and Latin—none of which he knew—and, finally, in English; so simple it was overwhelming, putting a lump in his throat.

I • AM • THE • WAY • THE • TRUTH • AND • THE • LIFE
NO • MAN • COMETH • UNTO • THE • FATHER
EXCEPT • THROUGH • ME
MY • NAME • IS • LOVE

For Julian, everything in the scriptures suddenly made sense. Or, rather, he sensed that it could … maybe. Surely, it couldn't be this easy. *Easy?* Could anything be harder?

He was startled by the king's voice. Philio was the only one waiting for him at the end of the esplanade. "It doesn't end there, Julian," the king said. "It only begins."

"What happens next?"

"What do you *want* to happen?"

Epilogue

Darius Block's promised sign manifested not long after. He missed it, he and his ilk. Or, rather, they misread it, not unlike they'd misread the gentle Galilean who'd ended war to become the King of kings and Lord of lords without a shot fired in anger.

They say it started in a soup line in the LA zone. Compton, some say. Inglewood, say others. A single mother with several pre-adolescent children failed to openly give thanks for her soup to the church warder's satisfaction. Her soup was taken away, as were the cups from her children, and she was publicly beaten. The uprising spread from there, unstoppable. When it abated, Philio's kingdom was complete, remaining so without challenge since. So many wonders followed, great and small, all the generations of mankind reunited, as cannot be contained in these pages ... or any others, not fully.

To this day, nearly a thousand years after, old men still speak of the End Times, questioning how it got to where it did, and why the ancients of the twenty-first century allowed it to get there. What was it about their perception of God that drove them to the edge of total destruction? Yet the world remains, new worlds explored and colonized even as the galaxy shrinks, the universe expanding. Truly, mankind *has* taken to the heavens, those that wish to go.

Some ask if Philio was no more than a myth—this King Love—arguing that death didn't end, not really; we simply lost our fear of it, becoming more spiritual beings. On any road, whatever lies ahead, the age of priests and kings is over. And, with it, the flesh of kings.

THE END

978-0-595-68213-3
0-595-68213-8